GW00375079

Paul Reizin began his career in newspapers and radio before switching to television, where he has worked on both sides of the camera. He is the author of three novels plus a forthcoming work of non-fiction detailing an odyssey through the lonely hearts columns of a national newspaper.

He lives in London with his wife and daughter.

Also by Paul Reizin

Dumping Hilary?
Don't Try This At Home

FIENDS REUNITED

Paul Reizin

<u>headline</u>

First published in Great Britain in 2004
by HEADLINE BOOK PUBLISHING

First published in paperback in 2004
by HEADLINE BOOK PUBLISHING

10 9 8 7 6 5 4 3 2 1

ISBN 0 7472 6870 3

Typeset in Perpetua by Palimpsest Book Production Limited,
Polmont, Stirlingshire

Printed and bound in Great Britain by
Mackays of Chatham plc, Chatham, Kent

Headline's policy is to use papers that are natural, renewable and recyclable
products and made from wood grown in sustainable forests. The logging and
manufacturing processes are expected to conform to the environmental
regulations of the country of origin.

HEADLINE BOOK PUBLISHING
A division of Hodder Headline
338 Euston Road
London NW1 3BH

www.headline.co.uk
www.hodderheadline.com

For
Tina Jenkins and Nicola Gooch

My grateful thanks once again to Clare Alexander for much wise counsel along the way; to my editor Harrie Evans for her surgical interventions; and to Martin Kelner for the film and musical advice.

I've got amnesia and déjà vu at the same time.
I can't remember what happens next.
John Cooper Clarke

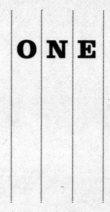

ONE

1

Fade up on a school playground some time during the first of Margaret Thatcher's three terms in office. It is the mid-morning break. Somewhat on the edge of the roiling turmoil, a small boy stands alone, eating from a packet of crisps.

A bigger boy, red-faced from playing football, comes juddering to a halt alongside him, hands at his hips, thick plumes of steam issuing from his nostrils following a thunderous charge up the wing.

The smaller boy is paralysed, a single crisp frozen midway between bag and mouth. The bigger boy is Neal Hooton, a notorious bully whose idea of fun, legend has it, is to wrestle you to the ground, sit astride your chest and gob into your open mouth. To the obvious question – why would your mouth be open in a situation like this? – the answer is that it tends to be when someone has a vice-like grip on your knackers.

As Neal Hooton recovers his breath, he studies the smaller boy, who, with a shrivelling certainty, now knows something bad – possibly something very bad – is about to happen.

'What flavour are they?' enquires the brute.

'Cheese and onion,' stammers the smaller child.

Hooton nods, as though these are the words required. In a single motion, he crushes the boy's crisp packet between the palms of his two hands.

'Got more now, haven't you?' he declares and lumbers off to rejoin the game.

In the catalogue of playground torments, the fragmentation of one's confectionery is an almost laughably trivial occurrence. Intact curls of flash-fried potato have been reduced to dust, true, but you have escaped unscathed. You have had a close encounter with the power of the beast as he destroyed your snack; but then he passed on. Your body has remained un-pummelled.

The smaller boy feels like cheering at his escape. More than two decades after this incident, he still recalls the sweet sensa-tion of relief – oh thank you God – that he was not selected that morning for Hooton to have some proper sport with.

In fact, the boy was never one of childhood's regular victims. And despite the terror, pulverised crisps was the worst crime that he could lay at the door of the infamous thug. But as he readied himself for tonight's reunion, fifteen years since leaving their unremarkable north London academy, as he climbed into his best suit and selected an appropriately colourful tie, some part of me – all right, I may as well stop with the literary thing right now – some part of me that had never left the playground was still cacking itself at the prospect of once again coming face to face with Neal Francis Hooton.

'How do I look?' I asked Squeaky, my girlfriend, as I prepared to depart.

'Truth?' she replied.

'No. Say something nice.'

Her head fell to one side as she considered the options. My fingernails found themselves raking through the hair above my right ear in a reflexive sort of fashion.

'I shouldn't worry about the, er, hairline issue.' She smiled. 'Everyone there is bound to have . . . moved on a bit.'

An unexpected wave of affection chose this moment to roll through me. I hugged her and told her I wouldn't be back late.

Then I asked, 'You don't think it's too much, do you? The tie.' It was the extremely colourful one by Georgina von Etzdorf. 'You don't think it's trying too hard?'

'What's that thing you always say?' she replied. 'You never get a second chance to make a first impression?'

This was true, I reflected as I exited the flat, with the singular exception of a class reunion. Tonight I had just such an opportunity – we all did – to make a second first impression.

The minicab rocketed along the North Circular towards the Carpenters Arms and I felt a small fist of anxiety take up residence somewhere around the top button of my jacket.

So what are you up to these days?

That was the way they'd phrase the question.

Oh, you know, I could reply. Still writing the column (I wouldn't need to explain about how the contract wasn't being renewed). Still talking rubbish on the radio.

Married yet? Any kids at all? (Not a poof, are you?)

I'd be able to report that I'd been going out with someone for a couple of years – there were no kids, no – there would be no reason to spell out the terms of the agreement that Squeaky and I had reached after much heart-searching and not a few tears.

So all in all you've done pretty well for yourself then?

Hmm. That was a tricky one. Had I?

Was it better to be a freelance media practitioner than . . . an accountant, say? Or a civil servant. Or a research chemist for a pharmaceutical company. These were the solid, honourable professions I imagined my classmates had mostly fallen into (though Hooton I more easily pictured as a nightclub bouncer. Or high-security prison inmate).

For some reason I felt as wobbly that evening as when I was a spindly eleven-year-old clutching my shiny new briefcase on the first day of term.

Who were my friends going to be? Was there going to be anything to say to them? Afterwards, was I going to feel better or worse about myself?

In short, was this a good idea?

2

Naturally I didn't want the hideous embarrassment of being the first to arrive, so I'd timed my cab to turn up half an hour after the advertised kick-off, by which time the event would be nicely under way, I calculated.

Hideously, I was the first to arrive.

For five excruciating minutes in the upstairs room at the Carpenters Arms, a horrible great barn of a place off a dual carriageway, it was just me and the barman. I sat on a stool and swallowed a large whisky in the hope it would do something about my damp palms. When I glanced into the mirror behind the optics, the gaze that returned mine was not that of a contented young man, fulfilled in his work, happy in his romantic life, eagerly relishing the prospect of catching up with some dear old pals. This bloke looked haunted.

Then in walked Roger Desouza.

'Oh, hello, Nicholas,' he said, as though it had been a fortnight rather than fifteen years since we'd last met.

I had never been particularly drawn to Roger Desouza. He was a brightish, hard-working, basically decent but ultimately dull boy; the kind who was admirable from a distance, which was where most were comfortable to keep him.

'I hear you on the radio when I'm driving home,' he remarked. 'Very amusing.'

Something rather awful seemed to have happened to Roger

Desouza's face. Once almost handsome in its youth, the flesh had thickened, and the expression upon it had dimmed by about ten degrees. Whatever early potential he may have shown – and it wasn't much – had apparently resolved itself into the countenance before me. The horrible thing about this was: I was sure the exact same thing had happened to me.

'So what are you up to these days?' I asked quickly to change the subject.

'Partner in a law firm.' He handed me a business card for a high street solicitors' practice. 'We do a lot of personal injury. Where there's blame, there's a claim, sort of thing.'

I popped the card into my breast pocket. 'I could slip on a tomato in Waitrose and end up in the fracture clinic,' I ventured.

'I'm your man,' said Roger.

It was fitting that we should be discussing personal injury compensation, because next to arrive was Neal Hooton.

The monster had broadened and, yes, thickened too in the intervening years, but had also somehow shortened. Or maybe it was me who had grown taller. Either way, he didn't seem nearly as impressive in his blue suit and shiny black shoes as he used to when he rampaged through the playground like a silverback gorilla in a school uniform. The wild hair had given way to a neatly barbered cut; and more importantly, much of the violence that used to leak from his person like an aura had evaporated. Indeed, so unthreatened did I now feel that – emboldened by the double Bells, possibly – I actually said to him after some opening pleasantries, 'You were a bit of a hard nut, as I remember.'

The old ruffian looked rueful. 'I did go bad for a bit. Fell in with a dodgy crowd outside school. I'm in the police now. Detective sergeant at Kentish Town.' There was a pause. 'Your face, honestly. You should see your face. Here, this'll make you laugh; I've put in an application for the murder squad. What are you drinking?'

Bloody hell, I thought. Hooton, a detective. But it sort of

made sense. They always needed people to beat the confessions out of the crims, didn't they?

The place was starting to fill up. All around . . . *men*, you'd have to call them, were shaking hands, punching each other in the shoulder, drinking beer from bottles, lighting fags. With a terrible shock of recognition, I clocked Phelps; back then, an impish shortarse of a kid; tonight, still short, but somehow horribly fleshed-in, his once ginger hair turned salt-and-pepper, his youthful freckly face darkened and creased by . . . by *life*, I guess. He was standing by himself, tapping a foot, looking around for someone, anyone, he used to be friends with.

Hooton had grabbed us a couple of glasses of the free wine that were being lined up along the bar. He clashed his against mine and leaned in to my ear. 'I know I was a bit of a cunt in them days. Sorry if I ever, you know . . .'

'No, not at all. You were never terribly unpleasant to me. The worst thing you did was crush my crisps. You crushed my crisps and said that meant I had more now.'

He winked at me. 'Good one.'

And then something happened. A molecular disturbance in the air; the funny atmosphere just before an earthquake measuring force eight on the Richter Scale turns your neighbourhood into a war zone. I swear the actual light in the room changed.

Everywhere seemed to darken subtly except for the doorway. Framed in it, Jay Bryant stood surveying the scene before him. He wore the same finely sculpted, almost feminine features; the same blazing, winning smile.

Hooton sniffed. 'I see your little friend has arrived.'

I nodded, unable to speak for some reason.

Jay clocked me, cocked his thumbs and trained two index fingers on my chest.

His first words in almost fifteen years – in nearly half a lifetime: 'Well fuck my old boots, look who it isn't.'

If I opened my mouth, I still wasn't wholly confident about what would come out. I reached for his hand and squeezed.

'Hello, Bryant,' growled the burly detective sergeant.

'Hooton, you old savage,' replied Jay with affection.

Instantly another scene in the playground came to me: Hooton astride a writhing weaker boy – it is Kapper; weird, disagreeable, a favourite target – his arms immobilised by Hooton's bulk, Hooton's free hand rooting to gain purchase between his victim's legs. The unequal struggle intensifying. Hooton's knuckles whitening as he squeezes . . . the terrible call of agony that we can all feel in the depths of our own trousers. The gleaming glob of saliva forming in the winter sunshine, now descending on its thread – Hooton has aimed well – straight between Kapper's gaping jaws.

The universal cry of revulsion among the spectators. Victim and assailant climbing to their feet, the grisly ritual over. And then Jay Bryant materialising alongside Neal Hooton, calm, almost friendly, asking if he can have a quiet word. As Kapper takes himself off to wherever the traumatised take themselves for a post-violation sob, the two boys in conclave by the wire fence, both rather solemn. Jay doing most of the talking, Hooton most of the listening and nodding. We never discover what they are, but the words spoken that morning must be very magical because, as it turns out, the torturer doesn't trouble Kapper again.

'What are you doing with yourself?' asked Jay.

'Met Police,' replied Hooton with a bit of a smirk.

'Murder squad,' I croaked.

My old friend laughed, shook his head in wonder at the funny turns that life took. And when Hooton went off to fetch more drinks he said, 'Fucking hell. If a psychopath like Hooton can redeem himself, there's hope for all of us.'

'And you?' I asked. 'What about you?'

He gave me a level look. 'Actually, don't tell PC Plod, but I just got out of prison.'

I sprayed Chardonnay over the Georgina von Etzdorf. 'You're joking, aren't you?'

Something about his expression suggested he wasn't.

'Jesus. What did you do?'

He paused. Released a huge smile of affection in my direction. 'Bit of a long story. Hey, it's *great* to see you, Nicholas.' He gazed at me fondly through the pitiless beam. 'It's *really* great to see you.'

'You too, Jay.' I meant it. It was.

There will be plenty to say about Jay Bryant in the course of this tale. It's probably already obvious that I was a little in awe of him, even perhaps a bit in love with him. Not in the way that Sprague was in love with Wilson, but in a nobler, purer way (and certainly with no question of the ghastly fumblings that Sprague and Wilson were said to go in for). Even at the time it occurred to me that our relationship might be a little unbalanced: if it wasn't hero-worship exactly, perhaps it wasn't far off.

It began in the third year when he joined our class. At the age of fourteen, Jay Bryant was everything I wasn't; he was cool and exceptionally good-looking; girls giggled and blushed when he spoke to them at the bus stop. I fell under his spell almost instantly.

Jay was gazing at me now, eyes flickering all over my face, the great arc-lamp of a smile almost too blinding to look into.

All I could think of saying was, 'You're looking great, Jay. It's amazing.'

'So are you, Nicholas,' he replied, but I knew he was lying. I could feel the waistband of my trousers biting into my stomach. Each morning, a few more hairs trapped in the teeth of the comb.

'How long is it? Since we last met?'

'Long time. Too bloody long.'

Whose fault is that then? I wanted to yell above the hubbub. Why didn't you reply to my letters? The last one returned by the post office. *Not Known At This Address*. The old telephone number, unobtainable.

'Must be at least ten years,' I suggested.

But I knew exactly how long. It was fourteen. That long summer at the end of our first year at university. The garden of a pub in Highgate. At first just me and Deano – I'll come to him in a moment – nursing our drinks, thinking that he wasn't going to turn up. We'd long been growing apart, the three of us. Nobody knew, however, that this was going to be the last time.

Hooton was standing a little way off with our wine, waylaid by some of the other violent inadequates he used to hang around with. Were they police officers too? It didn't seem impossible.

I reminded Jay of the day he'd taken Hooton aside in the playground. 'What did you say to him? I've always been curious.'

Jay smiled. 'Funny, you remembering that. I told him Kapper had a genetic illness. That nobody else knew about it. That the doctors reckoned he wouldn't live past the age of thirty. That one day the drugs would stop working and his bones would dissolve. That it was the worst death known to medical science.'

'Jesus.'

'I appealed to his better nature to let his short life be – well, not a happy one exactly, but at least not too miserable. It was all utter bollocks, of course.'

Kapper's tormentor returned with our drinks.

'Sorry to interrupt you two lovebirds,' he quipped. From his jacket pocket he produced a packet of crisps and tossed them at me.

'Cheese and onion, wasn't it?' He grinned.

3

Deano was a bit of a shock. He was wearing a tweed jacket and he'd grown a beard. In fifteen years he looked like he'd aged thirty.

'Who told you that beard was a good idea?' I quipped.

'Good to see you, Nicholas,' he replied, unfazed. 'You're looking very prosperous.'

I felt a little stung. 'You mean fat, don't you?'

'Not at all. Healthily prosperous, I should say.'

'Prosperous always means fat. I see you're prospering means I see you've put on weight.'

'It suits you,' he said warmly.

This was another surprise, Deano's new air of relaxed confidence. Although he always knew his mind, the old Deano could be a fidgety soul. I wasn't at all sure I preferred the Mark Two version.

Despite the nasty facial fuzz – there was plainly no *plan*; he had simply allowed it to form round his jaw like lichen – and the dreadful jacket – he could have been a geography teacher or scout leader – Deano still most resembled one of those wading water birds, the sort whose knee joints hinge backwards in wildlife programmes. He had been a shy, gawky boy, saved from worthlessness and potential victimhood by possession of an inner intensity and a strangely disorganised intelligence. At school, he flew below the radar, thereby failing to draw attention to himself as either (a) heroic sportsman; (b) cheeky monkey; or (c) unfortunate misfit who needed to be cruelly teased and/or brutalised. As it happened, I preferred to operate at this altitude myself. Apart from anything else, it was safest.

'So what are you doing with yourself these days?' I asked, to get in first.

'Systems,' he replied. And noting the blank look on my face, he added, 'I design software that allows machines to talk to other machines.'

It was such a grown-up answer, and the fact that he chose that moment to jangle some coins in his pocket left me with an odd urge to sob. What had happened to my twitchy old ally in the blackboard jungle?

In our way, we were a delicate pair of plants, Deano and I. Like me, Deano had not shone at any sport. Nor had he possessed a tribal loyalty to any football club. Nor had he been in the habit of talking publicly and graphically about sexual matters, a trait which for some reason was often constellated with success at games and footy fanaticism. In those days, the fact that sex consisted exclusively of desire and masturbation had done nothing to prevent the heartier of our classmates from supplying details we should have been horrified to voice.

Although no one else paid us much attention, I think Deano and I shone in one another's company. We were both helpless gigglers, for one thing. We loved to piss ourselves at the shortcomings of our teachers and fellow classmates. Beneath the pudding-bowl haircut, Deano's currant-bun eyes would glitter as he labelled Pugine 'a fat boy trying to get out of an even fatter boy'. Of Mr Porteous who taught German: 'What a loss to the unemployment register.' Of Tony Garibaldi — the first eleven's star striker — 'How much respect can you have for a person who's half-human, half-biscuit?' The fact that these cruel commentaries emerged from someone who looked like he should be mooching across a mudflat in search of worms made them all the more amusing to me.

Heavy sigh. Well, maybe you had to be there.

Of the time before Jay arrived, I seem to remember Deano and I mainly just 'hanging out', as it wasn't called then. I recall us playing chess (him winning every time); fooling around with his chemistry set (we made a *very* bad smell); but mainly talking. I picture two thirteen-year-olds in school uniform walking to the bus stop; a gawky one, small eyes in a pale face; the other darker, fleshier; both lugging *briefcases*. Cackling perhaps at the memory of one of Collins' – the class clown's – more hilarious statements (when asked to name an African country that shared a land border with Upper Volta, he famously ventured Lower Volta). Or discussing the technology in *Star Trek* (beyond me, but Deano was obsessed). Or speculating what terrible revenge Hooton would wreak on Knightly for whatever it was Knightly had done to Hooton (rumour spoke of fire damage to a West Ham scarf).

And then Jay Bryant turned up, and everything changed.

By rights, as a latecomer, he should have always been treated with suspicion. But there was something so effortlessly charming and bright about him – a natural intelligence rather than a results-based, academic excellence – no hint of shyness or awkwardness at being parachuted into a new circle of potential rivals and competitors, that he took his place in the scheme of things almost instantly, and without demur. It's true, some of the alpha-male types, those good-looking, sporty characters who were a little cute themselves in the charm and brightness stakes, may have viewed him warily in those early days. And his name itself – no one was called Jay back then – drew comments and the odd asinine remark. But by and large, he was so immediately like-able, so unthreatening to any of the various vested-interest groups (footballing, drug-taking, pop music, stamp-collecting), his overall moral superiority so incontrovertible, that within weeks it seemed like he'd been with us since the beginning.

I don't recall exactly how Deano and I fell under his influence. Looking back on it, there seems to have been no defining moment. Perhaps we sensed he might be our passport to a different sort of childhood; one that contained some greater challenge than writing space invader games for Deano's Sinclair ZX 81. Perhaps Jay sensed our admiration from afar, and in the manner of astronomical bodies our orbits were slowly captured by his stellar gravitational mass.

And Jay was the star all right, impeccably cool at dealing with the key *dramatis personae* in the world of the early teenager: teachers, other problematic boys, and, of course, *girls*.

There is a famous TV comedy sketch, much shown in this era, in which John Cleese, Ronnie Barker and Ronnie Corbett, dressed as upper-, middle- and working-class types respectively, stand alongside one another in descending order of height, offering humorous comments about their distinct positions in the social order.

'I am upper class,' intones Cleese. He turns and gazes upon Barker, 'so I look down on him.'

'I am middle class,' says Barker. He peers camera-left at the tall man in the bowler hat towering over him, 'so I look up to him' – now he flips his head camera-right to Corbett in flat cap and muffler – 'and down on him.'

Cut to close-up of Corbett. His expression is one of long-suffering. 'I know my place.'

Of course it wasn't like that for Jay, Deano and me – except in one respect: coolness. Jay was the *captain* of cool. Maybe the coolest boy in the whole school, out-cooling boys who were several years older. Deano and I were decidedly *uncool*. Nevertheless, like the comic class stereotypes, we had an instinctive regard for each other's place in the league table.

What was it that glued our triumvirate together? For my part, I admired Jay of course, and I appreciated Deano's hidden qualities (I imagined that I had hard-to-spot hidden qualities too). Deano I'm sure was equally in thrall to Jay. What Jay saw in *us*, you'd have to ask him. But we came to accept his leadership – almost – without question. Even when he let us in on some of his secrets – he wasn't above cheating in exams ('After all, what do exams test? Only your ability to pass them'), and the fact that his dad was some kind of fleet-footed entrepreneur – these only served to confirm his heroic status in our eyes.

It can't have been real, however, can it? Because it didn't last. Come college, and life beyond, it all evaporated.

I guess one has certain friends for certain times. Not everyone goes the distance.

'Who's Jay talking to?' Deano interrupted me in the middle of a rather tedious account of where I got my ideas from (he started it, he asked me).

Across the crowded room, Jay stood in the centre of a small knot of admiring . . . I was about to write 'boys'.

'It's Charlie Phelps. Boxer. Stephens. And, fuck me, it's Wanker. Jesus, Deano, this is faintly hideous, isn't it?'

Of course what I meant was *ageing*. When I first knew them, the people before me, Phelps, Boxer, Stephens, Wanker, they were – *we* were – *children*. I could still remember chasing around the playground playing off-ground-touch, for Christ's sake. *Now look*.

I suppose you'd have to admit there were still *traces* of youth about them – but more obvious to me were the creases and lines, assorted flaps and appendages of flesh that were wholly new. There were grey hairs, beer bellies and stoops. There was that crushed cast of carriage people assume after too many years journeying on Connex South Central. And the energy level of the group had changed. It felt deeper, heavier, more ponderous than before. An expectant rumble rather than a possible riot. And all this had been achieved by time. The simple, glacial accretion – day by day – of age to their, to *our* cases.

Was this fun, or was this excruciating? It was one of those events where the border between the two concepts is highly porous.

Wanker – Colin Wilkes, if memory served – was shaking Jay's hand, Jay smiling munificently.

'Christ, Wanker,' I said. I shook my head at the sorrow and the pity of it all. 'Wanker, Jesus.'

Here was Deano's opportunity to recall a funny remark from the Wanker era. How Kleenex shares had gone through the roof when Wanker hit puberty. How one might have powered a small Welsh village if only one could harness the kinetic energy of Wanker's right hand. How no one at Argos could understand why Wanker's self-winding watches were always at least eight hours fast. How some had suggested that Wanker's hand was actually at rest . . . and the whole of the rest of the world was frantically moving backwards and forwards at incredible speed. But this new, mature Deano – there was something disturbing about his sense of solidity – this Deano only said, 'Do you remember how we saved Wanker that day?'

I did. I'd never forgotten it. But Deano was rewriting history if he thought it was *we* who'd saved Wanker.

Wanker Wilkes was just the sort of worthless, nervy creature that boys who were only slightly less worthless themselves loved to torment. He was painfully short on social skills, not notably adept at any particular academic subject, and – particularly damning – crap at games. The fact that he was once found masturbating in a toilet cubicle was not in itself decisive either way – if one of the sportier boys had been discovered in the act, it might have been celebrated as a cheeky expression of a lively libido, a horny affirmation of the pleasure principle or some such bollocks. In poor Wilkes, however – such a gift that his surname was alliterative – it was seen as pathetic fumbling, a moral weakness on a par with bedwetting and who knew what other nameless shames.

Also he was a train-spotter. Trains were his passion. He ogled their photographs in specialist magazines. He logged their numbers feverishly in notebooks. He sent away for their collectible ephemera, tickets, timetables, guards' whistles and whatnot (this was in the days when guards had whistles. When trains had guards. When there were trains).

And he wore glasses (still did, I noted).

Oh yes, and he blinked a lot. .

As I say, none of these things *in themselves* was enough to condemn him. But taken together, he was so obviously a walking, talking (and yes, wanking) example of utter worthlessness that there was no serious dispute on the subject.

One lunchtime, Deano and I watched as a group of six or eight boys formed a circle round him in a hidden corner of the playground. There was a queasy half-smile on Wanker's face, as he spun round trying to ascertain the group's intent. Were they just teasing? Or did they mean to beat the shit out of him? The half-smile was there for protection: if it was all to be a laugh, well then he, Wanker, would want to be the first to join in (after all he, Wanker, understood better than anyone his lowly position in the food chain. He *felt* it every day).

They began to prod gently at him. A poke in the shoulder, a tug on the jacket. A ruffle of his hair. Wanker was turning like a top, blinking horribly, unable to bear the uncertainty, the thought of the violent assault coming from behind.

Deano and I were looking on. Neither taking part, nor doing anything to stop it. (We were powerless. We were fascinated.)

And then, probably only seconds before it would have got nasty – Wanker's smile had dissolved, any moment someone would have gone for his glasses – up walked Jay. He stepped calmly into the vicious circle, hands in his pockets.

'All right, Wanker?' he enquired kindly.

Wanker couldn't believe what was happening. Couldn't even speak.

'Any problem at all?' His persecutors began to turn away slowly. Jay had that kind of moral power over them. There was a plain, even pleasant expression on his face.

'Everything's fine, Jay,' Wanker managed to croak.

'Good, good. Just checking.'

And Jay just stood there, breezy as you like, as the mob slunk off.

After a bit, Deano and I wandered up to join them, probably a little ashamed that we hadn't helped Wanker in his hour of crisis (only that term in Modern History we'd copied down the phrase: *For evil to thrive, all that is necessary is for good men to do nothing.* Perhaps Deano and I didn't think of ourselves as good men at that point). Wanker was polishing his glasses on his tie, confused, and no doubt embarrassed to be at the centre of the rescue drama.

'Wanker,' said Jay quietly, 'next time anyone takes the piss, just fucking whack them, will you? They won't be expecting it. A smack in the face, a kick in the balls, whatever. They won't mess with you again.'

Deano and I nodded sagely, as if this was just the advice we would have proffered ourselves, and we left Wanker pondering this radical new approach to his personal safety.

Once we were out of earshot Jay said, 'Poor dumb fuck.'

I quipped, 'Aren't kids cruel?'

There was a very long pause, and Deano added, 'Yeah. But he is a bit of a wanker, isn't he?'

We all laughed.

4

Deano and I stared across the floorboards to where Jay was still deep in conversation with the older, apparently wiser, Wanker. Jay was laughing a lot, so either Wanker had developed a sense of humour, or he had some very funny news to impart.

The two of us strolled over to join our old friend.

'You'll never guess what W . . . what *Colin* does for a living these days,' cried Jay as we joined them.

Wanker was looking rather pleased with himself. He'd smoothed out somehow over the years, and thickened slightly. He was still doing the blinking thing, but his glasses didn't have thumb marks on the lenses or Sellotape round the hinges. I was also relieved to see he didn't have a top pocket full of biros, and that his fingers, when he put them out for me to shake, weren't covered in blue ink. I resisted a powerful urge to say, 'I hope you washed your hands.' I suspected that Deano was thinking the exact same thing.

'Something to do with railways?' I said.

Wanker raised his eyebrows comically. 'I do occasionally travel to work on the train, yes. How are you, Nicholas?' Hot brown eyes blazed into mine in a not altogether friendly fashion.

'Internet millionaire?' ventured Deano.

'It's true that more and more of our business is being done on the web.'

'Give them a clue,' said Jay quietly, the way he always spoke to Wanker.

Wanker furrowed his brow for a few seconds to denote thinking. Then he did a mime: reaching into the air to grasp something; a book. He mimed opening it, turning the pages. And then, the extraordinary thing. Glancing around, as though making sure there were no teachers about, he closed the thumb and index finger of his right hand into a circle and, in the time-honoured fashion, shook it suggestively in the region of his flies.

I think my mouth may have dropped open, because Wanker giggled.

'No change there then,' Deano muttered.

'Have you got it?' asked Jay.

'Loss adjuster?' I hazarded.

'Tell them,' said Jay.

'Adult magazines,' said Wanker. He didn't look at all embarrassed at the admission. If anything, the reverse.

'What? You mean, like . . . ?'

'What you would call porn, Nicholas. We're Britain's fourth largest supplier.' A bit of a stunned silence followed; Wanker continued. 'I prefer to use the term adult magazines, as our material does not deprave and corrupt. We needn't rehearse all the old arguments, but at bottom, we do live in a free society, thank goodness.'

There was a new confidence in Wanker too, I couldn't help noticing. A pedantry in his tone that he would never have dared display in the days when he was being tormented on a regular basis. Why had he said *at bottom* like that? Was he trying to be funny? My head swam a little. The evening was turning out to be a major mind-fuck. First Hooton was reinvented as a policeman, and now Wanker, a pornographer. There was something perverse yet oddly satisfying in the full circle the two class deviants had travelled.

'Would I have heard of any of your . . . your publications?' I stuttered.

'I doubt it. Though we're actually in the course of launching a new title called *Ripe*. For those with a penchant for farmyard scenarios. Might that be something of interest to you?'

'What . . . *animals*?' I blurted out, a little offended that he thought it might be.

Wanker's eyes shone irritably, as though I were a tiresome pupil who'd just made a particularly foolish comment. 'Not animals, Nicholas. *Ripe* is about milkmaids, and farm girls and the like. Research shows agricultural fantasy is a significant niche market, particularly in semi-agrarian societies.'

'Your parents must be very proud,' I said, and immediately regretted it. But Wanker was unabashed.

'You might like to pay us a visit some time. There's a pub nearby with an excellent carvery.' He handed round business cards. Golden Arm Publications. Colin Wilkes BSc. Chairman and Managing Director. An address in Vauxhall.

'And what about *you*?' Wanker asked with a bit of an edge to his voice. 'What are you doing with *your* life?'

I attempted to babble amusingly about my struggle to find material to fill 'Aimless Days', the weekly chronicles of a pointless urban thirty-something. It used to be the fifth-best-read part of the newspaper apparently, even though the newspaper itself was largely consumed by people over fifty, so who knew what was going on there? Why some bald bloke in a cardigan, pushing a lawn-mower round his garden in Nuneaton – for that was how I pictured the typical reader of the paper – why he, or for that matter his wife, who I visualised in slippers with a fag on, watching daytime telly, should have been remotely interested in the semi-fictional doings of a louche metropolitan boulevardier, I couldn't have begun to say. It was a profound mystery, albeit a profitable one from my perspective. As I jibbered on to Wanker about the imperative to keep coming up with new stuff about bars, restaurants, dates and the 'author's' gaggle of ghastly yuppie mates – I didn't bother to mention the depressing recent research that had talked of 'serious negatives' and 'reader hostility' – I wondered why it was that of the two of us, I suddenly felt like the flaky one.

The upstairs rooms at the Carpenters Arms was falling into the comfortable mainstream phase of the evening. The milling around, pumping hands and loud exclamations had given way to a more settled atmosphere. Small stable groups were forming, roughly along the same lines you would have seen in the school playground twenty years before. Coke and Fanta had been upgraded to Beck's and Grolsch; nevertheless I had the odd feeling that any moment someone might start dribbling a metal bottle top across the carpet. Jay, Deano and I found ourselves a table and gave way to speculating how the jumpy train-spotter could possibly have become a pornographer.

'There is something about trains and sex, isn't there,' I argued. 'All that insistent, rhythmical forward motion. Da-da-da-DAH! Da-da-da-DAH! Da-da-da-DAH! Da-da-da-DAH!'

'I feel sorry for your missus,' mumbled Deano.

'That climactic, getting faster and faster thing . . . and then coming to a complete standstill just outside Rugby.'

'Actually, a background in train-spotting could be useful to a pornographer,' announced Jay.

Deano and I stared at him. He took a deep glug of his bottle of lager and I thought, damn it, why isn't my jaw as firm as that?

'It's the attention to detail,' he continued. 'And the obsession. You'd want to exhaust the pornographic fantasy, capture it from every possible standpoint. Rather in the way you'd want to record every particular type of locomotive. You'd want nothing to elude you.' He smiled at me. 'They're both a bit banal in the end, aren't they? Porn and railways.'

'Is there a Mrs Wanker?' I enquired. 'I forgot to ask.'

'I'll find out,' replied Jay. 'We're having lunch. There's a certain little . . . *cause* of mine he seemed interested in discussing.'

'Really?' I didn't realise Jay was the sort of person who had causes. 'What's that all about then?'

'Funnily enough,' he said with a bit of a look in his eye, 'it's something you might be able to help me with, Nicholas.'

5

Three English gentlemen in a curry house shortly before midnight. The conversation filtered through a mulch of Bangladeshi food, top notes taken out by several hours of bottled lager and warm wine in the Carpenters Arms. It's an indistinct, low, throaty burble that reaches your ears, somewhere between eating and talking. Dialogue in fragments, like the poppadums.

'Long you been married?' asked Jay.

'Eight year,' replied Deano.

'What's name?' That was me.

'Megan.'

'Nice name.' Jay.

'Welsh?'

'Irish 'riginally. Grew up Lincoln.'

'Kids call?'

'Connor. Gaynor.'

It went silent after that. Well, not silent exactly, but nothing you can write down in words. There was a general chewing, a creaking of jaws. The clink of spoon against dish. Okra being speared. Cushions of naan parting with a sigh. The quiet felt like part of some religious ritual.

'Wanna talk about it?' I said, nodding towards the ring sitting on the third finger of Jay's left hand.

'Theatrical prop.' He spooned an extra-large portion of rice into his mouth. Chewed for a long time, waving his hand, buying time.

'Long story. But cutting it short . . .' Heavy sigh, like he was deciding which version to tell. 'I had to pretend to be married. All to do with one of those visa thingies. The girl needed it to stay in the country, blah blah blah. We bought the ring for five quid in Camden Market, to wear when the bloke from the Home Office came round. They visit to make sure you're not taking the piss. Which we were, of course.'

'So you're married.'

'Only in the eyes of the law. She's a lesbian. And now I can't get the fucker off my finger. Hasn't half cramped my pulling style, I can tell you.'

In the laughter, Deano mumbled, 'I don't know. Women are often attracted to married men.'

'It shows they can commit apparently,' I added. 'Women find that attractive.' I knew about this. We had been yacking about it on the radio programme only a few days before.

'Jay. What you were saying earlier. About what you've been doing lately.'

'You mean being in prison?'

Deano sent a shower of yellow rice grains pattering across the tablecloth.

'In many ways, it was a fascinating experience,' said Jay. 'Not for everyone, of course. But I really think . . . do I think this? . . . yes, I really think I might have regretted it if I hadn't gone. It was a bit like school to an extent. Only with better drugs. And more interesting cell-mates. Present company excepted, naturally.'

We were both staring at him, a little wide-eyed I expect.

'Don't look so shocked. It was one of those nice, friendly open prisons full of bent businessmen and perjured MPs. No one really nasty or violent or anything. I made some good contacts. There's an open invite to a castle in Scotland, when parole for a certain viscount comes through any day now. That was coke. He was fucking mad for coke, that one.'

Jay smiled at me. I had to ask. 'How, er . . . ?'

'What did I do? Another long story. It was a corporate thing, to do with a company I got involved in. Cutting it short, it went tits up, there had been some . . .' He scratched a pair of inverted commas in the air. '. . . some *irregularities*, which were technically illegal. According to the lawyer, it all boiled down to a case of someone having to go to jail for a year. Me or the bloke who actually started the company. It was one of those where you could present the facts one way or the other.' Jay ran a swab of naan round his plate. 'Jerry had a family. And a sick wife. And let's just say he made it well worth my while.'

'What sort of company was it?' I couldn't say why I wanted to know.

'Financial instruments.' There must have been something unpleasant in my expression, because he added, 'I had nothing to do with it, Nicholas. I just took the blame. Like I say, I've never been paid so well for . . . what was it? . . . eight months' work in my life. Cleared all my credit-card bills. Got very fit in the gym, and, as I say, made some intriguing new friends. Anyhow,' he said, 'changing the subject, was it The Flask? Where we met last time.'

'I think so,' I replied.

As I have said, I *knew* so.

'I had that MG. Fuck, what a useless car that was. Gorgeous, but useless. Do you remember it? You and me in the front, Deano in the back. That day we drove down to Brighton.'

'No.'

'No, we never did that, did we? We always said we would, though.'

We laughed about that one for a bit. But it wasn't the red MG that I especially remembered from the last night at The Flask. It was the person who stepped out of the passenger door after him. The luminous beauty who haunted my waking thoughts in those days, and then drifted through my dreams at night. As if in slow motion, I could still see her closing the car door. It made no sound, like silence in the aftermath of a bomb explosion. She seemed to float round to my side of the table in the beer garden, settling on the rough wooden bench next to me – I couldn't bring myself to look, but I imagined her lovely soft limbs spreading against the splintery timbers – the amazing pale face in its cloud of dark hair, and her perfume, that intoxicating mix of leather jacket and some particular brand of fragrance which, even years later, whenever I caught a whiff of it, in a bar or on the street, made my stomach lurch at the sudden, somehow shocking thought of *her*.

Her.

6

I allowed a few minutes to pass before asking.

'Whatever happened to that, er, very striking girl you used to go out with at university?'

He smiled. 'You were rather fond of her, weren't you, Nicholas?'

Did I blush? I hoped not. I couldn't say for sure.

'She was a stunner, Jay.'

Stunner. Stunner didn't even begin to convey it. Her almost painfully good looks. The huge grey eyes, full of light; eyes that somehow seemed too well drawn, too detailed (you suspected eyes penned in so much detail would *see* in too much detail). Those amazing long lips (lips with an independent existence, lips that seemed like a separate creature). The sinewy voice clothing her words, one minute warm and amused, the next bruised and philosophical. The slim, almost slight physique. The way she moved (a lightness of motion so very different to the ground-based plodding of my 'girlfriend' of the time). It wasn't just me. Plenty of male heads turned when she entered a room, though most weren't perhaps quite so obsessed. To me, she was more fascinating than any movie star. I was captivated by the blank, beautiful face, which in repose invited you to write anything upon it, and when troubled – as it often seemed to be by some nameless perturbation – well, then you just wanted to come flying to her rescue. Cancel stunner. To me Caroline Stamp was a full-blown goddess.

Okay, look at it another way: I was a nineteen-year-old male.

She wasn't his first, of course. Jay went through girls (they weren't *women* in those days) at a rate that seemed extraordinary to me. In our latter days at school, when I was still fumbling my way around Astrid Margolis and Deano was doing . . . whatever he was doing, Jay was dating all manner of exotic creatures. *Extremely* attractive girls were often to be found waiting for him on the park bench opposite the school gates, a new one every few weeks it would seem. At university – though we went our separate ways, he to Sussex, I to Manchester and Deano to Brunel – I calculated that in the ten months that I plodded on with my first college girlfriend, Jay had been through at least six – what he called – 'serious relationships'. But then came Caroline Stamp. And suddenly he was a one-man woman.

They met at a party in Oxford – Jay had gone up for the weekend to visit his older brother and check out the 'posh totty'. It was one of those 'chemical things', he told me. They laid eyes on one another and, as he put it, 'bam, that was it'. By his account, they spent the next forty-eight hours in bed (I remember wanting to ask, *but what about the eating arrangements, the toilet arrangements?*). Until Jay got his MG, they both became highly familiar with the public transport connections between their respective university towns.

He brought her back home for the long summer holiday, his eyes full of love. And even as my mouth went dry and speechless and my stomach flipped whenever I looked at her, I recognised the validity of his claim. They belonged together. They were one of those golden couples you meet every so often. Blessed in their beauty and charm to the wider world, absorbed in their animal attraction to each other.

'Yeah, we had a nice time,' said Jay. 'But you know. She was like the MG. Gorgeous but uphill.'

'What is she doing? Do you ever hear from her?' I carried on eating, eyes locked on to my postbox-red tandoori chicken.

'Yeah, we talk every so often. Working for a record company.'

'Married now, I suppose. Children and what-have-you.'

There was no reply, so I looked up. Jay was staring at me with a small smile on his face. 'No, she's not married, Nicholas. I think she might even be single at the moment. Why? You interested?'

A trapdoor opened in my gut. I made a ridiculous noise, adequately covered by the word 'guffaw'. Waved my fork about meaninglessly. Felt a tandoori hue creep into my complexion.

'I'll introduce you if you like. Re-introduce you; I mean, you have met.'

'A long time ago.'

'I'm sure she'd remember you.'

'Really?' I didn't know if this was a good thing or a bad thing.

'You're probably more her type than me.'

I struggled to keep my voice under control. 'How do you mean?'

'Oh, you know. Deep. She likes deep. She can be a moody cow at times.'

The conversation replayed itself in my head as my cab bowled along the Finchley Road. I gazed upon the passing pavements and shops, but I didn't see them. In their place was a vision of Caroline Stamp on my brown leather sofa. Her legs were crossed at the ankles, there was a drink in her hand, and she was staring at the ceiling, her face clouded by some ongoing personal puzzle. I came up behind her, put my hands gently on her shoulders, leaned over and kissed her on the lips. Upside-down, as it were. We stuck with it for a minute or so, chewing at one other in this delightfully unfamiliar configuration.

'I always had a funny feeling about you,' she said eventually (upside-down, her mouth looked like it belonged to someone else).

'How so?' I replied.

'The way you used to go all quiet. I knew you were . . . thinking things. Deep things.'

I peered into the enormous grey eyes. 'Well, you were dead right about that, matey.'

The lights were off when we pulled up outside the flat, so I took it that Squeaky had retired for the night. A relief, to be honest. My head was so full of the raised ghost of Caroline Stamp I could almost smell her perfume. Jay's words were echoing in my head like a mantra. *You're probably more her type than me. I'll introduce you if you like. She might even be single at the moment.*

I sat on the sofa for half an hour, staring into space, running through the events of the evening. Jay was married to a lesbian and had a prison record. Deano had acquired a beard, a tweed jacket and a family. Beyond the general goodbyes and it's been greats, we'd made no plans to see one another again.

Squeaky sighed when I crept in beside her. 'Nice evening?' she murmured.

'Very pleasant.' I threw my arm around her and gently bit her ear lobe. She wriggled lazily. After a while her breathing grew deeper and I could feel my thoughts beginning to get all bendy, the way they do in the moments before dropping off.

'Met a couple of old pals this evening,' I mumbled. 'Thought we could have them over for dinner.'

'Did they know you when you were a little boy?'

'I fear so.'

'I'll make lemon chicken.'

'Mmm.'

'And that vegetable dish of mine you like.'

'What vegetable dish of yours that I like?'

A half-hearted kick beneath the duvet.

'Was a joke, darling.'

A pause. Then, 'Nicholas?'

'What?'

'Did you meet any of your old flames?'

'Old flames?'

'Sweethearts. Exes.'

'I went to an all-*boys* school. I think you knew that.'

'Ah.'

She grew silent. I began to think about Wanker Wilkes. For some reason he was crooning into a microphone 'If You Were The Only Girl In The World (And I Were The Only Boy)'.

'Nicholas?'

'Yes.'

'So *did* you meet any of your old flames?'

A giggle. And we were asleep.

TWO

1

The next morning I woke up feeling flat. Flat and a bit foolish even. Jay Bryant who I'd so admired at school, for all his handsome heroism and occupation of the moral high ground, was now an ex-con who'd married a lesbian for money. My old pal Deano – jittery, giggly Deano – had turned into a whiskery scientist. In grotesque counterpoint, the class sadist had mutated into an officer of the law and the class wanker – make that the *school* wanker; actually, make that the biggest wanker within the entire local education authority, quite possibly – had evidently become a successful publishing tycoon (albeit of visual aids to semi-agrarian self-abusers).

Was there a pattern here? If there was, I couldn't see it. Certainly my own story was not inspirational. My newspaper column was certain to be axed; the ominous silence from Nigel who edited the section it appeared in could surely only mean one thing.

So, flat and still woozy from the night before, I contrived to make things even worse. I blundered clumsily into an argument with Squeaky, my girlfriend. My not-quite-fiancée.

She was getting ready to leave for work; I was preparing to hang round for an hour or so, drinking coffee and generally summoning up the energy to go out and buy all the papers prior to my regular guest appearance on Yack FM 24:7, as they styled themselves. I wondered whether, once I was no longer 'columnist' Nicholas Pitt, they would continue to book me.

The opening exchange was pretty innocuous.

'Your old schoolfriends,' she said. 'What are they up to now then?'

I didn't feel much like talking. The Scotch, the warm wine and the couple of beers in Tandoori Nirvana had taken their toll. 'Oh, you know. The usual.'

You can tell I made my living as a professional communicator, can't you?

'Solicitors, accountants, programmers . . . ?'

'Oh, totally. Married, kids, pets. The whole nine yards.'

Was there a trace of contempt in my voice for this picture of bourgeois domesticity? I fear so.

In a quiet voice Squeaky said, 'Really?'

In my head, an air-raid siren began its lonely wail. I attempted a recovery. 'One of my best friends has actually married a lesbian.'

Ominous pause. 'Is that so?'

'Yes.' Horrible long pause.

Squeaky perched herself on the edge of the brown leather sofa and stared at her fingernails. Her expression became rather serious. Oh fuck, here we go then . . .

'Nicholas . . .' she began.

'Anita . . .' Another horrid pause. Deep breath. 'I . . .'

'Have you been thinking about what we decided, Nicholas?'

'Of course I have. You know I have.'

'There isn't much time left, you know that.'

'I know.'

'A month.'

'Five weeks, I make it. Nearly six actually.'

Why do these things always come out of a blue sky? Squeaky's face reddened. After what seemed like an age, a couple of fat teardrops plopped on to the hide cushions, darkening where they landed. Squeaky tried to brush them away with the back of her hand. I sat down and put an arm round her shoulder. A sob shuddered through her, and a very large tearstain appeared on the sofa. I knew from experience that it would eventually evaporate, leaving behind the faintest ring of salt.

'I hate to be the one always bringing this up, Nicholas,' she snuffled.

'You're not.' She was.

'Don't want to be on your case the whole time.'

'You're not.' Not the *whole* time. 'Really, I'm very aware of what we decided.'

What we decided.

Six months previously, after yet another one of those Where Are We Going conversations reached no definite conclusions, we agreed that we needed a deadline. Actually it was Squeaky's idea, although in all probability, Catherine had put her up to it at one of their girly lunches. Either way, I could see the force of the argument: two and a half years together was plenty of time in anyone's book, and more to the point, easily long enough *To Know*. However, so as not to put too much pressure on anyone, we agreed we would come to a decision about our relationship by the third anniversary of the date we first met. It was an easy one to remember; Catherine's birthday, 1 September; the day Hitler invaded Poland. And when I say that 'we' would come to a decision, of course I meant *me*. Squeaky had already made her mind up. As far as she was concerned, I was her Mr Right, but she wasn't prepared to waste her life waiting for me to propose. She'd give it until Catherine's next birthday, which was now just under six weeks away. Or forty days and forty nights, if you want to get all biblical. So like I say, I had been thinking about it.

Squeaky raised her tear-stained face and, fixing her sad blue eyes upon me, let me have it, both barrels. An expression of such misery that my heart twisted in its cavity and I very nearly blubbed myself.

'Look, darling. Perhaps now isn't the best time . . .'

'Why won't you say it, Nicholas?'

'It's not that, it's—'

'So what that we like different things? That I don't get Woody Allen, and you weren't very keen on *The Ice Storm*—'

'Not very keen? I couldn't *stand* that movie.'

'Or that I don't care for Chinese food and you could live off it.' I'd forgotten that one. Very damning, don't you think? 'Or that I couldn't get on with *White Teeth* and you thought it was brilliant. What does any of that stuff matter?' Squeaky began dabbing at herself with a tissue, sniffing, and all that other female repair activity. 'Yes, I know what you say – that none of it matters in itself. It's what it's symptomatic of that's important. But I don't think it's symptomatic of anything. Lots of people don't get Woody Allen.'

True, this last. But it was tough to go out with someone who could sit through a picture like *Love and Death* stony-faced.

'You don't like the Marx Brothers,' I threw in softly, to lighten the mood.

'I do like them.' Loud sniff. 'Well, not all of them. Not that one with the silly hair.' A giggle. Barely audible, but I clocked it.

'You can't like only *some* of the Marx Brothers. That's like saying . . . What *is* that like saying? That's like saying . . . that you only like the top half of some great painting. Or two out of the Three Graces.'

'He's very irritating. The one with the stupid hair.'

'Harpo.'

'That thing when he puts his leg in your hand, it's terribly annoying.' And now a definite silvery tinkle. She blinked back a tear. 'Don't you find that annoying? And that bicycle horn all the time?'

'It's meant to be comically anarchic.'

'The Italian one is a bit trying too.'

'Now you're definitely pushing it.'

'The awful bits where he plays the piano.'

'Ah, well I'll give you that. Those are painful.'

Shafts of sun poked through the stormclouds. Squeaky's mood seemed to be lightening.

'So when you say you like the Marx Brothers, it turns out you only really like Groucho.'

'Which one is he?'

'*Which one is he?* The one with the moustache.' I waggled an imaginary cigar around my lips, put on the voice: 'Mrs Claypool, ever since I met you, I've swept you off my feet.'

Long pause. No giggle.

I tried another. 'Outside of a dog, a book is a man's best friend. Inside of a dog, it's too dark to read.'

'Oh yes,' she said. 'Him. He's a bit irritating as well, isn't he?' Now a full-scale peal. 'Still, it would be a dull world if we all thought the same, wouldn't it?'

I kissed her on the eyelids.

'Can I have my hangover now, please?' I asked politely.

She poked me in the chest and gathered up her handbag. 'Silly sausage,' she said.

2

Squeaky's given name is Anita Margaret Chivers. But the moment I heard her open her mouth (about half an hour after I was smitten by the sight of her long, blonde body on the other side of the room where we first met), in the seconds that it took her to say in that silvery cheeping tone of hers, 'You're Catherine's friend, aren't you? Apparently we share several common interests. Oh, that sounds terrible doesn't it? I mean interests in common. You know what I mean' – well, the word just popped fully formed into my head and had remained up there ever since. Of course the disjunction between the tall, elegant creature and the noise that came out of her face at first served to make her all the more sexy. It was the fascinating flaw – the small mole, or scar – that one couldn't quite take one's eyes (in this case, ears) off.

I can remember rather disloyally telling people around the time we first became an item, 'It's like going out with a budgie. Or a canary.' They would laugh and request amusing details. 'It's the hardest voice to imitate,' I would say. 'Very high. Quite sibilant, rather posh, and she's got this tinkly laugh. Like a bell.'

Squeaky and I didn't technically live together, though we might as well have done for all the time we spent with one another; sometimes in her fussy, rather-too-girly-for-my-taste apartment near Marylebone High Street, sometimes in my agreeably disordered, vaguely minimalist flat in Chalk Farm. There was some-

thing a bit Weimar Republic, a bit Bauhaus, a bit modern movement about Squeaky's look – the tall, thin frame, the short blonde
hair – that seemed to go terribly well with my high ceilings and
modernist furniture. During the week she wore a lot of those
handsome dark suits cut for women in business. Some evenings
after work, as she arranged herself along my Conran sofa with
a glass of dry white in one hand and takeaway menu in the other,
I could almost persuade myself that we belonged together.

Almost.

The truth was that we had reached the point where we should
either get married or split up. Both outcomes seemed as plausible, or to put it another way, as equally far-fetched. Yes, we
rubbed along fine, we didn't bore one another, we could stand
each other's friends (actually, she had an appalling friend called
Chloe, but let that pass). We'd successfully ticked all the basic
couply boxes – going on holiday together, passing time in bars
and restaurants, plodding round Tesco. We'd been to movies and
the theatre (okay, we saw *Art*. It was mercifully short). We'd had
quiet nights in front of *Big Brother* with a 17, a 28, two 41s and
a portion of prawn crackers. She'd met my parents, I'd met hers.
She'd looked after me when I had flu (and vice versa). She'd
seen me at my worst (being sick into a hedge after a party) and
I at hers (farting raucously when she thought I was out of the
flat. My, how I laughed). In short, as a couple we'd been tested
in all the categories that couples get tested in, and not been
found seriously wanting. By rights, the next thing that should
have happened is I should have dimmed the lights, got down on
one knee, whipped out the old diamond-peaked band, and, in
a shaky voice, uttered the 'M' word. I felt the weight of expec-
tation – the feeling that Now Is The Time For Him To Ask Her
To Marry Him, What Is He Waiting For, Fucking Christmas? –
hovering over our relationship like the mother ship in
Independence Day.

And yet. And yet.

My secret worry was that Squeaky was ultimately too . . . too posh for me, too *brittle* I think is the word. The idea of us going the distance, facing the *long haul*, actually growing *old* together . . . all that seemed impossible to contemplate. The alternative, however – shaking hands and heading our separate ways ('it's been fun, but there comes a time to let go . . .') – whenever I attempted to visualise that scenario, it wasn't long before I found a lump in my throat and felt a need to list her good qualities.

Squeaky was warm and generous and almost always cheerful (although that could become a little irritating after a time). She was smart (she got better A levels than I did). She could run faster than me (as I discovered when we chased a taxi down Oxford Street one evening). She would laugh at my jokes (even the wide-mouthed-frog one), and although she didn't tell jokes herself, she was often very amusing (her best line: 'Mmm. I'll give you four hours to stop doing that'). If she'd been a country, she would have been somewhere intelligent, good-looking and upbeat; somewhere like Denmark or Singapore. If she'd been a colour, it would have been orange. Day of the week: Wednesday. Department store: Harrods.

Her only serious negative was that she liked pot-pourri.

Oh yeah, and she ate soup 'properly' – i.e. she pushed the spoon *away* from herself, and then did something perfectly horrible with her face when the spoon rose to meet it, wrinkling her nose and extruding her lips to form a funnel. I dare say the Queen would have approved, but it always made me want to jog her elbow at the critical moment.

Anyhow, get married or call it a day. An odd choice to be faced with really. For a while it was my theory that – in terms of Where Are We Going? – maybe we were just where we were: a pleasant enough place, to be sure, but not necessarily the slip road to the Great Highway of Life. I once attempted this line of argument with Squeaky and it didn't play nearly as well as I'd hoped (think cup of cold sick).

In truth she should probably have gone out with a Toby or a Giles or a Hugo. One of those big-boned boys with small eyes who worked in property or finance (not a media whore like me). Chaps' chaps who played rugger and cricket and drove posh cars; chaps who wouldn't have been seen dead in a seven-year-old Toyota.

We didn't even *look* alike (often cited as a factor in why people are attracted to one another). Squeaky was dramatically pretty (though, lacking the mythological element, you probably wouldn't have said beautiful). She had a very sweet face, not at all like mine, which was rather weird.

During all our time together, I couldn't escape the feeling that I was somehow dragging her down. That she was degrading herself, slumming it in some way. Though that of course did help to make the sex quite exciting.

3

The headquarters of Yack FM 24:7 are to be found on the ground floor of a windowless building in a small industrial estate off the North Circular Road – not far from the World of Leather superstore, if you know the area – about three-quarters of a mile from the Hanger Lane gyratory system. The general environs would seem more appropriate to the manufacture of small electrical appliances or the assembly of ready meals than to the dissemination of wit and repartee to a potential audience of the entire population of the United Kingdom. But then, as the refreshingly blunt Australian manager who ran the place put it, 'Rule one. It's fuckin' *radio*. No one gives a shit where it comes from. You can do it in a fuckin' hole in the ground.' And, he was known to add with a bit of a glint in his eye, 'What we haven't pissed away on poncy offices in Covent Garden, with fuckin' . . . carpets and atriums all over the place, we can apply to you people.'

Yeah, right.

The Big Yack (11 a.m. – 5 p.m.) was what they call a 'rolling zoo format'. That is to say, there was a central presenter and an ever-changing roster of guests and panellists who stopped by to shoot the shit about the day's 'top talking topics'. Listeners were meant to gain the impression that they had joined a particularly lively debate about the issues of the hour, both serious and trivial. Indeed, they were constantly entreated to 'phone in and have *your* say'. At its best, *The Big Yack* might have kept you from falling asleep if, say, you were stuck in a slow-moving contraflow system somewhere outside Birmingham (and none of the other thirty-odd stations available on your radio dial was to your liking). At its worst, it was a vivid confirmation of Sartre's dictum that hell is other people. Nevertheless — and here was the nub of the thing — they did pay me actual pounds sterling simply for turning up and saying the first thing that came into my head.

That afternoon, it was a panel of the usual shameless gobshites that I slipped in alongside, while an advert played for a haemorrhoid preparation. There was Judy, the hysterical women's magazine writer (not *funny* hysterical alas, the *other* sort of hysterical). There was Angus, the smelly ex-Member of Parliament who lost his seat at the last general election (ha ha bloody ha). There was a woman who used to work for the BBC who'd written a book about dating secrets of the ancient Greeks. There was a minor TV chef. And there was me. We sat round a circular table heaped with newspaper cuttings and plastic cups, from the centre of which sprouted five microphones like a flower arrangement.

Squatting at the head of the table, presiding over *The Big Yack*, was the considerable figure of Clyde Folger, a giant toad of a broadcaster who'd worked in speech radio for so long, his limbs seemed to have atrophied, leaving behind mainly belly and face. He probably measured only five foot five, but in every direction, his body a mere life-support system for his mouth. And what a mouth. Issuing from it was the deepest, darkest, most wonderfully well-modulated male voice you have ever heard. If it told you to buy Brand A (and it would have) you would buy it. Ditto Brand B. If it suggested you load a shotgun and blow away your granny, you'd probably have the dear old thing sighted along the barrel before reason prevailed. Sadly, however, what Clyde said came almost totally unmediated by anything you'd call a thought process. Like an actor, his words arose from the diaphragm, and he seemed happy to rely on that organ for their content as well. In short, he talked absolute bollocks . . . but bollocks delivered with such conviction that you didn't care. He could read out the telephone directory and you'd beg him to do the Yellow Pages for an encore.

The commercial ended.

'Yack FM for a Tuesday,' Clyde intoned like he was announcing the outbreak of war. 'Writer and columnist Nicholas Pitt joins us in the sand box . . .'

Sand box? 'Hello, Clyde,' I said, my voice sounding terribly thin all of a sudden.

'I think you know your fellow astronauts.'

Astronauts? 'Certainly do.'

Clyde barely looked at me, his red-rimmed eyes skittering behind their half-moon specs at the drifts of newspaper in front of him. His headphones only just fitted over his huge cranium. A slim panatella burned between stubby yellow fingers. The fuzzy brown beard completed the illusion that you were having a chat with an overgrown tree-stump.

'So, what gives, *muchacho*?' he asked. 'Anything shaking apart from the leaves on the trees?'

'Well, I did a dangerous thing,' I replied. 'I went to a reunion of my old school.'

There were various *oohs* and *aahs*. The women's magazine writer went as far as to say *wooo*.

'There's usually a reason that one doesn't see people in a long time,' she added to demonstrate her deep understanding of the complexity of human relationships.

'On a scale of one to five,' boomed Clyde, 'I'm guessing we're talking six.'

Oddly, I knew what he meant. 'It was fairly weird, yeah.'

'Don't tell me. The sad little squit who no one liked—'

I said, 'That would be me, actually.' They were polite enough to laugh.

'Don't tell me, Johnny No-mates is now Jack the Biscuit. Am I right?'

'Not quite. But it's funny you should say that.'

The great broadcaster suppressed a belch. 'Uncle Clyde's Life Lesson one hundred and eight: ignore the loud buggers. It's the quiet ones you've got to watch.'

Debate was duly engaged. The women's magazine writer said attachments formed at school were often the most powerful in one's life, though she herself was no longer in touch with any of her classmates. The TV chef talked about how he had been 'teased rotten' because he was the only boy in his year who took cookery; when his potatoes *dauphinoise* came third in a nation-wide competition, he'd been quite badly beaten up behind the science block. The ex-MP recalled a reunion at his old prep school where he discovered that the boy who had regularly come bottom of the form had gone on to become Secretary of State for Wales. And the woman from the BBC said she'd recently discovered that the girl she'd sat next to in French had married the owner of the second biggest bank in Belgium and had four children. 'The funny thing was, she always used to say that she'd marry a banker and have four children,' she added.

Clyde looked like his past life was flashing before his eyes. Then, suddenly, everyone had stopped talking.

'*Can* you go home again? *Is* the past another country? Or is it more like Portsmouth?' he boomed. 'Phone the Yack Line and have your say.' He gave the number. 'We're remembering the days of the old school yard . . . here on Yack FM.'

A commercial played, for heartburn tablets. Behind the glass in the control room, a pretty girl in camouflage gear and metal piercings raised a lady-thumb into the air. 'Very nice, everybody,' she alleged in an antipodean accent through the loudspeaker. 'We'll do another ten minutes on schooldays, then asylum-seekers, then the Spice Girls reunion.' It was Meredith, the producer.

The rest of my hour on the show went by in a bit of a blur. Clyde took calls from members of the public. There was Brian 'hands free on the M6', a woman from Torbay with a canary in the background, and Kenneth, a 'first-time caller', who asked Clyde to be patient with him because he was 'very nervous'. Clyde said he needn't worry, because 'there's a first time for everything, up to and including folk dancing, my friend'. The woman who wrote for a women's magazine was replaced by a man who wrote for a men's magazine. The TV chef by an agony aunt. We opined. We joshed. Someone called Sandy called from Sheffield to say we were 'a lot of smug southern tossers'.

'Hard to quarrel with that,' I purred, drawing laughter from my fellow tossers.

After an ad for a rheumatism remedy, Clyde, without once lifting his eyes off the papers in front of him, said, 'Thanks to writer and columnist Nicholas Pitt. Good trenchant stuff, *compadre*. We'll see you on the next one. I think you know the way out.'

As I slipped away, I once again reflected on the fact that I'd never witnessed Clyde in a standing position. His stomach seemed to have actually grown into the side of the table, the way an old tree will envelop a garden railing. Legend spoke of a secret hose arrangement that carried away his waste products during the six hours he was anchored to the microphone. On one occasion I did ask him how he managed such a long stint. Every other atom of his body remained still as his lips parted and in his dark brown voice he replied, 'Never drink milk on air, old love. Promotes mucus.'

'Very nice, Nicholas,' said Meredith as I put my head round the control room door. 'Good stuff with the reunion.'

Behind the glass, in the studio where I had so recently been sitting, the yack-fest continued. The former MP was making the case that 'There are certainly no easy answers, and things will probably get worse before they begin to get better, but that is not a reason for standing idly by and doing nothing.' The engineer sitting in front of a bank of knobs and faders said, 'I think we're losing him, Merry.'

Meredith glanced at Clyde, leaned over and flipped a key on the engineer's control panel.

'Clyde, mate.' She was speaking into his headphones. The human toadstool appeared to stir from a reverie. Or possibly deep sleep, it was hard to tell. 'Only another three and a half hours.' She flipped the key back. 'He's a great pro. I've learned a lot from him.'

'It's *The Big Yack*,' announced Clyde like the Voice of God. 'All yack, all the time, twenty-four:seven, from now till Kingdom come. More from the pork barrel after the following miracles and wonders.'

4

After flirting with Jamie, Nigella and even Delia, Squeaky finally settled on Nigel: a recipe of his that we called 'pornographic lamb'. It was a week later; the evening of the dinner party for my old schoolfriends.

One Sunday morning, I'd turned a page in a colour supplement and come upon what can only be described as hardcore food porn. Filling the frame in its lustrous depravity, a gleaming chunk of pink mammal flesh reclined suggestively on a crib of cute baby onions and wedges of roasted potato. 'Fuck me, get a load of that,' I'd commented to Squeaky at the time. She'd thoughtfully clipped the article.

Deano was the first to arrive. With Mrs Deano. Megan. A rather plain dark-haired woman with a faint regional burr to her voice. Deano had completed his transformation from nervy schoolboy to stalwart of the suburbs. He was wearing a pair of what you might describe as *slacks*. Pale brown, quite nasty, with sharply defined creases. Teamed with the burgundy V-neck pullover, he reminded me of a model in a leisurewear catalogue for the middle-aged. Standing in the sitting room, back to the mantelpiece, glass of Scotch in one hand, spare hand down the trouser pocket, he struck a solid figure of patrician virtue. Mrs Deano perched on the edge of an armchair, gazing at him with something like admiration.

Squeaky had gone into minor-member-of-royalty mode.

'And is Colindale *convenient*? For getting into town and what-have-you?'

'Well, Dean drives,' said Mrs Deano. 'And there's always the Northern Line.'

'Actually, we don't go into town much,' growled Deano. 'The West End's become a zoo.'

I nodded in silent agreement, even though I actually rather liked London at night; its dark promise of Entertainment.

'Quite a do the other night,' I remarked to Deano. 'Seeing old Wanker again.'

'*Wanker?*' shrieked Squeaky. 'There wasn't a boy there called Wanker?'

'That wasn't his real name,' said Deano.

'No. His real name was Masturbator. Wanker was just a nickname.'

Some awkward laughter. Mrs Deano looked at me a little oddly. Squeaky said, 'I'll just check on the oven.'

'Looks very nice,' said Deano, nodding towards the dining table laid for five, candle burning at its centre. 'Typical Jay. Always late.'

'Remember that morning when he was late for assembly?'

The whole school in the big hall. Jay trying to sneak in quietly through a side entrance. Not during a hymn, where he might have got away with it unnoticed, but during some routine announcements. Heaps, the headmaster, clocking him.

'*You*, boy. You are *late*! Who is that boy? . . . *Bryant*. Why are you late? Everyone else has contrived to arrive here on time. All were no doubt subject to the same vagaries of public transport, traffic congestion and the like. So what is *your* excuse? Hmm? I think we should all like to hear it. *Hmm?*'

Every head swivelled towards Jay Bryant as he completely failed to lose his composure in the face of the withering verbals.

'I'm terribly sorry, sir,' he said in a clear, firm voice. 'The man next door fell down his stairs and fractured his skull. I helped look after him until the ambulance came.'

Later he confided to Deano and me, 'When it's a lie, always make sure it's a big one. And make sure it's a lie that makes you look *better* than you would have looked if you hadn't needed to tell it in the first place.'

The doorbell. He was here.

I opened up, but my smile faded when I realised that Jay had brought someone with him. And then my stomach fell through the floor as I found myself staring into a pale face set in a cloud of dark hair; huge grey eyes that seemed to have too much *detail* about them. As though eyes which had been so intricately drawn might have been able to *see* more than other eyes. Might have been able to see straight through your own eyes, for example, and read the writing on the back wall of your head. The eyes in question were lit by an expression of wry amusement.

Long lips began to slide against one other.

'Hello, Nicholas,' they said. 'Long time no see.'

5

A memory.

A summer in the mid-eighties. Me, Jay and Caroline at the cinema. One in Camden Town that isn't there any more. Her in the middle.

'I'll feel like a gooseberry,' I'd suggested when the expedition was mooted.

'Don't be silly,' she'd assured me. 'We'd like you to come.' As though they'd discussed it.

'Won't you want to, you know . . . ?' Snog in the back row or whatever.

She'd smiled.

'I think we'll just about manage to keep our hands off one another.'

But about an hour into the movie – *The Unbearable Lightness of Being* – she leans towards me, rests a hand on my upper arm and moves her lips very close to my ear. She whispers something that in my confusion I don't catch. I have to ask her to repeat it.

I can feel her hair brushing against the side of my face. 'Prince Charming has fallen *asleep*,' she breathes.

I glance over her shoulder. Jay's head has lolled sideways and a faint gurgling can be heard.

'It's not the most gripping film I've ever seen,' I whisper back.

She giggles. 'Shall we leave?'

'Sorry? What, you mean . . . ?'

'Shall we creep out and leave him?'

To my horror — a trapdoor opens in the pit of my stomach — she appears to be serious.

'Where will we go?' I hiss.

She clasps my wrist and tugs. Moments later, we are on the street.

'Don't look so worried, Nicholas,' she says. 'He'll probably find us.'

She leads me to a nearby pub. Miraculously, we locate a corner to snuggle into with our drinks.

'What's he going to think when he wakes up?' I babble.

She doesn't answer. Smiles at me conspiratorially. 'Tell me about Manchester. Have you got a girlfriend up there?'

I am proud to reveal that there is someone, yeah. (Helen Malpas; no goddess, alas, but a game companion to be sure and one who appears as interested as I am in 'nookie', as she engagingly calls it.)

'Are you in love?'

The question is an embarrassing one. The truth is: of course I am not in love. But to admit this may make me sound callous. However, to claim I am in love might diminish my prospects with the enquirer (*I know, I know*). To equivocate seems weak and unimpressive.

I go for weak and unimpressive.

'I don't know, to be honest.'

Then she says a surprising thing. 'Do you ever wish you'd gone out with more people before meeting her?'

As I had previously 'gone out' with precisely one other person — Astrid Margolis — if 'going out' can accurately describe our fevered gropings in the back of her father's Mark Two Cortina — I'm not sure how to play this one.

'Per-*haps*.'

'I sometimes think it would have been better if Jay and I hadn't met yet.'

'Met *yet* . . .'

'If we'd met, I don't know. In five years' time or something.'

She looks serious and a bit sad. 'Why's that, Caroline?'

'Perhaps you don't feel this about Helen, but I sometimes think Jay and I might have met too early in our lives. The timing scares me a little. The randomness of it all.'

I don't really know what she's talking about, except I have the vague and ridiculous notion that somehow she is talking about me. That it if weren't for the fact of having met Jay Bryant, she and I would be free to go out with one another. At this point she is everything I can imagine ever wanting: beautiful rather than obviously sexy, if you understand the distinction; one moment smart and sophisticated, the next enigmatic and mysterious: her face occasionally going totally blank, as though a plug's been pulled somewhere, or she's receiving a transmission from a parallel universe. There are other exotic moments (what can be going through her head to produce expressions of such helpless desolation?). But then she'll bat her eyelashes, shudder, and say something wickedly funny. Other girls do not warm to her. Plenty of boys can't see why they'd bother. But I am fascinated.

The timing scares her, apparently; luckily, I know a joke on just this topic.

'Ask me what I do for a living. Then ask me the secret of my success.'

A warm look in her eyes tells me she's up for it. Or perhaps it's pity. 'What do you do for a living?'

'I'm a comedian.'

'What's the sec—'

'Timing.'

She laughs, a little helplessly; a wondrous sight. I realise I don't care if I never see Jay Bryant again.

Then in he saunters. Beaming as ever. He fires off a wink in my direction and slides an arm round Caroline.

'You were dead right, ducky,' he tells her. 'We should have gone to *Fatal Attraction*.'

6

The dinner party was an awkward affair. Squeaky was initially appalled that there'd be an extra person to feed. '*FHB*,' she hissed at me in the kitchen, Chivers tribal shorthand for Family Hold Back. But it turned out that the unexpected guest ate like a ghost.

'Honestly, just the tiniest sliver,' purred Caroline Stamp when Squeaky waved a serious clump of *insalata tricolore* at her. 'No one told you I was coming.'

'Go on, there's plenty,' said Squeaky, with a bit of an edge in her voice.

'Really. Just a crumb of cheese. And a leaf.'

'Oh well, more for everyone else then,' she said. But there was an ugly set to her jaw and I knew she was furious. Because of the disturbance to the dinner arrangements. And also because of the fact that Caroline had aced her in the tiny portions department. Normally Squeaky was the one in any gathering fluttering her wrist and saying *no, no, no, I couldn't possibly*. The slim, good-looking one. The one towards whom the male heads inevitably rotated, like sunflowers. With that instantaneous sense women have of other women, Squeaky had recognised a rival who had turned up and begun weeing all over her patch.

Not that I had been drooling and drivelling. If anything, I think I had been remarkably quick in recovering my composure. Of course it was a shock to see her standing there again after all these years. And to discover that the passage of time had done little to diminish the sheer *impact* of the woman. I found myself in the same ridiculous brain-emptying swoon that I always used to fall into in her presence; red in the face, barely able to mount a coherent thought beyond the one that goes: *Fuck, you're lovely*. However, I did discover a new reservoir of social bibble-babble that wasn't there before, some ready-to-use words and phrases with which to mask my embarrassment, so clearly I'd learned something in the intervening fifteen years. During the intro-ductions I even managed to sound a little hail-fellow-well-met, chuckling, 'Of *course* I remember Caroline,' rather as though she were the grown-up kid sister of a chum, and not an almost myth-ical creature whose image once colonised my entire imagination and desire. I very deliberately hadn't been paying her any more attention than would be appropriate, didn't pour her wine first, or fuss round her in any way . . . and yet. And yet women always *know*, don't they? The small tremors in your body language, the way you blink – or fail to blink – something about the set of your eyebrows, it all serves to give you away. Every time I caught Caroline's gaze there was something *in* it that made me want to go, '*What?*' And Squeaky intuitively grasped the nature of the problem.

'Well, cheers everybody,' said Jay, raising his glass aloft.

'Cheers,' cheeped Squeaky a little louder than usual. General gulping, followed by the sound of six humans going about the business of chowing down tomato, buffalo mozzarella and basil leaves.

'Nicholas tells me you've married a lesbian, Jay,' Squeaky trilled. Megan looked faintly shocked, fork pausing momentarily on its trajectory towards her mouth.

Jay recounted the tale, this time in a little more detail. His wife was called Myrna, she was from Croatia, a 'smashing girl', and the five thousand quid she evidently forked out to become the first Mrs Bryant was 'smashing' too. Caroline had clearly heard the story before. When my eyes flicked towards her, I found hers already upon me, a sensation that was almost physical, like a blow. Naturally she'd aged. But her face was, if anything, even finer, the Dresden china-like quality even more heartbreaking, as if it had reached some sort of apogee. It occurred to me that this might be the high-water mark of her legendary beauty. Black hair spilt over a lady-cardigan of baby blue. Something precious and pearl-like hung on a fine chain against the white of her breastbone. Even if I couldn't see them through the glass-topped table, I would have been able to tell you from memory about the exciting legs contained in the pale silk trousers. Her knees were pressed together gently, ankles splayed pigeon-style, heels raised slightly off the ground.

'More *insalata*?' With surgical accuracy, Squeaky placed the dish over the exact spot on the table affording such a fine view of the knees, ankles, heels, etc. described above. See what I mean? I'm not even sure she realised she'd done it. It was probably entirely instinctive.

'So what were these two like at school then?' asked Mrs Deano.

Deano did something with his mouth to connote thinking-about-it. 'You used to tell jokes,' he said, looking at me.

'Did I?'

'All the time. You couldn't wait when you had a new one. Knock knock.'

'Who's there?'

'Nicholas.'

'Nicholas who?'

'Knicker-less girls shouldn't climb trees. That was one of yours, as I recall.'

There was good-natured laughter. Even Squeaky seemed genuinely amused at the adolescent period piece. The set of her jaw returned to something like normal.

'What goes in dry, comes out wet and gives men satisfaction?' enquired Deano. 'That's another one.'

'Er, what?'

'Tetley tea bags.'

'Fuck, I remember one now,' cried Jay. 'You had loads. How do you know if your girlfriend's too fat?'

'How?' I croaked.

'When she sits on your face, you can't hear the stereo.'

Squeaky looked as if she had just received some piece of particularly bad news. Megan didn't seem to have quite understood. Caroline chose this moment to dive into her wine glass. 'I don't know why you're blaming all these on me,' I protested

But Jay was not to be put off. 'What was that really *disgusting* one you used to know?'

'Shall I clear your starter plates?' said our hostess. 'That is, if everyone's *quite* finished.'

7

It wasn't so great that Caroline turned out to be a vegetarian. This little revelation caused Squeaky's face to make that ice-cracking sound. But it was clear that Caroline wasn't one of those women who bond readily with other women. She was more obviously what they call a man's woman, relishing only male attention. Or perhaps she was actually her own woman, needing not very much from anybody at all.

Squeaky offered to microwave her some fish fingers. Caroline insisted she was perfectly content with the vegetables and the wine. While Squeaky stomped off to make final pre-launch adjustments to the lamb, Caroline and Jay lit cigarettes. Through the wreath of smoke, I marvelled at how little the golden couple had changed. They seemed utterly unreconstructed; aged, yes, but only technically. Only in years. Cloaked in their personal cloud of fumes, it was as if time had stood still for them, save for an update in the fashions and the fact that they were no longer going out with one another.

The pornographic lamb received raves all round. It helped to raise Squeaky's temperature back above freezing. Cheered by the reception, she went on the attack.

'So tell us, what do *you* do, Caroline?' she asked. When you're not refusing food, smouldering languidly and generally looking gorgeous, you cow, was what she meant.

'Nothing just now really. Delicious baby onions, by the way.'

'Really?' cheeped my girlfriend. 'I thought you were involved in the music business.'

'I was. I've been — what's the word? — rationalised. Our label was merged with another label. They didn't need two people to do what I did.'

'There's a lot of that,' said Squeaky with a note of pleasure in her tone. 'How perfectly horrible for you.'

And then Caroline did something that made me remember another of the reasons I was so fascinated by her. Her shoulders slumped and a kind of resignation appeared in her eyeballs (already described at length above). I felt her fragility; the invisible veil of disappointment. Was it the closing-off of options, the creeping realisation that life wasn't working out as well as it had promised? Tragic beauty being so much more interesting than happy beauty, I'm afraid I found this sense of loss irresistible. Perhaps because it chimed so well with my own. When you are nineteen — to say nothing of thirty-three — the idea of rescuing a sad, beautiful woman is a powerfully stirring one.

'It isn't very nice, no,' she admitted.

'Still,' said Squeaky cheerily, 'there's probably other work you can get.'

'I *suppose* there is,' Caroline said, although she didn't look all that convinced.

'You could re-train,' was my girlfriend's next helpful suggestion. 'I know someone who used to be quite senior in personnel and she re-trained to be a vet. She lives in Chippenham now.'

Caroline looked totally defeated (I expect it was the reference to Chippenham). 'I've been trying to write a novel,' she murmured. 'But it's all a bit silly. Actually, it's ridiculous.'

'Oh, I *bet* it isn't.'

The words were out of my mouth before I could stop them. And Squeaky looked at me like I'd run her through with a kebab skewer.

8

In an uncomfortable little moment, just the two of us in the kitchen, Squeaky and I clearing away the last of the plates, prior to the lounging-around-on-soft-furnishings part of the evening, she said to me quietly, 'What is it that you see in these boys exactly?' She twisted a knob and the dishwasher began its taxi up the runway.

'What do you mean, what do I see in them?'

She came up close so she could whisper. 'It's not exactly *The Three Musketeers*, is it?'

'Sorry?'

'You don't seem to have very much in common.'

'Shared suffering. That can be very bonding.'

But how to explain it to her? Or myself, indeed. About the depth of feeling I had for these chaps. Would it have made any difference if I'd told her the story about the football match? A lost Wednesday afternoon, somewhere in the early eighties. A pitch in the local park, the whole class (apart from the cowards and weaklings who had notes excusing them from 'games') standing around the halfway line as the two captains nominated for the afternoon, Jay Bryant and Anthony Bourne (sporty, like-able), prepared to select their teams in the time-honoured method. For the non-athletic, it was always vaguely humiliating. Naturally, the stars were picked off first, those precocious talents that any captain wanted on his side. (If Captain A began by naming

Paulo Casillas, a Brazilian boy who could run at forty-five degrees to the horizontal, Captain B would inevitably go for Tony Garibaldi, who at one time seemed destined for a career as a professional.) Then came the middle order – a series of cruelly fine judgements about who was less worse than who – and finally it was down to the cripples. The worthless fat ones who wheezed about hopelessly, the disastrously myopic who didn't see the ball until it struck them in the face. The ill-coordinated, the plain terrified, the delicate flowers who found all that chasing around in the mud just so . . . *gruesome*. In short, the duds; the luckless creatures who each week were forced to undergo this brutal public confirmation of their lowliness of status.

On the occasion in question, it came as a serious shock when, for his first choice, Jay nominated Pugine. Pugine, for whom the phrase *great heaving lummox* might have been invented. No one was more startled at his preferment than the GHL himself, his huge upper thighs rubbing together as he trod his fat-boy tread across the grass to take his place behind his team captain. Next, Jay called up Lagasse, a feeble, jug-eared specimen whose glasses were so thick and heavy they had to be fastened to his head by means of elastic. Then Kapper, a nervous, dislikeable fellow (a senior public servant now, I gather); Wanker of course, Wanker elated at being *included in* – included in even such a perverse line-up – as opposed to being singled out for special torture. Various other misfits and oddballs followed; Ritblat, who once famously tried to take a penalty and his boot flew off into the goalmouth; Conway (you only had to shout his name and he'd pass the ball to you, it didn't matter to him what side you were on). Last but one he chose Deano. And last he chose me.

Bourne, meanwhile, had selected his side on merit.

I think I shall always remember Jay as he captained his squad of duffers that afternoon: running his lungs out all over the field, covering twice as much ground as anyone else, gesticulating, bellowing commands, pointing towards empty space, yelling encouragement, slapping backs, issuing words of consolation ('bad luck, fatty'; 'good effort, Wanker'). Inspired, we played our hearts out for him. The lazy were moved to *run*. The timid, who could normally be frightened off the ball by a thunderous approach and some bad language, actually committed fouls. The hopeless and ill-coordinated were still hopeless and ill-coordinated, but now with a passion.

Of course we lost horribly. The word *massacre* would not be overstating the final result. But that day I think we all experienced a rare feeling of achievement, moral uplift even. And there were several glorious moments. One when a powerful on-target drive from Cretikos was blocked by Pugine's mighty arse (his howl of pain turning to one of triumph when he realised the slinky Cypriot striker had been frustrated). Another when Deano and I managed to thread together an exhilaratingly perfect one-two, passing a bewildered Hooton. And above all when Jay's cross rebounded off Lagasse's head (it would be unfair to say that he headed it) and the ball dropped into the goal. The look of astonishment on Lagasse's jug-eared, bespectacled face as we ruffled his hair and pounded his shoulders (I think Conway may even have kissed him) was a profound joy.

As we trooped back to the dressing room, savouring our magnificent defeat (23–1, if memory serves), it was with a curious sense of elation and the exciting thought that *things were possible*. I dare say we felt oddly *empowered* (even though the word had not yet been invented). It was Jay Bryant who had brought this about, and I loved him for it.

The match became a school legend. The day Jay picked a team of . . . *spastics*, in the cruel argot of the era, and they went on to receive an epic tanking (although it should be noted that Deano and myself were not technically spastics, being the last and the last but one to be chosen).

One afternoon, when the three of us were loitering on our favoured park bench, and the conversation turned to the game, I finally asked Jay what had made him do it.

'Dunno really,' he replied. 'I think I just wanted to see what would happen.'

'Dunno really,' I said to Squeaky. 'I think you had to be there.'

9

We'd reached the stage in the evening where coffee, brandy and the recreational herbs had been broken out. John Barry film themes were playing agreeably on the stereo.

Caroline passed across an ashtray bearing the glowing joint from her sofa to the one where Squeaky and I were beached. Squeaky took a token sort of puff, didn't inhale – she didn't really go in for narcotics much, she'd read somewhere that they were ageing – passed it on to me, and then, given the time of night, asked what was to my mind a highly impertinent question.

'What do you plan to do for work, Jay? When your savings run out.' When you've spent that pile you got for going to jail was what she meant. I think it was her way of trying to get everyone to leave.

Jay was perfectly sanguine about the flagrant breach of etiquette (bringing up the vulgar topic of work after drugs have been taken). 'As it happens, Anita, I'm just in the process of putting something together. I was only talking to Wanker about it yesterday.'

'To *Wanker*?' I interjected woozily.

'I need some glossy brochures doing. Prospectuses for potential investors. Wanker knows all about printing and that.'

'What's the, er . . . the investment exactly?' Sorry. I couldn't help myself.

Jay gazed at me. 'It's the project I mentioned at the reunion. You really want to know?'

I've wondered since what would have happened if I'd replied, *no, not really*.

'Sure.'

He took a deep breath. Clocked each of us in turn to make sure we were listening. Then he began . . .

'You know how the sexiest ideas are often the dullest, right?' I nodded. I didn't actually know this, but I nodded all the same. 'Well this is an *extremely* dull idea. This idea is on a par with . . . ooh, I don't know. Manufacturing rubber soles for trainers. Or dog food. Or tile grouting.'

'In other words, real stuff that real people actually need in their real lives . . .' As opposed to newspaper columns and radio shows, I was thinking.

'Exactly!' He beamed. 'You know when you fill in an application for a credit card? Or an insurance claim? Any of those irritating forms where they tell you to use block capitals and you have to write each letter in a separate square, right? Eventually that information has to be inputted into a computer. Usually by a human sitting at a PC. Where do you think that happens?'

'Head office?' I speculated.

'Correct,' Jay replied. 'In head office, by head office people all getting paid head office wages.' He paused. Re-clocked his audience. 'Imagine if that work could be done somewhere else. Like India, for example. Or China.' He paused. 'Or Africa . . .'

It was the New Big Thing apparently. Something called overseas data processing. Telecomputing, to give it another name. A strange light appeared in Jay's eye as he warmed to his theme; how he wanted to put a thousand educated Ghanaians in front of computer terminals in an office building in Accra and link them to the United States by satellite ('The bird's already in place,' he said, 'in a geostationary orbit over Equatorial Guinea. You rent slots on it'). Thus connected, 'my people', as he phrased it, could now be doing exactly the same work that a thousand people in New Jersey were doing. Or people in Akron, Ohio. Or Macclesfield, Cheshire. But – and here was the gist of the thing – for a fraction of the wage bill. Split into three eight-hour shifts, they'd work round the clock, processing health insurance claims, or inputting credit applications . . . 'basically any kind of DP scenario where you need a load of people sitting at PCs typing stuff in'.

'Like those call centres,' I piped up. 'When you phone to renew your car insurance, and you end up speaking to someone in New Delhi.'

I was exactly correct, apparently. Africa was the new frontier for telecomputing. And the beauty of the scheme was that it was 'economically progressive'. One would be spreading wealth from the first world to the third. You paid your guys – though actually it was mostly women – three hundred dollars a month in places where the average wage was four hundred dollars a *year*. And when you paid one decent salary in the city, it was reckoned that you were helping to feed *fifteen* other people. Up to thirty-five in rural areas. He seemed to have all the facts at the tips of his fingers.

'And what's your . . . your involvement, as it were?' I asked.

'I'm going to raise the seed capital to open one of these places.'

'Christ, Jay. It sounds awfully grown-up.'

'Not really. Anyway, it's better than sitting round the house smoking dope and watching daytime telly.'

'I'm truly impressed,' I confessed.

'Caroline's been helping me a little, haven't you, ducky?'

The grey eyes rolled from Jay's face on to mine. 'I've been helping him dream up names for the company. He wasn't terribly fond of Let's Put A Lot Of Our Own People Out Of Work and Employ Others Much Cheaper Abroad . . . Dot Com.'

'You might be able to assist, Nicholas. If you were interested. And you too, Deano. Nice to keep it in the family, as it were.'

Deano and I looked at one another.

'How could I help exactly?' growled the scientist. But he was intrigued, I could tell.

'On the technical front. It's not cutting edge or anything, but it would be great to have you on board.'

Deano took another slug of firewater. 'You wouldn't necessarily need a satellite. Not for a low-resolution application like data capture. Broadband internet connections could be just as effective, and with the right software, as secure. And about a zillion times cheaper, of course.'

'You *see*!' Jay clapped his hands. 'I *knew* you were the man for this. You've probably saved us a fortune right there.'

Deano was a little embarrassed. 'Depends on your exact throughput, obviously.'

'Say you'll help out.'

Deano and Mrs Deano looked at one another.

'It would just be a few meetings,' entreated Jay. 'You could be a consultant. Nicholas, you'll help, won't you? You could help me write the brochure. Being a top words man and all.'

'I'd be happy to. If you really think I could bring anything to—'

'Oh definitely. You know all those fancy phrases for everything. You're the guy.'

I gazed with enormous fondness at my old friend, the ten-kilowatt beam back on his handsome face. Still at it, still Making Things Happen.

'You'll get your people to call our people, right?'

He laughed. 'I'm actually really excited about this. There are serious amounts of money to be made here. Imagine how much the big corporations can save by getting their data-crunching done in places where labour's cheap as chips.'

'Really? What do you call serious?'

'Oh, millions. Tens of millions. Maybe hundreds over time.'

The joint that had been burning down quietly between my fingers finally reached skin. I yelped with pain and mashed it out in the ashtray.

'Are you serious? Did you say *tens* of millions?'

'Oh definitely. This is my pension fund. Once this baby comes off, I'm never working again.'

10

'Is he serious?' asked Squeaky snapping off the bedside light.
We'd got ready for bed exchanging barely a sentence.

'Jay? Perfectly, I imagine.'

'He doesn't seem quite . . . capable.'

'Because of the easy manner, and the way he speaks? Don't
be fooled.'

'There are laws about people involved in corporate failures.
He went to prison, Nicholas.'

'He did, didn't he? Still, we don't know the exact ins and
outs. I'm sure he will have thought it all through.' Squeaky rolled
on to her side and prepared to submerge herself in sleep. 'Jay
Bryant is one of those people who is capable of anything.'

It was true. He was. And in fact, the more we discussed it
over further joints and brandies, the less far-fetched the whole
idea became. Jay had learned a lot, he told us, from his old boss,
Jerry. 'Jerry was a lovely bloke. A dreamer,' he said. 'A fucking
hopeless businessman, by the way, but a natural entrepreneur.
There was always some new scheme he was trying to get off the
ground.'

One month apparently it would be a service to prevent people
rifling through your rubbish to obtain your credit-card details
from discarded statements (Security Garbage UK). The next, it
would be a chain of restaurants called Yellow, that only served
yellow food (pasta, pizza, pilau rice, omelettes). There were plans

for a nationwide chain of greetings card outlets; he toyed with nursing homes; he got excited about fitness centres. Debt consolidation – where you turn a lot of little debts into one big debt – had been the Big Idea for a while. And his proposal for virtual golf courses – perfect for places where there was no room for a real one (Manhattan, Japan, etc.) – had been described by one investment banker who Jerry had tapped up as 'either brilliant or lunatic, I really can't decide'.

Of course none of his wheezes ever came to anything – few were sufficiently dull to have the smell of success about them – but through Jerry, Jay became very familiar with the world of venture capital, and the various channels that existed to bring people with a potentially profit-making idea together with the funds needed to make it happen. Even Squeaky and Mrs Deano fell a little silent as Jay talked about 'business angels', those speculative investors who, instead of being taxed at forty per cent on the interest their pile of gold was accruing, preferred to take a tax-free punt on a new business if the business plan was 'sweet'. That is to say, if the basis of the scheme was convincing and the investor himself stood to make plenty of money out of it. An angel might even be drawn in on the basis of his previous expertise, enjoying the role of *éminence grise* while the young people did all the running around exhausting themselves.

'Where did remote data processing come from?' I asked. 'Was it one of Jerry's?'

Jay sucked hard on the joint, holding the smoke down for maximum hit-value.

'If you want the honest answer,' he croaked, 'I read an article about it in an old *FT* I picked up on a train.'

There was laughter, but it felt true. It was how things happened in the world. One minute someone muses that it would be a fine thing if slips of paper could carry an adhesive edge – the next, the world has been festooned in Post-it Notes.

'There's some extremely serious moolah to be made here,' said Jay rather seriously. 'And I know . . .' And at this point he stopped to eyeball us each in turn. 'I just *know* that I can do this, boys. I was born to do this. *We* can do this. This is a *highly* dull idea. It will probably make us very rich indeed.'

I had a vivid flashback to opening the mail only that morning; queasily extracting the monthly Visa statement from its envelope. Some *statement*. Kick in the kidneys, more like. The old flexible friend must have been rubbed with extraordinary vigour to clock up such a sickening total. None of the individual payments, all for strictly non-luxury items (curry, CDs, petrol, dim sum, books, Tesco Direct, Oddbins, sushi, cinema tickets, fifty quid on *something* at Gap), seemed horribly excessive in itself. Taken together, however, the overall effect had brought about a powerful sinking feeling.

'Count me in,' I declared firmly. I think it was the magic of the phrase *extremely serious moolah*.

Very rich indeed probably helped as well.

We both looked at Deano. His lips pursed. His brows put an additional half-inch between themselves and the small, enigmatic eyeballs below.

'Might work, I suppose,' he admitted.

Jay's face blazed with happiness. If it hadn't been for all the brandy, I think I should have found it hard to look into that smile.

'Fucking great,' he said. 'You know something? This is going to be fucking great.'

And he slapped Caroline's knee so hard that she gasped.

'I think you're a little bit in love with him,' murmured Squeaky. 'And her.'

I reached behind me and squeezed a pyjama-clad buttock. 'Don't be ridiculous.'

'Not ridiculous.'

'Great pornographic lamb, by the way.'

Her breathing was slowing and deepening. 'Bloody rude,' she slurred.

'Who?' As if I needed to ask.

'You don't fancy her, do you?' she said sleepily.

'Of course not.' Someone's words came back to me. *Never tell the truth, it's the surest way of being found out.*

'Can always tell when you're lying,' she mumbled. 'Your lips move.'

'What are you talking about?'

But with a gentle snore, Squeaky slipped below the radar.

I lay still, replaying the events of the evening over in my head. *Goodnight, Nicholas. It's been fascinating to meet again after all this time.* What she'd said on the doorstep as she and Jay were leaving. And reaching up, the long, pale hand emerging from the baby-blue sleeve of the cardigan, she'd brushed a polite kiss against my cheek, I likewise on hers. And then the over-detailed eyes and the well-drawn lips with all their intriguing planes and edges had seemed to settle into an expression of *well, aren't you going to say you'd like to see me again*, and I'd found myself saying, 'I hope we'll be seeing you again.' Though of course I hadn't meant *we*.

What would happen to those eyes during sex? I wondered. Would they perhaps lose some of their sharpness of detail? And the lips. Might they too perhaps blur and become indistinct? And would that be a good thing or a bad thing? Would it make her more or less attractive?

How fascinating to be able to find out.

THREE

1

I woke the next morning with a powerful sinking feeling.

Squeaky had left for work wearing a bit of a boot face (remembering all the horrid moments from the dinner party, no doubt). There was certainly no question of a restorative you-know-what, merely a chilly smile, a perfunctory 'see you then' and the door slammed with rather more force than was necessary to close it technically. As I lay in bed listening to her heels striking their familiar tattoo on the paving stones, I realised that I had been dreaming about Caroline – a memory that was swiftly followed by the sickening realisation that I must have spoken her name aloud in my sleep. I had been known to vocalise while unconscious (my best was yelling, 'Go on, ask him about the fucking daffodils!' No one ever managed to work that one out). The C-word appearing on my lips would go a long way towards explaining Squeaky's somewhat frosty departure.

But this wasn't the main reason for the PSF. The primary source of my nagging sense of disappointment that morning lay in the bombed-out ruins of the Ghana thing. Over the narcotics and liqueurs the night before, amid the general bonhomie and big plans for us to become millionaires, it all seemed perfectly plausible. Even as crusty white bits started to form in the corners of Jay's mouth as he rattled on about this posh bloke he'd met – in prison, I'm guessing – who knew lots of people who might be persuaded to invest in the project, the idea seemed eminently *doable.* With his energy, with Deano's scientific know-how, with my . . . with my 'way with words', there didn't seem any particular reason why we couldn't open up a data processing facility in Accra. The potential profits were enormous. And if we got it right in Ghana, Jay had said, his voice dropping suddenly, as though worried about being overheard, we could 'roll out the package' through Africa and the rest of the third world.

Ultimately there was billions in it. Satellite, telephony, the internet . . . they had all served to shrink the globe. If Africa and Asia could be trusted to manufacture our TV sets and our trainers, why couldn't they do our office work as well?

The next morning, however, it all looked like bollocks.

Who were we to think we could behave . . . like proper business people? Jay, who, for all his charm, was unemployed, watched daytime television and had been in jail. Deano, who was a salaried employee if ever there was one. And me . . . well, I wasn't one of those blokes with briefcases you see moving purposefully through airports. I was a media flim-flam man; someone who could turn you out eight hundred words on Why We Feel So Awful About Everything At The Moment. Or Fifty Reasons Why We Should Be Cheerful Today. Who could go on the radio and natter about everything and nothing.

It had been great to see Jay again. And Caroline had re-entered my soul like a virus. But were we really going into business? I don't see the guy for fifteen years, and all of a sudden we're palling up to be rich together? Don't make me laugh.

'Never going to happen,' I said aloud to the empty bedroom. Like that trip in the MG to Brighton.

And sure enough, for several days nothing did happen. Squeaky found all sorts of reasons why she couldn't come round. Staying late at the office to work on a proposal document with Rollie; meeting up with Chloe for one of their monthly chinwags; and once, 'Actually, Nicholas, I think I could do with a quiet evening sorting the wardrobe,' which I took to be code for *you are a grievous disappointment to me and I think I had better begin to re-organise my life*. Neither of us had the bad taste to bring up the subject of our looming deadline.

In the end I called Jay. A weekday mid-morning.

'I speak him,' said a woman in a strong foreign accent, Myrna I took it. As I listened to the sound effects from the other end of the line (footsteps, a single cry of 'Telephone!'), it occurred to me that I didn't even know where Jay lived these days. When I finally got round to checking the dialling code – only many months later – it turned out to have been Southwark. Then a door opened, TV sound in the background, followed by the rhythm of different footsteps, a slapping noise, like leather slippers against lino.

'Yellow,' he said. He did, he said Yellow. A cross between Yes and Hello.

'Jay, it's Nicholas.'

A terrible, crushing pause. Less than a second, probably, but it told me all I needed to know about the place I occupied in Jay Bryant's thoughts. He was thinking, Nicholas *Who*? I just know he was.

'*Nicholas!*' he exclaimed eventually. 'I was just thinking about you.'

'How are things?' I asked, a little sulkily perhaps.

'Things? Things are good, yeah.'

There was a thick, vague quality to his voice. The sort of thick, vague quality you tend to get after smoking several spliffs. I wanted to ask him: what were you doing when I called? Were you lying in bed watching *Call My Bluff* as I suspect?

'Excellent. Pleased to hear it. I was just wondering whether there was anything I should be doing.'

Another killing pause. My old friend was being very slow off the blocks that morning.

'About the DP thing!' he said at last. Like it was a guessing game.

'If there was anything I could be doing.'

'Shit, sorry, Nicholas. Yeah. No. I've been meaning to get back to you. I had a great meeting with Wanker the other day. He's totally cool about doing the brochures – actually old Wanker's turned out to be a bit of a laugh. He was very funny about the porno business.'

I don't know why, but I found the idea of Wanker becoming a bit of a laugh a little irritating.

'Do we need another session?' I asked. 'To go through everything properly.' To get real about this thing. If this *thing* really was real.

'Definitely. Great dinner, by the way. How's Anita?'

'She's fine.'

'Caroline was telling me how much she enjoyed the other evening. Said how much you'd changed.'

'Really? Changed how?' Changed for the good . . . or the other?

'Said she never realised how amusing you were.'

'Amusing?'

'We need a conflab, don't we? I'm going up to Scotland tomorrow. All day on the fucking coach; mega-bummer, really. I'll get back to you the second I return. Is that all right?'

'Of course.'

'Thanks, mate. If you can leave it with me for now . . .'

After we hung up, I tried to picture the scene: Jay plodding back to the bedroom, skinning up another little number perhaps, maybe flipping to *Wipeout*.

'Never going to happen,' I said out loud to the empty room. 'Never going to happen.'

2

But I was wrong, it turned out. Things did begin to happen.

Some days later, I was sitting in the flat bashing out some notes for what I calculated would be my final 'Aimless Days' column. My inspiration was the treacherous line that fell out of Deano's mouth when we met at the reunion. When he said, 'You're looking very prosperous.' Meaning that I'd put on weight. As my parting offering, I would serve up a collection of similar phrases in modern usage — weasel formulations that sound rather good, but in fact are very bad.

Interesting. When someone says, I read your article. Or I heard you on the radio. I thought what you were saying was very . . . interesting. That always means, I thought you were crap, doesn't it?

Bubbly. That's another. Women are sometimes described as bubbly when what you mean is inane. Or barking. Or fat. Or all three. (You'd never label a man bubbly, would you? Interesting, that.)

Darling, I think we need to talk. I think I should tell you I've been seeing rather a lot of Mandy Whatnot lately. Yeah, your best friend. Sorry.

Comfortable. The victim suffered fractures to both arms and legs, severe bruising to his head and neck, several cracked ribs and possible internal injuries. A hospital spokesman described his condition as 'comfortable'.

The cheque's in the post. That's just an old lie, isn't it? Like *I promise not to come in your mouth*. They don't count.

Leave it with me. I shall do nothing about it, now go away and leave me alone.

Wacky. Pain in the arse. Knows all the words to the Monty Python parrot sketch. (Also see *zany*.)

God, that must have been awful. Tell me everything. Leave nothing out. Omit no unpleasant detail. Especially the bit about how you thought you were all going to die.

Please continue to hold. Your call is important to us. Yeah, right.

As I stared at the crack in the ceiling in search of further inspiration – and then out of the window at the windows of the flats opposite, and then up at the crack in the ceiling again (no, still nothing) – the doorbell went. At this hour of the morning in Chalk Farm, it could only be a delivery for a neighbour. Or someone from the north of England selling dishcloths.

'It's Caroline,' squawked the voice on the intercom. *Uh?*

'Sorry?'

'It's Caroline Stamp.'

Uh?

'Can I come in?'

'Sure.' My brain suddenly laid on a graphic display of the meaning of the phrase *flat spin*. I was wearing my shabbiest rags, grubby tracksuit bottoms, three-day-old T-shirt (including pasta stains). I was unwashed, unshaven, there was hardened sleep roosting in the corners of my eyes. I was generally in one of those conditions in which One Should Never Be Seen, especially by goddess-like figures (the others, for the record, being: at stool, masturbating, and queuing for a sale at Radio Shack). The sitting room had a fetid fug about it. A pair of boxer shorts hung off a radiator. A cereal bowl with its pathetic residue stood next to my winking laptop. The downstairs front door slammed. I calculated I had thirty seconds – tops.

I flung open a window, raced into the bedroom and pulled on a fresh T-shirt. I jammed my feet (not my best feature, big toenail like an assassin's stiletto, according to Squeaky) into a pair of deck shoes, and careered into the bathroom. There I splashed water round my face hopefully, aimed a blast of Eau Sauvage up the T-shirt (Gap, black), took a few deep breaths, and sauntered as calmly as possible into the hallway. Grasping the handle, I inwardly chanted a secret phrase, specifically designed to boost confidence and facilitate charm on this sort of occasion.

Oh fuck it, here we go then.

Then I opened up.

'Nicholas. Sorry.' A faint smile occupied the pale terrain between and including her eyes and lips. She brandished a large, fat envelope at me. 'These are the papers Jay wanted you to see.' Something in my expression made her pause. 'Jay *did* call to say I'd be coming?'

'Er. Yes. Of course. Actually. Actually, no, he didn't. But come in anyway. Sorry for the . . .' Filth and squalor that you find me in.

The huge grey eyes seemed particularly well penned today. I could feel them sucking up all the details of my wretched appearance. The stubble. The unmentionable *marks* on the deplorable sweat pants, the general idea of sleep (and possible nocturnal emissions) that I felt clinging to my every pore. As she shimmered in – she was in baby pink that morning, rather than blue – I caught the familiar gust of vanilla, and a fleeting suggestion of bare midriff beneath the short, fashionable lady-mac.

'Please.' I indicated the sofa with an insouciant wave of the arm. But she didn't take her cue. Instead she began prowling the room, peering at my bookshelves, checking out the view of the street, skirting the boxers (not too horrendous, the ones with playing cards on; rather rakish, I fancied) to examine the CD collection.

'It looks different in here during the day,' she commented at last.

'Yes. That'll . . . that'll be the daylight,' I riposted. 'Would you like anything? Tea? Coffee? Gin and tonic?'

She turned towards me. In the daylight, so satirically referred to above, I now saw what I'd missed over dinner the other night. Though her skin was still marvellously taut across her bones, delicate lines of age, like cracks in fine china, had begun to etch themselves into her face. An endearing little spray at the corners of her eyes. Two faint tracks journeying down either side of her nose to the zone where her lips finally ran out of steam. A pause as she allowed me to take in Time's opening foray with the wrecking ball. And now the surfaces and planes of her lips began to rearrange themselves. The eyes widened and I could feel my brain voiding itself until there was nothing left but the rear wall of my skull, and me backed against it. My final thought was this: *a slightly faded goddess is still a goddess, right?*

'Do you have any ordinary tea?'

'What, like English breakfast tea? Or what's that other tea? Earl Grey tea.' *Stop saying the word 'tea' like an idiot, will you?*

'I'd love a really strong mug of builder's tea. Full fat, not skimmed, if you have any.'

As I mucked about with mugs and teabags and milk and the like, she inspected the glass-fronted cabinets, the fridge magnets, Squeaky's list of things 'we' needed.

'Draw-string bin bags,' she purred.

I wanted to die. Or crawl into one of those holes. Or perhaps it would have been better if the ground had swallowed me up (though if it had, I should only have ended up in the flat downstairs with Eric and Toby and their fucking Jack Russell).

'Uncle Rudolf's Swiss-Style Muesli. With fifty per cent fruit and nuts in brackets.'

'That's Anita,' I replied, crushed. 'She's very keen on . . .'

There seemed to be no way to avoid saying it. 'On muesli.'

'Ah,' said Caroline. 'I generally have piles of toast in the morning. Sometimes with marmalade. Sometimes with peanut butter. Sometimes both.'

'Not on the same slice, surely?'

She shot me a quizzical look. The lips did some lippy realignment thing, and the eyebrows set themselves at an interesting new angle.

I remembered that look.

It took me back to that long-ago summer, the same era as the trip to the cinema; Jay and Caroline and me and Deano at The Flask. We were enjoyably recollecting some of the absurdities of our schooldays, when Jay brought up the famous Spotty Ferguson Wing Mirror Incident. In mixed company, Deano and I probably wouldn't have chosen to talk about Norman Ferguson's obsession with our English mistress's underwear, but Jay was not subject to such reservations.

'She had this great bod, but a face like a slapped arse,' he recalled. 'Didn't she?' I was obliged to nod my assent. 'And she wore these short skirts. Whenever she walked past Spotty's desk, like during a test or something, he'd always drop his pen so he could bend down and try and sneak a quick shufty.'

If Caroline was entertained, she was betraying no sign of it.

'So one day he invented this device: it was a car wing mirror taped to the end of a sawn-off broom handle. Like those things they use to check under vehicles for unexploded bombs.'

I still remember the morning vividly. The excitable Ferguson, acne aglow, waving his contraption in the air like a Tartar leading the charge, the whole class hysterical with excitement. And then later, the moment; in silence, Miss Fischbein patrolling slowly between the lanes of desks; Ferguson awaiting his chance. A turn of the shoulders; a blur of broom handle; the entire room holding its breath.

'*White!*' he yells, disguising the news as a cough. The class erupting. Poor Miss Fischbein knowing that *something* has happened . . . but not what.

'Perhaps someone would like to tell me what is so funny . . . ?'

Thirty minds – thirty *teenage male* minds – all resting in the same place; thirty pairs of teenage male eyes – all containing the same thought. The surge tide of red rising up her neck as she slowly intuits she has been the victim of some unknown humiliation. For a second, I think she will cry.

'You are such little . . .' Words are Miss Fischbein's stock in trade; the language of Shakespeare is her lifeblood. 'Such little *shits!*'

And there is uproar.

Caroline's expression then was the one that faced me now. A mixture of amusement and contempt. Back then, she said, 'God. Boys are such . . . *boys*, aren't they?'

Now she merely cocked her head through fifteen degrees, as though waiting politely for my next priceless comment.

What was it that Jay had called her?

Gorgeous but uphill.

A moody cow at times.

Hey, who needed easy?

Mmmoooooooooooooooooo.

3

The papers she had brought round were all about telecomputing. A great pile of cuttings and other technical material now lay strewn across the coffee table. There were photographs of serried rows of earnest-looking Ghanaians seated before desktops in well-lit offices; schematic diagrams of satellite uplinks and down-links, broadband connections and multi-channel ISDN feeds (all Greek to me); complicated documents from Ghana's Education Ministry about standards of academic attainment and what have you. But more important than any of that, Caroline had placed herself down one end of my leather sofa with a mug of builder's tea while I occupied the other. The baby-pink cardigan clung winningly to her slender ribcage. Interesting white jeans did much to outline the rest of the fascinating picture. I found it hard to keep my eyes off the adorable little roll of exposed flesh at her middle. We were making progress.

After a brief discussion about what I was supposed to do with all this stuff — read, inwardly digest, await further instructions seemed to be the gist — we got on to what was to my mind the more rewarding topic of what we had been doing with our lives since we last met.

I rattled through my story, moving rapidly on to the recent developments, so I could speak with enjoyable ennui about my so-called career. With a nod towards the winking laptop, I explained about the weasel-isms.

'Colourful,' she said. 'People are always getting described as colourful, aren't they?'

'You're right.' You're so right.

'He was a Colourful Character. In quotes.'

'It means complete pain in the arse, doesn't it? Loud, annoying. Big drinker. Possible alcoholic.'

'Not for us.'

'Not for us!' Of course. Not for us.

'We admired your play stroke article stroke novel stroke whatever but unfortunately, for one reason or another, it's not for us. Or to put it another way—'

'We hate it! It stinks. Stop wasting our time, you cretin. Do you mind if I use those, Caroline?'

She made no objection and went on to talk with a complementary enjoyable ennui about her career pathway through the music business; promoting bands, doing record label publicity, looking after various 'silly young men who thought they were going to be stars' who were 'lied to on an almost hourly basis'. There was a lot of stuff about 'product', lavish parties, life-threatening amounts of coke. It all seemed to have ended up in a reasonably senior and well-paid position where the biggest challenge was 'dressing ten years younger, and having to say things like pants when you mean rubbish'.

I wanted to throw my arms around her and shout, Yes! Yes, I know exactly how you feel. We're so alike, we two. How has it taken this long to find one another? But what with the deplorable tracksuit bottoms, and the just-got-out-of-bed funk, and the general wisdom of keeping it cool, instead I remarked, 'I wouldn't worry if I were you. Something else is bound to come up.'

She cast her big eyes upon me. 'I'm not really sure I could cope with another job.' Again that sad look that made me want to fly to her rescue. 'I haven't applied for anything. Actually, I think I might be unemployable.'

It was odd. I knew just how she felt.

I asked, 'What do you think are the chances of Jay's thing working out?'

A shrug. 'Impossible to predict. Triumph or disaster. There are never any in-betweens with Jay. Perhaps you knew that.'

'Hmm.' Actually I didn't, but I *hmmed* all the same. 'It's all entirely . . . legal, is it? What with him having gone to prison.'

'He wasn't disbarred from being a company director, if that's what you mean.'

We sat there looking at one another for a moment. It suddenly occurred to me that perhaps, having no job to go to as such, this woman didn't have anything else to do today but drink my tea and turn me into a gibbering idiot. For some reason the thought drifted into my head: *she's lonely*.

'Have you seen anything of Jay?' I asked. 'Since we last met.' What was it with you two, anyway?

'Not really. He's gone to Scotland. To visit a viscount.'

'Have you ever met Jay's wife?'

'Myrna. Yes, I have. Perhaps I'm a bit old-fashioned in this respect, but I'm afraid I rather disapprove of anyone who can treat marriage so lightly.'

'Really? But what about . . . ?'

'Oh, I *totally* disapprove of him,' she said fondly. 'I've even given up disapproving of each new outrage. He's covered by a sort of blanket disapproval.'

With a small, thrilling shock, I realised she was smiling. She'd swivelled round and feet and knees were both aiming straight at me. If she had been a submarine, this was the moment her captain would have unleashed the torpedoes.

I found myself saying, 'Caroline, I don't suppose I could buy you dinner some time. Apart from all this stuff . . .' I waved at the paper-work on the coffee table, '. . . there are a couple of things I'd love to pick your brain about. For the column. If you wouldn't mind.'

Perhaps no one had asked her to dinner in a long time. Because the smile only grew in intensity and she said, 'I'd like that very much, Nicholas.'

Slight confusion when she left, about whether to shake hands or social kiss. In the end, we did both.

But still, not bad, eh? For a bloke with serious unidentified *marks* on his sweat pants. A date with a goddess.

4

Five days later, Jay Bryant had turned my living room into a reference library. Papers, books and documents covered every available surface; the man himself occupied one corner of the sofa that wasn't heaped with business publications; I perched before the laptop, fingers poised.

We were writing the business plan. We were going to be rich.

Jay had come back from Scotland in a terrific mood. He turned up on my doorstep in a mini-cab with two cartons of paperwork in the boot ('Not to be removed' from a certain university business library, I noticed).

'This is going to take a whole day. Maybe two. Maybe a week,' he'd told me on the phone the night before. 'Can you clear your diary?'

I told him I thought I could arrange it. Apart from my slots on the radio, my fortnight-at-a-view diary contained one entry: *Lottery tic expires! Buy new!!*

'You'll love Guy – he's the viscount,' he'd said. 'Absolutely top posh bloke – fantastic attitude to life, though he's a fucking hound for Charlie.'

Apparently after tooting a lot of coke and generally reacquainting himself with his old prison pal, this viscount had readily agreed to ring round his buddies to see if anyone wanted in at the ground floor of an exciting new investment opportunity. As a result, we needed to get started on the glossy brochure a bit sharpish.

Actually, it was an insidious little gem, an artfully woven conflation of facts and assertions that we synthesised from the pile of stuff Caroline had brought round and dumped on my coffee table. Jay had clearly done a load of reading on the subject; additionally he'd laid his hands on a ton of . . . I was about to write *real* prospectuses, from which to crib the general style in which these things were couched, viz. a quietly confident corporate prose. No extravagant claims, nothing flashy or vulgar, the whole shooting match oozing what he liked to call 'full Monty probity and rectitude'.

I particularly liked the line about the company seeking to raise £1.25 million from angel investors, 'to ensure it remains in a strong negotiating position with venture capital investors from whom it is subsequently seeking up to £15 million to fund and build a sustainable business. Equity stake negotiable; exit by share sale, trade sale, buy-back or refinancing' (whatever the fuck any of that may have meant).

Jay handled all the complicated financial stuff himself, the columns of numbers and projections of 'revenue streams' and 'repayment schedules', the opportunities for Enterprise Investment Scheme and Capital Gains Tax re-investment relief. Together we bashed out the pin-striped mood music, including, in a personal statement from the Chairman of JB Holdings, his view that the project represented a 'uniquely ethical investment in what is an increasingly complex world market in which to do business'.

Naturally we had to take a few liberties with the CVs of the key personnel. The management team, I typed, 'combines strong electronic engineering, sales and marketing and general management (board level of a fully listed IT company) background' – embroidery, let us say, that I was initially a little concerned about.

'You've never actually worked for Nokia, have you?' I asked Jay.

'I had one of their mobiles.'

'And this stuff about you being involved in setting up major data-handling networks for UK blue chip companies throughout the Far East.'

'Indicative,' he replied with a grin. And when I didn't grin back, he added, 'Firstly, everybody does it; secondly, no one ever checks at this stage; and thirdly, it's the power of the idea we're selling. Investors are only looking for reassurance about the core team.'

'I can't really say I've done consulting for all these corporations, can I? AOL, Microsoft . . .'

'You're a communications specialist, Nicholas. The point is you *could* have.'

This, I have to admit, defeated me. But I must say it had all been rather enjoyable, just the two of us sitting in the flat hour after hour, hammering the stuff into my PC, and sending out for takeaways.

Night had fallen, and I could feel the creative juices starting to ebb. So by way of knocking it on the head for one day, I rattled in the statutory paragraph from the 1986 Financial Services Act, the one about investment in a new business carrying 'high risks as well as the possibility of high rewards' and how one should 'seek your own independent advice in relation to the information contained herein' and generally watch your step, trust no one, and avoid talking to strangers.

'This has been fun, you know,' I admitted.

Jay beamed. 'It's been great. Been great to hook up with *you* again.'

Did I blush? Maybe I did. I didn't really care.

'Drink? I'm as parched as a . . . as a highly parched thing.'

'You and your way with words, Nicholas.'

We cracked open a couple of beers and I turned off the computer. Jay settled his feet on a pile of company reports on the coffee table and took a deep chug on a Beck's.

'This is how it all starts, you know,' he said, reading my thoughts. 'Two blokes in a room with an idea.'

'I guess so.'

'It might all seem a bit daft at this stage, a bit . . . what's the word? *Hypothetical*. But my old boss Jerry once told me a good thing: money can't sit still. It has to chase other money.'

'Like a shark,' I tossed in.

'*Very* like a shark,' Jay gurgled, wiping a trail of beer off his chin. 'If money lies around doing nothing, it goes into decline. Bits fall off it. Money has an almost physical need to grow. To seek more money. So that's why this DP thing is bound to find a backer. The Forces of Money will inevitably chase down the Scent of Profit. It's one of the laws of nature.'

'I'm pleased you're so confident about it.'

Jay looked at me, a slow smile spreading across his handsome face.

'Anita thinks this is all cobblers, doesn't she? I'm guessing.'

'There is a certain . . . scepticism on her part, yes.' Why had he asked?

'I don't think she entirely approves of me.'

'I wouldn't say that exactly . . .'

'It doesn't matter, mate. It won't break my heart.' He paused to download another tranche of German beer; did that narrow-eyed thing when alcohol slides over the soft tissue of the throat. 'You two been together a while now,' he said finally.

I told him everything.

How it had all been great . . . *but*.

How *she* was great . . . *but*.

How we'd reached that point on the runway where the pilot has to either pull the throttle back and take off . . . or abort. Get married or split up. How we couldn't decide.

'Meaning *you* can't decide.'

'Correct.'

I told him about the deadline.

'Good move,' he confirmed. 'Concentrates the mind.'

'I mean in many ways, Anita's a terribly good bet.'

Jay cocked his head to one side and shot me what I believe is called an old-fashioned look.

'Go on,' he said.

I listed as many of Squeaky's qualities as I could think of, up to and including good in bed. I cantered through the reasons why we were good together. I attempted to outline how I could do a lot worse. I was surprised how long it took me to get through all this.

Jay nodded thoughtfully. Sucked on the beer bottle. Lit a cigarette. Said, 'Caroline tells me you've asked her out.'

'Yeah. Yeah, I did actually.'

And then I'm positive that I blushed.

5

Jay's phrase still echoed through my head days later. The one he employed after he'd stopped laughing like a drain.

'You've turned into a right little fanny-rat, haven't you?' he chortled. 'Christ, who'd have thought it?'

Fanny-rat. I didn't know whether to be flattered, outraged or humiliated. What did he mean, *fanny-rat?* And come to that, what did he mean, *who'd have thought it?*

But Jay was having no equivocation. He practically slapped me on the back and congratulated me for 'having a crack at Caroline'.

'You don't mind then?' I shouted from the kitchen, my face cooling nicely in the fridge, where I'd inserted it, ostensibly in the hunt for more beer.

Jay was grinning when I returned with a couple of Beck's.

'Mind? Why would I mind? Me and the Princess are ancient history, mate.'

'Even so . . .'

'What?'

'You know . . .'

'What? Residual jealousy? If I can't live with her, I can't bear anyone else having a go?'

'Sort of thing.'

'Don't be daft. Besides, they say into each life some rain must fall,' he replied. 'Cheers.'

'Cheers. What's that mean then? The rain thing.'

'Just. Well, she is a difficult woman, Nicholas.'

'Moody. You told me.'

'Moody would only be the beginning of it, really.'

'You seemed to survive all right.'

Jay looked at me . . . I guess *reflectively* would be the *mot juste*.

'Six months of heaven. A year of happiness. Another year of non-*un*happiness. And then a year, year and a half of sheer fucking grief. What's that come to?'

'Four years?'

'That sounds about right.'

What went wrong? I wanted to ask. Why didn't it work between you? Whose fault was it all? Hers, I presumed. Being moody and difficult and all that.

'If you knew then what you know now . . . ?' I trailed off.

'Would I have gone anywhere near her? Interesting question.'

Jay glugged some more beer. Flicked an uneaten pizza crust around its cardboard box. And his reply, when it came, surprised me. My old schoolfriend, who was always so sure of everything, actually shrugged.

'Dunno, to be honest. It's about fifty-one, forty-nine. That close.'

'Which way, though? On balance, probably . . . . which?' He was glad he'd gone out with her, or he regretted it?

'On balance, yeah. Yeah, very probably.'

And he sat there beaming at me. Like he'd answered the question or something.

We finished the business plan the following evening. At the door on his way out, Jay brandished the black diskette containing all our confident predictions and subtle phraseology that Wanker was now going to turn into a spiffy-looking brochure.

'I've got a good feeling about this, Nicholas.' He sniffed the slim plastic casing. 'Know what this smells like to me? This smells like the answer to fucking everything.'

'I fucking hope so,' I replied in all sincerity.

Rather suddenly, he grabbed my shoulder and squeezed it quite hard. His handsome brown eyes stared down into my own.

'If one hopes to discover new land, one must be prepared to lose sight of the shore.'

'Bobby Davro?' I ventured.

'Something like that,' he replied, and vanished down the darkened stairs.

FOUR

1

Wanker's brochure was an absolute triumph.

I have to admit, the idea filled me with unease at first – asking a pornographer to turn out a classy business document – but Wanker did us proud. It was a symphony in shades of grey; from the impressive marbling effect on the front cover, to the small typographical flourishes that interrupted the blocks of text – which themselves floated stylishly alongside the well-chosen photographs and diagrams – the whole thing sitting amid masses of luxurious white space and positively *reeking* of full Monty probity and rectitude, not a tit, bum or the other thing in sight.

'Fucking good, isn't it?' Jay had gushed when I called him after finding my copy in the morning post. 'Wanker says it's got class coming out of its arse. That's how classy it is.'

I laughed. And it was true. The document felt substantial. It had *heft*. The suspicion had to be that a booklet that weighed this much, that was printed on paper this posh and that contained so many blank spaces – '*air*, Wanker calls it', said Jay, 'the more air, the more class apparently' – the presumption had to be that people with the good taste to produce such a splendid-looking document wouldn't have the bad taste to piss all your money down a drain (sort of thing).

'You know the best thing about it?' crowed Jay. 'It's not glossy.'

It wasn't. From the stiff covers to the almost parchment-like pages, the business plan eschewed all gleam and shine. Even the photographs (obtained from a photo library, no doubt) – downtown Accra; serried workers; fingers at keyboards, all that malarkey – had been subtly bled of pigment, making them appear dream-like, yet somehow all the more realistic as a result; as though one were looking at a finished reality, not a business proposition.

'Who knew Wanker could be this . . . this sophisticated?' I pondered.

'I don't think he did it himself. One of his layout guys probably fancied a change from the usual wall-to-wall beaver gallery.'

'Weird, isn't it? Wanker. All those years ago. Who'd have thought?'

'What? That he'd end up helping us out?'

Actually I was thinking: who'd have imagined we'd ever again lay eyes on the strange and disturbing masturbator, never mind solicit his professional services?

So as I say, the brochure was a hit. But the fly in the ointment turned out to be Deano.

'Nicholas, I can't put my name to this,' he said quietly down the phone the evening he received his copy. 'Someone's been playing very fast and loose with the facts.' On the line from Colindale I could hear a child crying – and the theme tune for *Inspector Morse*.

'The slight, er, embroidery about our previous expertise—'

'Lies, I think would be the technical term.'

'You shouldn't worry,' I attempted to reassure my old chum. 'For a start, everybody does it . . .'

'I'm not everybody.'

'No one checks at this stage . . .'

'When do they check then?'

'And thirdly . . .'

'Yes?'

'Thirdly . . .' For the life of me, I couldn't remember what thirdly was. 'Thirdly . . .' Oh yeah. 'Thirdly, it's only what they call indicative.'

There was a longish pause. Followed by a heavy sigh.

'I think you may want to leave me out of this one, Nicholas.'

'Deano,' I cautioned. 'Please don't make any decisions until you've had a chance to talk to Jay.'

'Nicholas. It all sounds very plausible. It might even work, though that really isn't the point. The point is there are serious untruths in this document, and I can't allow my name to go forward alongside them. By the way, where did you get the idea that I was a PhD?'

Dr Dean Sheridan. Jay thought it had a nice ring to it. Together with all the colourful details about our extensive collective experience in the data capture industry.

'It shouldn't be taken entirely literally . . .' I blustered.

'Jay was always a bullshitter, Nicholas. If you and Anita can manage it, we'd love to have you over for dinner some time. But leave me out of this Ghana thing, okay? Now if you don't mind, I have a five-year-old who won't go to bed.'

'Deano. There's a saying. If you hope to discover new land, you must first be prepared to lose sight of the shore.'

Did he hang up on me? People with squalling five-year-olds can be forgiven for their abrupt telephone manner, I guessed.

The bullshitter remark troubled me, however. Yes, Jay was a bullshitter. Of course he was – but in a good way. He was a *noble* bullshitter – he bullshitted for the greater good. Anyway, who ever got anywhere in life without a little . . . embroidery along the way?

Bloody old Deano. I recalled the solid, patrician way he'd leaned against my mantelpiece; the way he'd jingled his change in his trouser pockets at the reunion. People who jingle their change are rarely going to be prepared to lose sight of the shore, are they?

Scientists, I concluded. They set far too much store by the truth.

2

The following days passed in a bit of a blur. I found it hard to concentrate when there were so many Caroline issues yet unresolved: where to take her on our date, for a start. Somewhere posh? One of those deeply reassuring old-fashioned places with white tablecloths and old-git waiters and nursery food you could suck up through a straw. Where the clientele consisted of old gentlemen in skilfully cut suits with their ageing mistresses. Or should it be somewhere unexpected and groovy? A converted toilet in Archway with low lighting and a mercurial new chef who does 'amazing things' with soba noodles and Iberian chicory and what have you; one of those hot, buzzy restaurants of the hour that can only do you a table at 6.30 or 11, that six months later has turned into a Starbucks.

Or maybe one of those dependable old warhorses. Been there a million times. Or how about the all-time-favourite Chinese in Soho? Sublime menu, but toilets like an open sewer.

Toilets *matter* to girls, don't they?

Hmm. There was further thought needed on this one, clearly.

There was also the question of What To Wear. My familiar and comfortable uniform of black shoes, black trousers, black T-shirt and black leather jacket? Or something a little less, er, black. Surely not a suit (and certainly not the only suit that still fitted, the Graham Greene cream linen jobbie). In an ideal world, I would have worn the midnight-blue Ralph Lauren cords and the

John Smedley polo — but the Ralph didn't technically do up any more (well, it did, but not without risk of internal injury) and the John, if memory served, featured the residue of a food strike in the shape of the Falkland Islands.

Hmm. (You see, this was a two-hmm problem as things stood.)

Another thing. Should I pick her up or not? Advantage: women love to be picked up. It's manly, chivalrous and romantic and, in complete contrast to the behaviour of their usual dysfunctional boyfriends who arrange to meet them in crappy pubs and are twenty minutes late, you begin the evening with a whole stack of brownie points. Disadvantage: you have to pick them up. You have to find their place. Then somewhere to park. And beforehand clear out all the empty cans of Diet Coke and sweetie wrappers, and yellowing newspapers and *Roxy Music's Greatest Hits* cassettes. Above all, you have to *drive*. As in, operate heavy machinery. Never advisable after a cocktail or two and a river of Chilean merlot. On the other hand, picking her up would mean ringing the bell, entering the sanctum — the bedroom door cracked open a few tantalising inches — while she floats about extinguishing lamps, setting answering machines, burglar alarms and man-traps. And then afterwards. Driving her home. Smooth, masculine gear-changes. *Nicholas, thank you. I've had a lovely evening. Would you like to come in for a euphemism?*

Hmm. (Make that a three-hmm problem.)

Who paid was not an issue. I would insist (though I hoped she would protest just enough to seem sincere without becoming tedious). After all, it was my idea. And I could put it through on the newspaper's expenses (I'd think of *something*).

So between where to take her (somewhere with *oysters*, maybe? Something very sexy about seafood), what to wear (perhaps I could have the midnight-blue cords *let out*; oh, the shame of it) and whether to pick her up or not (fuck it, pick her up. If I pulled in from the right, and led her round the back of the car, maybe she wouldn't notice the dent in the passenger-side wing) . . . with a constant bubble of anxiety pinging around inside my ribcage, I found it rather difficult to think of anything else.

3

Happily, my contribution to the output of Yack FM 24:7 took up very little neural processing capacity.

The underlit vivarium that was Clyde Folger's studio smelt of curry and cigar smoke as I slipped into my seat. Takeaway food cartons mingled with piles of newsprint. Round the table were a flamboyant astrologer, one of those TV makeover people who turn your sitting room into a Turkish brothel, the London bureau chief of a Dutch news magazine, a woman who'd written a book about teaching your cat to paint . . . and me.

'Columnist Nicholas Pitt has entered the amphitheatre of dreams,' boomed the human tree stump. 'Now hear this, brothers and sisters. Eating seaweed can improve your memory, so says new research. Would you eat seaweed for a better memory? Call the Yack Line and have your say. Mr Pitt, sir. What say you?'

'Sorry, what was the question again?'

'Do you mean the seaweed you get in Chinese restaurants?' asked the flamboyant astrologer. 'Because that isn't seaweed. It's deep-fried shredded cabbage.'

'That stuff reminds me of pubic hair,' revealed the TV decorator. 'Mind you, my first husband *was* a Martian.'

Debate was engaged. The London bureau chief of the Dutch news magazine talked about samphire, or sea asparagus as it was sometimes known. The woman who wrote the teach-your-cat-to-paint book rattled on about feline memory. Apparently experiments had shown that cats could remember the location of a tin of pilchards placed in one of three containers up to *five* years ago, but not birthdays or anniversaries. My own contribution was to talk about something strange that had happened only that morning when, sorting through some old books to take to Oxfam, a postcard fell out of a copy of *The Dice Man*.

It had long been my habit to tuck letters and postcards from friends between the pages of the volume I was currently reading so that when the book eventually went up on the shelf it would contain within it a fragment of the past: a time capsule, to be accidentally discovered at some point in the distant future, when I wanted, say, to check a particular passage in *Zen and the Art of Motorcycle Maintenance*. Or re-read *Lord of the Rings*. Or maybe just finish the bastard.

So the postcard lying on the carpet I knew would be redolent with nostalgia.

It was from Spain. A photograph of the bullring at Ronda. Postmarked the October of my last year at university. And addressed to my parents' house.

Dear Nicholas,
   Unbelievably baking hot here, but having a fine old time. Reading, swimming, boozing (of course), guzzling seafood and wishing you could have come. Day trip to Tangiers tomorrow on the ferry. If I am sold into white slavery, you may have my stereo! Keep well.
   Lots of love, Karen XXX

An innocuous enough text, but just one problem. Who was Karen?

It bothered me all morning, and then for much of the afternoon, that I couldn't remember being close to anyone of that name. And it certainly appeared that we *were* close, didn't it? The wishing that I'd come. The lots of love. The XXX. The bequest of the stereo. I thought back to my circle in the last year of college. The gang from the hall of residence. The people who I liked in English Lit. The assorted drugsters and wasters who I used to hang around with in the student union coffee bar. In none of the tableaux that came to mind could I find anyone called Karen.

I scrutinised the card for clues. The parenthetical *of course* after *boozing*. Was she someone I used to get pissed with? (It might help to explain why I couldn't remember her.) The remark about *white slavery*. An odd phrase, that. Was she some *Daily Mail* reader from the Home Counties whom I had taken a shine to? *Reading? Swimming? Guzzling seafood?*

Who the hell was Karen?

'It's a really rather disturbing thing,' I said with unusual frankness in what was after all a forum for small talk and cheap gags. 'It's like finding the face of a stranger in your holiday snaps. It's not as if there's a *blank space* in your memory waiting to be filled in. This is more like . . . a nothingness. Where once there was a person. A bit of one's life, presumably.'

The flamboyant astrologer pulled a face at me, somewhere between a sympathetic smile and a wince. The woman who taught cats to paint said people often forget other people, but rarely a cat who's done a few watercolours.

'Nothingness,' thundered Clyde. 'A big word for something you can't weigh, measure up for a suit or spread on a dry cracker. So we have a mystery. The Lady Vanishes. If you're out there in Radioland, Karen, give us a call. If you are Karen the disappearing postcard writer who took that holiday to Spain, that day trip to Tangier, who pledged Nicholas Pitt the Younger all of your worldly stereo systems, phone the Yack Line and put him out of his amnesia. And now Frank. Frank calls from Grange-over-Sands. What's in the bank, Frank?'

Frank told a sad tale about his mother, who was suffering from senile dementia. His voice caught as he described how she no longer recognised him. Dave from East Lothian reminded us that the brain was a muscle. Use it or lose it was his recommendation. Darren on the M6 talked about mnemonics and quoted one for remembering the colours of the rainbow: 'Richard of York gave battle in vain' – red, orange, yellow, green, blue, indigo, violet. Philip in Peterborough said there was a phrase for the order to pot snooker balls in, but he couldn't think of it just at the minute. A woman from Sheffield phoned up to call us a lot of 'smug southern tossers'. When Clyde pointed out that Lars, the bureau chief, was actually from Rotterdam, she apologised and called him a 'smug Dutch tosser'. Clyde told the time and waggled a finger. The red light snapped off and an advert played for a constipation remedy.

4

The following afternoon found me in a spectacularly grotty pub at the end of an evil-smelling cul-de-sac near High Holborn.

'Christ, this must be the last unmodernised boozer in the country,' I remarked, casting my gaze through the fug of tobacco fumes. A profound alcoholic lassitude had settled on the exclusively male clientele. They looked like they'd been there since 1962.

'I love this place,' beamed Jay. 'They keep a very decent pint of bitter.'

He was wearing the same slim black suit from the reunion – rather worn, I noticed, yet still somehow effortlessly stylish. The shirt collar too had seen better days, buckling against his firm jawline, unshaven that afternoon – though by default or design, I couldn't have said. He drained the remains of his beer and came straight to the point:

'Deano's being a bit of a prick, isn't he?'

'You've spoken to him.'

'Bit fucking precious, isn't it? I told him the document was indicative.'

'What did he say?'

'That he didn't know what I was talking about. Silly fucker.'

He rolled his eyes and started on the next pint. Tipping the workmanlike brown liquid down his throat like he was following a recipe: *then add 100 ml of John Smiths Bitter. Allow to settle. Repeat a few moments later*. I poked a finger in my vodka and tonic and waggled the ice cubes about.

'We don't actually need him, though, do we? He's not . . . not *crucial*, as it were, to success.'

Jay looked at me a little oddly. Was it the way I'd said *we* didn't need Deano?

'He's our *boffin*, Nicholas. Our scientist. You and I know diddly about all that shit.' He did the next 100 ml, and now it was my turn to look at him a little oddly.

What did he mean, he was our scientist? Weren't there thousands of people out there with the necessary technical know-how? Why did it have to be Deano?

'I'm sure we can find someone else.'

Jay sighed. 'We probably can.' Smiled wistfully. 'Would have been nice to keep it in the family, though.'

'Who'd have thought?' I added philosophically. Who'd have thought Deano would prove to be so picky about a few facts? was what I meant. But then Deano was always the most reluctant member of our threesome. The slowest to draw out of his shell; the one least likely to agree to anything illicit. 'He wouldn't even take the short cut on the cross-country runs, remember?'

Cross-country runs. What a ridiculous phrase. The route — past a petrol station, a DIY superstore, along suburban streets, and then through playing fields backing on to a huge rusty gasometer — was hardly 'cross-country'. Nor could the sort of hopeless puffing and blowing that we went in for be accurately labelled as running. I loathed cross-country for the complete lack of enjoyment one derived from the process of utterly knackering oneself. Deano, I know, felt even more bitterly on the subject. Jay, who found the six-mile enforced slog round the local environs less physically challenging, nevertheless held the event in contempt for its total lack of interest ('no goals, no wickets, a waste of a perfectly good afternoon').

It was a gift that the circuit was an approximate figure-of-eight formation, affording the bold an opportunity to lop off at least half the course by judicious back-doubling at the crossover point. There was a handily situated loitering area — a small rubbish-strewn dip behind a stand of trees next to a footbridge over a dual carriageway — where the enterprising could lounge about before rejoining the 'run' to limp the last quarter of a mile home. Very occasionally, strategic points along the route would be policed by teachers with sinister clipboards, but more often than not, an honesty policy was in force.

It was Jay's practice — and then mine too — to duck into this fume-filled hollow, where he would loll against a pile of old tyres, smoking cigarettes, glancing at his watch and gazing at the traffic on the North Circular Road.

'Really, what is the fucking point of that?' he'd mutter from our vantage point as we gazed upon the parade of pale legs in plimsolls staggering across the pedestrian walkway (the leaders would be back about forty minutes later).

'Poor saps,' I'd reply; ironically, I imagined.

Pugine always afforded us a bit of a laugh, his huge blood-engorged thighs lumbering up the spiral stairwell; Wanker, too, the comic way his ankles splayed: he runs like a *girl*, was the usual taunt. Kapper, Ritblat, Conway among the stragglers; Deano too. Deano who, no matter how hard we tried, could never be persuaded to take advantage of the malingering facility.

'Think of it as an energy-saving scheme,' I suggested.

'It's cheating,' he replied, red-faced, chest heaving, as he finally made it home.

'Who does it cheat, exactly?' Jay enquired, quietly amused by the principled stand.

Deano didn't have an answer to that in those days. He was too bright to reply, *yourself*, the individual who cheating was always supposed to afflict — an argument that I personally have never found terribly persuasive. Today I guess he might make reference to the concept of success being the fruit of one's own efforts. An honourable position, though as Jay and I saw it, a somewhat foolish one.

'Where are you taking Caroline?' Jay asked me now, with a bit of twinkle in the optical department.

'Dunno. Actually, I was going to ask if you had any suggestions.' I neglected to mention that this question had more or less occupied my every waking moment since she agreed to be seen in public with me.

Jay did something thoughtful with his lips. 'Tough one,' he conceded. 'First date sets the tone.'

'And I don't want to leave it to her to decide . . .'

'Quite right. Girls like to be *taken*. Even the Princess.'

'I was thinking maybe the Savoy . . .'

Jay was shaking his head. 'You can't impress her like that. She's been everywhere. I should go for something a bit different, if I were you. Some trendy tapas bar in Hoxton. No, forget that. She hates fucking tapas. Spent our last holiday together complaining about the grub.'

He effected a rueful grimace, drained his pint. And I was assailed by sinking feelings on all sides. Go for somewhere *a bit different*, he said. Yes? Like where, exactly? By definition, I Knew Where I Knew. How was I supposed to find somewhere a bit different? (And don't say look in a book, or ask someone.)

Our last holiday together. Suddenly I was aware of the immensity of the task – of the futility of trying to impress the goddess. What hope had I got? I had the instant crushing realisation: the woman was out of my league. Caroline was a creature of another world – the world of those handsome people you saw in magazines or walking around in expensive parts of London. The world of good-looking women who went out with blokes with firm jaws; blokes whose top trouser buttons weren't too tight; whose modern woollen knitwear wasn't stained with black bean sauce. These were *knowing* women. They *radiated* knowingness. They held themselves differently because of what they knew. And the men who got them knew stuff too (and not just where to take them).

People like me didn't get goddesses. People like me were obliged to make do with the Squeakys of this life — and then only if we were lucky.

And at the thought of Squeaky — another sinking feeling. Which would be worse? I wondered. To cut her loose — or to slink back and attempt to make a go of it?

'How's Anita?' asked Jay, reading my thoughts.

'Fine. Yeah, great.' I hoped he wouldn't call me that thing again. Fanny-rat.

'And the deadline business?'

'We haven't really talked about it.' Being as how it was a fucking great ten-ton weight hanging over our heads.

'How long to go now?'

I shrugged. 'Fortnight or something?'

But I knew exactly. It was nineteen days.

Nineteen days, five hours and twenty-two minutes, if you wanted to get all Seiko Quartz Timing about it.

'Getting close then.' Jay lit a cigarette.

'What would you do?' I found myself asking. 'In my position.' Not that he would ever be in my position. Things always seemed clearer to him.

'I think you'll know what to do when the moment arrives.'

'What? I'll just know? As in sudden certainty?' As in breaking the habit of a lifetime.

Jay peered at me a little intently. 'You know how when you get food poisoning, right?' He broke into a little smile. 'When you get the raging shits, or you're puking up your guts. If you think about it for half a second, don't you always know what did it? When you cast your mind back to what you've eaten, don't you always get a mental picture of what poisoned you? Those fucking prawns. Or that chicken. Or the little bits of scrambled egg hanging around in the Singapore noodles. You always *know*, don't you?'

'Yeah, you do, sort of . . .'

'It's the same with girls.'

'As food poisoning?'

'You just *know*, Nicholas. It's a gut thing. You go with your guts.'

As a technique for diagnosing the causes of gastric trauma, I could accept the plausibility of the thesis. As a philosophy for living the rest of one's life, however, it seemed a little underpowered. Where was the higher mental functioning? The intellectual agony that is the essence of the human condition? The to-ing and fro-ing of the arguments in the old cranial debating chamber? On the one hand, this; on the other hand, that; on the third hand, the other thing.

'I don't seem to be a terribly . . . *gutty* sort of person,' I confessed.

'You had the guts to ask the Princess out.'

It was true. And what was more, I had found myself asking her out before I had consciously thought about it — a sure sign of Guts In Action, no?

'I suppose.'

'Course you did.'

We sipped our drinks for a bit. Someone put some money in the jukebox — that's how unreconstructed this pub was, they still had a jukebox — and an Elvis song came on. 'A Little Less Conversation'.

Eventually Jay said, 'Still. Bloody Deano, eh?'

'Scientist,' I replied, as if that explained everything. 'All brain and no guts.'

'You're dead right there, mate. Anyhow, don't worry about him. I'll think of something.'

Only later, in the taxi, did it occur to me that I hadn't been worried. Nor had I felt that there was anything that especially needed to be thought about. As in *I'll think of something*. No, as I bowled away towards my next appointment, I was much more struck by the figure I saw crossing the road in front of my cab, apparently heading in the direction of the pub I had just left. Walking along the pavement, a trifle urgently, but also perhaps with a small air of amusement. And yes, with the faintest suggestion of splayed ankles too.

Colin Wilkes.

Colin — if memory served — *Herbert* Wilkes.

Wanker.

5

There was good news and bad news from the world of print journalism. The bad – though not unexpected – news was that my column was finally humanely put to rest. Over a long lunch and two decent bottles of red, Nigel, who ran the section that it appeared in, definitively ruled out any prospect of a reprieve.

'Sorry, mate,' he said. He even went to the trouble of looking like he meant it.

So here it was. My journalistic career, having apparently reached its high-water mark, was now commencing its gentle decline. There were no doubt hordes of hotter, sharper, more trenchant columnists out there, writers whose words were more in tune with the ever-shifting Zeitgeist. And yet. And yet, when I asked myself how I felt about all this, I discovered I didn't seem to mind as much as I once might have. With the prospect of Jay's data processing project before us, I appeared to be moving towards the field of wealth creation; the production of text was now a means to an end, not the end in itself. I should soon probably have to buy a briefcase.

The good news that I mentioned was that Nigel tossed me a consolation bone. The paper's restaurant reviewer was taking a 'well-earned' break and could I fill in for a week while she was away? There was a new place in west London that had just opened up called Ovation.

'The building used to be a clap clinic,' he told me. 'Hilarious, isn't it?' he added without the trace of a smile. 'Do you know anyone you could take along?'

So while life was far from settled, this piece at least was perfect.

It was with the nice warm feeling of reservations for two booked at the capital's hot new eatery that, a day or two later, I practically *bounced* up the steps to Caroline's block of flats and pressed the doorbell. It didn't matter if the restaurant turned out to be crap: I was *reviewing* it. We could be delightfully disapproving, or delightfully . . . delighted. With nothing invested, we could simply take as we found.

Weirdly, it turned out she lived about five minutes' walk from Squeaky, in one of those red-brick mansion blocks close to Marylebone High Street.

When I reached it, her doorway stood ajar. From within came weird, soft jazz music; formless improvisational stuff, the sort that typically doesn't have a beginning, middle and end, but just swirls around moodily for half an hour, then looks at its watch and calls it a night. Evening sun spilled on to a polished wooden floor.

'In here,' a voice called.

I crossed the hall and stepped into a huge, bright, empty sitting room. Two pale sofas faced each other across a pale rug. A lamp on a side table had a length of pale silk draped across it. About the only other object was a compact disc player with a heap of CDs nearby on the floor. At the far end, on a huge marble mantelpiece, actually *standing* on this huge marble mantelpiece – and not at all safely, by the look of things – was the slender figure of Caroline Stamp. She was adjusting the position of a small brown painting hanging above it on the wall.

'Christ. What are you doing up there?' I blurted out, even though it was perfectly obvious.

'Is it level? I can't seem to get it right.'

It was a study of a pair of reddish-looking fish lying on a plate. Rather old I should have said. Done in oils. Set in a brown frame. There was something terribly sad about the fishy duo (red mullet at a guess). Maybe it was the darkness of the background. Or the candlelit gloom in which they'd been executed. Or maybe because they were dead.

'Perfectly level, I'd say. Listen, Caroline . . . you don't look one hundred per cent *safe* up there.'

She didn't. She was flattening herself to the wall, like a climber, to stay on board the mantelpiece's narrow ledge. Which isn't to say that it wasn't rather *exciting* to see her from that angle, pressed against the cream paintwork, pale orange blouse above pale green trousers, an inch of pale skin in between. I noticed she was in bare feet. Slowly she turned her head round and smiled. Her eyes locked on to mine, and at once I felt the data draining from my head, as though it were being downloaded on to a hard drive.

'If you don't mind me asking,' I asked, 'how did you get up there?' No chair or stepladder stood nearby. A funny chill chose that moment to run through me.

'We used to go to the mountains a lot as children,' she replied. And at that, with an extraordinary, almost *ape-like* facility, knuckles whitening on the various hand-holds involved, feet and *toes* right in there too, nuzzling into the marble's handy crevices and curlicues, she scrambled back down to the ground. The whole fluid operation took about five seconds, and I was speechless with admiration.

Just as suddenly, she clicked back to goddess mode, practically *gliding* across the floor like a ballet dancer to survey the picture. She turned, standing directly in front of me, her palms resting in the small of her back. I was close enough to see the fine down on her neck, to smell her perfume, vanilla and something else, perspiration perhaps. I had a powerful urge to lay my hands on her shoulders and lower my chin on to her head (not normally considered polite on a first date, I expect).

'What do you think?' she asked with a certain ambiguity. Did she mean the angle of the picture? Or its quality? The monkey trick I'd just witnessed? Or just things in general?

'I think you're marvellous,' was what I wanted to say.

'Are they red mullet?' I enquired weedily.

'I believe so.'

'I very much like the sadness in the painting. The air of . . . of gloom hanging over the scene.'

She peered round at me, that strange look of desolation across her features once again; the one that said *I'm not happy*; the one that made me want to rescue her each time I saw it. Rescue her from *what*, I couldn't have said.

'I've always found it rather peaceful. It was my grandmother's.'

We both gazed upon the fish for a bit, trying to extract their deeper meaning.

(No, I'm sorry, but it really was rather gloomy, you know. Two fish, mullet or otherwise, but in any case very much devoid of the life force, lying in a black bowl. The bowl standing on a brown table, lit by some unseen guttering candle. The whole cheerless prospect framed in brown. Quite possibly a brutal civil war or a medical epidemic raging just off-canvas. Peaceful as in The End of Struggle, possibly.)

'Do you think they'll have whitebait?' she asked. 'Where we're going.'

I was impressed. Most of the women I knew were squeamish about whitebait. 'Don't all those little eyes put you off?' I jested.

'No, I rather like them, actually.' She was looking at me seriously. 'It's probably a need for attention.'

There was a pause, and then a little miracle: she spluttered with laughter at her own joke. I felt a powerful urge to wrap her slender frame in my arms and squash it against my body.

6

They didn't. Have whitebait, that is.

It wasn't that sort of establishment at all. And I could tell right away it was going to be a dud. All the signs of dud-ness were in place. The great roiling bar full of tanned young people rather too obviously Dressed Up For A Night Out; the specially commissioned challenging art works (a series of oils on venereological themes); the sinister touch-screen ordering system speaking of the horridly efficient restaurants-to-pubs-to-petrol-stations conglomerate that in all probability owned the joint. The feverish quality and sheer noise level from the clientele that was generating the self-fulfilling buzz about it being the buzzy new restaurant that everyone was talking about.

Except none of it bothered me.

I couldn't have cared less.

My companion was a goddess. She glided a little in front of me as we were steered to our table, and I felt the eyes of other men (and women, come to that) lift from their plates to regard her as we passed. A few flicked on to me by association, and mostly flicked quickly off again. Those that remained plainly framed the unspoken question: *uh?*

I watched Caroline's great grey irises as they danced across the words of the menu, the usual meaningless mixed metaphor of superfluous adjectives, sub-clauses and general fol-de-rol. (Do you really need to know that your fish was *line-caught*? Or that your duck was *pan*-seared. Where else are they going to sear a duck . . . in your hat? And why is it that when you ask the waiter what the difficult word in French means, it always turns out to be *portion*?)

I went for the roast chicken (how badly could they fuck that up?). She for the 'baby baa lamb', as she put it to my great amusement (I do love women who are unsentimental about these things). She decided she was going to start with the goat's cheese thingy. I, the octopus salad.

'I believe you can train an octopus to unscrew jars,' I said when it arrived (to indicate that I was safely un-squeamish about these things as well).

'You mean for the elderly. Or infirm.'

'Yes, though they can make a hash of pickled cucumbers. The cucumbers tend to float off. Hang on, Caroline. Aren't you meant to be a veggie?'

'Not *always*,' she replied, shooting me a rather particular look.

'Really? So when exactly?' I enquired with some interest.

'Every now and again I get an urge to taste a warm-blooded creature's actual blood. Does that make me a very bad person, do you think?'

'I'm terribly shocked.'

She ate with a certain feline intensity, with none of that air of distaste and face-pulling that Squeaky brought to the task. (And at the *thought* of Squeaky . . . a definite tug of guilt in the abdominal region.) I watched as Caroline operated her fork, pulling layers of lamb away from the bone, moving the knife thoughtfully through her new potato at interesting angles. She brought the glass to her lips; they parted; she admitted a quantity of red wine between them. I had the thought: she is a complex living organism engaged in *feeding* – which, if you remember your biology, is one of the seven characteristics of living organisms (the others being response to stimuli, respiration, locomotion, digestion, defecation, and reproduction). I had the same thought about myself. Under the veneer of sophistication, beneath the Gap trousers, Gap shirt, Gap boxer shorts and whatnot, there was a largely hairless ape (one who had learned to walk upright, manipulate symbols, order a pizza by telephone, that sort of thing, but an ape nonetheless). I remember reading somewhere how it's our old 'animal' brain that fills most of our skull. Our new 'human' brain is a thin layer of cerebral cortex on top, like a serviette wrapped round a grapefruit. Underneath, we're monkeys.

Was I having these peculiar thoughts because of the ape-like display on the mantelpiece earlier? Or did these musings about the characteristics of living organisms arise because she was making me feel more *alive*?

'What shall I say in my review?' I asked. 'My companion's *gigot* of lamb was . . . ?'

She thought about it for a moment. 'Scrummy.'

'Not really a restaurant review word, scrummy.'

'Heaven, then.' She was being funny.

'Some sort of *commentary* would be nice.'

'My companion's senses were flooded, no, were *overwhelmed* by her lamb's tender pink juices. A lapsed vegetarian, she felt a guilty pleasure that was almost physical. As though she'd personally crept up on the helpless creature in a field and sunk her teeth into its neck. How was your chicken?'

'Oh, you know. Chickeny. No, I can't say that, can I? *Plausible*. My chicken was plausible without being in any way memorable.'

'Can chicken be plausible?'

'It was . . . *workmanlike*. Without being in any way . . . exceptional. Remarkable. My chicken was *un*remarkable, without being in any way . . . in any way what?'

'Implausible.'

'That's it! My chicken was unremarkable without being in any way implausible. I think we've just invented a whole new school of food journalism, right there.'

'Can I ask you something, Nicholas?'

'Sure.'

She was looking at me a little oddly. 'Why didn't you ask Anita to be your . . . your dining *companion*?'

A handful of lies popped into my mind, like a drop-down menu on the laptop screen. She's out of town. She's got food poisoning. She's busy this evening. She hates restaurants. We had a row. She's left me. She died very suddenly, of a brain haemorrhage.

Finally, when the truth presented itself, it was — as always — beautifully simple.

'Because I wanted to ask you, Caroline.'

I took a deep swallow on the pointlessly expensive New Zealand cabernet sauvignon. She was still thinking about that one, her eyes fixed on mine, so I added a little weakly, 'After all, it's a free country.'

She smiled. *Thinly*, I think is the word for it. 'Would you be terribly offended if I picked up the bone?'

'Of course not.'

'You wouldn't think I was a savage or anything?'

'You go right ahead. I like to see a woman enjoying a piece of red meat.'

Did that sound a bit like I thought it sounded? Her eyes held mine for a few more seconds. Then she grasped the lamb bone in both hands, her lips wrapped themselves round it and her teeth deployed in a manner I could feel in the depths of my flat-front chinos.

But the question was a good one. Why *had* I asked her out? She was beautiful, of course, and naturally I desired her, although I didn't fancy her *rotten*, as they say; she wasn't one of those women whose blatant geometry played straight to one's monkey brain and made one's eyes stick out on stalks. The truth was that, beyond Jay Bryant, we didn't have anything in common. We didn't even particularly *click* on a personal level. There must be something about her that chimed with my psychopathology, I concluded. Perhaps it was to do with her secret sorrow; maybe there was something about the enigma that lay at the centre of her that I needed to penetrate (in a *nice* way, thank you). Or did she represent *worth*? Was she someone in whom I could dissolve my unconscious feelings of worthlessness? I certainly perceived her as a cut above the average female, even though she probably went to the toilet in much the same way as all the others.

By the time she was finished gnawing, there were grease marks at both corners of her mouth.

'Sorry about that,' she said, dabbing at her face.

'Not at all. Lick the plate if you want to.'

7

The ride back to Caroline's flat was, if I say it myself, a master-
class in smooth, manly gear-changing. I even reverse-parked the
car in *one*, thank you God. When we stopped, she got straight
out as though she was expecting me to do the same (none of
that would-you-like-to-come-in-for-coffee bollocks).

So while she rattled round in the kitchen, I placed myself at
one end of one of her pale sofas and thought hard about how to
make progress. At dinner she had been friendly, but not flirty.
We had touched upon all the polite conversational topics, but
there wasn't what you'd call active chemistry. There were
certainly none of those green-for-go signals a chap can't fail to
notice – spooky eye contact over the wine schooner, twirling of
hair (including chewing), girl's hand resting on man's arm a fraction too long, etc. The thing to do, I decided, was to follow the
guidance of Barry White and simply hang on in there.

Caroline returned with a tray bearing two steaming mugs and
a bottle of Courvoisier. She set it on the floor and draped herself
along the sofa opposite. Something mellow and improvisational
was playing on the stereo. Perhaps that was what prompted me
to attempt a little improvising of my own.

'Tell me about your unlived life, Caroline. What you might
have done if you hadn't gone into the music biz. What you might
still do.'

It was a reasonably bold enquiry, and she felt the need to

dispense generous slugs of brandy into the black coffees while she considered her reply. When her eyes next met mine they contained a familiar blend of regret mixed with acceptance.

'I'd live in the mountains,' she said a little sadly. 'I'd get into climbing again. I'd write. Learn to cook. Grow alpine plants. Maybe there'd be . . .' She trailed off. 'Actually it seems to have taken all my imagination to live one life. How about you?'

How to convey it? My recurring bucolic fantasy. Bring up the sound effects first. Birds twitter. Sheep bleat. The low of distant cattle. Now fade in the vision: a country cottage, beehives in the garden. From an open upstairs window comes the thin tappety-tap of a laptop. It is me, at work on my latest book, the eagerly awaited ninth volume in my acclaimed series of detective novels. Downstairs, doing her thing in the kitchen, or maybe it is the sitting room, perhaps the garden . . . well, to be honest, this is where it's a little hazy, but there definitely is a *she* about the place. (Is she a writer too? Or a painter, or sculptor?) I can't quite picture her face, but I am certain she is the most glamorous creature for fifty miles in every direction. For some reason, the beehives are a particularly important element in my fantasy. There are two of them, in the long grass between the ancient apple trees. Every time I look up from my keyboard, I can see the bees arriving and departing on their fascinating flightpaths, always leaving and returning at the same magic angle (it has something to do with the sun; or is it the moon? Some bee-bollocks anyway). The bees do their work. I do mine. The months roll by. And then the years. Pollen accretes to the honeycombs, words to the hard disk of the laptop.

'I'd be a writer too,' I confessed. 'I'd live in the country and write thrillers. There'd be beehives in the garden,' I added to appear a little enigmatic myself.

She offered up a bleak smile. 'Just what the world needs. Two more failed writers.'

It was hard to quarrel with that sentiment. I nodded philosophically. But how to warm up the temperature of this
encounter? I was sort of stranded on one sofa, while she was
pretty well hunkered down on the other. Spread along it in the
most eye-catching fashion, it had to be said, but in such a configuration — viz. flat out — that it was impossible for me to imagine
how I might contrive to make the journey across the rug and
join her upon it.

'Would you say you were a happy person, Caroline?'

The question fell from my mouth before I could stop myself.
Her brow clouded. A couple of question marks appeared in her
eyeballs. Upper lip seemed to slide ever so slightly against lower
lip, rather in the way a reptile rearranges its jaws in the instant
before the vile red tongue snatches the moth off the twig.

'How do you mean exactly, *happy*?'

What I meant was: why did she so often resemble an eight-
year-old whose hamster has just died? It was as though she lived
in a universe that was very slightly different from the one
everyone else occupied. It contained all the same objects, so she
didn't bump into the furniture or anything, but it was plainly a
more tragic place.

I said, 'On a scale of one to ten, where one is utter misery
and ten is ecstasy, where would you put yourself, do you think?'

She thought about it for a moment. 'What would five be?'

'Neither happy nor unhappy.'

'Five.'

'Fucking hell, *cheer up, love* . . .'

No. Much as I wanted to, I didn't say it.

Instead, I trudged off to the CD player. The music collection
seemed to be deeply hardcore and sophisticated. There was a
heap of obscure cerebral jazz (the sort of stuff that showed its
working-out, if you know what I mean); loads of Central
American and Arabic that I'd never heard of; plus a handful of

gloomy classical (lute concertos, a requiem mass or two, say no more), all of it grossly unsuited to a late-night boy-meets-girl scenario, in my view. The only stuff I could relate to were the obvious freaks. *The Monkees' Greatest Hits*, the soundtrack from the movie *Dumb and Dumber*, and a trashy compilation called *Eighty Big Ones From the Eighties*.

For a moment, I was paralysed with indecision. This sort of thing could matter very much. Pick the wrong recording, and one's stock value was liable to nosedive.

But what to choose? The depressive-looking jazzers — from Germany by the look of things? (Jesus, German jazz. What could that be like?) The guys from the Maghreb with the instruments made out of clay? Surely not the lute concertos?

And then, because I noticed the song title on the sleeve, and because I love them, and also because life is too short to agonise about this stuff — I whacked on The Monkees. I twisted the volume knob up, pressed PLAY and it came bursting out of the sound system like a great soggy explosion of pop happiness.

'I'm a Believer'.

And then it happened. Caroline was suddenly on her feet, on a stretch of the wooden floor near one of the speakers, and she was *dancing*.

Her head was shaking about, her elbows were raised, her wrists were doing funny rhythmical things. Every now and again her knees bent and her whole body sort of shuddered in the direction of the floorboards. I couldn't say it was the most *convincing* display of bopping I'd ever seen. In fact, there was something curiously *fettered* about it, a restraint in her move- ments which for some reason I found tremendously attractive. The thought passed through my head: *go and join her, you idiot*.

Ah yes, all very well to have that thought, but I was no dancer. Never had been, unless I had on-boarded a life-threatening amount of alcohol. She had her back to me now, slender hips wiggling – she was communing with the loudspeaker, it would seem – so I used the opportunity to take an enormous swallow from the brandy bottle. Then another. And then one more for luck.

A great surge of forty per cent proof fire entered my belly. And now – oh Jesus, what must this have looked like? – my elbows were in the air, my knees were knocking into one another, my shoulders were rolling around the place, and technically I too was 'dancing'. As I jigged over towards her, she spun round, and a huge smile lit up the miraculous face.

'I *love* this song!' she yelled.

'Me too!' I cried. Then I added: 'You must have crept up to six or seven now, *surely*?'

'*Five and a half!*' she bellowed.

What are those quotes? About the strange potency of cheap music. And the other one, about dancing being the vertical expression of a horizontal desire. Well here you had it. Caroline and I were face to face, flogging ourselves about to the Monkees' chugging chords. This song is as cheaply potent as any I know. The vocalist was outlining his – by now celebrated – views on the subject of love and fairy tales. His suspicion about things happening for other people and not for him. And how everything changed when he caught a glimpse of her face. I was watching *her* face as her body shivered and spasmed in its oddly controlled manner. Her eyes were dividing their time between my own and my *feet*, for some reason. When I glanced down at her bare toes splayed against the blond flooring, I noticed a small tattoo at her ankle. For a moment I felt the absurdity of the situation, prancing around like a fool in someone's *sitting room*, even one as free of objects to knock over as Caroline's. But then the music kicked up – or maybe the Courvoisier kicked in – and I just Went For It a little. She seemed to respond, becoming more animated. There was a spell where our eyes were locked together

– it fell at the point in the narrative where the singer tells of how all traces of doubt have been removed from his mind, he now feels free to declare that he is in love, and that he is a believer. I suddenly realised that I had been singing along with the words, which in my book is about as uncool as reading with your lips moving.

The song faded. We stood there panting, staring at each other. A strand of black hair was sticking to her forehead. I had a strong urge to wipe it away. She was smiling, her head was tipped back, she was looking at me in a certain way, and I had the sudden shocking thought: *she wants me to kiss her*.

Another half a second and I probably would have done. But two things interceded. First, the next track on the CD burst into life, 'Last Train to Clarksville' (never liked it).

And secondly, at the exact same instant, into the sitting room, a nuclear grin blasted across his handsome features, stepped my old schoolfriend Jay Bryant.

'Brilliant news!' he yelled above the racket. 'We've found our angel.'

And then he walked over to the spot where Caroline and I were standing only inches apart from one another and flung his arms round us both, squeezing us into a fierce three-way hug.

'We're going to be *rich*,' he hissed. A rib cracked, mine possibly.

'Fantastic,' I managed. Caroline's face seemed to be buried somewhere in the region of my right armpit.

'Hey, Nicholas,' said Jay when he eventually released us. 'How do you fancy a trip to Spain?'

FIVE

1

Squeaky was not thrilled when I broke the news to her that I was going to Majorca on business.

'What business?' she asked rather sharply, stabbing several *fusilli* on to her fork with more than a little *brio*. She was pretending to have forgotten. Or not to have taken it seriously in the first place.

Squeaky and I had spent a few evenings together since the dinner party. But calling out Caroline's name in my sleep, combined with the approaching deadline, seemed to have darkened the cloud across our relationship. We had cooked, watched TV, even slept together (although Nothing Else. *That* was clearly out of the question). An atmosphere of brooding anxiety hung between us.

Now I reminded her gently about the Ghana project. How Jay had been searching for people to put money in it. And how his new friend the viscount (I didn't feel the need to detail the circumstances in which the two had met) had apparently provided him with an introduction to a chum of his. An angel investor, so-called; a rich bloke in Majorca who needed to find a tasty-looking scheme to park a million quid in to avoid the attentions of the British tax authorities.

We were having dinner in Squeaky's favourite local Italian. The owner always made a big fuss of her, kissing her hand – she lapped up that slobbery old schtick, tipping her head back and squeezing off a full-bore carillon – shaking mine, and telling me how lucky I was (to be allowed to fuck this fine figure of a woman, I think would have been his general drift).

'You're not really going to get involved with it, are you?' she enquired.

Pausing for our host to dispense the usual red fluids from the raffia-clad flask, I outlined The Plan.

Tudor Owen Pickstock – known to all as Teddy – had recently inherited a rudely large amount of money from the estate of his long-standing male companion, who had died suddenly from an undetected aneurysm. For fifteen years, it would seem, the couple had lived the high life in the hills behind Palma, a location the late party had loved for its warm climate, dramatic scenery and friendly people – but principally for the fact that it wasn't Great Britain. For his part, Teddy, although relaxed and baked to a biscuit brown, had felt himself becoming increasingly homesick. Each new day, as the sun climbed into another cloudless blue sky, the exiled Welshman would retreat into the darkest corner of the villa and pine in secret for drizzle-soaked Machynlleth. Only loyalty to his lotus-eating boyfriend had kept him on Spanish soil. Now, through tragedy, Teddy was in a position to fulfil his atavistic longings, the Inland Revenue had begun taking an interest in the pair's financial affairs. It would appear that Teddy's late partner, Raymond Veale – where had I heard that name before? – was something of a financial fancypants who had employed all sorts of nimble footwork to shelter his earnings beyond the reach of Her Majesty's tax inspectors. If Teddy hoped to bring his fortune back into the UK and protect it from the depredations of Inheritance Tax, Capital Transfer Tax, and regular old unpaid Income Tax, accountants, among other measures, were recommending a 'platform' of investment vehicles.

'And that's where we come in,' I said. 'Teddy Pickstock puts a million into our scheme, escapes all tax on it, and only takes a hit on the profits much further down the line – if at all.' I may not have got the details exactly right, but it still sounded magical to my ears.

Squeaky offered me a look of deep scepticism (she knew I was no businessman). 'And your role in this would be what exactly?'

I explained how everything had been carefully thought through. How Jay was the chief executive, front-man philosopher-king, the guy with the original vision, as it were. 'He'll do most of the talking.'

'Yes, he'd be good at that,' chirped Squeaky a little sourly. 'And you . . . ?'

I admitted I was to be called Director of Communications. I would be overseeing the way in which the company communicated both internally and with the wider world ('making sure the leaflets look spiffy and everything's spelt right' was the way Jay put it. 'So we don't appear to be a bunch of complete and utter dickheads').

If I failed to mention Caroline's part in the scheme, it was perhaps because I didn't want to see my lady friend's face go all mean and tight at the thought of me sharing planes (and hotels presumably) with the goddess.

'So the plan is, you're going to Majorca to meet up with this millionaire character and sweet-talk him out of . . . *how* much?'

'A million pounds, yeah. Million and a quarter actually.'

It did sound a bit ridiculous, the way she put it like that. But essentially, that indeed was the nub of the thing. 'The one point two five million represents the seed investment. To get us to the point where we invite the venture capitalists to pile in.'

Squeaky was staring at me in dismay.

'What?' I said. '*What?*'

She spoke quietly. 'It isn't real, is it, Nicholas?'

For some reason my heart sank. 'What do you mean?'

'It's not real. It's just one of Jay's pipe dreams.'

'I'm not aware that Jay has pipe dreams,' I replied, a little hurt.

'You know what I'm saying.'

Perhaps I did.

Perhaps I did because I'd put the very point – not in quite such high relief, as it were – to Jay the night he arrived with the good news about The Angel. He was in very fine spirits, as I've remarked, and didn't seem at all surprised to find me in Caroline's flat. Nor did he seem to notice that I wasn't over-joyed to see him at that exact moment. (Oddly, it was only months later that it occurred to me that he must have had a key to let himself in.) Jay had thrown himself on a sofa, bashed out a few lines on Caroline's coffee table – she didn't, we did – then immediately began filling us in on what the viscount had told him about Teddy Pickstock. As he got to the bit about how there was fifteen – some said twenty – million quid that the taxman would feel free to claim first dibs on, unless it was cleverly tucked away in various tax-exempt investment opportunities, funny white crusty stuff began to appear at the corners of his mouth.

'Can we really do it?' I asked him soberly after he'd finished.

'Sure. Why not?' he replied with a grin so bright, you could practically hear the filament buzzing.

I couldn't think of a single argument against. 'Like, how hard can it be?' I echoed.

2

If Squeaky wasn't thrilled that I was going to Majorca, then I wasn't exactly overjoyed to discover that the pornographer would be coming with us.

'He'll just be standing in,' Jay explained. 'Until we find a proper technical person. He's doing us a favour actually.'

'But *Wanker*, though . . .' I trailed off. Mere mention of his moniker, I assumed, would be sufficient to carry the force of my objections.

Jay elaborated on the long conversation he'd had with Deano. How the bearded scientist had been unbudging in his refusal to assist with the project.

'I just need you to come and shake hands with the guy,' Jay had entreated. 'He may be coming up with one and a quarter million pounds, so the least you can do is nod and smile, sock him with a bit of scientific stuff, and head back to the sun lounger. Think of it as a free holiday.'

Deano had apparently replied that there was no such thing as a free holiday.

'It's a confidence issue,' tried Jay. 'We could introduce you as an adviser. Not even part of the core team.'

Deano mentioned the thing about the *embroidery* in the business plan, although he deployed a different word.

Jay said there'd be a fee. Deano said he wasn't interested.

'Please,' said Jay.

'Sorry,' said Deano.

'For your old mates,' said Jay in desperation. 'What about loyalty?'

'What about honesty?'

'The people in Africa. They need this to work,' said Jay.

'I hope it does,' said Deano.

'Why are you being such a fucking stubborn prat?' Jay had yelled at him. 'Just do it for me and for Nicholas.'

'Just fuck off, will you please.' (And Deano hung up.)

So now, apparently, solely for the purposes of the initial meeting with this investment angel, Wanker would be playing the part of our technological guru.

'But Wanker knows fuck-all about science,' I'd objected. 'Remember the time he tried to mate two male hamsters for the biology project?'

Jay giggled. 'People grow. They move on. Besides, hamsters are famously difficult to tell apart.'

The point I had to grasp, apparently, was that Wanker was no longer the inadequate adolescent that I remembered from school, but a respectable – okay, not respectable exactly – fully functioning adult. More importantly, he'd done a brilliant job on the brochure, and was prepared to throw himself into Deano's role at a moment's notice.

And at the airport, it was true, Wanker did seem to have matured a bit. We found him waiting for us on the concourse, a small suitcase between his feet, wearing a rather unpleasant lightweight grey suit over a maroon polo shirt in an artificial fibre. A mobile was pressed to his ear as he issued last-minute instructions to a subordinate; something about double-checking the page proofs, squaring the Derek business with Alec – or possibly the Alec business with Derek – and nagging the wholesalers again about you-know-what. And no, he didn't want any excuses about the other thing. Someone had had long enough to decide, and an answer was needed by the close of play Friday, or they would go ahead without her. It was his – Wanker's – view that they knew full well that he – Wanker – had had enough of playing silly buggers.

As Jay and I stood there waiting for him to finish, the pornographer's eyes blinking rapidly as he spoke his commands, I felt my enduring distaste for Wanker's actual person suddenly counterbalanced by a new if grudging respect for his general air of action and enterprise. Even if one regretted his taste in shirts and suitings, here, one felt, was a busy man with Things On His Plate.

'Nicholas. Sorry,' said Wanker when he eventually ended the call. He offered me a hand, just as he'd done at the reunion.

It was the same faintly damp grip, but there was a new poise in his demeanour, that perhaps I hadn't clocked at the Carpenters Arms. Now I had a reason to study him more closely, I saw that the nervy, blinky boy who always had a half-smile playing about his features (*see, I'm smiling, I am no threat to you, please don't stick my head down the toilet* would be the general subtext) had become one of those slightly intense characters whose gaze blazes a fraction too strongly for comfort. The hurt that once lived in his hot brown eyes had been replaced with something a little less damaged: a certain briskness of manner; irritability, maybe. I had the sudden, rather surprising thought: perhaps this bloke doesn't suffer fools gladly.

'Colin.' I forced myself to use his first name. The first time ever, probably.

'Well, this is all very jolly,' he burbled, not sounding particularly jolly, it had to be said. 'Not to say unexpected.'

'Good of you to help out,' I said.

'A fascinating project. I wish I'd thought of it.'

In the business class lounge – 'Of *course* we're going business class,' Jay had snapped at me when I'd expressed surprise, 'we're businessmen, aren't we?' – over Bloody Marys, Wanker produced a photo from his wallet of Mrs Wanker and the three little Wankers.

'This is Christine. And the littlies are Kerry, Sean and Poppy. Twelve, nine and four.' An attractive young woman and her brood stared confidently out of the laminated print. They were grouped along one side of a wooden picnic table in what could be a pub garden.

'It doesn't seem possible.' It came out before I could stop myself.

Wanker's eyeballs skittered over my face. 'What doesn't?' He was smiling, although his gaze contained something else; something beyond amusement.

'That you've got this . . . this terribly grown-up family,' I stuttered.

'We started early, Nicholas.'

'So I see.'

But what I meant was: it doesn't seem possible that these happy, pleasant individuals in pastel leisurewear could be Your Family. That you could even *have* a family. You, who were the object of derision, pity and occasional violence. How was it possible that Wanker – and here I pictured the terrified schoolboy, encircled in the playground, turning like a top, dreading the coming blow from behind – how could this . . . this worthless worm have turned into an economically active member of the community with a wife – yes, dammit, a *good-looking* wife – and three sunny-looking children? Wanker, who even the teachers felt sorry for. Wanker, who – if you'd asked me at the time, what's going to happen to old Wanker then? – I'd probably have replied: nothing. He'll live with his mummy and never leave home. When she finally dies, he'll use the money to move into an old signal box, and one day his body will be found surrounded by train-spotting magazines and used Kleenex.

Perhaps what I also meant was: where was *my* family?

3

The late-afternoon flight to Palma was fairly surreal. Up to this point, the whole Ghana project had been all talk and a stylish brochure. But once the plane's undercarriage had rumbled up into its belly and the captain had cancelled the seatbelt signs, now it seemed that we were on our way to something, the very *oddness* of the situation struck me. Across the aisle, Jay Bryant was clamped between a pair of Walkman headphones. Next to him, curled into a fragile ball, our remaining travelling companion was asleep. 'I like the idea of waking up in another country,' she announced before turning herself off like a piece of electrical equipment. I was sandwiched between a window and Wanker, who was keying stuff into a laptop (when I sneaked a peek it appeared to be rows of figures). Through the perspex, a very long way down, we were crossing a coastline. I was leaving behind . . . what exactly? A discontinued newspaper column and a failing relationship. Also, it might be asked, equally and oppositely, what exactly was I approaching? A new life as a business executive?

Hanging between the earth and sky in the company of a jobless ex-con, an unemployed music PR and a pornographer, I confess I felt a little ridiculous.

It was raining when we arrived, which didn't seem to be a particularly good portent. The hire car too took an age to wrangle out of the agents, a detail that did nothing to lift my spirits. But as the lights of Palma gave way to the darkened roads of the countryside and the storm clouds parted to reveal mountain peaks and the moon even popped out to silver the tarmac under our wheels, a brief shudder of adventure rolled through me.

'Somehow, I don't think we're in Kansas any more,' I quipped.

Wanker dealt me a bit of a dirty look, from which I understood he had never seen the 1939 film version of *The Wizard of Oz*. If he had, he might have been more amused by my ironic movie referencing.

It had been the viscount's suggestion that we stay at the Finca d'Angelo. Dramatically lit, the walls of the old sandstone farmhouse arose from the blackness as we drove into the grounds, moths dancing in the floodlamps, the last few guests polishing off their dinners on the terrace. We successfully pleaded to be fed and, after a quick visit to our rooms, hastily reconvened for a late supper.

The night was warm and contained that magical smell of abroad. Clinking glasses of the local red in the candlelight, we drank to the success of our venture.

'Remember the last time we went abroad together?' said Jay.

'Boulogne, if I recall correctly,' said Wanker.

'Boulogne,' I added with a bit of a dying fall.

The school trip to Boulogne. Crossing the Channel in the juddering ferry; going in cafés and ordering things with *frites*; trying to smoke a Disque Bleu and feeling nauseous; buying cheese to take back to my parents (the same stuff, it turned out, that you could get in Waitrose). Above all . . . the sheer *Frenchness* of the place: the fish-faced old geezers playing *boules* in the dusty square; the bow-legged widows with their shivering poodles; and the French kids, sulky-looking boys with bad haircuts, the olive-skinned girls with their fascinating brown eyes.

Late in the afternoon, Deano and I find Jay in conversation with one on a bench near the open market. She looks older than him, in the way that girls in their early teens always look older. In a turquoise dress, twisting a dark plait between her fingers. Jay is laying on the full charm offensive – no simple matter in O-level French – except when we draw near, we discover they are talking mainly English, the local educational system being clearly more advanced than our own.

'This is Natalie,' he announces. 'These are *mes amis*, Nicholas *et* Deano.'

'*Bonjour*,' I essay, and bow slightly for some reason.

Natalie giggles, and stares knowingly at Jay. Deano becomes hypnotised by his shoes.

'*Enchanté*,' she replies. '*Qu'est-ce que vous aimez*, Nicholas?' she asks, putting a delightful local pronunciation on *Nicho-LASS*.

Oddly enough, our French teacher, Miss Saltman, had posed the same question only a few weeks ago. I am prepared.

'*J'aime bien* . . . *le rockgroup* Queen.'

'*Ah, oui. Moi aussi.*'

'*L'écriveur* George Orwell.' We have just read *Animal Farm*. I pronounce him *Georges*. '*Connaissez-vous* George Orwell?'

'*Oui. Naturellement*,' replies Natalie, a little outraged that I might think she doesn't.

'*Mais je n'aime pas* . . . Margaret Thatcher.' Who has been in the news recently for being Prime Minister. A rather sophisticated piece of political commentary, I fancy. Perhaps a job at the United Nations beckons.

'*J'habite à Londres*,' I continue (Miss Saltman would have been proud of me). '*Où habitez-vous?*'

I can still picture Natalie's healthy French limbs emerging from her cotton dress. The fine dark hairs on her arms lifting in the breeze. She selects one of her plaits and twiddles it playfully.

'*J'habite à* Muswell Hill actually,' she replies in perfect Received Pronunciation. She and Jay fold with laughter.

'She's English,' he splutters. 'She's on our *boat*!' He slaps his thigh a needlessly large number of times. Even Deano begins to giggle.

I colour, a deep shade of *rouge*. 'Then may I congratulate you on your French.'

It feels like a betrayal.

Nearly twenty years later, Natalie's co-conspirator in my humiliation suddenly jumped to his feet.

'Right,' said Jay. 'That's me done. See you in the morning, everyone.'

Horribly, I realised that Caroline was also standing up. Wanker and I were left to nurse our brandies on the terrace; the mismatch between the loveliness of the Majorcan night and the company was a powerful disappointment.

Since I appeared to be stuck with him, I decided to draw him out about the porn business. But before I had the chance, he said rather suddenly: 'Tell me about Caroline.'

'What about her?' I think I was a bit startled by the impertinence of the question.

'She and Jay were once an item, I gather.'

'They were.' What of it?

'But now they're not.'

'No. They're not.' Where was this leading? I wondered.

'You're rather taken with her, if I'm not mistaken.'

'Really?' It slipped out. 'Why do you say that then?' And by the way, what made him think I gave a fuck what he thought (although I was intrigued, obviously)?

'You're a brave man,' Wanker remarked, draining his glass. 'She wouldn't be to everyone's taste.'

Cheeky sod, I thought. 'Not your type, then. If you were still single.' It occurred to me that he might be a little pissed.

'She's what I would call strong meat, Nicholas. It isn't for everyone.'

The metaphor revolted yet strangely stirred me. 'Strong meat.'

'What I mean is, the prize might be very great, but think of the price to be paid. I imagine a woman like that could make one's life exceptionally difficult.'

The *prize*. Another disturbing yet simultaneously thrilling idea. It felt surreal sitting on an island in the Mediterranean discussing women with Wanker of all people. Only that morning I had been emptying the dishwasher in Chalk Farm.

'You prefer your . . . your own meat a little blander. Your price a little more economical.'

Wanker twisted in his seat. 'Let's just say we all make our choices in life.'

4

Breakfast must have made a peculiar sight to our fellow guests on the terrace the following morning. Three Englishmen — a handsome one; a second sporting the most appalling leisure-wear known to man; and, er, me — plus one goddess-like Englishwoman. This last currently lurked behind a pair of Audrey Hepburn sunglasses, and turned the pages of a day-old copy of *The Times*.

'You could have read that in London,' said Jay, his mouth full of cornflakes.

'I know,' said Caroline, not looking up. 'But news always seems more interesting when you're on holiday. I mean, away on business.'

The new day had revealed the finca's excellent position. It stood amid well-tended gardens in a mountain valley of terraced olive groves. This morning, the silence was only broken by the mournful clang of sheep bells (and the cornflakes. And the rattle of the newspaper. And the comments reported above).

'Must drive them fucking nuts,' Jay had remarked when we first laid eyes on the strangely goat-like indigenous sheep dotted all over the landscape. Fastened round the neck of each beast by a thick leather collar was a brass bell.

'Imagine having one of those tied to you,' he said. 'You'd never be able to sneak up on a lady sheep.'

At this, Caroline offered Jay a particular look — the one where her features shuffled around a bit and then returned to base — and he went off to make phone calls.

The day was startlingly still and clear. One of those confident blue skies with a few Toytown clouds hanging around in it by way of providing something for your eye to settle on. Distant bells clanged in the olive groves, terrace upon terrace of ancient twisted trunks, said in the guide to have been planted by the Romans. Of my companions at the table, Caroline was giving out very clear I Want To Be Alone signals, hiding first behind the shades, and secondly behind *The Times*. I felt a little cheated. I should have loved a glimpse into those huge grey eyes first thing in the morning, still a little misty perhaps from sleep, something unprepared in them, some remnant of a dream maybe, or nightmare. Wanker, meanwhile . . . oh Christ, as I glanced at him I caught a hideous snapshot of his open mouth, an appalling slurry of liquid egg and sausage and God knows what else. I looked away. Above a distant mountaintop, a very large bird circled. The thought passed through my head: what the fuck am I doing here?

Again, in a Newtonian sort of fashion, this thought was quickly followed by an equal and opposite thought: what the fuck would I have been doing at home? Dreaming up ideas for thousand-word articles to try to sell to features editors. Feeling morbid about Squeaky. Summoning the strength of character to take the bags of defunct paperbacks to Oxfam.

'Here's something,' said the voice behind the newspaper. 'Scientists are warning the end of the world really could be at hand.'

'Is that so?' I said brightly. 'In that case I definitely shouldn't have paid off my Visa card.'

Caroline ignored my *bon mot* and brought the paper closer to her face. 'A strange subatomic particle produced in an atom-smashing experiment could, in theory at least, tumble to the centre of the planet and start eating the globe from the inside out.'

Wanker raised his eyes from his fried food and gave her what I would call a *level* stare.

She read on. 'Or a random quantum fluctuation in distant space could trigger off a bubble of destruction that would advance at the speed of light, shutting down all creation in its path.'

'And it seemed like such a lovely morning.' You've got to admit, I'm a trier.

'Light would stop shining,' she intoned. And now she repositioned the sunglasses from her face to the top of her head. Her eyes were full of fear and wonder, as though she believed this stuff. 'Electricity would no longer work and atoms would spontaneously break up. The universe, the Earth and the stars would disintegrate. And this bubble of death would expand at the speed of light so no one could know of its coming.'

Caroline cast her eyes to the sky, picturing these Ends of the World, grey irises shining almost blue. Light flooded the pale face, illuminating every fine line and plane. A tiny breadcrumb sat in the corner of her mouth, at the source, as it were, of her long, meandering lips. I had the urge to wipe it away. To put my arm round her and say, don't worry about any of that, newspapers love printing scary stories. They tend to sell better than those headlined: Everything All Right Just At The Moment.

But the bubble of destruction was rather a good one, wasn't it? One moment, the mountains, the valley, the terraces of olive trees, that sheep over there, this woman's face. And the next . . . pop. The very fabric of space-time ripping apart with unimaginable violence.

Jay was marching back across the terrace. He dropped into his seat and fastened each of us with a bit of a determined look.

'Teddy will see us tomorrow night. Which means we have two days to really hone our pitch, sharpen up the act and rehearse our lines. On the other hand . . .' A great grin started to spread across the unforgivably handsome features. 'On the other hand, so we come over as breezy, likeable, nice people to work with, we could just relax, unwind, and have fun. What do you reckon?' And with that, he gave Caroline a playful, if painful-sounding slap across the knee.

5

'A narrow winding path takes you past the olive groves and up the hill. After twenty minutes you will pass by an interesting rock feature. If you are lucky, you will see two or three mules tied up there. Turn right and walk through a small furt.'

'A small *what*?' She stopped to tie the two loose ends of her blouse together. I found it exceptionally difficult not to stare at the fascinating new section of exposed midriff.

'A small furt. F.U.R.T.'

I was quoting (verbatim) from the Finca d'Angelo's helpful guide to local hiking and rambling trails. Caroline and I were doing the route up to the site of the old castle (duration: three hours. Difficulty: piss easy, by the look of things; no mention of the need for stout boots, reliable weather, crampons or the like). Earlier Jay had announced he was driving into Palma on an errand; Wanker declined the offer to join us (hooray), decamping instead to a sunlounger by the pool with his thriller.

So It Was Just The Two Of Us Then.

'Path, rock feature, mules, furt.' Caroline summarised the likely highlights of the next half an hour or so and set off again at what was, to my mind, an ambitious pace, given the heat. Slender legs emerged from khaki shorts and terminated in white trainers. She'd gathered up her hair and jammed it through the back of a baseball hat. Ethereal, slow-moving Caroline had metamorphosed into athletic Caroline, the same

Caroline who shimmied down the mantelpiece like a sexy ape.

'Mules only if we're *lucky*,' I pointed out by way of satire.

Delicate lady-elbows pistoned back and forth as she forged up through the olive groves. The rocky path was narrow and I was forced to follow. No companionable sauntering along side by side on this bit, from the look of things. None of the leisurely conversational ebb and flow that I had imagined when she suggested it might be a nice idea to go for a 'stroll' in the hills. She'd set off at such a lick that I was struggling to keep up. Already I could feel the shirt sticking to my back, and a warm, swampy feeling spreading through the depths of my shorts. My visual field narrowed to her two feet in front of me, which seemed to be picking their landing spots with a mysterious deliberation. Some stroll, I was thinking.

The track became narrower and rockier. And steeper. A fascinating moist patch appeared on the back of her blouse. I was just beginning to wonder what was making that ugly rasping noise, when I realised that I was.

'Christ, Caroline. Are we in a hurry or something?'

I leaned against an olive tree to stop myself from collapsing into the dirt. The day was exceptionally still. Mountains folded away into the distance. We'd left the sheep so far below, their bells were a tiny, distant tinkle. Caroline had stopped and was gazing at me with something like pity.

'Sorry. I was looking forward to getting to the interesting rock feature. Water?'

She passed me the bottle of fizzy and I glugged like a shipwrecked sailor. But had that been a dig? Did she think I was a ruin? Because my lungs were going like bellows and I could barely see for the Zambesi of sweat pouring off my eyebrows.

'This can't still be the path, can it?'

'It probably comes to the same whichever route we take,' she replied. The castle is generally sort of . . . *up*.'

We pressed on, and after a while I just *knew* we weren't on the nice easy track recommended in the book. Nice easy tracks suitable for elderly tourists wound gently through trees; they felt trodden and worn by the passage of feet. Occasionally they featured small piles of stones along the way, or a flick of paint applied to a trackside boulder to signify: *People Have Passed Along Here Before. Don't Panic. Calm Down. This Be The Right Way.* Nice easy tracks were – above all – nice and easy. Our current route no longer seemed worthy of the technical term 'track', being more a sort of rocky outcropping that wound precariously up and round the side of a hill. Stubby, wind-blasted trees huddled against the side of this . . . actually, *hill* doesn't quite do it justice. *Peak* might be overstating the case; *mountain* would definitely be over-egging the pudding, although *mountainous* does give a flavour of what was going on here, in the sense that instead of walking, I now realised – it had happened imperceptibly slowly over the last ten or fifteen minutes – Jesus Christ, we were *climbing*.

Her feet were above my head. I was having to grab hold of things to haul myself up. Rocks, tree stumps, other rocks; actually, that was about it for items to grab on to. Caroline of course was springing through the landscape like the Missing Link between humans and apes. High, high overhead, the broken remains of an old castle had come into view. But there seemed to be nothing between it and us but the implausibly steep . . . no, I'm sorry, it wasn't a track. It was the side of a near-vertical slope. There was no sign of mules, nor interesting rock features; no hint of any kind of furt whatsoever, small, medium or large. This Was Not The Way.

And then I did it.

I looked down.

It was the swifts that turned my bowels to liquid. A pair of them wheeled about way, way below, and below *them*, the panorama was of the type more normally admired queasily from the seat of an aeroplane, a soothing beaker of whisky clenched between sweaty fingers. *Terra firma* seemed to be shelving away from the sky at a disturbing angle, as though one were banking on to final approach. A very long way down, I noticed a ribbon of road snaking between low hills. A white van moved along it like a toy car. My knees had turned to custard. My grip on the rocks, I realised, was directly equivalent to my grip on life. Loosen it, and by a simple law of gravity I should plummet into the treetops. I felt sick. I could neither advance nor retreat. When I opened my mouth to speak, nothing came out.

'Hey,' I finally managed to croak.

Ahead, the Goddess paused. With an almost reckless insouciance, she took a hand and foot off the rocks to swivel round and peer down at me.

'Everything all right?' she called.

'Er. Not really.'

In ridiculously few seconds she had scrambled back to within a few feet of where I was pinned to the hillside, sweating and breathing heavily.

'You look a bit white, Nicholas.'

'I'm sort of . . . pausing here for a tick.'

'Pausing.'

'To be honest, Caroline, I'm not terribly good at heights.'

'We're nearly there now. We've saved ages by not sticking to that zig-zaggy path. This is much quicker.'

'I, er. I don't seem to be able to actually . . . make progress, as it were.'

'How do you mean?'

'I'm . . .'

This was exactly how tragic accidents happened, I wanted to tell her. Out of a blue sky. You do something just a bit unfamiliar and then – bam. The horse throws you on to a dry-stone wall. The tyre bursts on the hairpin bend. The newspaper headline:

BRITON KILLED IN MAJORCA. I'm shit scared, I want to cry. I want my mummy.

'Are you stuck?'

'Not stuck exactly. More sort of . . . frozen.'

'The thing is to keep going. Don't stop, don't look back. Think about something else.'

'Easy for you to say, mountain girl.'

She smiled. 'Come on, give me your hand . . .' She reached for me and I yelled.

'*NO!!!!!*'

My cry of horror may have been heard for miles around. She stared at me rather solemnly, the huge grey eyes peering into mine, and for once I didn't feel my brain doing its usual trick of voiding itself of all useful data.

'What are you worried about?'

'Since you ask,' I replied a bit irritably, 'since you ask, I am worried about falling off this . . . this fucking . . . this fucking *treacherous peak*, and turning into Christopher fucking Reeve. If I fucking survive at all.'

After a bit she said quietly, 'I'm sorry, Nicholas. It's my fault for bringing us this way. But you're perfectly safe, I promise. Nothing bad is going to happen to you.'

What I wanted to say was, oh yeah, and where do you get that idea from? But I rather liked the clear, confident way she had spoken just then. And I badly wanted to believe her.

'Now,' she said after a pause. 'Should we carry on or go back?'

'I don't think you quite understand, Caroline. I can't do anything. I am, as the saying goes, rigid with fear.'

'Well, we certainly can't stay here. Actually, we could, but it would become awfully boring.'

And that was what broke the spell. The sudden thought that I might *bore* her. Oddly, it was more powerful than the idea that I could fall to my destruction.

And somehow – maybe because I'd stopped thinking about it for a bit – my right leg took a step. Off its own bat, as it were. The way, first thing in the morning, you sometimes find you've got out of bed without consciously deciding to get up. Now my left leg did the same. My arms too seemed to be working again.

I didn't think. I climbed. Arm leg arm leg arm leg. It was an arm-leg thing. I didn't for a second try to think what we must have looked like from, say, the perspective of a passing buzzard. I didn't think about anything. Above all, I didn't look back. I just climbed. Caroline was behind me this time; very wisely, she was offering no words of encouragement. Just following.

At the summit, I stumbled towards what was left of the old castle walls – a pile of rubble mostly – and subsided exhausted amongst it.

'I'm alive! I can't believe I'm alive!' I gasped satirically. Did she think I was a great big nelly for bottling it back there?

She joined me; we sat side by side, panting against the ancient masonry, gazing a little stupefied at the majestic panorama that unfolded before us: hills, valleys, mountains, fields, trees and other large-scale nature stuff along those lines. She lit a cigarette.

'Sorry,' I said after a bit.

'For what?'

'Being a bit of a big girl's blouse.'

Under the baseball hat, she turned her great grey eyes on me and smiled softly. 'I enjoyed that "treacherous peak" speech. I admire people who aren't afraid to show their feelings.'

Really? 'Sorry. It just came pouring out.' That's what it's like with us people who aren't afraid to show their feelings.

'We'll go back the long way.'

'I'd appreciate it.'

We sat in silence for a bit under the hot blue sky, she smoking, me dreaming up an elaborate cover story for my cowardice. As boys, I decided to tell her, my brother and I were playing on a high roof. And he fell – or did I push him? – and I'd never felt the same about heights since. I don't actually have a brother, and it's the plot of a Hitchcock film of course, but if she mentioned it, I would go all deep and mysterious on her. *She likes deep*.

'That story in the paper,' she said after a while, 'about the world coming to an end. I don't believe it could happen. Do you?' She was gazing off towards the mountains. They didn't look particularly vulnerable to a deadly particle or quantum fluctuation, it had to be said.

'Nothing lasts for ever,' I replied after a pause for timing (deep, wasn't it?). 'You. Me. Even this old castle is showing signs of wear and tear.'

'No. Nothing does, does it?' She'd gone all dreamy. Into a tobacco trance, as someone once wrote.

Did I dare say it? 'There are exceptions.' *No, I couldn't.* 'Things that are supposed to defy the rule.' *Coward. Say it.* 'That outlast their actual existence, as it were.'

Say it.

Oh fuck it then. Here we go. 'Love. The memory of love.'

I fancied I could hear the whirr of servo-mechanisms as Caroline's head rotated back in my direction, a micro-clunk as it came to a halt. A barely perceptible mechanical whine as the grey eyes focused upon me.

'I've never known whether or not I believe that,' she replied. 'What Larkin said. "What will survive of us is love".'

I suddenly remembered an old line from a Woody Allen picture. After death, he said, your hair and fingernails continue to grow, though your phone calls taper off. I took it as a sign of my improving sense of how to deal with this woman that I did not quote it.

'No. I don't know whether I believe it either,' I said. You see. We agreed about stuff.

And because she was staring at me rather intensely, and because we were sitting close together, side by side against the decayed ramparts of the castle, and because lots of stuff must have happened within these walls over the centuries, and all the people involved were now dead (and their descendants and their descendants, dead too; and the castle itself crumbled to ruin) and because I'd just had a near-death experience and because the sun was very hot and the sky was very blue, and because a large bird was circling high overhead, and because there was something timeless and yet impermanent about this scene, and because if one wants a great prize, one must be prepared to pay a price, and because there was a sort of luminousness about her, behind the gauze of cigarette smoke, and . . . and because I very much wanted to, I leaned towards her slowly and, being careful not to bark my head against the bill of her cap, I placed my lips gently on hers and pressed against them a little. She smelt of cold cream, vanilla, female human and Marlboro.

Her mouth did something in reply that reminded me of a small animal settling itself in its cave prior to three or four months of shut-eye. I was about to pull away when the serpentine lips parted and suddenly she was upon me. Her eyes closed and there was a wonderful languor about the way the creature went about its business, unhurried but thorough, if you know what I mean, with an excitingly mysterious bit held back in reserve. I answered in kind (I could do languor + mysterious too, it turned out). It seemed like we'd jump-cut from that instant in her flat when 'I'm A Believer' had just stopped playing and she was looking up at me . . . straight to this moment in the rubble of the Arabic fortress. As if the intervening weeks had been snipped out, thrown away, and the two ends spliced together. Years of fascination and desire dissolved in the smoky taste of her mouth. With appalling pleasure, I realised that the idea of this woman must have been squirrelled away in some corner of my mind through all the years we were apart. From that long-ago evening in the pub garden in Highgate – to the night when she reappeared so unexpectedly in my doorway. *Hello, Nicholas. Long time no see.*

'Who knew you'd be such a talented snogger?' she said quietly. We seemed to have separated. I was looking into her face again, the exact same expression as from a minute ago – intense, puzzled – except the lips had lost their well-executed edges and planes. They seemed a little blurred now.

The grey eyes bored into mine. A line from 'The Love Song of J. Alfred Prufrock' came to me. The one about being pinned and wriggling on the wall.

'You,' she said, a little oddly. 'I always had a funny feeling about you.'

Something in my gut fell through a trapdoor. I could barely bring myself to speak the line.

'How so?'

She took a big drag on the cigarette that must have been burning throughout our smouldering clinch. Allowed the smoke to drift from her lips in a long sigh.

'What sort of funny feeling, Caroline?'

Smoke was mixed in with her words when she answered. 'A *funny* funny feeling.'

'Funny ha ha or . . . or the other funny?'

She turned away to regard the mountains once again. Something in the distance must have been very interesting to her, because she didn't answer. With a pang of loss, I felt the moment we had just shared retreating into memory.

'*Which?*'

Oh shit. Had that come out a bit sharply? In the most sensitive, seductive voice I could manage I muttered, 'I'm sorry, it's just that I'd really like to know . . .' and brought my lips towards hers.

'I'm starving,' she declared. 'Let's have lunch.'

'No, wait. Just one thing . . .'

She put a hand to my face and gently pushed it away. Smiled.

'First things first,' she stated firmly. And that apparently was an end to the matter.

6

She walked ahead of me all the way back to the hotel. I laboured behind, my gaze locked on to the fascinating sway of bare flesh at her hip like a raptor's. Caroline seemed distracted. Our joyous sixty-second snog wasn't mentioned. And nor did there seem to be any polite way to bring it up without becoming tiresome. Over and again, I replayed that scene in the ruins of the castle. The way I moved to kiss her. The way – after that odd animal-like shiver – she accepted, responded. No, it was more than that . . . she was *at* me, for Christ's sake, her mouth hungry, needy even. But with something held back, an intriguing hesitancy, suggestive of caution or inhibition. And by association, suggestive of caution *removed*, inhibition *dropped*. That thing she'd said: *who knew you'd be such a talented snogger?* I felt a certain afterglow of pride at the compliment. Although, *was* it altogether a compliment? Could it have been more an expression of amazement: who in the world would ever have imagined *you* – you of *all* people – to be a talented snogger? And now the mystifying way she was acting almost like it had never happened.

But *first things first*, she'd said, hadn't she? With its clear – and to my way of thinking, thrilling – implication of Second Things Second. Perhaps to be followed in due course by Third Things (far too early to be thinking about Fourth or Fifth Things).

She was an odd one, there was no getting round it. The way to play it, I decided, was long. And most probably deep as well.

We reached our rooms. 'See you later then,' she said with an enigmatic smile. And she vanished behind her door, the lock clicking into place, before my intended reply – 'Looking forward to it' – had a chance to tumble from my open mouth.

From my bedside, I called my answerphone. It seemed I wasn't exactly Mr Popular. There were no messages.

I dialled a familiar number, and when it appeared in my ear, I found I was curiously relieved to hear the familiar cheeping note as she said hello.

'Hi. It's me.'

There was a sort of sniff. Or perhaps a sharp intake of breath.

'Nicholas, why didn't you mention that . . . that woman was coming with you?'

Oh, shit. 'What woman, darling?'

'The vegetarian.' She couldn't bring herself to utter her name. How had she found out?

'Caroline? Didn't I mention it?'

'No.'

'Perhaps I unconsciously sensed she wasn't your favourite person.'

'I see.'

'Incidentally. How, er . . . ?'

'The other boy's wife rang to invite us to dinner. You didn't mention he wasn't going.' *Mrs Deano.*

'No.'

Another silence. I could picture Squeaky's mouth all crimped with disapproval. Knuckles white against the phone receiver.

After a while I came in with 'I wasn't trying to hide anything, if that's what you're thinking. I mean . . . what *are* you thinking exactly?'

Her voice was almost a whisper. 'I don't know what to think, Nicholas.'

'Do you suppose we're having some . . . some torrid affair?

Is that what you imagine?' That was better. Pour scorn on the idea.

'It came as a bit of a surprise. That you hadn't mentioned her.'

My turn for a heavy sigh. 'My mistake. It's just . . . just that you did seem to have taken against her in a big way. Nothing sinister.'

'I see.'

And then I said something *really* stupid. 'I know Caroline can be a bit uphill and everything, but she's all right once you get to know her.'

'Have you kissed her?'

'Sorry?'

'Have you kissed her?'

'What do you think? Oh yeah, sorry, you don't know *what* to think. Christ, what must you imagine I'm like?'

After a pause. 'Was there a purpose to this call?'

'Oddly enough, I think I just wanted to hear your voice.'

'How touching.' She didn't sound particularly touched, to be honest.

'Look, if you're going to be all frosty, perhaps I'll try you again another time.'

'Perhaps you should.'

Click.

Women. They always bloody *know*, don't they?

7

Several hours later, I plonked myself on to a barstool and ordered a large vodka and tonic. Wanker was already in position. He was sporting an unusually tasteful tropical shirt featuring representations of palm trees and coral islands (though best skip over the accompanying brown 'slacks').

'Vodka is the best medicine,' I said, lifting my glass.

'Cheers,' he replied. He was nursing a Johnnie Walker rocks by the look of things.

I took a deep breath. Tried to think of some subject to mount a conversation about. And then in she walked, and everything changed.

I believe I may have gasped. She was standing in high heels, sheathed in one of those flimsy little black dresses that hang by two thin straps from bare shoulders and come to an end just above knee level. Small bright objects sparkled at her throat and ear lobes. She'd done something with her hair — it looked a bit more mucked about with than usual (sorry, that's the best I can offer) — that spoke of trouble being gone to, effort being made. There was something different too about the way she walked into the bar. A wanton sway of the hips that I didn't remember in her previous locomotive repertoire. Maybe it was a high-heels thing. They're bound to make you walk funny, aren't they? Even Wanker looked a bit startled by the transformation. I think a couple of coconuts may have fallen off his polyester shirt.

'Golly,' I jibbered. 'You look . . .' Beautiful, was what I wanted to say. Just more lovely than anyone I had ever seen. 'You look amazing.'

She smiled, and I swear to God I could feel the data banks crashing in both hemispheres of my brain. I opened my mouth to speak, but the only sound that emerged was a throaty salival gurgle which I attempted to bury under cover of a cough.

172

'A glass of champagne would be lovely, thank you.'

Caroline insinuated herself on to a barstool, lit a cigarette and regarded Wanker and me with an expression of wry amusement.

She continued, 'Our leader has telephoned to say he won't be joining us this evening. He's met his friend, the viscount. There's some talk of a party on a boat in the marina in Palma. So it's just the three of us.'

'Fine,' I managed. Brilliant, would have been more like it. But how to get rid of the pornographer?

'I've been thinking about roast baby baa lamb all day. It must be those endless bells. You haven't had a chance to look at the menu, have you?'

We dined on the terrace under the stars. Candles flickered, red wine spilled into fine glassware, waiters shimmered silently between tables. The air was scented with orange and lemon, and all the other soft herby fragrances that wafted about in this part of the world after dark. I couldn't have been happier. Opposite me sat a living goddess in a sexy frock with her hair up (okay, there was a weird bloke with shiny eyes in the next chair along with pineapples and stuff all over his upper body, but let that pass for the moment). She was being oddly charming, even flirtatious, you might say, with lots of interesting eye contact, lip business and half-smiles. Some of the traffic was going in Wanker's direction, but a good seventy-five per cent was aimed at me, and consequently I was feeling a lot more cheerful about life. (I still wished he'd bugger off though.)

'Caroline nearly killed me this morning,' I informed my old classmate, trotting amusingly through the story, leaving it — I hoped — unclear whether I was really shit scared, or just pretending for comic effect.

'He was very brave,' she cooed.

Our main courses arrived with a bit of a flourish. Caroline and Wanker had both gone for the lamb option; I, the fish, to show my independence and keen intelligence. The waiter dispensed the remains of our wine directly into Caroline's glass. His momentary look of confusion — *oh dear, it's all gone; what happens now then?* — prompted me to ask for another. A fat white moon rose behind a distant mountain.

'How's your dorade?' she asked me after a while. The last few minutes had been devoted to cutting, munching, swallowing, stuff like that mostly.

'Very plausible,' I answered. 'If unremarkable.'

Wanker looked at me and produced a sort of snorting sound. It's our little joke, I wanted to yell at him. Why don't you just fuck off back to your room and leave us lovebirds in peace?

'The lamb?'

Caroline did a bit of intensive chewing, flapped her fingers about in front of her face. Finally she was ready to pass comment. 'Sublime,' she said. 'It tastes like someone's just bopped it on the head, hacked a lump out of its bum and chucked it on the grill.'

The wine must have loosened Wanker's tongue. Because the chump felt free to give a somewhat over-honest reply when Caroline asked him — only to be polite, I'm sure — about our schooldays.

'Nicholas was always telling jokes, I hear,' she said.

'Was he? I couldn't say. We weren't particularly close at school. I was a rather solitary boy. I didn't make friends easily. Actually, I was bullied rather a lot. Nicholas was never one of my torturers, however.'

'People were a bit unpleasant to you,' I conceded nobly.

Actually, unpleasant doesn't begin to cover it.

By some sort of bush telegraph, by some sort of nasty schoolboy collective fever, every few weeks it would be decided that someone's head was due to be put down the toilet, and more often than not the head in question would be Wanker's. Across the playground, the cry would go up, *'Where's Wanker?'* and the hunt would commence. Scores of small boys dashed about hysterically, searching in all the likely places where Wanker might be lying low (round the back of the tuck shop; the area behind the science block; the library). Although I never actually took part in any of these actions, it would be false to deny that my heart didn't thump a little faster as eventually, pale and terror-struck, a dozen hands tugging at his grey V-neck jersey, Wanker would be hauled from his hidey-hole and frog-marched off to his humiliation. Alongside his executioners, as it were, ran the pack of excitable spectators who, even if they weren't actually prepared to assist in Wanker's downfall, didn't wish to miss a moment of it either. The mob, baying with the cry *'Wank-ker! Wank-ker!'*, would surge into the cold, smelly latrines, and if one was near the front, one could witness the pitiful spectacle of Wanker being forced on to his knees – his head threshing wildly, fear glinting off his spectacle lenses – followed by the awful moment.

Other victims (Kapper, Ritblat) would relax at the denouement. The inevitable had arrived, why struggle any longer, was their attitude; a philosophy, frankly, that disappointed the mob. Not Wanker, however. Wanker went to his destruction magnificently, howling and struggling to the bitter, filthy end. His neck would arch, his legs would flail. It took as many as five or six boys to force his face down into the toilet bowl and hold him in position while another pulled the chain.

Confession. Despite Wanker's assertion that I was never one of his 'torturers', there was one occasion where I was more than a little complicit. The scene was just as I have described, Wanker bucking and wriggling at the death, his head three-quarters of the way down into the bowl. I think one of his shoes had come off, just as they often seem to in newspaper photos of the aftermath of a shooting (a body lies on the ground, and almost always there is a shoe nearby, have you noticed?). I had an excellent view of all this, having climbed on to the toilet seat in the next stall along and peered over the partition.

'Pull it!' screamed his tormentors. 'Pull it.'

Sickeningly, I realised they were shouting at me. The half-dozen lead bullies had their hands full holding Wanker down, and I was in the best possible position to bring on the deluge.

I like to imagine that I froze for a few seconds. I was not the sort of boy who terrorised others; yet, not uncommonly, I clearly had a fascination with violence and retribution. There was a horrible deterministic reality about the scenario: below, face down in the white porcelain, was Wanker; above, the cistern; between them, covered in grey flaking paint, a downpipe; six inches from my right hand, the lever that operated the ballcock.

If I didn't do it, someone else would, I reasoned.

Afterwards, when he came up coughing and spluttering, glasses wet with who knew what unimaginable slime, the crowd would usually linger for a few minutes to enjoy his discomposure. Having your head put down the toilet was the *ne plus ultra* of childhood tortures; nothing else held the same symbolic power, nor so dramatically demonstrated one's lowliness of status. If the punishment was a dark and terrible thing to receive, it struck no less a chill in the hearts of the spectators.

Perhaps worse than the actual lavatorial dunking – no, perhaps not worse, but right up there in the same league of ghastliness – was the fact that Wanker always blubbed. He couldn't help himself, his distorted mouth a wound, sobbing as he clawed at his soiled collar, toilet water running down his neck into the old-fashioned vest he was known to wear beneath his shirt. 'Shouldn't be such a fucking Wanker, should you?' I remember one of the lynch mob lecturing him in these closing seconds, as if this was the moral of the incident.

I suppose it was possible that he had indeed drawn something from the experience, because today there was a sense of quiet determination about Wanker that had replaced the creeping hesitancy of his boyhood. And irredeemably weird as he still was, he nonetheless didn't look like the sort of bloke you'd particularly want to mess around.

Wanker drained his glass of red. 'There was a thing where they would surround you in a circle. And then they'd all start pushing and prodding.' For some reason he found it necessary to remove his specs and begin polishing them on the edge of his shirt. 'Once they flooded my desk. I opened the lid, and it was full of water. All the books . . .' He trailed off.

Yes, I'd forgotten that one. The look of amazement on his face had been exceptionally comic, I seem to recall.

I don't *think* I sniggered. I'd say it was more of a sharp exhalation of breath. Nonetheless Wanker turned on me.

'It wasn't *funny*, Nicholas.' His hot brown eyes shone with hurt anger. 'Stuff like that can ruin your life. I'm lucky. I got over it.'

The next few moments were lost to the scrape of silverware against china. The low murmur from other tables. I concentrated on separating the flesh from the bones of my little white fish. My ears felt like they were on fire.

I couldn't help it. I flicked a glance up at her.

She was looking at me. There was a subtle smile playing in the long, expertly drawn lips; something soft, sympathetic even, lying behind the reflection of the candle flame in the huge, over-detailed eyes.

8

It was Caroline who finally got rid of him. We were still lurking on the terrace, having drained our brandies and smoked our cigars – the embarrassing little outburst long past us – when Wanker yawned, one of those loud, public yawns, arms outstretched, that squished all the flesh up on his face.

'Probably time to turn in,' she said, and started dropping fags and things into her handbag, ready to leave. No, don't go, I was thinking.

Wanker hauled himself to his feet. 'Yup. Big day ahead,' he said. And a small look of surprise appeared on his face when Caroline remained in her seat.

'Goodnight, Colin,' she said quietly.

'Yeah, 'night,' I added in triumph.

Finessed, he scuttled off to his crib.

But honestly, what had he been hanging around for? Couldn't he feel the sexual chemistry between the two of us? The mysterious connection that he wasn't part of. He had, however, offered one helpful remark. When, apropos of a somewhat tedious story – of what one of his children had said to the other when he (Wanker) had been forced to brake rather sharply in a Sainsbury's car park – he'd asked Caroline if she wanted 'littlies' one day.

She'd thought about it for a bit, taking cover in a cigarette that she had just fired up.

'Littlies,' she said eventually.

'I call them littlies,' he added pointlessly.

'Yes, they might be quite fun.' As though she were talking about the guest list for a dinner party.

'Hard work, of course,' commented the sage. 'Worth it, though. The funny things they say.'

'They talk a lot of crap as well,' I said, to be controversial. (It's true, though, they do. I once asked Squeaky's four-year-old nephew Henry if he knew who had stolen his daddy's Volvo. The little boy stared at me solemnly for a moment or two before replying: 'Goblins.')

She smiled. 'Perhaps they would be rather fun,' she said a bit wistfully.

'What about you, Nicholas?' Wanker enquired.

'I think so,' I replied. 'But it has to be with the right person. It's no good,' I continued, and here I fixed on Caroline, 'it's no good at all unless it's with the right person.'

'How are you supposed to know when you've found the right person?' she said softly. And suddenly, Wanker, the waiters, all the other people on the terrace were no longer there. It was just me and Caroline. And the moonlight. And the unanswered question.

Without taking my eyes off hers, I replied, 'Some things I think you just know.'

We held one another's gaze. The over-detailed irises locked on to mine, and this time I thought I could read the need in them. The hunger. And in that instant, I came to a shocking little realisation.

Wanker managed to leave a decent pause for respect before he crashed in with: 'The Germans will be first to the sunloungers. That's one thing you just know.' He was rather pleased with his joke.

'The sun goes round the earth. That's another,' said Caroline, dissolving the spell of our odd little moment. 'I mean, the other way round.'

I couldn't actually speak the thought that was in my head. Instead I gabbled, 'The value of your investment may fall as well as rise. That's one, isn't it?'

But what I was actually thinking was, 'I'm going to sleep with you tonight.' I felt oddly certain about it.

I guess I had Wanker to thank for getting us to that point.

9

So it was just the two of us now. But somehow it had been easier when my tactless old classmate was around. So we talked about him for a bit. She said she couldn't imagine Wanker being bullied because he seemed such a self-contained sort of person. Nor did Wanker seem like her idea of a pornographer. If she'd had to guess, she'd have thought Wanker was a civil servant. She didn't actually refer to him as Wanker; she called him Colin.

'I think when you've been to school with someone, they become a bit like family,' I found myself saying. 'You may not even like them particularly, but you retain a kind of background fondness.'

The night was warm and still. The waiters had all departed and the candle on our table had long since guttered. The black of Caroline's dress bled into the darkness. The Goddess was reduced to a head and shoulders. And long, pale arms that glowed in the moonlight.

'How's Anita?' she asked softly. I think maybe a few moments had gone by with no one saying anything.

'Anita?' Fuck. How to put this? 'Well.' Deep breath. 'Since you mention it. We're actually at a sort of crossroads.'

'Ah. One of those.'

'Hmm.'

'A good crossroads? Or the other sort.'

Heavy sigh. 'The other sort, I fear.'

If I said any more I should spoil it. So I adopted a sort of moody silence, conveying, I hoped, appropriate sorrow combined with an adult facing-of-the-facts.

After a bit she said, 'Anita reminded me of someone I went to school with. Faith Leith. I always thought that was a very unfortunate name. It's difficult to say, isn't it? Faith Leith. Her parents must have had no sense of . . . what's that word?'

'Euphony.'

'Anita reminded me of Faith Leith. She had the same . . . interesting way of talking.'

I smiled. 'The voice.'

'She used to get teased for it. Which was unfair, because everyone was pretty posh.'

'Faith Leith. Yes, it is quite hard to say. Faith Leith. Whatever happened to Faith Leith?'

She shrugged. 'Married with . . . with littlies, I should think.'

Something about the way she described the probable fate of Faith Leith brought me to a halt. I sat there looking at her for a few seconds.

'Do you fancy a nightcap, Caroline? There's a lovely view of the other side of the valley from my balcony. Of course we won't be able to see it now. What with it being dark and all.'

It just popped out of my mouth. How about that?

She stared at me a little crazily. Then she just nodded and stood up. I followed her lithe, swaying body across the terrace and into the silent hotel. Through the deserted tiled lobby, past the antique olive press. She walked with a thrilling silky, swooshing sound. She was in bare feet, high heels dangled from a hand. Her long white toes splayed against the flags of the stone staircase as we climbed. At my door, she had a change of mind. Curled an index finger at me.

'Mine,' she whispered.

We stepped into her room. I clocked a ripped-open carton

of Marlboro and one of those electric curling tong thingies that women use to torture their hair. She snatched something insubstantial off the back of a chair and flung it into the bathroom.

'You didn't see that,' she said.

'I didn't see that.'

Her balcony, I was gratified to see, was configured exactly as my own, with a small side table and a single wicker sofa. I positioned myself at one end of it and awaited developments.

She emerged with a bottle of Spanish brandy. The brand wittily entitled *Soberano*. As she placed herself at the other end, the sofa erupted into a symphony of crackling. Every delicious motion of her flesh against wicker was translated into wicker-language. It was comically loud against the hush of the Mallorcan night. Into a pair of tooth mugs, she poured two encouragingly large measures. We raised our glasses and clinked gently. She lit a cigarette. A moth endlessly circled the lamp over the balcony door. I knew how it felt.

And now I didn't know what to say. Because sitting down on the sofa had caused the little black dress to travel up her legs. And there they were, long and slender, and the way they lay against one another, the way they emerged pointing at me, then pivoting at the knee and travelling away again at a different trajectory . . . merely perceiving the manner in which the legs brought off this effect had taken up all the spare processing capacity in my brain (the capacity that hadn't been engaged chewing over the bare arms and shoulders and face and all the rest of it). There was no thought in my head that could be adequately expressed in words.

The drink was in my hand again; I swallowed, my every movement echoed in the snaps and pops of the sofa (Christ, I'd never heard such a noisy piece of furniture). Caroline's glass was resting on her knees, her head bowed, hair falling across her face so I couldn't see it.

'Are you all right?' I hissed.

She looked up at me slowly. 'Yes thanks. Why are you whispering?' she whispered.

'Don't know really.' So Wanker didn't hear us. 'Don't want to wake the sheep.'

I took another deep glug on the Soberano. Christ. That had been a full glass a moment ago.

'May I?' I refilled the mugs. We clinked again.

I threw my left arm along the back of the sofa and regarded the view. Stars, moon; olive groves painted in various shades of inky blackness. A long way away, car headlights weaved through the trees, illuminating them at impossible angles. It was the magical wide old world out there, I thought to myself, full of beauty and mystery. How ridiculous to suppose it could be swept away by some vulgar subatomic *fluctuation*. It was *we* who would be swept away. We, the short-lived life forms who crawled about this planet, full of our pathetic dramas and crises, alarms and excursions. It was we who fluctuated. The hills, the trees, the mountains, the stars, they remained supremely indifferent to our foolish fluctuations, and who we might – or might not – fluctuate with.

There was something a bit odd about the way she was sitting. She had her glass in both hands, resting on her thighs. Her shoulders had drooped forward. She looked . . . was it demure? A bit defeated perhaps? Or simply pissed (we had rather been going at it)?

I took another deep swallow. And as the fire hit my stomach, I felt it again. As in the moment our eyes had met and I'd said *some things I think you just know.* (Okay, not Socrates, but still true.) I felt the lurching tug of *certainty*.

She brought her glass to her lips and admitted a serious dosage.

I said, 'You know when we were up at the old fortress today?'

Her face had gone a little fuzzy. Must have been all the brandy she'd been necking. 'Yes, Nicholas,' she replied softly.

'What we did. Do you think it was a good thing or a bad thing?'

She rearranged herself slightly to consider my enquiry. Plenty of sofa-static as she sat herself up straighter (in the process, the legs grew even longer. Sorry, couldn't help noticing).

'How would it be a bad thing?' she said after a further contemplative gulp at the sauce.

'Well . . .' Heavy sigh. 'I don't know really.'

I used the opportunity afforded by this small interregnum to drain the remains of my Soberano.

'Top-up?'

She extended her glass and I refilled. We re-clinked.

'So it wasn't a bad thing?' Me again, after a quick quality-control check on the latest tranche of brandy (yes, it was the same as before).

'Far from it, I should have said.'

Kissing, I suddenly realised, was like getting up in the morning. One moment you were lying there stewing and fretting *I really must get up*. And then the next – mysteriously – you were on your feet. Somehow, the logical intervening stage – a conscious sequence of commands to arms and legs – had been skipped. Your body appeared to have performed the act for you, and it was the same here. One moment I was staring at this lovely woman, stewing with desire and thinking *I really must kiss her*. And the next, I was doing so. Without any distinct conscious instructions – put the glass down, move towards her slowly – my glass was on the table and my lips seemed to be engaged with hers. There was no odd animal shrug from her this time. She seemed to recognise the moment had arrived as soon as I did. Her mouth tasted of brandy and tobacco and healthy female tissue. Again I felt her exciting sense of *restraint*, a delicious lack of abandonment. Her languor. Her curious *thoroughness*.

The sofa played wicker-nocturnes as we fluctuated gently upon it.

'Wait.' She pulled away. Mashed the cigarette that was between her fingers into the ashtray. Made a bit of a meal of it, actually. Seeming to need to ensure each tiny ember had been fully extinguished; in the seconds I sat watching her, maybe reaching some decision.

She said, 'You were saying something . . .'

At some point in the minutes that followed, an empty glass fell from the table, shattering on the tile floor, but I was barely aware of it.

Eventually, with a drowsy smile on lips whose planes and edges had grown indistinct and blurred, she asked if I'd care to come inside, 'for a rest'.

'Yeah. Nice idea,' I replied

We passed the next eight hours resting like rabbits.

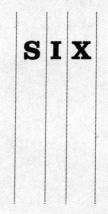

SIX

1

I was awake before I knew I was awake, if you know the feeling. I realised that I had been aware of the mournful tolling of sheep bells for some time, and it occurred to me that by virtue of having this thought, I must be awake. I opened an eye to confirm the hypothesis.

Jay Bryant stood at the foot of the bed, hands on hips, light-house grin plastered across the criminally handsome features. He was shaking his head slowly from side to side.

'Well, well, well.'

I closed the eye, and waited a few moments. I had the strong impression that were I to re-open the eye, I should find my schoolfriend in exactly the same position.

(I was right. I did – he was.)

'Well, well, well.' He was repeating himself. 'Well, well, well.'

'Could you stop saying well well well like that,' I croaked. 'Can you try saying some other words.'

'Don't you know how to knock?' Caroline's snarl from under the bed sheet was cured in brandy and tobacco smoke.

'Sorry, loves. I didn't want you to miss breakfast.' He pulled a jokey ooh-err face for my benefit. 'Guy's here.'

'Who's Guy?' I groaned.

'Guy. The viscount. We've been to a great party.'

I couldn't quite seem to summon the moral fibre to resist Jay's enthusiasm. Instead I closed the eye – it didn't help – so I opened it again. I tried nodding gently; this was definitely a bad idea.

'It was on a boat and everything. And right, this is how seriously trashy it was, okay? They had some of those women with painted-on clothes? Who are actually bollock naked? People were snorting lines of coke off their tits. You look fucking dreadful, by the way.'

'Bit of a late night.'

'Guy's having a swim. Claims it blows away the cobwebs. Hey, princess?' He reached under the sheet and made to grab her foot. She began to kick and flail like an animal in a trap. Jay laughed. 'Hates anyone touching her feet.'

When the short, painful commotion had subsided, I elevated an eyelid again. Jay had gone.

'Did I just dream that?' I muttered after a minute or two.

There was a long pause. 'Did you just dream what?' She sounded a bit hungover, to be honest.

'Was Jay just here?'

'He never learnt to knock.'

'Is it true, the feet thing?' I sent my own foot in search of hers, and was rewarded with a bit of a lazy kick. I placed a hand on a hot skinny hip. She had her back to me, so I moved closer and pressed myself against her.

'That was a lovely evening, Caroline.'

She returned some of my pressure. Wiggled about a little.

'An unexpected conclusion,' she said.

'Think so?'

'Don't you?'

'Hmm.'

I buried my face in the side of her neck and tried nibbling her ear lobe (this had been quite well received last night, I seemed to recall). Possibly I nibbled a little too hard, because there was a sharp cry of pain and a bony elbow drove into my ribs.

'Jesus!' She jabbed me quite hard, actually.

'You bit me.'

'I got carried away. Sorry.'

She struggled free, rolled on to her other side and looked at me. Lids half closed over the huge grey eyes, a wry smile folded into the twists and turns of her lips (their planes and edges restored to normal, I noticed).

'You *were* carried away, weren't you?' She was talking about last night.

I felt a little embarrassed about it now, to be honest. The sheer . . . *erotic delirium*, I think would be the phrase, that we tumbled into. Now, in the fresh light of morning, hard sunshine banging away beyond the open balcony doors, sheep to be heard on the march through the olive terraces, we seemed to be in a parallel universe to the one of only a few hours ago. Our clothes, scattered across the floor, bore testament to that other, contiguous world. That world contained intimate little revelations. Eyes that seemed to fill with crushed ice at the moment of rapture. Lips at first blurred, then stretched taut and sinewy. Long legs that flailed against the white sheet. Dangerous hands that pulled at my hair, fingernails that dug into my flesh. And yet throughout . . . throughout, the strange feeling of *something held back*. As though, almost against herself, she couldn't quite let it go. As if she needed me – needed *someone* – to batter whatever it was out of her. This morning, the storm seemed to have passed.

'Do you do this a lot, Nicholas?'

'Not a lot, no. What do you mean?'

'Seducing women. And with such . . . *application*.'

Was she taking the piss? It was so hard to know with this one.

'You *are* a dark horse,' she said, placing a Marlboro in the eastern outskirts of her mouth and a horrid heavy ashtray on the bedsheet between us.

She fired herself up and went quiet for a bit. Smoking and

regarding me oddly between the veils of smoke. She seemed content to puff away and not say anything, rather as though she was watching rain through a window.

After a while, I grabbed her arm and pulled her towards me. She resisted for a bit, then allowed her smoky lips to be kissed. I put it like that because I didn't feel her answering. Not a question of restraint or lack of abandonment this time – just a certain deadness.

'Shall I see you at breakfast?' she asked, floating out of bed. My eyes didn't miss a microsecond as her naked body travelled across the floor towards the bathroom. In the doorway, she turned.

'Would you see if they'd do me a kipper?'

The hiss of the shower.

As I stole away, I glimpsed a distorted, water-streaked vision of Caroline through the plastic curtain, head tipped back, elbows aloft. It was hard to tell, but I had the feeling she was humming.

2

The viscount was one of those very tall, aristocratic, incredibly self-contained Englishmen who have almost become extinct. He seemed about eight foot six as he rose — and kept on rising — from the chair to shake my hand. High forehead, marvellous Roman conk on him, pale, translucent skin revealing blue veins below twinkling grey eyes. His public school floppy hair was almost white. His posh, slightly thin voice had a faint undertow of camp, investing his words with a vague sense of hilarity.

'Nicholas.' *He said Nick-less.* 'I understand you and Jay were in an institution together.'

'We were.'

'Same here. More recently, of course.'

'So I gather.'

'I found him excellent company. And very free with his tobacco, which is important. How did you find him?'

'Much the same,' I quipped.

I liked the viscount enormously. He was obviously one of those people who were effortlessly at ease in the world, but somehow without arrogance or side. There was a sense of calm and confidence about him that was terribly attractive. We were sitting in the shade of one of the finca's huge white garden umbrellas, Jay, the viscount and me. And just the way he'd settled himself himself into the Adirondack teak chair — the blue polo shirt, the long white shorts, the sockless oxblood slip-ons — the way one knee rested atop the other, the way he occasionally turned the pages of a glossy magazine as he chatted to us . . . in some people it could have been incredibly irritating, but in him it seemed utterly natural and unaffected.

'Guy seemed to know half the people at the party last night,' said Jay. And of the two of them, he suddenly looked like the junior partner.

The viscount smiled. 'Weren't they a deplorable bunch?' To me he said, 'My mother spends most of the year on the island. Some of her friends are a bit of an acquired taste.'

'Something about girls with their clothes painted on . . . ?'

'Oh, that's Raul, who has the boat. He thinks it's the height of sophistication. So terribly nineteen-eighties, don't you think?'

'Sounds rather fun to me.'

'It is quite *clever*. The level of detail. The way they paint in the seams of the girls' jeans. And the little red label on the back pocket. But such a dreadful *waste*. What is the point, after all?' Guy's eyes were glittering with mild amusement.

'Fun,' said Jay. 'Fun and girls and parties. We used to talk about fun and girls and parties, if you remember. Late at night.'

'He's absolutely correct. We did. We used to lie awake, dreaming up the perfect party. Great days, eh?'

They laughed. And I could see how sharing a cell with either Jay Bryant or the viscount might have made a spell in jail more bearable.

Guy turned some more pages of his magazine. I glanced over at Jay and he winked at me. Because of the viscount or because of Caroline, I couldn't say.

'Do you believe this?' said Guy. 'There's a management guru here offering hints for acquiring gravitas. Listen to this. "You should look slightly above the person you are talking to, as if the point you are making is more important than the person." Do you think that would work?'

He looked at me. 'Do you think that could possibly be true?'

'I've no idea. Who is this guru?'

He studied the article for a few moments. 'Here's another one. "Think about your natural body space, then imagine it twice as great."' He stopped, looked up. Thought about it. '"Then imagine it fills the room. Hold that thought and your body language will automatically increase your presence." That's *insane*. You'd look constipated.'

'Go on, try it,' said Jay.

Guy was concentrating, his lips growing pinched. He breathed in, swelling his chest. Then he looked at me – or to be more strictly accurate, he picked a spot about one inch above my head – and began to speak rather oddly. As if – yes – as if he hadn't had a proper crap for weeks.

'If one hopes to discover new lands, one must first be prepared to lose sight of the shore. Now how did that sound?'

'Very, er . . . very plausible.'

The viscount exploded into silent laughter. 'What absolute rot. The idea of acquiring gravitas. It's like acquiring fins and scales.'

'I shall try it on Teddy,' said Jay.

'I shouldn't bother. Teddy is not one of those people who can be impressed by such artifices.' Looking at me, he added, 'He's Welsh, you know. Incidentally, there's, er, no particular reason why he should be made aware of the circumstances under which Jay and I became acquainted.'

Jay said, 'I thought of telling him we were at school together.'

'Not very likely,' said the viscount, twinkling.

'You don't think I could pass as an old Etonian?'

'Let's say Oxford. How about . . . St Cat's?'

'The piss-artists' college.'

They laughed about that one for a bit. And I laughed along with them. Not because I thought it was funny, but because I wanted to be a part of it.

My stomach did a little swan dive. Swaying towards us, along the path from the terrace where she'd obviously just finished breakfast, was Caroline. I had an instant flashback. Her sudden sigh, her neck arching. The huge grey eyes filling with crushed ice, like a dead woman's.

'Morning, ducky,' chirped Jay.

She released a slow, enigmatic smile. Extended a slender hand for the viscount to shake.

'Guy,' he said. He stood up for her. 'Delighted.'

'We were just talking about gravitas,' I gibbered. 'If you look over the top of someone's head, apparently . . .'

But she was ignoring me. Perhaps it was because I had failed to order her kipper.

3

A little later, I passed Wanker doing laps in the swimming pool. He made an alarming sight, the goggled Englishman churning up rather too much water for the actual progress being made. A couple of guests looked up irritably from their news magazines to gaze upon the source of all the plopping and splashing.

As he hauled himself out, not for the first time did I note Wanker's resemblance to an animated cadaver. The alabaster skin, the sunken abdomen, the painful, sinewy limbs. I followed the trail of drying Wanker-prints to where they ended at his lounger.

'When did you become such a water-bird?' I asked in a friendly fashion. In our class, Wanker, famously, was the only boy who couldn't swim, another source of his worthlessness and disgrace.

Wanker paused from towelling himself off. He was sporting the sort of micro-swimming-trunks that tend to sharply define the terrain beneath (nothing to write home about, I should have said). Rivulets of water travelled through his dark body hair – some pooling, I couldn't help but notice, in the hollows between his neck and shoulders.

'The littlies like it,' he replied. 'We go to the family evenings at the local leisure centre.'

'Sounds fun.'

Wanker blinked at me. Without his specs, I guessed he couldn't see much beyond my blurred outline.

'You should come and join us some time. There's an all-you-can-eat buffet afterwards. And they usually have a bit of cabaret. No one you'd have heard of, of course, but they generally get a good reception.'

Was he taking the piss? Off the top of my head, I couldn't think of anything worse than bobbing around in a chlorinated broth with Wanker and his brood – followed by the entertainments listed above. I could easily imagine the echoing tumult of the municipal pool, the rings of red pepper hanging around in the cold rice salad, the bloke in the dodgy lounge suit singing 'Angels' by Robbie Williams. Characters like me don't spend their evenings in leisure centres, I wanted to tell him, we inhabit bars and restaurants. On the other hand, however – it would be a chance to meet Mrs Wanker, to learn more about Wanker's extraordinary personal metamorphosis. If one hopes to discover new lands, and all that . . .

'Thanks. I'd like to.'

Wanker looked a bit taken aback. Perhaps he was being sarcastic after all.

And then the balloon went up.

Jay was running towards us, waving his arms. Teddy Pickstock's people had called to ask if we minded bringing today's meeting forward – to right away. Jay, being a can-do kind of operator, had said of course we didn't.

So it was that half an hour later the five of us were bowling through the Majorcan landscape, the viscount at the wheel of a powder-blue Mercedes – 'Mother's' – Caroline alongside him in the front passenger seat, me, Jay and Wanker in the back. Guy piloted the vehicle through the scarifying twists and hairpins in the scenery with the natural ease he obviously brought to everything, proceeding neither showily too fast, nor cautiously too slow. Mountains towered above us. In the distance the sea. As we threaded our way down through the olive groves

I had one of those odd moment-of-destiny moments, one of those existential episodes where one feels oneself at the cutting edge of a perpetual present. The feeling that the viscount's Merc contained all our futures. The feeling that *this* was . . . well, you know. *It*.

'Well, this is it,' I added superfluously.

No one replied, each lost to his own thoughts. Jay, I noticed, was chewing the edge of a thumbnail; a small smile played on the lips of the viscount; Caroline hid behind her Audrey H sunglasses. I had an excellent view of one bare shoulder and an arm, limbs that only – what was it now? – only six hours ago were conjoined with mine in a frenzy of orgiastic carnality. I was still in something of a post-coital fugue; part hungover, part sleep-deprived, part lovesick. One of those peculiar states where everything looks vaguely unfamiliar – except, that as everything actually *was* unfamiliar, it was hard to tell how much to put down to being abroad, and how much to being what Jay once (many years ago, unforgettably) described as fuck-struck. As somebody once observed, the hard part about being a barman is deciding who is drunk and who is just stupid.

Caroline and I had had only one private exchange since I left her in the shower (I found I couldn't stop thinking about those needles of hot water drilling against her flesh). She was making her way back to her room to change for the visit to Teddy.

'Sorry about the no-kipper thing. They didn't have any,' I lied.

'One of the Germans had a kipper,' she observed.

'Blimey. They even get to the kippers first,' I quipped.

She stepped through her door, and I attempted to follow. She stood in the way, with a bit of a look on her face.

'What?' I said.

'Sorry?'

'Can I come in for a second?'

'What is it, Nicholas?' She didn't budge.

I glanced left and right and whispered, 'I'd like a minute alone with you.'

She smiled, like I was some sweet but tiresome child. Ran two fingers down my cheek, and then on to my chest. Shoved me gently into the corridor.

'Later.'

We were flashing along the clifftop road between Soller and Valldemossa. Tall pine trees whipped by. Between them, far below on the turquoise Mediterranean, little white sailing yachts bobbed under a flawless blue sky. Every few minutes, through another pair of high gates, another path led off to some millionaire's mansion. Jay flicked nervously through a copy of the investment brochure, scanning the columns of figures as though last-minute-revising for an exam.

'We *can* fucking do this, you know,' he muttered.

Here it was. If this went well, we were going to take delivery of one and a quarter million quid. The telecomputing scheme would fly. I would enter the World of Commerce. I'd become some sort of Business Executive, engaged daily in the Creation of Wealth (not a crummy jobbing journo, hanging round the house unshaven, in dirty tracksuit bottoms, tap-tapping cultural froth into a fliptop computer. Or talking crap on the radio). I would be up and out there. A player. One of those guys you see at airports with briefcases who make the world turn.

I'd have serious money. I'd buy the place with the beehives.

How hard could it be?

The viscount braked sharply and we swung off the road through a pair of tall iron gates. In a layby opposite, two men in a parked car stirred from their newspapers. As I looked back, one of them appeared to raise something to the passenger window. Sunlight glinted on what may or may not have been a camera lens.

4

Teddy Pickstock must have been nuts.

I very nearly asked him: why would anyone in their right mind want to cash in their chips and move from a lovely spot like this one – to Machynlleth? Wherever the fuck that might be.

We were all gathered on his terrace, admiring the spectacular vista. Land, sea and sky was what it stacked up to, indecently large amounts of each; more, indeed, it was my feeling, than any one person should be properly allowed to lay claim to. A whole length of coastline stretched away into the glare, sunlight spilling through the pine trees as they stepped down gently to a glittering Med. Below the terrace, Roman columns, stone porpoises and the like adorned a heart-shaped swimming pool; small birds chirruped in the orange and lemon trees growing in the gardens around it.

I found I was oddly moved. 'It's beautiful,' I heard myself saying. 'Oranges and lemons and everything.'

Teddy Pickstock smiled sadly. 'Ray got a big kick out of those. He used to love going down to pick a lemon for our evening G and Ts. Said his old mum would have never believed it.'

Teddy Pickstock had been aptly nicknamed. He was one of those big, bluff blokes, knocking sixty at a guess, with a kindly face and soft brown eyes beneath a fine head of silvery hair. A large, warm right hand enveloped my own as he ushered us inside, yet despite his general height and bearing – he must have been six three or four, wide and long-limbed — there seemed something oddly insubstantial about him, a little weightless. As if beneath the rumpled cream linen suit, the salmon and cucumber tie, he might indeed have been filled with stuffing and straw. We hadn't been offered a drink yet, but in the few minutes it took us to progress from the entrance, through the villa, to the jaw-dropping panorama on the other side, I had already learned a lot about Teddy Pickstock. And, more to the point, about the late Raymond Arthur Veale.

'Guy.'

'Teddy.'

The two tall men had embraced stoically at the door.

'*So* sorry to hear about poor Ray,' said the viscount.

'Thank you,' replied Teddy, assuming that brave, business-as-usual expression the recently bereaved are forced to adopt.

We followed them into a huge marbled sitting room filled with rugs, paintings and antiques. Dozens of box files and scrap-books spilled from a chintz-covered sofa on to a nearby ottoman and then to the floor.

'Sorry for this,' said Teddy, waving a paw at the disorder. 'There's a mountain to sort out.'

An album of newspaper cuttings lay open. 'Hundreds Attend Funeral of Local Character' read a headline. In smaller letters, a sub-heading recorded: 'Clergyman Pays Tribute to Warmth and Generosity; Makes Light of Rumours of Criminal Past'. An obituary filled the facing page; a photo of a middle-aged man dominating the piece, grey hair, chiselled cheekbones, and an unsettling expression that was half smile, half *what the fuck are you looking at?* 'Raymond Arthur Veale 1945–2002' read the legend. Picked out in white letters inside a black box, the further announcement: 'Retired Businessman Haunted by Allegations of Armed Robbery and Drug Trafficking'.

Teddy noticed me staring and chuckled ruefully. 'Ray used to say, "I don't care what they write about me, Teddy, so long as they spell my name right."'

A squadron of silver photo frames fanned out across the black lacquered surface of a grand piano. In the largest, two young men in black tie were captured at a posh dinner – some time in the late sixties, judging by the haircuts and the cigarettes that everyone seemed to be smoking. Teddy and Ray. Ray, thin as a rail, wiry-faced and oddly camp-looking, eyes that seemed to contain charm and menace in equal measure. Teddy, taller, wider, calmer. The 'straight' one, I concluded. The pair sat there, holding your gaze; the spunky little terrier, the big laconic gun dog.

'Drinks,' said Teddy. 'Go through to the terrace and Guy and I will rustle up something long and cold.'

Teddy and the viscount trooped off into the shadows and I was left thinking: of *course*.

That was where I'd heard that name before.

It was *that* Raymond Veale.

5

Teddy Pickstock seemed uninhibited by the presence of so many strangers. As we sat on his terrace sipping home-made lemonade and gazing out at the Mediterranean, he more or less recounted the whole tale. It was directed at Guy mainly – though he'd been well brought up enough to flick the odd glance round the rest of us to make sure we were still awake.

'That's where he died, Guy,' said Teddy. 'The chair you're sitting in.'

The viscount was un-spooked; shook his head in sympathy. 'Unimaginable, Teddy.'

'We were reading the English Sunday papers together. Ray stood up. And then he sat down again. And then he made this noise. A long sigh, it was. *Aaahhhhhh*. Like he'd suddenly got the answer to a crossword clue or something.'

'Ghastly, Teddy.'

Teddy shuddered. 'Not a bad way to go, really.'

I think we all felt a little embarrassed to be party to such intimate revelations. Guy touched Teddy's shoulder. 'You poor thing. It must have been quite terrible,' he said quietly.

'It's funny, I never could imagine Ray growing old. Old age wouldn't have suited him.' Teddy seemed to be peering back through the veils of his own memory. 'I wish you could have known him as a young man, Guy.'

In his deep, bluff voice (with just the merest hint of Wales),

Teddy recalled how he'd only just come to London, only just taken his first job in the antiques business, working in a shop on the New Kings Road, when one morning Ray Veale walked in.

'I had no idea who he was; of course he wasn't anyone much at all then, but you know what I mean. He was very smartly dressed. Cocksure of himself, young as he was. Said he was looking for a handsome tallboy. It became our little joke.'

Polite giggles all round. And I tried to remember what I had once read about Raymond Veale in the *Evening Standard*. Dodgy Londoners living it up in the sun would have been the theme of the article; Veale, one of a dozen so-called 'faces' or 'ex-faces' who, the paper reported, were currently toasting themselves in warmer climes. The phrase 'allegations of armed robbery and drug trafficking' certainly had a familiar ring.

Apparently it had been ages before Teddy began to twig what Ray did for a living.

'He could have an awful temper at times. People were very frightened of him. But he was always very kind to me. I was quite good-looking in those days, believe it or not. He used to call me his big taff Teddy.'

Our host's voice suddenly faltered. He shook his head and seemed to find something exceptionally interesting to look at in the sky directly overhead. Curiously, I discovered a bit of a lump in my throat: it wasn't exactly Abelard and Heloise, the romance between the camp crim and the boy from Machynlleth, yet there was something in Teddy's tale that spoke of the evanescence of love – a topic that has always cracked me up. Two people meet in an antique shop, live together for the next forty years, and then one Sunday morning, to a little low sigh, the walls of a weak blood vessel rupture and their story is over.

The sea would remain, of course. The sunlight would continue to glitter on the blue Mediterranean. And in time Teddy himself would go. And then, many years later, the last person alive who still remembered Teddy and Ray, he or she would go. And then no one would ever think of them again. And then, and only then, I've heard it said, Teddy and Ray and their love for one another would truly be dead.

I couldn't help it. I looked at Caroline. She was gazing out to the horizon. Lips that the night before had surrendered their expert penmanship, the great grey irises that kaleidoscoped with ice chips, today formed a mask of total inscrutability. The viscount had assumed a noble faraway stare; Jay was nodding mechanically. Only Wanker betrayed some sort of inner turmoil, his brown eyes shining furiously behind their unfashionable tortoiseshell frames.

6

'Are you really giving all this up to go back to Blighty, then? Welsh Blighty, I mean.'

It was Jay who finally asked the question that had been buzzing round my mind since we arrived at the villa. Teddy had pulled himself together after the waterworks and had topped us all up with further home-made lemonade.

The big man twinkled ruefully at him. 'I should like to spend a little time there. Before . . .' He trailed away.

'Machynlleth,' essayed Jay.

Teddy smiled. 'Actually you pronounce it Machynlleth.' Like someone bringing up phlegm, apparently. 'Ray would never have gone back, of course. He always said he never missed the UK for a single second.'

'What's to miss?' asked Jay. 'The rain? The cold? The public transport?'

'The smells, funnily enough,' said Teddy. 'Autumn. The pong of the Underground blowing up into the street. Dry ice at the theatre. We used to love all the musicals, Ray and I. He'd buy a box, even if it was just the two of us. If you're going to do it, do it in effing style, Teddy. That was his motto.' Teddy shook his head in wonderment at his loss.

A small plump man in a smart suit stepped on to the terrace, dark-eyed with a well-trimmed beard. Lebanese was the word that immediately flashed through my head. He carried a briefcase and wore a white shirt with the sort of silvery-flecked tie favoured by people who work with money. He stood before us, breathing audibly, looking at each of us in turn. As his cool, not unfriendly gaze met mine, I felt myself being sized up, and a small shiver rippled through me.

'Christos,' said Teddy, rising to pull him a chair. 'Christos is — was — oh dear — Christos is Ray's personal banker. Guy, perhaps you can do the introductions . . . ?'

Much later, when I had a chance to replay it all in my mind, I realised the banker barely uttered a single word that afternoon. During Jay's pitch, he mostly confined himself to nodding, releasing the occasional wintry smile, and scribbling notes in the margins of our spiffy brochure with a small gold ballpoint. And smoking. I'd never seen anyone smoke so many cigarettes at a sitting. Never mind like a chimney; this was the whole industrial estate.

'Shall I start?' asked Jay rather quietly.

The banker, not Teddy I noticed, signalled assent with a microscopic head movement. His eyes opened and closed in counterpoint. Teddy furrowed his brow to denote paying attention and wrapped some fingers round his chin for added emphasis.

Jay took a deep breath. 'I want to do this for Africa,' he began.

Even Wanker sat up and took notice of that one.

'We live in a post-national age. Modern corporations have their parts made in Taiwan, assembled in the Philippines, tested in China, fitted into a sub-component in Malaysia, plugged into another component in Brazil, loaded with software designed in India.' Jay cast an eye round the terrace to see how he was doing. 'As with manufacturing, so with the handling of data and services.'

Advances in telephony and the internet, he continued, had broken the historical link between service provision and location. 'When I book a ticket for the Leicester Square Odeon, I speak to someone in Stoke-on-Trent. When I phone my insurance company helpline, I am connected to Bombay—'

'Really?' blurted Teddy Pickstock (he hadn't been back home for a while, had he?).

East Asia, south-east Asia, South America, Central America and eastern Europe had all felt the benefits of globalisation – Jay didn't mention Stoke-on-Trent again – but poor old Africa had largely been excluded from the club. This represented both a challenge and an opportunity. The challenge was to bring work to some of the neediest people in the developing countries.

'And the opportunity . . .' Here Jay affected a dramatic pause. Eyeballed Teddy and the banker – the banker *especially*, I felt – and sipped at his lemonade. When he resumed, it was in the small, understated tone he used for maximum impact. 'The opportunity may be a once-in-a-lifetime one. When you come to examine the figures, you'll see that our revenue projections are all on the conservative side. The potential is actually rather amazing.'

The banker's biro vibrated furiously as Jay rattled through it. All the stuff about the leasing of the office buildings, the installation of the technology, the recruitment and training of the workforce, the liaising with the relevant ministries, the agreements with the satellite providers and their regulatory bodies – plus the tapping up of the major US and European companies (insurers, credit houses, financial service providers); some five hundred of them – it was news to me, but there you are – who'd expressed strong interest in our product. Teddy had been trying to follow, but he was clearly a little out of his depth. At one point I noticed him attempting to yawn with his mouth shut (never easy), his sad pale eyes watering at the struggle. Jay continued – about the scheme's potential impact on corporate profits; of first and third worlds coming closer together. And this was no coke-fuelled rant (no white bits round the corner of his mouth), no hash-induced daydream. This was a sober, measured performance radiating intelligence, sincerity, probity and . . . what was the other one? Oh yeah. Rectitude. There was a little modesty in there too, in the face of the sheer potency and inevitability of the idea ('the market dictates that whatever can get done in a more cost-effective environment *will* be done in a more cost-effective environment'). He was even a tiny bit nervous. At times his voice sounded dry, and once he stumbled; it was on the phrase 'venture capital' (he actually said *ad*-venture, but I'm not sure anyone noticed).

And fuck, you know something?

I even believed it myself.

When he was finished, Christos stared at him for a long moment, the dark eyes weighing up the earnest Englishman. He leaned in close to Teddy and appeared to whisper a word, maybe two, into the bereaved party's ear.

Teddy cleared his throat. 'I am reminded of the, er, question of systemic corruption . . .'

Jay nodded, a small, sad smile travelling through his handsome features. 'Sadly, Africa is indeed a notably corrupt continent. However, all the essential . . . lubricants, shall we say, have been included in the budget. In Agenda C. Items 57 through 62. Supplementary maintenance on buildings and equipment, I believe we have them down as.'

I had to make a conscious effort not to laugh. My clever old schoolfriend, one jump ahead as per usual.

'The document should fill in most of the blanks,' said Jay. 'But we're here to answer any questions you may have.' As he threw open his palms to include Wanker, Caroline and me, I noticed his hands were trembling. A powerful sinking feeling followed. Oh fuck. What if someone asked me something? Teddy I could probably bluster, I thought. But the banker looked like he'd rumble me in seconds. May already have done.

Christos, however, set down his pen. Signalled *no, no further questions* by doing something subtle with his beard and eyebrows. And then Teddy made what I would call a rather unwise speech.

'There is apparently the need to act quickly,' he mumbled. He shot a glance at the financial guru, who micro-nodded. Legal claims, he continued, were expected to be laid within weeks, maybe days, in relation to the assets. There would almost certainly be a claim from Ray's wife – I think we were all a bit thrown by that one – 'They married very young,' Teddy explained. 'No children, thank goodness, but they never divorced. Ray used to pay Cynthia a sort of pension, the rent on her place in Broadstairs, it amounted to.' According to Christos, her lawyers were stirring the pot for half the estate. The banker confirmed the accuracy of the last statement with a long, owl-like blink.

'It's all rather vulgar and tiresome,' sighed Teddy. He cited the Inland Revenue as another of the circling vultures, although as things stood, they couldn't touch the fortune while it remained outside the UK. Ray had evidently used banks all over the Mediterranean to squirrel away the loot (he didn't employ that precise phrase). There were even accounts in northern Cyprus, which, as he put it, made life 'interesting'. The Levantine money man clicked his fancy-looking biro on and off by way of adding, *you can say that again, matey*.

In addition, and rather late in the day it was felt, the Spanish authorities too had begun showing an interest. 'You may have noticed two gentlemen in a car outside . . . ?'

I piped up. 'You know, I'm sure one of them was photographing . . .'

'When I went to have a word, they said they were bird-watching.' Teddy laughed grimly. Christos permitted himself a facial twitch.

The priority, explained Teddy, was to liquefy those assets that weren't held in long-term bonds and the like, and source appropriate new investment vehicles for them. Apparently speed and discretion were of the essence. In consultation with Christos, he was considering a number of proposals. A significant advantage of our project from his point of view was that it was UK-based. Investment funds could be brought into the country without attracting UK taxes – and released further down the line, when the project had moved into profit. He and the banker would put their heads together – we would have a decision very quickly.

'We must do what we can to protect the family silver,' he said, rising to his feet, the interview clearly over. 'It's what Ray would have wanted,' he added, entirely without irony.

Again, only much later did it occur to me that what Teddy Pickstock was suggesting – in his mild-mannered, slightly helpless sort of way – was that we enter a conspiracy with him to help launder the proceeds of criminal activity.

7

It was an oddly subdued meal we enjoyed that evening, Jay, Caroline, Wanker and I. Under the stars, each of us seemed incapable of puncturing the bubble of our thoughts. Jay was as pessimistic as I'd ever seen him, gradually losing the struggle between the urge to charm and the need to drink himself into a stupor.

'No, I'm sure of it,' he slurred after a long silence. 'We're fucked, and that's an end to it. Sorry.' He spilled the remains of the red wine into his glass and necked it with indecent haste.

Caroline cast her grey eyes upon him. Couldn't bring herself to say, 'You can't possibly know that,' for the tenth time that evening.

It was Jay's view that as neither Teddy nor the banker had asked us any questions — aside from the corruption issue — the project was a non-starter in their eyes.

On the car ride back to the hotel, I had tried to jolly him up. 'Your speech was *very* comprehensive.'

'If you're interested, you want to hear more, don't you?' he retorted. 'We're fucked.'

'They need time to absorb the document,' I'd persisted.

Jay stared bleakly through the windscreen. 'Colin. What do you think?' he said eventually.

The pornographer removed his glasses and started polishing them on his shirt. I felt a little hurt that Jay would bother to solicit Wanker's view (over my own, for example).

'I am reminded of one of the quotations of Richard Nixon,' said Wanker, pompously. 'Once you have them by the balls, their hearts and minds will follow.'

I couldn't help it. I snorted.

Wanker continued. 'It's my guess that you may have Mr Pickstock in just such a position.'

'How do you work that one out then?' It just slipped out.

Wanker ignored me. And months later, when it all finally made sense — well, nearly all — I realised that Wanker's next statement should have given me the clue that there were layers to this that I wasn't entirely party to.

He told Jay: 'It strikes me that Teddy needs you more than you need Teddy.'

Jay merely shrugged and allowed the passing landscape to slide across his eyeballs.

Now, over dinner, Wanker seemed to have retreated into his shell. On the phone to 'the home office', he reported, Mrs Wanker had given him the news that their youngest littly had swallowed a ten-pence coin and they had all had to go off to the hospital. I considered cracking the 'I expect he could do with the change' joke, but Wanker hadn't looked like a man in the mood for humorous badinage.

Actually, I was more than a bit downcast myself. Caroline had paid me little attention on the journey back to the finca. As we peeled off to our rooms for the customary late-afternoon lie-down, she served up a chilly smile and said, 'See you at dinner?' hanging a question mark on the end of the sentence, like I might have had other plans. The only character capable of entertaining us, the viscount, dropped us off with a noble wave and declared that he was having dinner with 'Mummy' that evening. If he 'ran into' Teddy, he'd put in a word.

So our last night in Majorca made a pretty dismal picture. A cloud of uncertainty hung over us. Jay no doubt was contemplating the prospect of resuming his relationship with afternoon TV; Wanker, although assured his littly was fine, was obviously rattled and plainly did not want to be here. Caroline – well, whoever knew what Caroline was thinking? – and I too was succumbing to the general mood.

If I had a plan, it was to follow Jay's lead and drink deep of the local red – and wait for the Goddess to thaw out.

Wanker was the first to peel off, mumbling goodnight as early as decently possible and beetling back to his room, no doubt to place more anxious calls to Mrs Wanker.

'Fine fellow,' gurgled Jay when he had disappeared. 'Looks a bit creepy, but a top bloke is Wanker. Sounds daft to say it, but there's a strong sense of decency there. Of doing the decent thing. Comes of being a victim of injustice. Do you fancy some brandy, Nicholas?'

'I won't, but you carry on.'

Jay continued to burble garrulously, staring into the face of the full moon and giving us the benefit of his thoughts on a selection of topics: the essential decency of Wanker ('top bloke, despite the porn thing'); Guy (another 'top bloke. Fucking mega-posh, but doesn't rub your nose in it'); Teddy ('bit of a soft-boiled egg to be honest, but I bet that fucking banker knows the difference between shit and chocolate pudding'). Inevitably these meditations led back to his feeling that Teddy – and more importantly Christos – wasn't going to bite on the Ghana biscuit. At one point he banged his fist on the table, making the cutlery bounce. Caroline and I were forced to watch, a little spellbound in my case. In adult life I'd never seen Jay so fully in the grip of drink, and it made for a grimly absorbing spectacle. Caroline regarded him a tad sceptically; her expression, devoid of any note of affection, seemed to be saying: *see what I mean, this is what he is like.*

Eventually he wobbled to his feet; there was a shambolic kiss for Caroline – 'Night, ducky' – a painful slap on the back for self – 'Look after her, Nicholas' – and he lurched off to bed.

In the silence and the darkness we looked at one another. She was eyeing me very *squarely*, if you know the one; the way people do shortly before launching into some particularly unwelcome piece of dialogue like, *I'm afraid there's something you should know*. In return, I struggled to nurture a small smile on my face, and holding her gaze, attempted to convey the message: *I know you're difficult, but hey, you know what? I don't mind. Actually, I find it attractive.*

'Are you all right, Nicholas?' she asked quietly. 'You're looking a bit odd.'

I opened my mouth and the following words fell out: 'You know, Caroline, I don't really care if this Ghana thing happens or not. I feel I've already had a result, bumping into you again.'

In the moonlight, it was hard to tell, but the look on her face seemed to pass from square to sour. I pictured warm urine splashing over a serving of chips.

'It seems to have been rather a long day,' she said. As she rose, her black dress made a swooshy noise against the silence.

'Yes, it has.' That was the pearl of wisdom that passed from my lips. 'It has been a long day.'

She floated before me in the darkness, pale limbs, two huge grey eyes containing . . . I couldn't have said what.

'Are you coming?'

'Sorry?'

'Are you coming to bed?'

She was standing before me and I thought: What do you mean, are you coming to bed? Did she mean, like, coming *with* her? Or just coming to bed, as in retiring to one's own bed. As in not sitting out on the terrace all by oneself. It seemed foolish to ask for clarification.

'Sure.'

For the second time in twenty-four hours, I followed her lithe, swaying body across the deserted lobby of the finca and up the staircase. I felt a little light-headed, there being nothing in the movement of her hips, or the way her long, slender toes splayed against the cool flagstones, no hint, glance or sign, frankly nothing whatever to indicate whether it was *she* who was going to bed – or whether it was *we*.

We reached her door. This was the point where she could turn round and bid me goodnight – fond or otherwise. But she did not.

Instead, she walked straight in. And I followed.

8

I was lying in Caroline's bed. She was in the bathroom, doing all that stuff with the cotton wool balls and the tiny expensive jars in French. One made some claims about *jeunesse*. Another was billed as *crème de nuit* (couldn't help looking, could I?)

On the side table were a copy of *Vogue*, a travel guide to Central America and a shockingly bad novel of recent years. This last disappointed me — somehow one expected goddesses to have better taste in reading material. If she'd told me she was actually enjoying it, I should have been seriously under-impressed.

Suddenly the room light snapped off, and I was joined under the sheet by a hot, skinny presence. I turned towards her, planting a kiss behind an ear. She stirred slightly, then lay silent. I brought my lips up against hers and put in a spot of tentative chewing. She *sort* of answered, but not with much conviction, to tell you the truth. Her eyes were closed, which could have signalled rapture — or the first stages of sleep, it was hard to tell. I rested a hand against a bony hip and tried a bit more chewing. This went hardly better than the first attempt.

'Aren't you going to make love to me?' she murmured.

'If you like.' Actually, I'd thought I was doing.

'Go on then.'

Now I don't know about the next man, but I have always found that sex is a bit of a two-way street, if you will pardon the metaphor. Perhaps it's not very macho of me, but I do like to see a bit of involvement from the other party. Doesn't need to be a great roiling fracas, but one does appreciate *some* kind of input; the reassuring feeling that the party one is having congress with is volitional, and not, say, in a persistent vegetative state. Only twenty-four hours ago, you could have lit a medium-sized townhouse with the volition that came off this woman. Tonight, it felt like someone had cut the cable.

Nor, while I'm on the subject, was *go on then* a particularly romantic sweet nothing to whisper to a lover.

What? Was she just going to lie there like a sack of potatoes? A very attractive sack, of course. But a sack nonetheless.

'Caroline. Wouldn't you like a little . . .' Don't say foreplay, for Christ's sake. The worst word in the English language. After pelvis. And mucus.

'Little what?'

'Little . . . you know.' Serious snoggery, like we did the night before.

My hand drifted off her hip and headed south. She squirmed, and shuffled her head against the pillow, as if seeking a more comfortable position. She *was* just going to lie there like a sack of potatoes.

After a while she moaned, 'Never mind about all that. Just do it, would you.'

Some blokes, I guess, would have risen to the challenge. But I'm afraid her words — *just do it, would you* — had a powerfully negative effect. They echoed round the walls of my brain, cancelling all the 'Go For Launch' lights and generally flooding my system with a major sinking feeling.

I lay silent for a while (two could play at this sack-of-potatoes thing), listening as her breathing deepened and slowed.

'Has been a long day,' I mumbled. 'Perhaps in the morning . . .'

There was no reply.

Perhaps in the morning things would look different. In the

morning we would wake refreshed. The sun would have risen in the valley. In the morning there would be no *go on then*. No *just do it, would you*. We would fall at one another and make love joyously to the sound of sheep bells.

Except when I woke, eight hours later, she was gone. I stumbled into the bathroom and splashed cold water on my face. And when I looked up, in the mirror, floating across the haunted reflection that returned my stare, was a perfect impression in red lipstick of a wide, serpentine smile.

SEVEN

1

My finger hesitated over Squeaky's doorbell. I took a deep breath. This, I was certain, would be a ticklish encounter.

'So,' she said, after a rather off-hand greeting. She allowed me to pour myself a drink — waved away an offer of one for herself — and settled into a position on the sofa that could best be summed up in the phrase, *Okay, let's hear it, buster, and this better be good.*

'So,' she said, repeating herself. I raised my glass.

'Cheers.' A fiery slug of Scotch blitzkrieged its way down the passages. 'So.'

'So.'

Light flashed off Squeaky's specs in a rather unpleasant way (like that Nazi in the leather coat in *Raiders of the Lost Ark*). She fiddled with the quick of her fingernails, pushing them back and reddening the surrounding skin.

Over the years I'd learned something. That the best way to deal with a situation like this was to confront it head on. Be direct and to the point. Lance the boil. Draw the poison.

'So, er. What have you been up to while I was away, then? Oh, sorry. Nearly forgot. This is for you. You like ham, don't you?'

Squeaky was not as impressed with the sexy vacuum-packed segment of Majorcan pig flesh as she might have been.

'It's tapas,' I told her. 'You eat it off little sticks. They didn't have any of that perfume you like. White Luggage.'

'Linen.'

'Yeah. White Linen. They didn't have any.'

'Thank you, Nicholas,' she said stiffly (she wasn't all that impressed with the ham, to be honest).

'This is prime piggy, you know,' I said trying to make her laugh. 'It came from a beast who ate nothing but acorns.'

'Really.' She wasn't buying the pig thing, I could tell.

'Pigs are crazy for acorns. It would be like us eating nothing but lobster and smoked salmon and caviar and chocolate truffles and that. It makes the flesh especially flavoursome.'

'Thank you,' she said. 'It's very thoughtful of you.' She placed the piece of pork on the coffee table and resumed the assault on her fingernails.

I'd found the pig in the gift shop at Palma airport. I was staring blankly at the shelves, when Caroline wandered up alongside and said, a bit pointedly I thought, 'Buying something for Anita?'

'What do you think she might like?' I replied, to seem breezy and man-of-the-worldish.

'The art is to choose something utterly unexpected,' she said. 'Something the recipient didn't know she needed that will change her life in surprising and delightful ways.' She picked out the fist-size specimen of swine-flesh, tossed it to me with a definite *look* in the grey, detailed eyes. 'So much more surprising than a bottle of boring old Canal Number Five,' she said.

'Actually, she does go for a bit of ham.'

The scene in her bedroom — the sack of potatoes incident, as I call it — was never mentioned again. On the flight, Caroline had sat by herself reading *Vogue*. On the train to Liverpool Street she dozed behind huge sunglasses. At the station, there was a peck on the cheek for each of us — even Wanker, his shiny eyes wobbling behind their brown frames — then she snagged the first taxi and sailed off into the night.

Squeaky turned to look at me. Her mouth had gone a little tight and mean.

'Why didn't you tell me she was going with you?'

Aha. Here it was.

'Caroline,' I said wearily.

'I saw the way you looked at her, you needn't pretend.'

'When?' It was a tactical error. Not denying the charge, but asking for details.

'When she came for dinner that evening. You looked like a goldfish, your mouth was hanging open so long.'

'That is so . . .'

'Nicholas!'

'. . . preposterous. What?'

'Don't.'

'Don't what?'

'Just don't. Besides.'

'Besides what?'

'Besides – do you know what the date is?'

'September the . . .' Oh shit.

The deadline.

Our deadline.

September the first – the day Hitler invaded Poland – had passed the day before.

A fat old teardrop landed noisily on the sofa. Followed by another. Squeaky's eyes closed, her shoulders began to shake. As her hands flew to her face, I couldn't stop myself, I moved up and put an arm round her.

'Hey, darling. For God's sake . . .'

She pushed me away, to an appalling medley of sobs and wet snuffling noises.

'Don't *call* me that!' she bellowed. 'I'm not your, your . . . *darling*! Don't call me that!'

'Darling. Anita. *Please* . . . don't.'

Squeaky was in the eye of the tempest, her body racked by great heaving convulsions. Behind her fingers, her face was red and tear-streaked. I tried a cautious hand on the shoulder.

'Fuck *off*!!!' she screamed. A first. She'd never before used the f-word in my presence and hearing, except that time when a pile of spaghetti she was carrying slid off the plate and fell to the kitchen floor with a sickening slap. Dear me, that was funny.

I backed away and drained the remains of my Scotch. 'Might have to have another one of these, actually. You sure you don't want . . . ?'

Squeaky turned a mask of absolute anguish upon me. Pale green snot descended from her nostrils; a skein of saliva hung across her tortured mouth.

'How have I allowed you to do this to me?' she wailed. 'Why do I have so little pride?' The questions were followed by more boo-hooing and SFX of general liquefaction.

The situation seemed past saving. It was hard to think of anything that might suddenly soften the mood. I *could* have mounted an outright denial of the Caroline business – I could have put it down to Squeaky's overworked imagination; through sheer dogged *insistence* I could have *eventually* staunched the tears and set things straight again. Fuck it, I could have *proposed* to her. But what would have been the point? I reflected sombrely: well, perhaps this was it, then. Perhaps this was the end of the road for us. Not how I'd imagined it, but maybe this was the moment, eight fifteen on a Monday evening, when we were forced to recognise that – fond as we were of each other – we were incapable of making one another Happy. When the tracks of our lives began to bifurcate.

And at the thought – the bifurcation thing – of Squeaky going off somewhere and doing her thing, and me going off and doing mine, I felt a powerful wave of sadness roll through me. Not because We Were Meant To Be. But more because . . . well, I suppose I couldn't quite bear the idea of never seeing her again.

'I'm sorry,' I said quietly. 'I honestly thought you liked ham.'

There was further coughing and spluttering, and then the miracle. Garlanded in mucus, a small silvery outburst.

'Poor Nicholas,' she said, blinking and sniffing, followed by a prolonged and unattractive snort. 'You can't help it, can you?'

'Help what?'

'You are *such* a silly sausage.'

2

'You're listening to Yack FM, your old mucker from way back, Clyde Folger, with his feet on the pedals. Wise was the man who sayeth, there are more questions than answers. And wiser still the one who added: the more you find out, the less you know. Back after this one, *amigos*.'

The red light snapped off and an ad played for a pet vacuum cleaner ('give Rover a once-over').

A cloud of cigar smoke hung above the veteran broadcaster like bad weather viewed from a distance. He squatted unseen at the edge of a pool of lamplight that illuminated a mound of newspaper clippings, publicity handouts and takeaway menus. Occasionally, through the fumes and the gloom, one was aware of a pair of small red eyes skittering behind half-moon glasses.

I'd only been out of the country a few days, but somehow it felt like years. Everything was achingly familiar – the rainy drive along the North Circular Road to the Yack FM 24:7 building; the usual D-list of gobshites – and yet all was oddly different. I couldn't quite seem to care any longer. They say when you go on the radio, they pay you as much for what you don't say as for what you do. As much for not saying *oh fuck this for a game of soldiers, you're all a bunch of boring cunts, and I'm one too for being here* as for saying *yes, that's rather interesting. As Cho En-Lai observed about the French Revolution, it's too early to form a judgement*. On this occasion, however, I wasn't sure what they were paying me for. My mental tectonic plates felt like they had shifted.

Apart from myself, Clyde's think-tank contained a nutritionist who reckoned the answer to everything was to eat more oily fish; a bloke who'd just written one of those compendiums of the world's richest people (including tips on How To Become One Of Them); a woman from a tabloid newspaper who was there to talk about the week's telly offerings; and a woman who'd had an affair with a government minister, then wrote a book about it, and had now recorded an album of love songs entitled *Corridors of Passion*.

Clyde released an enormous belch and picked up a cutting from the drift in front of him. 'Mental health,' he said a bit flatly, because we were off air. 'There's more of it than ever. Or less, depending how you measure it.'

'Sounds good for half an hour,' said Meredith over the talk-back from the control room. 'Stand by.'

The ON AIR sign re-lit. '*Caramba!*' exclaimed Clyde. 'Now here's something to put in your picnic basket. Mental health is on the increase, according to health chiefs. Pressure groups, however, are accusing the authorities of massaging the figures. So, what seems to be the trouble? Is it time for a large cash injection, or will we just feel a little prick?'

'You mean mental health as in *wellness*?' I enquired. 'As opposed to illness.'

'Nope,' said Clyde. 'Mental health as in mental health. And you can take that to the bank.'

The telly woman rattled on about the soaps, whose current storylines involved characters who were cracking up (all of them, apparently). The fish oil man talked about the role of fish oil in sanity (key). The guy who'd written the book about rich people expanded on the theme of megalomania and wealth creation (not uncommon bedfellows). The mistress revealed that the minister was always rather terrified of madness (his granny used to take her nightie off and shout in the street). And I couldn't think of anything to say.

Not a thing.

There was no warning. When I opened my mouth to speak, nothing came out but a small, dry, choking sound. Naturally, I hadn't given the slightest thought to what I might actually pronounce on the subject. I never did on this show; in my experience it didn't help.

'Didn't catch that,' boomed Clyde. 'Did you say *egh*?'

'I did rather, didn't I?'

'Pithy – if a little obtuse.' He was taking the piss. 'You want to go again on this one, *muchacho*?'

Again, I opened my mouth and took a breath. But instead of the usual stream of flip verbiage and recycled gags, there spilled forth – nothing.

'Er, I find I have no actual view here, Clyde.'

What followed was an audible hush. The four heads of my fellow gobshites turned slowly in my direction. I became aware that Meredith and the technician were scrutinising me from the control room. Our host's slim panatella paused on its way to his whiskery face. A stool of grey ash broke off the end and landed with a mighty crash on a page of script. Clyde's crimson irises danced over my blushing face.

I had committed the worst crime in speech radio. I had admitted that I had nothing whatever to add on a particular topic – sensible, insensible or otherwise. It would have been better to say, 'Do you realise mental fatigue is only a consonant away from metal fatigue' – someone would have thought I had made a bloody good point. It would have been better to say, 'Fuck this for a game of soldiers, you're all a bunch of cunts' – at least the station would have gained some free publicity. It would have been better to say 'Yibble yibble yibble' – it would have made the red needle bounce around in the sound engineer's meter and most listeners wouldn't have noticed. It would have been better to have hummed the theme from *Knots Landing*. To have performed a selection of farmyard impressions. To have rushed out of the studio screaming that my brain had been invaded by radioactive cockroaches. To have done almost anything.

But to admit to having *no actual view* was the starkest possible confirmation of one's own pointlessness – and the station's uselessness in booking you.

You know that moment when you blow up a child's balloon and then let it go, and it makes that amusing farting noise as it bats about the room, deflating? That's what it felt like. I knew with sickening certainty that I had just lost my one remaining job. That I would never be invited into Clyde's cockpit again.

'What a shame, mate,' said our ringmaster quietly. He looked upon me a trifle sadly, I fancied, the way a racing trainer might on a stable favourite after its back legs had gone. 'Let's go to the phones,' he rallied. 'Nicholas Pitt confesses to no actual view. But what of the Great British Public?'

Munro from Kelvinside phoned in to say he regularly heard voices coming out of his radio. Marcia from Fleetwood said her brother was in a terrible state until he was prescribed some orange and green capsules. Now he was well enough to drive a mini-cab. Lance from Kidderminster said that for many years he was crippled by shyness. When Clyde asked him what he'd done about it, the line went dead. And Sandy from Sheffield called up to say we were a lot of smug southern tossers.

'How dare you! I'm from Leicester!' howled the TV writer.

'Still south from where I'm sitting, love,' replied Sandy, to laughter.

Eventually, a commercial played for Laxatives Direct ('relief is just a click away'). In the break, I felt the producer's hand on my shoulder. I was removed from the salon and replaced with someone who claimed to have crossed the Alps with Hannibal in a previous life as an elephant.

'Keep it real, man,' murmured Clyde as the heavy studio door wheezed shut.

In the office outside, Meredith handed me a slip of paper with a telephone number. 'Message for you. Called after the show last time? Says she used to know you? Someone called *Karen*?'

3

At this point, I began to feel quite sorry for myself. The pillars of my professional life were in ruins and things on the romantic front were hardly more cheerful. Caroline had gone off the radar like a downed airliner; I had to admit I was thoroughly confused. We had had a night of sublime carnality followed by a night of indifference ('just do it, would you') followed by complete radio silence. If I didn't know any different, I would have said she was trying to ease me out of the picture.

In regard to Squeaky, notwithstanding the beam of sunshine that had poked through clouds at the end of the last meeting, it was pretty clear that It Was Over. After the major waterworks, she went into one of her brittle fake-jolly moods, and the subject – *US* – was never raised again. I didn't stay the night; we parted with a perfunctory hug and an agreement to 'have a drink sometime soon', an event, I felt certain, that would seal our unspoken decision. Despite my lowness of morale, I still hadn't felt the urge to rush round with a huge bunch of flowers and a diamond-peaked band and tell her what a fool I'd been.

The days passed with no word from anyone. Nothing from Jay – I had a growing sense of doom about the Ghana project – not a peep out of Squeaky. And nothing from the Goddess.

I found effective – if temporary – solace in the wines and spirits department of Camden Town Sainsbury's.

'You know something, Nicholas. This is bloody ridiculous.'

I was at home, lying on the carpet listening to one of those octogenarian Cuban guys, when I realised I had spoken out loud.

It occurred to me that if there were a small dog around the place, or cat, to whom I could have addressed such remarks, the creature could in return have rubbed its head against my leg, or rewarded me with an expression of quizzical intelligence (though such expressions in small dogs are often undermined by the position of their *ears*, don't you find?). If there had been another living entity living here, I calculated, a caged bird, or reptile in a tank, let's say, then at least I wouldn't have been Talking To Myself.

I began to feel like I was going slightly mad. The way you can when you haven't spoken to another human for several days. By way of therapy I took myself into Camden Town and exchanged dialogue with some shopkeepers.

I returned home with the London evening paper, a copy of *Time Out* and – I don't know why, because I couldn't bear to play it – the Monkees' Greatest Hits. While I was out, my answerphone told me, I'd received no messages.

I unscrewed the whisky bottle, fired up the telly and cast myself adrift on the sofa armed with nothing but the remote control and a takeaway curry menu. I was halfway through Channel Four News when it suddenly struck me.

Karen.

Rather a lot seemed to have happened since her postcard tumbled from the copy of *The Dice Man*. I retrieved the scrap of paper that Meredith had handed to me and considered the number written there. From the impressive number of digits involved, I imagined it was safely out of London.

I made one last attempt to cast my mind back to those dope-perfumed days in Manchester.

No. It was still a great yawning blank.

Hmm. This could be kind of awkward, actually. Nonetheless, I dialled.

'Hello?' A flat voice, with a bit of an edge to it. A rasp, even.

'Is that Karen?'

'Yes.'

'Karen, this is Nicholas Pitt. You left your number with the radio station.'

A pause. Then a funny wet creaking noise, like she was swallowing.

'Nicholas. How good of you to call. I gather you've been suffering from memory loss.' The accent was no help. It placed her anywhere south of Birmingham and east of Bristol. Half the UK spoke like this. But fuck, something told me I *knew* this voice.

I played for time.

'You heard me joking about that postcard, then . . .'

'Oh. Was it a joke? Because it sounded very like you really couldn't remember me.' Unapologetic. On my case straight away. And maddeningly familiar.

'Did you catch the whole programme?' I blustered. 'Or just a snatch perhaps. It's such a zoo, that show.'

'I heard enough, Nicholas.' A sigh. 'My God, did I mean that little to you?'

Fuck fuck fuck. She wasn't letting me off the hook. 'It's not that.'

'No?'

'It's more. Well. Well, you know.'

'You have a degenerative brain disease?'

I took the chance to laugh. 'I couldn't think of a way of tracking you down.'

'Really?' Like she didn't believe a word.

'So what have you been up to then?' I enquired cheerfully. 'Tell me everything that happened after you and I . . . were last in touch, sort of thing.'

Now she laughed. 'You've got some nerve, haven't you?'

'Have I?' Trying to seem likeable.

'You haven't a clue who you're talking to. Admit it.'

I took a deep breath. Prepared to further bluster, prevaricate, evade, avoid, dodge, feint, fade, duck, dive, bob, weave and all that other shifty stuff. But instead, in a quiet tone, I found myself saying, 'Sorry, Karen. You're quite right. Perhaps I am going senile.'

She chuckled. 'There's only one reason why I'd ever have remembered *you*, actually.'

'Only one. Well, that's a relief.'

'I saw your column in the newspaper.'

'You buy it.'

'The man who came to unblock my drain had a copy.'

'I see.'

'I guessed it must be the same Nicholas Pitt.'

'It's not an uncommon name.'

'The article had your smarty-pants tone.'

'I see.'

'Still can't remember me, can you?'

'Nope.'

Heavy sigh. 'Shame.'

'Come on. I've had a hard life. Give me a clue.'

She chuckled again, a throaty, rasping sound that I knew I'd heard before. I reviewed the clues: she was bright, ironic and combative, tempered by a softer side. She believed in intellectual and emotional honesty. She'd had her drain unblocked in the last four years. It seemed absurd that I couldn't remember anyone like that.

'Okay. Does this ring a bell? *Take me home and fuck me.*'

'Sorry?'

'*Take me home and fuck me.* Does that phrase ring any distant bells at all?'

Hideously, it did. In the distance, in the extremely distant distance, I could indeed discern a faint tolling.

'Er, go on.'

'You can't have forgotten the world's greatest chat-up line, Nicholas.'

Take me home and fuck me. Not exactly a cliché or a common-place. And yet there was something horribly familiar, something powerfully close to home . . .

'I'm a little hazy on this, actually . . .'

'Imagine the impression you would have made on an innocent first-year student from Ely. Goes to only her second party in the big city, and this drunk staggers into her, spills wine on her blouse, and by way of apologising says, *Take me home and fuck me.*'

I think there may have been a long pause.

'Ely, you said.' *Ely*.

'Ely. It's in Cambridgeshire.'

'Yes.'

'Famous cathedral.'

'Yes.' *Fuck. Ely*.

'Coming back to you now?'

'This party . . . ?'

'It was in Furness Road in Fallowfield. Somebody I knew in Zoology knew somebody who knew somebody who knew somebody who was going out with the person giving the party. The usual story.'

'I see.' *Zoology*.

'We never worked out what you were doing there. You didn't seem to know anyone.'

'Zoology, you said.'

'Zoology and Botany'

'You did zoology and botany.'

'I did.'

Ely. Zoology and Botany. Something was stirring in the muddy pool.

'I did English.'

'I know, Nicholas. I'm not the one with pre-senile dementia.'

Ely. Zoology. Zoology and botany. The breathy, raspy quality to this woman's voice. There was something tantalisingly familiar about all of it, accompanied by an undertow of unease. It felt as though the answer to the puzzle lay just beyond the edge of my peripheral vision. Every time I turned to face it, it eluded me.

Ely. Zoology. So terribly close . . .

She laughed. 'You had a row with Oliver about it once. He said all English students were tossers.'

'Oliver.' *Oh my God.*

'My brother Oliver.'

'Of course.' *Oh my God.*

'Funny, because he teaches English now.'

'Oh my God.'

'Yeah. He's working in Botswana on a literacy project.'

Fucking hell. Jesus Christ on a bike.

That Karen.

A phrase rose from the muddy pool, the silt and slime of the ages dripping off it.

The Girl With The Biggest Nose In The World.

A vision of her came back to me now. The pale, pleasant, brown-eyed creature with the nose that seemed impossibly too large for her face. Actually, it was hard to imagine *what* face it would have fitted. Even the word *nose* was too small to do it justice, deploying a mere four letters to encompass what was truly an extraordinary edifice, a marvel of engineering, a wonder of nature. This one was a whopper. A conk among conks. An *über-conk*.

'Are you all right, Nicholas? You've gone terribly quiet.'

'No. Yes. Fine, thank you.'

I dimly recalled the drunken party where we'd met. Some sort of loose gathering of students and dopers. I was probably in a morose state; I must have been exceptionally pissed – *Take me home and fuck me* – I certainly had no memory of how we ended up in Karen's bedroom in a shared house in a profoundly working-class area of the city. Come to think of it, Karen must have been pretty pissed herself – or lonely, or desperate, or curious – to have taken me up on my suggestion.

I seem to remember that *take me home and fuck me* became a bit of a running joke in the – what was it? – the month or two that our relationship lasted; if 'relationship' can be the word for turning up on her doorstep during the hours of darkness and, after some elementary pleasantries, driving myself into her pale, skinny loins.

Actually, she may have been quite good-looking. It was so hard to tell for sure, so hard to get past . . . *it*. I recalled black hair, warm dark eyes and lips which, despite the fact that they never saw the sun, were full and smiling.

Three vignettes came swimming back to me.

Karen naked, coming back to bed from the bathroom. All knees, pelvic bone, elbows and beak. Like some sort of sexy stork.

Karen's long, spindly body sprawled across an armchair, with her nose *literally* in a book; a work of zoology or botany, no doubt.

Karen sitting opposite me in a Greek restaurant. The only time I ever took her out anywhere, such was my reluctance to be seen in public with her. Feeling the waiter's eyes upon her each time they brought another course of our *meze*, sneaking amazed looks at the extraordinary protuberance.

'Ancoats. Was it called Ancoats where you used to live?'

'It was Miles Platting. You'd probably have gone through Ancoats.'

'Jesus Christ. Miles Platting. Sounds like an actor, doesn't it? Or a novelist.'

'A *poor* novelist.'

What did we talk about in those days? I hadn't the faintest clue. I recalled a well-brought-up, intelligent girl, humorous – though without the present-day feisty sarcasm – normal in every respect, save one.

She was remarkably unselfconscious about the monstrous extrusion of skin, bone and cartilage; so much so that it occurred to me that perhaps *she didn't know*. Perhaps she and her older brother Oliver – who was similarly afflicted, though not to such a dramatic extent, I now recalled – had been educated at home, kept separate from other children. Or maybe sent to a special school for the sons and daughters of the well endowed in the nose department.

She never – not once – mentioned *it*, so nor did I. Indeed, sometimes it was possible to forget the fact altogether: when she had her back to me, or when we were making love. But then she would turn, or I would look up, and my gaze would be *skewered* by the sheer offensive magnitude of the thing, like a harpoon through the eye.

I remembered feeling increasingly sick at heart about calling round to shag her in secret, as it were, as if in confirmation of the vivid Mancunian dictum of the era that one didn't need to look at the mantelpiece when one was poking the fire. (Snogging was always straightforward, of course. You could *only* go left or right – there wasn't the remotest question of Mr In Between.)

In the end, I think the bad faith got to me. The idea of having sex with someone I couldn't quite stand the sight of. I didn't remember any fiery bust-ups; no tender *it's not you, it's me* scenes. I had a horrible feeling that one day I simply didn't turn up pissed on her doorstep any more. So guilty did I feel about the whole thing, I'd unconsciously deleted her from my memory's hard disk, or, more strictly speaking, placed an *Access Denied* command across the relevant files.

'So what are you doing with yourself?' she asked. 'Are you married or anything?'

'Not really, no. No, I'm not married. Not at all. Yourself?'

'Me neither.'

'How's the nose? Still enormous?'

No. I didn't ask this question. But it was what I was thinking.

'You were a bit of a shit to me, Nicholas,' she said after a while, though not sounding all that angry about it, to be honest.

'I was, wasn't I? Sorry.'

'You were quite sweet as well.'

'Really?'

'Even though you were drunk most of the time.'

'Ah.' That old chestnut.

'Still, you did the job.'

'The job.'

'You know.'

'Sorry, not with you.'

'You took it.'

'Sorry?'

'You really don't remember, do you? You took it. *It*.'

'*It?*'

'God, do I have to spell it out? My cherry. You took it.'

There was a long pause.

'Aaaahh.' *Oh fuck.*

'*Yes*, Nicholas.'

'Did I really?' *Oh double fuck.*

'It was okay. I wanted you to.'

'I see.'

'I even quite enjoyed it.'

'Ah, well, that's good then.'

'You were older. The first-year boys all seemed so hopeless. I'd sort of been planning it.'

'To lose your cherry.'

'In the first year.'

'So it worked out quite well.'

'I actually got rather fond of you by the end.'

I think there may have been another long pause.

'Are you still there, Nicholas?'

'Yes, thanks.'

'You sound a bit shocked.'

'Yes. No. Well, you know. It's been a long time.' And I had *completely* forgotten. A lost evening in the eighties. Some tears. A little blood on the sheets. The beak burying itself into my shoulder.

'See what happens when you start mucking about with old books.'

'I shall never do it again, believe me.'

Only after we hung up did I realise that I hadn't even asked where she lived or what she was doing with herself these days.

4

And then we were rich.

As in – amazingly, miraculously – Teddy Pickstock came good with the money for the Ghana thing. £1.25 million.

Or, to put it another way: £1,250,000.

I think it looks better in full, don't you?

For a few glorious hours – and I don't think the manager of the Kentish Town branch will ever recover – it was even credited to my bank account.

At five o'clock one morning, I was woken by the phone ringing. It was Jay. So excited he could barely speak.

'Nicholas. Don't ask any questions. Jesus fucking Christ. Teddy's coming up with the fucking cash.'

'Oh my God.'

'He has to get it off the island first thing this morning before the bad guys serve an order freezing his assets.'

'Oh my God.' I snapped on the bedside light. Tried to shrug off the hangover that hadn't even had a chance to fully develop. I was in the immediate post-Squeaky phase, and had been consoling myself particularly heavily the night before with Sainsburys own-brand Scotch.

'Teddy's banker was tipped off by someone at the wife's Spanish lawyers. They're arriving at noon with fucking writs and subpoenas and everything. Teddy has to move his money out fast. It's happening.'

'Oh my—'

'Don't say oh my God again. Find your cheque book and give me your bank details. We'll park the cash in your bank until I can get a business account opened. I was so fucking sure this was never going to happen . . .'

'Why can't you put the . . . ?'

'Because I don't fucking *have* a bank account, Nicholas. Now will you please find your cheque book. The sort code is the three sets of two-digit numbers at the bottom.'

'Bloody hell, Jay,' I stammered after I'd dictated the details over to him. The last cheque I wrote, I remember noticing from the counterfoil, was to Camden Council's Parking Ticket division. Such irritants, presumably, would never concern me again.

'I know, mate.'

'I mean, bloody *hell*.'

'Teddy's going to be down at his bank nice and early this morning.'

'First in the queue, sort of thing.'

'I fucking hope so.'

We laughed darkly. But it all happened exactly as discussed.

I still keep a copy of the statement showing the electronic transfer from the Banco de Credito in Palma, Teddy's funds rubbing up alongside my personal fortune of £2,219.03 during the hours it took Jay to open a business account in the Channel Islands later the same day. When I went to sign the bit of paper moving the money on again, Jay suggested I retain some as an advance against salary.

'Sure,' I replied. 'How much?'

'How much do you need?' he asked breezily.

'Well. I don't know. What do you think?'

'Dunno. Thirty? Forty?'

'Forty?' What? Like, forty *thousand*?

'Fifty then. Take fifty Gs and we'll call it your signing-on fee.'

Two weeks later Jay was in Accra, doing the deal on the lease of an 'abso-fucking-lutely perfect' office building that was looking for a taker right away, owing to a loan default or similar 'prize Ghanaian cock-up', too good an opportunity to pass on, evidently.

And I – as they say – I was so happy, I could shit.

5

We celebrated that night in a private dining club in St James's. In a wood-panelled room lit only by candlelight, waiters in black jackets brought on a ceaseless chain of exquisite little morsels. Hardly anything was bigger than one's own thumb.

I was the first to arrive, followed a few minutes later by Wanker. His dark shiny eyes flittered about, probing the shadows.

'Well,' I said to him, by way of making conversation. 'What do you think?'

Wanker was wearing a terrible brown suit; one with a *grain* in the fabric, if you know the sort of article. I felt like asking him what kitchen catalogue he'd bought it from.

'Landing the big fish with your first hook? I don't think it gets much better than that, Nicholas.'

The viscount arrived in black tie.

'Are you going on somewhere afterwards?' I asked him, a little light-headed.

'Not at all. So rare that one has an opportunity to dress for dinner.'

Caroline, of course, looked like she'd stepped from the pages of *Vogue*, dressed in a devastating little black number, plenty of bare limbs on display, wrists, ear lobes and throat all ablaze with an impressive show of carat-power.

'You look wonderful,' I told her, raising a glass of champagne in her direction.

We hadn't met in the flesh since she'd waved us goodbye at Liverpool Street. I'd left messages on her answering machine but had received no reply.

'Well, Nicholas. It seems that we're going to be spending a lot of time together,' she said, news that I received as a tingling feeling in my lower back.

And then Jay Bryant came crashing through the doorway of our private room. He stood there for a few seconds, drinking in the scene, then he detonated a blinding smile and fell upon Caroline, sweeping her into a powerful hug. Her feet lifted off the ground, the backs of her shoes dropped away from her heels. I was worried for the integrity of her ribs in the sheer force of his embrace.

'We've fucking done it!' he hissed.

The viscount slapped him on the shoulder. '*You've* fucking done it.'

When she touched down again, the Goddess looked a little flustered by the physical assault – like a cat when you stroke its fur the wrong way – but a little pleased as well, I fancied.

Fuck it, though, I thought to myself. We were rich.

'I offer a toast,' said my old schoolfriend when we gathered round the table. 'To Teddy Pickstock.' He raised his glass. 'Half Welshman, half soft toy.'

'*Teddy Pickstock*,' we chorused (even Wanker, I noticed). '*Half Welshman, half soft toy*.'

'And Raymond Arthur Veale,' I added. 'If he hadn't pegged it—'

'Raymond Arthur Veale,' interrupted the viscount, hijacking my toast. 'Alleged master criminal and total sweetie.'

'*Alleged master criminal and total sweetie*.'

Empty plates were removed and replaced with fresh ones. These featured at their centre, I noted, a tiny whorl of caviar, intertwined with a spiral of something else, the pair contained within the overarching galactic tendrils of a third, equally mysterious ingredient. The entire creation could have fitted comfortably on a fifty-pence piece.

'What is it?' I asked.

'Dunno. But it's fucking lovely,' said Jay, snaffling the lot in a single action.

The viscount mumbled something in French that I didn't feel like asking him to repeat. He topped up all our glasses and performed the international hand signal for *remove this empty bottle and bring another soonest, would you please?*

'To commerce. Enterprise. And other words like those,' he proclaimed.

'Commerce and enterprise. And other words like those.'

There were further toasts. The exquisitely small portions of food kept on appearing. At some point in the evening, they began an imperceptible shift into the dessert shade of the spectrum. Sorbets and ices gave way to exotic fruits. Which gave way to doll's-house-sized tarts and tartlets. Perfectly kept little wedges of cheese appeared, almost too lovely to eat (although it turned out they weren't). Brandies were offered (and, by and large, accepted). Followed by vintage ports (ditto). The viscount ordered absinthe, so we all did. There was some funny business with a spoon, some sugar and a low purple flame that played over the top of the glass. Caroline couldn't finish hers, so I helped her out. Cigars were set ablaze. At a late stage in the drunken bonhomie, I leaned over to Guy and offered to refill his glass.

'Splash more absinthe, Viscount?'

'What did you call me?' he asked.

'Viscount?' His double-height forehead furrowed. 'Oh shit, sorry. Have I got it wrong?' Had I used the wrong form of address towards a toff? Should I have addressed him as Your Worship or something?

'I'm not a viscount. Where did you get that silly idea from?'

'I. I. I'm sorry. I thought you were.'

'Good God, no. Not at all. A *viscount*?'

I had to say I believed him. Real viscounts didn't as a rule deny that sort of thing, did they? And to be honest, he did look a bit peeved about it. When he slipped off to the bathroom I said to Jay, 'I thought you said he was a viscount.'

Even Caroline agreed. '*I* thought you said he was.'

Jay was unapologetic. 'He fucking acts like one,' he replied.

Through a haze of drink, I peered fondly at the faces round the table: Jay, defocused now, tie pulled to half-mast, his expression a mixture of delight, exhaustion and relief; Caroline, flushed, but still full of her ineffable *poise*; Wanker — well, perhaps he hadn't been drinking as heartily as some of the rest of us — a cautious smile had crept across Wanker's features, as his fingers drummed restlessly against the hefty silver handle of the cigar cutter.

With a wicked surge of glee, I realised I wouldn't give a fuck if Guy turned out to be a countess.

We were rich.

The evening degenerated into everyone doing their party piece.

The viscount (or rather the not-viscount) sang. In an unexpectedly fine voice he performed something sad and operatic in German, a bit of Wagner possibly. Even the waiters applauded at the end.

Jay did the trick with the tablecloth. The one where, if you whip it away in the right direction with sufficient speed, force and — above all — confidence, everything remains standing on the table underneath. He *almost* got away with it.

Wanker orated. Specifically that poem, 'If', by Rudyard Kipling. The one about how if you can keep your head while all around you other people are cacking themselves, then basically you're okay. If you remember, it also features the poet's controversial recommendations about meeting Triumph and Disaster and treating 'those two impostors' just the same. I swear Wanker's voice cracked and tears stood in his eyes as he came to the last line: Kipling's view was that if you could do everything he'd mentioned – including walking with kings (but not losing the common touch) and losing all your money on the toss of a coin (and not whingeing about it) – 'You'll be a Man, my son.'

The performance was curiously moving and generously received. Wanker seemed to need to blow his nose into a handkerchief for rather a long time afterwards.

Suddenly Caroline had kicked off her shoes and was climbing round the four walls of our private room, using the wood panelling for hand and foot holds. She got very stuck on one particular stretch, but was determined to make it all the way round without touching the ground. The sight of her splayed up there in her little black number, toes and fingers clinging on to the mouldings, her involuntary little grunts – her guttural cry of '*No!*' when someone offered to help – I remember thinking, I shall always remember this scene.

The not-viscount chipping in his words of encouragement. 'Oh, very good. Most impressive. Extraordinary dexterity.'

Her final, amazing, crab-like leap from one section of panelling to another. Her whole body held up by the sheer power in those finger and toe holds. Jay hugging her again when she made it all the way round.

And then it must have been my turn.

'But you must have a party piece,' said Caroline, being helpful.

'Everyone does, you'll find,' added the not-viscount.

'Come on, Nicholas, think of something,' entreated Jay.

I remember trying to juggle with some tangerines, to general booing and derision. I tried to tell the wide-mouthed frog joke, but fucked up the ending. The last thing I remember thinking was, I really should develop some sort of party piece. Then I must have fallen asleep, because the next thing, I was lying on a sofa and the not-viscount was shaking me and saying that my taxi had arrived.

Still, fuck it, eh?

We were rich.

6

It was fun being rich.

I suppose I did all the regular things that people do when they come into money.

I bought stuff. Stuff I didn't need.

I bought one of those leather and chrome Le Corbusier recliners that you always see pictured against blond wooden floors in estate agents' windows. I don't know why, but I've always fancied one. (Actually, it wasn't nearly as comfortable as it looked, and there was nowhere to put your arms.)

I bought a simply *huge* fuck-off TV set. Never mind watch it, it looked like you could *live* in it.

Actually, once they delivered the TV and the recliner, the sitting room began to feel a little undersized.

So I put the flat on the market. Toured a few groovy male lofts in fashionable and soon-to-be-fashionable parts of London. I tried to interest myself in buying a new car, but found I was utterly bored by the topic. Resolved to take cabs everywhere instead.

I had a suit made. I even paid extra so it would be ready in a week. It was the first piece of clothing I'd ever worn that actually fitted *perfectly*. That wasn't a bit too long in the sleeve, or short. Or a tad too narrow in the seat, or wide. That couldn't do with being taken up an inch, or letting out a gnat's. The trousers didn't cut into my stomach or balloon round my ankles.

The jacket buttons met their holes at precisely the correct place across my chest. I held myself differently when I wore the suit. I stood straight. There was a confident, fluent quality to my movements. Sorry, let me rephrase that. When I moved around, there was a confidence and fluidity that hadn't been there before. An animal assurance born of wearing clothes that moved with me, instead of being hauled along for the ride. Rich, successful people have this confidence in motion – and now I knew where they got it.

I loved my suit. I ordered three more in different patterns with different-coloured jazzy linings. When Jay came back from Africa we would have to hit the ground running, he told me before he set off. There would be offices in London to locate and staff up. Meetings, presentations, trips to the States. We would need to *radiate* confidence and success. Hence the suit.

'It'll mean six-day weeks, *seven*-day weeks. Twelve-hour – *sixteen*-hour days,' he said. 'You'll be, like, totally shagged and your brain will have turned to slurry. But every morning you'll have to get up and do it all again. We shall need fucking *industrial* quantities of drugs to get through this. Oh yeah. And nothing, but *nothing* will go as planned. You can fucking rely on that one. But in nine months. Maybe a year. Maybe a year and a half, when the revenue comes on stream, you should expect to start making a lot of money. I mean, a real *lot* of money. A life-changing lot. Even after Teddy has taken his slab.'

It was inspiring talk. And Jay was right about nothing going exactly to plan. The office block he had his eye on, for example. That turned out not to be the quick bankruptcy fire sale he'd hoped for.

'The fucking lawyers are all over it like a rash,' he told me over a crackly connection from Accra. 'But I've made friends with the head lawyer honcho – great name, Randolph H. Randolph. We went to this amazing bar, actually. The *women*.

Jesus. Anyway, he says it should all be all right in the end, and it's an absolute fucking *steal* at the price. Mind you, everyone expects a nice little sweetener along the way, even Randolph H. Randolph. *Especially* Randolph H. Randolph, actually. Seems to be par for the bloody course out here.'

'Can I be doing anything in the meanwhile?' I asked.

He laughed. 'Relax. Have fun. Spend bugalugs' money. There'll be plenty to do when I get this fucker sorted.'

Curiously, it felt as though bugalugs' money (the promise of more — much more — where that came from) was actually located somewhere *inside* me, rather like the contented, full sensation you receive after a couple of drinks and a good meal. If I wanted to be dramatic about it, I thought, where once there may have been a hole in my soul, now there was a warm, golden plug.

7

'You smell different,' said Squeaky as she brushed her cheek against mine, a little coldly. 'And you look different. Is that another new suit?'

'New shirt. Do you like it?'

She picked up the menu and studied it, her mouth crimped into the small, mean outline that I had come to know rather well of late. We were in Sheekeys.

'I'll have the roast cod,' Squeaky declared, and peered at me with a not entirely approving expression.

'Got to be the seafood platter, hasn't it,' I responded. 'Full Monty, additional oysters and lobster.'

I turned my palms inside out and clapped them together, while – at a lowish volume, so as not to disturb the other diners – effecting the sound of a peckish bull seal who has just received word of the imminent arrival of an important herring shoal.

Squeaky was not amused.

'So,' she said tartly. 'How have you *been*?'

I didn't much like the upward inflection on that *been*. Implying, as it did, something other than genuine concern in regard to my wellbeing.

'Pretty good, as a matter of fact,' I replied. 'Keeping cheerful.'

'What do you actually *do*, Nicholas? What are any of you actually *doing*?'

It was a good question. She'd asked it before.

Once again I explained how Jay was in Accra, tying down the building. How after that we would hit the ground running. The stuff about the six-day weeks. The fourteen-hour days. Squeaky seemed sceptical.

'Have you ever worked that hard before?' she asked unkindly. 'The stress could kill you.'

The two of us had fallen into a routine of meeting once a week for dinner. Not in any of our usual local tratts, but somewhere splashy in the West End. I couldn't have said why we were doing it, because it wasn't as though we had a great time or anything. An edgy badinage held sway between us, freighted with tons of unspoken dialogue. I suppose what it boiled down to was: I didn't want to be the one to say, *Well, it's over, isn't it? The deadline's passed. Let's move on, sort of thing.* And she didn't want to let me off the hook. The result was that we would pass a couple of hours together, neither officially declaring that it was all finished between us, nor the contrary.

I think maybe we were marking time. Allowing our hearts to catch up with what our heads already know. Checking in with each other, while awaiting developments.

(And it was rather good to see her, to be honest. I did have a genuine soft spot for Squeaky, as I have stated on several occasions in this account.)

She said, 'It's a remarkable transformation when you think about it. Media man to corporate man.'

'*If one hopes to discover new lands, one must be prepared to lose sight of the shore.*'

She shot me an acid expression. To have called it a smile would have been over-egging the pudding.

Our dinner arrived. Lobster and crayfish snapped their claws from the summit of my tower of seafood.

'*The road of excess leads to the palace of wisdom,*' I chucked in for good measure, applying lemon to several healthy-looking oysters.

She set about her cod with a bit of a look on her face.

If Squeaky knew about the one corner of my old life that I still clung to – the radio show – she wasn't saying. Oddly enough, after the incident when I ran out of bullshit opinions – like an H.M. Bateman cartoon (The Man Who Admitted He Couldn't Think Of Anything To Say On A Talk Radio Station) – they dropped me for a week, then promptly rehired me. I was so surprised and touched by their loyalty that now I couldn't bring myself to tell them that I was rich and no longer needed to drag myself along the North Circular Road to shoot the shit with a bunch of media whores. Also, I guess I enjoyed seeing Clyde. I got a kick out of staring at his stunted trunk while the amazing deep, dark voice boomed gobbledegook like, 'Eirwen calls from Goole on Humberside. What's battering your haddock, Eirwen?'

After some minutes of general chewing, I asked, 'So what about you, then?'

'What about me?'

'What have you been up to?'

'Up to? You mean, have I found a new boyfriend yet, so you don't have to go on feeling responsible for me?'

That last bit came out a bit sharply, actually. Squeaky set down her knife and fork and went rather red in the face.

'Not what I meant at all,' I said, trying to sound calm and reasonable. 'Have you seen the *size* of this thing?'

I waggled the bright orange head of a sea monster across the table at her. Then I pretended it was a glove puppet, cupping it behind my spare hand, and listening as it 'whispered' in my ear.

'He's just told me a very old joke,' I said. 'Did you hear about the prawn who went to a disco?' Pause for timing. 'Pulled a mussel.'

Didn't play at all well (think beaker of cold vomit).

'Actually, I've been seeing Rollie,' she said.

'You would do. You work together,' I said sensibly.

She hissed, 'I've been *seeing* him, Nicholas.'

'What? Sleeping with him?' That pompous bore? Surely not.

'We've been out for dinner a few times.'

'I thought Rollie was married.'

'Obviously, it's not ideal . . .' With an audible plop, a tear landed on Squeaky's roast cod.

Oh shit.

'*No*,' she said. 'I will not *do* this.' She sniffed; actually, it was more of a snort, a smidgen too loud, I thought, for a posh restaurant in London's Theatreland. She dabbed at her eye with a napkin. 'I will *not* make a fool of myself.' She fixated on my shirt collar with a glassy intensity. Took a deep breath. Even managed to crank a thin smile on to the features. Bloody well done, I wanted to congratulate her. For a moment there, I thought we were in for the full-bore waterworks.

'Actually, Rollie's left Loretta.'

'I'm sorry to hear that.'

'We have rather a lot in common, Rollie and I.'

'You do.' *You do?*

'It's silly really. We both like doing the *Telegraph* crossword over coffee. To get the brain cells ticking, as he says.'

'How touching.'

'Neither of us is over fond of Chinese food.'

'I'm sorry.'

'And Rollie *hates* the Marx Brothers,' she added a little triumphantly. 'And Woody Allen. All comedies, in fact.'

I splintered a crab leg with a vicious squeeze on the metal crackers.

She continued, 'He says comedies aren't nearly as funny as they like to think they are. He says some of them, when you really stop and analyse them, are actually quite sick.'

And then she did it. She squeezed off a small, fluttery peal of laughter – a giggle, more like – a sound effect, I realised, that I hadn't heard in rather a long time.

What I wanted to say was: 'Well, I hope the two of you will be fucking happy together, then.'

But nothing came out, owing to the presence of a small lump that had suddenly appeared at the back of my throat.

8

It was fun while it lasted.

Being rich.

Like it always does, the end came out of bright blue sky. Except I didn't recognise it as the end. To me, it looked rather like a dark Rover saloon that pulled up alongside the pavement one morning as I was leaving the flat. A door swung open and to my faint amazement, Wanker hailed me from the interior.

'Nicholas. Do you have a minute?'

It was out of my mouth before I could stop myself. 'Wanker! What are you doing here?'

Wanker affected not to hear. 'Do you think I could have a word?' he said, motioning towards the empty passenger seat.

I was wearing my new made-to-measure suit, a lovely lime-green shirt from Gieves and Hawkes and a beautiful tie from Paul Smith that shimmered orange or purple depending which way the light struck it. I was heading in the general direction of St James's, my intention to float a little aimlessly round the shops before dropping into that lovely Russian caviar restaurant for some restorative oysters and a flute of something cold and bubbly. I felt I had time to accommodate the strange pornographer.

'Certainly.' I climbed in as requested.

Wanker, as per, looked like he'd got dressed in the dark. Big old rubbery shoes and the same brown suit from the party. The grain in the fabric strobed unpleasantly on my retinas.

'I'll come straight to the point,' he said. 'I want my money.'

'I beg your pardon?'

'I want my money, Nicholas. It's not a particularly hard concept to grasp.'

Wanker's eyeballs wobbled with a shiny intensity behind their tortoiseshell windows. I didn't know whether to laugh or get angry.

'Would you like to start again, Colin?' I enquired. 'I'm not sure I follow.'

He spoke slowly, like he was explaining something to a backward child. 'As you are well aware, Jay Bryant owes me a great deal of money. There are the production costs on the brochure. There's my success fee. There's the first tranche part-payment as agreed. There are sundry expenses, again as agreed. It comes to a hundred grand, near enough, Nicholas. I want it.'

'Colin. Not being rude. But whatever financial arrangements you made with Jay are for you and Jay to sort out. He's in Ghana. I think you know that.'

'No he isn't.'

There was something in my old classmate's expression that I didn't like the look of. A new and unsavoury twist to his mouth, like there was a bad smell beneath his nostrils.

'I spoke to him a few days ago,' I said. 'He's out there tangling with the lawyers. There's this character, Rudolph H. Rudolph. No, Randolph H.—'

'*Bullshit*, Nicholas.' I was a little shocked, both by the language and by the sheer vehemence of Wanker's interjection.

'. . . Randolph,' I mumbled.

'Jay flew to Miami, Florida. I know because his so-called *wife* showed us his travel itinerary.'

'Myrna.'

'It took some finding.'

'I'm sorry?'

'My associates' powers of detection were thoroughly tested.'

'I see.' Actually, I didn't quite, but I didn't feel like quarrelling. Wanker seemed to be ahead of me here. It was all rather galling.

'As the saying goes, they had to take the place apart.'

'Really?'

'Down to the floorboards.'

'It sounds very . . . what's the word? . . . painstaking.'

'Indeed. In the end, they found it in a bin bag. Torn into pieces. Unfortunately for you, Mrs Bryant isn't very assiduous about the disposal of rubbish. She's from eastern Europe, I believe.'

I didn't like that *unfortunately for you*. It sounded distinctly menacing. If this wasn't the boy who'd been caught masturbating in the lavatory, whose head had been put down the toilet bowl on a regular basis, if this wasn't *Wanker* Wilkes, I should have begun to feel a little scared.

'He flew Virgin Atlantic Business Class. Seat 2A. We also found a bank receipt, Nicholas.'

'Did you?'

'Again torn into little pieces.'

'Really?'

'From a bank in Guernsey. In the sum of one million, two hundred thousand pounds. Transferred from an account in the name of Nicholas Pitt.'

'Ah, well, I can explain that . . .'

'Well that's excellent. Really excellent news, Nicholas. I propose that the two of us go off somewhere more comfortable, where we can sit down together, and you can explain it all to me in full.' Wanker began fastening his seatbelt.

'Shouldn't you be at work, actually?' I asked, a little stupefied by these revelations.

'Let's say I'm taking the day off.'

'You know something, Colin. I'm a little busy right at this moment . . .'

I turned and placed my hand on the passenger door handle. There was a sudden metallic *clunk* as the car locks popped shut.

'Have you ever been to Mill Hill?' he asked.

I felt curiously helpless. 'No,' I bleated. 'I can't say I have.'

Wanker thrust the gearstick into Drive. Then he put his hand on my knee and squeezed it harder than I should have imagined possible.

'You'll enjoy it,' he replied, not all that reassuringly, to be honest. 'It's a nice little run-out.'

As we rounded the corner on to Haverstock Hill he added, 'I suppose you know who was booked into seat 2B.'

My heart sank even lower

'Yes, Nicholas. The anorexic tart.'

EIGHT

1

I didn't know which to feel more perturbed about. Being locked in a car with Wanker. Or the news that Jay had flown to Miami and not Accra as advertised. Or the disturbing fact that Caroline had travelled with him.

'You know that Jay did phone me from Accra not that long ago.'

'I'm sure he *said* he was in Accra,' said Wanker, a little wearily (still with the backward child motif in his voice). 'Jay was always a very gifted improviser.'

We were bowling along a leafy boulevard lined by thirties villas topped with green roof tiles. Thirties-style bird-life twittered in the treetops. Unfeasibly healthy-looking blackbirds; robust little robins; entire avian species that were almost extinct in my own more polluted district of London.

'Mill Hill,' I murmured, somewhat depressed at the way events were developing.

'Mill Hill indeed,' sighed the pornographer with pride.

I thought back to the call. It was true, it hadn't actually *sounded* like an African capital – there had been no cacophony of car horns, crying of pedlars and the like – but then the inside of one air-conditioned hotel room would sound very much like the inside of another. Anyhow – what did he mean, Jay was always a *gifted improviser*? What the fuck would Wanker know about stuff like that?

'You wouldn't be taking me anywhere against my will?' I had asked him as we set off.

'You wouldn't be thinking of trying to get away?' he'd replied.

'You wouldn't be thinking of trying to stop me?' I'd come right back.

Wanker rearranged his fingers on the padded steering wheel, making the fabric creak a little. I thought about that bone-crushing squeeze; I could still feel it, deep in the ball and socket of my right knee. Not an assault, exactly. But highly intimidating nonetheless. It occurred to me that Wanker must have taken up some sort of martial art. It would serve to explain his new physical confidence, and the fact that I didn't entirely fancy my chances against him.

'I think you're going to come out of this looking rather foolish, you know, Colin. Jay is going to return from Ghana, and you will be seen to have over-reacted big time. It will call into question your judgement. I should relax, if I were you.'

'Thank you for that advice, Nicholas. I shall give it due weight along with all the other things you will have to tell me. In any event, here we are. Home sweet home.'

Chez Wanker smelt of furniture polish. Its parquet floors gleamed in morning sunlight. The place felt comfortable rather than flashy. Rugs curling faintly at the edges, a glimpse of kids' paintings fixed to the fridge, Harry Potter mugs hanging off a mug tree. It was all rather grown-up, like someone's *parents'* house. Wanker indicated the living room. The cushions on the World of Leather sofas had been recently plumped. Today's *Daily Mail* lay unopened on the coffee table. Through French windows, a well-kept lawn fell away past flowerbeds to a slide and a swing. An orange cat sat in the shadows, licking its genitals. All appeared unnaturally silent and still.

'Your family? Mrs Wa . . . Mrs Wilkes?'

'My wife has taken the children to visit their grandmother in Poole.'

'I see. Shame. I should have liked to have met them.'

'They are away for several days. We shall be quite alone, Nicholas.'

The signs were not encouraging. Wanker didn't invite me to sit down and make myself at home or offer me a coffee or anything. Instead he removed his jacket and laid it carefully on an armchair. His shiny dark eyes bobbled behind their lenses in an unpleasant way. He seemed to be leaving it to me to say something. Then he interlaced his fingers and produced that horrible cracking noise that always made me feel slightly queasy.

'So,' he said at last.

'So what, exactly?'

'So, you've had some time to think about it.'

'About *it*.'

'Nicholas. I don't like being lied to. Tell me where I can find Jay Bryant.'

'Colin. No one has lied to you. I can't explain why Jay and Caroline should have flown to the States, but I'm sure there will be a perfectly reasonable—'

I never reached the end of the sentence.

Wanker took a pace towards me and shoved me quite hard in the chest with the heel of his hand. I stumbled backwards a few steps and dropped into the sofa. I felt surprisingly winded (I think he might have got me in the solar plexus).

'You hit me.'

'Hardly *hit*.'

'You fucking hit me.' I couldn't believe it. Wanker had struck me, the *fact* of the blow more of a shock than its actual force.

'Sorry. Here. Let me help you up.'

He grabbed my Paul Smith tie, wound it round his fist a couple of times and began pulling. The knot closed tight against my collar and I found myself on my feet. Wanker's face was much closer to my own than cultural convention would recommend. What was more, a seriously unsavoury expression had broken out across it, all the more distasteful because one end of his mouth was curled into the suggestion of a smile. The fucker was enjoying himself.

'Where's the money, Nicholas?'

His breath smelt faintly of cooked bacon. He released the tie — fifty-five quid, if memory served — the gorgeous shimmery material now hopelessly creased and corrupted by the outrage.

'Colin. You'd better stop this right away—'

I felt a sharp stinging sensation across my cheek, accompanied by a loud slapping noise. I could feel my right ear glowing. My upper lip seemed to be thickening.

'Where's the fucking money? And don't tell me you don't know. Your nose has been in the trough, you shifty little cunt.'

A bolt of anger flashed through my brain, lighting up the squishy grey landscape. Perhaps worse than the physical attack was being called a shifty little cunt. By Wanker, of all people.

'How *dare* you!?' I roared at him. 'How fucking dare you?!' I allowed my fury to boil. 'Who the fuck do you think you are, you impertinent . . . squalid . . . fucking . . .'

I was not a fighter. I had never been in a serious scrap in my life. The truth was, I had no idea what to actually *do*, in terms of physical technique. I guess my plan was to worry about that when the time came: to trust that my fists would know how to harness the aggression that I felt spilling through my head and shoulders into my chest. What was that Arab proverb? Better to live five days as a lion than five years as a lamb. I flew at him, with madness in my eyes, I fancied.

Rather suddenly, my legs seemed to have altered their long-standing arrangement with respect to the horizon (viz. vertical). Wanker's parquet floor came rushing up to meet me at an alarming rate. On impact, I found myself in an excellent position to observe what looked like a piece of toast crust that the cleaning lady had missed under the sofa.

'That was a good trick,' I murmured. 'Where d'you learn that one?' Several of my teeth appeared to have loosened during the events of the last two seconds.

Wanker spoke a word I'd never heard of. It sounded Far Eastern. I felt certain they ran classes in it at the local leisure centre.

'It's a tradition that places emphasis on inner fortitude. Something you wouldn't know much about, Nicholas.'

Slowly, I hauled myself to my feet. My lovely new suit, I noticed, was ripped at the knee. My ankle was throbbing painfully from where Wanker must have kicked it out from under me. My shoulder too was aching (I landed on it, I dare say).

'I'm asking you nicely,' said Wanker (not all that nicely, truth be told). 'Where's Jay? Where's my money?'

'I'm telling you nicely, I don't know.'

'I thought you said he was in Ghana.'

'Yes. Yes. I believe he is in Ghana. Yes.'

'Then why did you tell me you don't know?' Wanker did the queasy thing with the fingers again and I flinched.

'Wa— Colin. This is not nice. You can't invite someone round and attack them in your own home.' My voice sounded peculiar to my ear. As though my mouth had gone puffy after a visit to the dentist.

'Where would you suggest I do it?' he drawled a little laconically.

I decided not to dignify his remark with a reply.

'You know he's not in Ghana, don't you?'

'No. I don't know he's not in Ghana. Too many negatives in that sentence actually.'

'Funny guy,' said Wanker. His fist buried itself in my stomach and when I next opened my eyes – after the pain in my guts had eased – I found I was able to strike up my old acquaintance with the piece of toast crust lying beneath the sofa.

'I think I'm going to be sick,' I gurgled. I began the long climb on to my knees.

'I advise against it.' Wanker's horrible clown rubber shoe lodged itself against my cheek. I could see the wear in the sole, the dirt from a thousand pavements. 'I shall ask again. Where's the money?'

'I really have no idea.'

Wanker sent me sprawling across the living room. I came to rest on a colourful rug, again with breadcrumbs in it, when one looked really closely. It occurred to me to raise the topic of his domestic cleaning arrangements, but decided on balance against.

Wanker stood over me, polishing his glasses on his tie. 'It won't just be me, you know. Teddy Pickstock isn't going to take kindly to being ripped off. Some of his . . . associates, shall we say, the late Raymond Veale's associates, they won't be as understanding as I've been able to be. Nor will the wife's people be happy. Nor, I might remind you, will the police. Theft is still considered a crime in this country, Nicholas.'

Wanker popped his specs back on. His dark eyes were shining unpleasantly. It crossed my mind that he was about to unzip his fly and urinate all over me, but I decided that even Wanker wouldn't pee in his own sitting room.

'Shall I tell you what it looks like from where I'm standing, Nicholas?'

'Er, go ahead.'

'It looks like the money passed through your bank account, you helped yourself to fifty grand before moving the rest to the Channel Islands where Jay no doubt emptied the account and buggered off to Miami. Now I'm guessing you know where he is. Would I be correct?'

The image of Caroline's bedside table at the finca came back to me. The copy of the travel guide to Central America. I suddenly felt profoundly tired. Wanker's last statement seemed to have punched a major hole below my psychological waterline. It was hard to take issue with any detail of the scenario he had just proposed, save the last. Wanker's rug seemed like an attractive place to grab forty winks. I closed my eyes.

'In all honesty, I have no idea, Colin.'

There was a lovely sleepy pause when nothing at all happened. But then we were on the move again. Wanker had me by the back of my collar and my trouser belt and was dragging me through the house on my hands and knees like a dog. And not all that carefully, as it happens, because my head banged against a couple of doorways as we passed. I felt the suit jacket rip as he manoeuvred me (think sack of spuds) into what I gathered was a small downstairs bathroom. I had an exceptionally clear view of the toilet pedestal and its shaggy green surrounding mat.

'Avocado,' I groaned.

'Correct,' said Wanker from somewhere above.

'Very seventies.'

'Very probably. Now, you mentioned something about honesty.'

'Honesty.' So *that* was what had set him off.

'Be honest. Tell me if you remember this.'

Suddenly Wanker had my ribs in a tight grip between his legs, as though I were a sheep in need of shearing. One hand was forcing my head down into the toilet bowl, the other pinioning my wrists together behind my back. I was grateful that the cleaner had done a better job here than in the sitting room.

'Does this scenario ring a bell at all, Nicholas?'

'Er. Now you mention it . . .' My voice echoed around the porcelain.

'It used to take six of them. You'll notice now it's just you and me.'

The landscape that met my gaze was depressingly featureless. The smooth sides of an avocado valley fell away to the waters of a bright blue lake. No little boats, no jolly pleasure craft bobbed upon it. Another bolt of fury bubbled up through my soggy and battered brain cells. 'You sick fucking . . . *fuck*.' I struggled furiously, but Wanker seemed to have me trussed up tighter than the proverbial Christmas turkey.

'It wasn't *me*,' I yelled, deafening myself slightly. 'I never . . .'

'You never what? Never took part, Nicholas?'

'Never.'

'Fucking liar.'

'I *never*.' My words rippled the still surface of the blue waters.

'I *saw* you, you idiot. You were there afterwards, laughing with all the others.'

'*No!*'

'You were complicit. As complicit as if you'd pulled the chain yourself.'

Well at least he never found out about *that* one, I noted.

And then I had another thought, rather a good one, given the circs, I fancied.

He hadn't got enough hands.

If he was going to pull the chain — or push down the handle, I guessed here — he was going to have to let go of something: my collar or my wrists, I reasoned. Unless the toilet had one of those electronic push buttons that he could operate with his nose, I was in with a fighting chance of somehow overpowering the fucker.

'Admit it.'

'What?'

'You enjoyed watching.'

'Oh fuck *you*, Wanker.'

There was a pause. 'I'm sorry. I didn't quite catch that.'

I repeated my statement: Fuck *you*, Wanker. As opposed to

Fuck, you *wanker*. A subtle matter of emphasis, but one, I was guessing, that he would pick up on.

'I see. So in your reasoning, the person with his head down the toilet thinks the person who has put him in that position is a wanker? Funny, I should have thought it was the other way round.'

'You're not *a* wanker, Colin. You're Wanker. It's your name.'

I felt him release his grip on my hands; here was my opportunity. But now I discovered that I still couldn't move them.

'What have you done to my hands, you sick fucker?' I yelled into the blue lake, disturbing its tranquil waters once again.

'I have secured them with a polypropylene tie. The sort the police use these days instead of handcuffs. Your ankles are also fastened in the same manner, but perhaps you didn't notice.'

Now he mentioned it, I realised my ankles were similarly trussed. The idea that Wanker had a source of polypropylene ties was an alarming one. I heard the creak of the toilet handle, as he waggled it playfully.

'I've waited a long time for this moment, Nicholas.'

I closed my eyes and braced myself for the deluge.

'A very long time.'

I remained braced.

'More than fifteen years.'

Still braced, though growing mildly bored.

'Fifteen years is a long time to wait for revenge.'

'Wanker, are you going to talk, or are you going to pull the chain?'

I heard him sigh heavily.

'Nicholas, you will perhaps allow me to savour the moment.'

'Ah.'

My heart sank. You know that phenomenon where, once you give up all hope, you immediately begin to feel much better?

It didn't happen.

'It's very sweet,' said Wanker.

'It must be.'

'One of the sweetest.'

'Right up there, I expect.'

'I don't follow.'

'It must be right up there with the sweetest moments. You know, having a baby, getting married. Wanking in the lavvie—'

Suddenly he had me by the hair and was thrusting my head deeper into the bowl.

'That hurts, actually.'

'Where's the money, Nicholas?'

He tightened his grip. His fingernails were digging into the back of my scalp.

'Would you fucking *stop that*.'

'Where's the fucking *money*, Nicholas?'

'No idea. But I'll tell you *something*. You won't be seeing any of it. And you know why?'

'Amuse me.'

'Because you're a fucking wa—'

It was worse than I'd imagined. Perhaps because he pushed my head right down into the boiling blue epicentre of the flush, perhaps because I was speaking at the time. My nose and ears filled with cold, poisonous water that seemed to take an age to subside. I must have swallowed some of the foul brew, because there was a vile taste in my mouth when, finally, he hauled me up, coughing and spluttering.

'I'm not going to ask you again,' he said quietly, once I had got my breath back.

'I see,' I gasped.

'You might like to know we replaced the cistern on this toilet last year.'

'Really.'

'The old one was slow and knackered. This new one refills in under a minute.'

'Is that so?'

'I believe it's German.'

'All the best stuff is.'

'Where's the money, Nicholas?'

'I thought you weren't going to ask me ag—'

It must have been a *very* superior cistern. I should probably have asked him for the catalogue.

The second tsunami felt even more powerful and protracted than the first. When I came up, my sinuses were on fire from the bleaching agent in the water, the back of my head bruised and raw where Wanker's claw was digging into it.

'Try to resist the urge to make flip comments, Nicholas. Confine yourself to the subject at hand.'

'Colin. I've already told you . . .'

I began to lose count after the sixth or seventh flush. We even took a break while he went off to answer a phone call, leaving me to lie on the bathroom floor and reflect on what a disappointing morning this had turned out to be.

When he returned, I noticed he'd rolled up his sleeves.

'That was the office,' said Wanker. 'Everything's fine. Nobody wants me. We've got all day, if we need it. Now then, let me see. Where were we?'

Once more I found myself gazing upon the surface of the blue lake. Something about it seemed terribly lonely and sad (maybe the absence of small boats and leisure craft, as I have indicated).

'Are you crying, Nicholas?'

'Doh.'

'You *are* crying.'

'*Not*.'

'I'm sorry. I must have been hurting you. We'll stop whenever you like. Whenever you feel like telling me where I can find Jay Bryant and my money.'

How had it happened? I wondered. How had Wanker become so strong and I so weak — and not just in terms of who was holding whose head down the toilet bowl?

My sobs were drowned in the roar of Wanker's new German cistern.

2

It crossed my mind that he meant to kill me.

When he bound my mouth shut with masking tape and dragged me out into the garden, I had the sudden and terrible thought: he's going to turn me into fertiliser for the roses.

But in fact all that happened was that he sat me on the children's swing while he went through my wallet in search of banking and credit cards. It was a beautiful morning; birds chirruped; Mill Hill looked splendid in the dappled sunlight. I might have felt inclined to whistle a merry tune, were it not for the fact that I was bruised, brutalised, half drowned and bound with nasty polypropylene strips, my gorgeous made-to-measure suit a ruin. Blood and blue dye co-mingled disagreeably down the front of my Gieves and Hawkes shirt.

'The garden isn't overlooked,' Wanker explained. 'It's one of the reasons we bought the house.'

'Hgmmmggfh.'

'Is the fifty grand still in your bank account, Nicholas? Just nod or shake your head.'

'Gmmmmfghk.'

'When I go to the hole in the wall, will this card give me a current balance?'

'Mmmghg.'

'That's excellent. Now I'm going to peel away this tape and you are going to tell me the pin number. If you cause any trouble,

I will hit you rather hard. If you give me the wrong number, on my return I shall hit you very hard indeed. Is that clear?'

'Ygggnfgfh.'

It seemed I had little alternative but to comply.

'C-can I just ask?' I said when Wanker had copied down the details. My voice sounded horribly weak and wobbly to my ear. 'What made you think that Jay had cheated you?'

The shiny brown eyes of my torturer blinked back at me through their tortoiseshell frames. 'It's in his nature, Nicholas. Which isn't to say he doesn't have several fine qualities.'

'No.'

'There was something about his voice on the line from – well, he said it was Accra. I thought it would do no harm to check. It turned out he was calling from Belize. It's in Central America, next to Guatemala.'

'Yes. I know . . . I know it's in Central America. Not that I know he was phoning from there.'

Wanker gave me a bit of a look. 'Perhaps I can best put it like this: I have a highly developed sense of when people are out to get me.'

He pressed the tape back across my lips before I had a chance to add: *yes, you would have*.

'There's a branch of your bank at The Broadway. I shall be back within the hour. I recommend you sit tight and enjoy the garden. We have a woodpecker who visits regularly. If you're lucky, you may get a sighting.'

Wanker's garden lay still in the heat. Insects buzzed and danced in the flowerbeds. When the ginger cat finally tired of licking his privates, he padded over and rubbed the side of his face against my leg, a small act of kindness in an uncaring universe that I found oddly moving. Wanker, I discovered, had secured my wrists to one of the swing's chains. There was indeed little for me to do but 'sit tight', as he'd put it.

Five minutes went by. Then another five. A further five followed suit. The ginger cat, having made a decent fist of leg-rubbing, stalked off back to the shadows and resumed his auto-erotic activities. If the woodpecker was going to show up now, I thought, it would be a curious sight that met its beady gaze: a grown man, soaked, gagged, and trussed to a child's swing. I stared up into the puffy white clouds that sailed cheerfully over Mill Hill.

What did he mean, *it's in his nature*?

As I sat on the Wanker family swing, swinging this way and that a little, for want of anything else to do, I examined Wanker's contention. It was true that Jay's father had not exactly been whiter than white. Fragments of a conversation floated back from down the years: Jay and Deano and me, talking about our dads; mine, who had worked for a non-glamorous bit of the BBC before he died; Deano's, who was a geologist working for an oil company. We were sitting on our favourite park bench, swigging Fanta.

'My dad's an entrepreneur,' Jay told us with a bit of a dreamy expression on his handsome face. 'He creates wealth.'

We knew he was about to tell a joke.

'He's a fucking con man, actually. He sets up companies that sell things to people, but the companies go bust before the people get what they've paid for. And then he sets up more companies that sell more things to more people. And they go bust as well. And he keeps setting up new companies. It's all to do with unit trusts and insurance and whatnot. It's even been in the papers, what a racket it all is.'

We must have been looking at him in a particular way, because he added, 'It's perfectly legal. And no one gets killed or anything. I only see him every other weekend. But still. Keep it under you bonnets, would you, chaps?'

The fact that Jay was the product of such a questionable background made it all the more obvious to me why he should be, if not a boringly upright character, then very much an honourable one. Perhaps you might even say a heroic one, rising above such plainly dodgy antecedents.

Then I thought of something else that didn't quite square with the idea of Jay as an all-round decent guy. He cheated at exams.

'I just cannot remember all those dates and fucking formulae,' he'd told us in the playground once. 'My brain isn't designed to retain that sort of information.'

It was true. He was more obviously able at stuff like English composition, where his natural talents could shine, rather than anything to do with rote-memorising. And in answer to the inevitable question about his consistent success in exams, he showed us – on pain of terrible reprisals if we ever told anyone – his miniature crib sheets; Rizla papers covered in tiny, closely crammed biro, ready to swallow if he ever came near exposure (which of course he did not).

It had been dishonesty that had got him expelled from his previous school. His own – 'Never write anything on the inside of a pencil case,' he'd advised us. 'It's too non-deniable' – and his father's: 'The cheques for the school fees kept bouncing. In the end, they bounced me.'

I wasn't appalled by any of it. On the contrary. I guess I found it faintly raffish, glamorous even; my dad being too dull to pull a fast one over anyone. And I being far too scared of getting caught to do anything as dangerous as cheat in an exam.

In Mill Hill that morning, waiting for Wanker to return from his mission, it was still obvious to me that Jay did have a moral authority that marked him out from others. An ever-present, highly developed sense of what *needed to be done* at any one moment. I guess it was a particularly attractive quality to possess during the swirling ambiguities of childhood. And even more so perhaps amid the swirling ambiguities of so-called adult life.

It didn't make him a thief, however.

Did it?

'The woodpecker never showed up,' I informed my tormentor when he ripped the tape away from my lips once again. 'Nice cat, though.'

Wanker ignored my attempts to cosy up to him. He was looking at me in a businesslike way that I didn't altogether relish. Another not-encouraging detail was that he had emerged from inside the house bearing what looked awfully like a child's cricket bat.

'Listen very carefully, Nicholas. Your new current balance is £46,028 and some pence. A wiser financial head would have placed fifty grand in an interest-bearing account, but we can let that pass. I have withdrawn the cash machine's maximum daily allowance of five hundred pounds to cover some immediate expenses involved in this investigation. However . . .'

There was a long, ugly pause. Something about Wanker's demeanour reminded me of a headmaster lecturing a recalcitrant pupil.

He continued: 'You have consistently failed to adequately explain where Jay Bryant or the rest of the money can be found, so here is what you are going to do. You will deliver £46,028 – you may keep the pence – in cash, to this address within four working days, a sum which will represent an on-account payment of the larger sum owed to me by your co-conspirator. Furthermore, you will use your best endeavours to locate the whereabouts of Jay Bryant and relay them to me within seven days; the four days and the seven days to run concurrently. Failure to comply with either of these requirements will result in very serious consequences. Do I make myself clear?'

'Er . . .'

'Here, again on account, as it were, to help concentrate your mind, is a small example of what I mean by the phrase *very serious consequences*.'

Wanker suddenly raised the cricket bat as though he had in mind to hit a match-winning six and be back in the pavilion for lunchtime. Sunlight glinted off his spectacles in a sickening manner. Behind them, his dark eyes shone with a nameless passion.

I cried out, 'Wanker, *no!*' but the fucker caught me in the ribs.

Outside of a dentist's chair, the pain was the worst I have ever experienced.

'That is a very tiny sample of what will happen if you fail to comply . . .'

And then he caught me again. The bat made a horrid noise against my flesh. I fancied I heard a bone crack.

'. . . and *that* is for calling me Wanker.'

I may have passed out for a bit. Because the next thing I remember clearly is sitting in Wanker's car as it pulled up outside an Underground station. There was something surreal about the familiar red and blue logo containing the words MILL HILL EAST.

'You didn't need to drop me off,' I remarked inexplicably.

'There's only one platform, Nicholas,' he said by way of a parting shot. 'It's all southbound from here.'

3

Since that morning, I have never felt quite the same about Mill Hill East. Even now, there remains to my eye something cruel, something hammer-like about the little spur on the Tube map between Finchley Central and West Finchley.

I remember little of the next seven days, beyond the fact that they passed in a kind of miasma of anxiety. I was paralysed by fear: fear of what had already happened; fear of what might be still to come.

Day One

Went to The Royal Free Hospital, where they told me I had a cracked rib and there was fuck-all they could do about it (I paraphrase). I told the medic I'd taken a nasty tumble down some concrete steps.

'Really?' he said. 'I'd have said those bruises are more consistent with being struck about the body with a blunt instrument. Anyhow, you'll probably find it's most painful when you cough or laugh. So I should try to avoid excessive laughter, if I were you.'

'Steer clear of amusing situations? Comedy clubs and so forth.'
'That's it.'

Day Two

Received a concerned call from the viscount. Or rather, the not-viscount. He'd had a conversation with Teddy Pickstock, who had somehow got the idea that Jay Bryant had disappeared with his money. Did I have any clue how he might have come by such a notion?

'Not the faintest,' I replied.

'You don't think he could have?' suggested the not-viscount, after a pause. 'Disappeared, I mean.'

'I very much doubt it. Anyhow,' I added with a powerful sinking feeling, 'I spoke to him in Ghana just a few days ago. The deal on the office building is just taking a little longer than expected.'

'Ah. Well that'll be it then.'

There was another long pause.

'Guy. *You* don't think Jay would be capable of . . .' I trailed off.

'Good Lord, no. Why do you ask?'

'Oh, nothing. No reason. Natural . . . you know.'

'Natural caution.'

'Understandable, really.'

'You were at school together,' he added.

'We were.'

'He'd never rat on a pal.'

'Never.'

'That's what I told Teddy.'

'You were in jail together.'

'We shared a cell.'

The conversation fell a bit flat after that. Eventually, after a few moments of *hmm* and *I see* and *right then* and the sound of the two of us breathing, the not-viscount said, 'You know, none of the telephone numbers he gave me ever seemed to work. Not even the mobile.'

'No. Me neither. But he did ring.'

'Yes.'

'We should hang on to that.'

'Wouldn't rat on a school pal.'

'Never.'

Day Three

The spotty young man in the dark suit who I took to be an estate
agent when I answered the door to him asked me (with an un-
necessary smirk, I felt) to confirm that I was Nicholas Adrian
Pitt. When I did so, he thrust a brown manilla envelope into my
hand.

'Legal document, sir,' he said, before legging it in the direction of Chalk Farm Tube.

The letter was from a firm of lawyers purporting to represent one Cynthia Veale, widow, of Broadstairs, Kent, advising me
of their client's interest in the estate of the late Raymond Arthur
Veale of Majorca, Balearic Islands, and announcing their intention to 'vigorously pursue all such goods, properties, chattels
and funds – whether wholly or severally owned – as did properly form the estate of our client's late husband on the date of
his demise'. Furthermore, they gave notice that they would be
lodging a claim for a rightful, legitimate and valid share of the
said estate, making reference to a brimming hatful of laws,
statutes, articles, regulations and other scary words. If I knew –
'or had cause to know' – where any of the late crim's loot was
lurking, I had better spill the beans within seventy-two hours of
receipt of the letter, or they would personally see to it that I
entered a world of shit, face-mask and paddle not included.

Again, I paraphrase.

Day Four

I took a mini-cab – somehow I couldn't quite face the Northern Line – to Mill Hill. All was silent within the Wanker homestead, as I stuffed seven bulging envelopes through the letterbox. It was one of those which are situated at ankle height to make life especially difficult for the postman. Forty-six thousand pounds in used fifties made a bundle roughly the size of half a dozen paperbacks. The first six volumes of *A Dance to the Music of Time*, perhaps. Or a single Stephen King novel. I straightened up painfully to discover Wanker's orange cat eyeballing me from the shrubbery. If it had been a witness to my earlier humiliation, it wasn't letting on. I felt a sudden urge to kidnap the beast and send Wanker a series of disturbing ransom notes fashioned from the cut-out letters of newspaper headlines; each week, a freshly severed paw.

As I walked briskly back to the car, I saw the bright green undercarriage of a large bird swing in over the rooftops, its flight path bringing it in to land somewhere in an area roughly contained by Wanker's garden.

Then I went to Camden Town Sainsbury's and with the remaining funds in my name made significant investments in wines and spirits.

That evening, I pulled the curtains and began to medicate my growing sense of agitation and loss. By the time a muted *Inspector Morse* came on, my insulted rib didn't so much as twinge – even during the most protracted and convulsive bouts of grief.

Day Five

Drunk. All day. From lunchtime when I woke, to the early hours of the morning when I fell into bed again.

In my head at first, and then out loud, I staged numberless imaginary confrontations with Jay. All of them begin with an overhead fan whirling in the tropical night. The bar of some hotel, Jay and Caroline on barstools, me watching them from the shadows. They aren't smiling and joking at their good fortune; rather, it's as though they're comfortable merely being in each other's company. Slowly, I walk up to them. A huge smile spreads itself across Jay's features. He throws open his arms, spreads his fingers: 'Nicholas. *Great* to see you.' After a suitable pause, my opening lines vary:

1. 'Is it? Is it really?'
2. 'Good to see you too, Jay. And you, Caroline.'
3. 'My God, you're a good liar.'
4. 'Let me tell you a story. It's about two old schoolfriends . . .'
5. 'You cunt. You treacherous, traitorous cunt . . .'

Then there's the version where I walk up, and after another perfectly weighted pause for timing, empty the contents of my cocktail over the front of his freshly tailored white linen suit. His smile never falters.

And then there's the one where I shake my head sadly, and produce a small black gun from my trouser pocket. I aim between his eyes and say one of the following:

1. 'You're dead, fucker.' (Nicked from an Oliver Stone movie.)
2. 'Goodbye, Jay.'
3. 'If one hopes to discover new lands, one must first be prepared to lose sight of the shore.'
4. 'Say goodnight, Dick.' (Don't know why. Just liked the sound of it.)
5. 'Bang.' Long pause. 'Did you think I'd actually do it?'
6. As 5 above, but then I shoot the bastard.

In my mind, I turned it over continuously, returning again and again to the central mystery: why did he bother bringing us in? Me and Deano, and when Deano refused, Wanker?

'It's ridiculous,' I called out to the empty sitting room. 'He could have done it without any of us.'

And as for trying to unravel *her* part in it all . . . well, I couldn't seem to get much further than my memory of travelling into her lithe, elusive body, her dark hair fanned across the pillow, her eyes full of crushed ice.

Drinking and fantasising were hardly mature responses to the pressure of circumstances, I admit. Yet the alcohol did help to dull the pain, and allowed the sensible part of my brain to reach a sense of acceptance in the face of the ugly facts. Finally I could see it.

All was lost.

The game was up.

Everything had turned to ashes.

Everything.

Jay had fucked us over.

The Middle of the Night Between Day Five and Day Six

And yet. And yet, I found it hard to think of Jay as pure villain. I woke with a very clear memory from childhood: the park opposite our school; a particular spot, a wooded rise that strategically overlooks several green metal benches on a circular path round a flowerbed. The site is a favourite with mothers with prams, old chaps smoking pipes, and – critically – younger boys who don't know any better. Concealed from more open public areas, it is an ideal location for surprise attacks.

The thrill is in stealing silently through the bushes until one emerges undetected at the vantage point above the chosen victim. The favoured assault weapon is a dried-up clump of soil, usefully solid and chunk-like when thrown through the air, but upon impact (with the top of someone's head, say) shattering harmlessly – though infuriatingly from the point of view of the victim – into many thousands of particles. As we are well aware, the effect of several well-aimed fragmentation grenades of this variety can be devastating. Dried mud gets in your mouth, in your eyes, in your crisps, down the back of your neck. By the time you've recovered your composure enough to wonder who is responsible for the outrage, the perpetrators are well beyond identification or capture, smirking innocently on some distant lawn.

Pugine, Kapper, Ritblat, Conway and, yes, Wanker. The worthless and the bullied have all been separately or collectively caught out in the park's killing zone. Indeed, the attack on Pugine is legendary, the corpulent adolescent having just settled down for an intimate *à deux* with his jumbo-sized lunch box. The sudden and terrible hail of earth spilt his drink and rendered his sandwiches inedible. The big fellow is reported to have wept in shock and disbelief.

One baking hot lunchtime in the early eighties, Jay, Deano and I, swinging past the flowerbed, come upon Frank Porteous, the single most unpopular member of staff in the whole school. Today, with the advantage of maturity and hindsight, I see the bullying and malodorous teacher of German as a troubled, possibly even disturbed, individual. The delight he exhibits in humiliating small boys who have failed to master some piffling point in the language of Goethe and Schiller one might label pathological (though his standards of personal hygiene would cause offence in any era). His nickname is Porkchops and on the afternoon we encounter him his nose is very deeply – very gloriously – buried in a book. As we walk past him, we are all thinking the exact same thought.

'We can't,' says Deano as we head up the grassy bank to the vantage point.

'I really don't think we can,' I echo.

But there is a look in Jay's eye that can mean only one thing.

'He deserves it,' he assures us. 'No one deserves it more. He's a stinking bully and he needs to be taught a lesson.' Jay's pace has picked up and we are struggling to follow.

'But he's a teacher,' whines Deano.

Jay comes to a halt. Fixes Deano with a powerful stare. 'I know he's a fucking teacher. That's why it's got to be done. Are you with us?'

Deano nods. And I find myself thinking: who's this *us* all of a sudden?

We steal through the trees towards our target, vaguely hysterical with fear and excitement. The clods of earth that day are in almost optimum condition. Below us, the unsuspecting Porkchops has not stirred. Deano is looking sweaty and nauseous. I feel almost physically sick with nerves. To lob mud-bombs at worthless younger kids is a valid exercise, and arguably provides both sides of the exchange with an important part of the experience of growing up. Mounting such aggression against *a teacher*, however, is an unprecedented escalation whose consequences are entirely unknowable

Jay looks into our faces. 'They've got to know they can't get away with it,' he whispers. And then he stifles a giggle. It is a relief to discover this isn't only a Cause Worth Fighting For. It is an old-fashioned good laugh as well.

In the way of military assaults, of the six missiles we launch, four fail to hit their target, shattering uselessly around his feet. But two make good contact. One on the shoulders of the loathed Porteous, and one – sublimely – on the back of his head. The head-shot (Jay's in all probability) explodes into a wonderfully satisfying dark cloud, showering him and his book in choking debris. The last vision I have before we effect our retreat is the German master staggering to his feet, coughing and spluttering, fingers raking the filth from his hair.

When we emerge through the bushes on the other side, swivel-eyed with adrenaline, Deano and I begin to run.

'Walk!' commands Jay. 'Clean under your nails and walk. We don't know anything about anything.'

But Porkchops never comes after his attackers. It's possible he never mentions the incident to another living soul. And curiously, though it could be my imagination, in the days and weeks that follow, he seems rather more subdued than normal. A little humbler, less driven to persecute the incompetents or miscreants in his classroom.

Although I don't boast about it widely – who knows what terrible reprisals he might yet mount – I feel terribly proud of my part in bringing about Porkchop's comeuppance. And I am especially grateful to Jay Bryant for putting the iron in my soul.

Day Six

Wanker phoned as I nursed the mother of all hangovers (actually the mother *and* the father. And the baby. And you could toss a few cousins in there as well).

'You found the money,' I mumbled at him after the opening pleasantries.

'Indeed,' replied Wanker. 'I'm calling, however, to remind you about the other part of our agreement. You have no doubt been busy making enquiries on my behalf.'

I sighed heavily. 'Colin. You must realise that I have no more idea where Jay is than you do. If I was part of a plot to diddle you, why did I post forty-six thousand quid through your letterbox the other day? Why haven't I vanished along with Jay?

Why am I not even now sitting on some fucking yacht in fucking Miami sipping fucking cocktails?'

When he didn't answer, I threw in an 'Eh?' for added emphasis.

All in all, a not-bad speech, I thought, for someone whose brain felt like a picture of the ruins of Warsaw in 1945 that I'd recently come across in a Sunday supplement.

Wanker, however, was unimpressed. 'None of this is germane,' he said. 'I seek to learn Jay Bryant's whereabouts. The minute details of your criminal relationship with one another is irrelevant.'

'You don't understand. He's taken *me* for a ride as well. There'd be no point trying to beat anything out of me. I don't *know* anything.'

Wanker spoke words that chilled my blood. 'No, Nicholas. *You* don't understand. You see, I should enjoy doing it.'

It was a nightmarish concept. The torturer who didn't mind whether or not his victims confessed. 'You're sick,' I informed him.

'I was badly bullied at school, I think you'll find.'

I did make it to the bathroom sink after he hung up, but with no seconds to spare.

Day Seven

Of course I tried all the numbers for Jay again. I trawled the internet for lists of the luxury hotels in Accra and phoned each in turn. It even crossed my mind to call International Directory Enquiries in search of a listing for Randolph H. Randolph.

I might as well have banged my head against a wall.

Actually, at one point, I did bang my head against a wall (a partition wall rather than structural; it was curiously satisfying).

I paced about the flat, uttering the worst f-words and c-words that I could summon to mind.

I cursed him.

I threw a cup at the wall (*extremely* satisfying; highly recommended. So good, in fact, that I followed it up with a plate, which wasn't as much fun. Then a wine glass, which gave a rather puny sort of effect. And then a soup tureen, which detonated fabulously).

I broke a biro in half (ineffective).

And then he rang.

I thought it was going to be Eric or Toby from downstairs, about all the crashing and banging.

But it was him.

'How funny. I was just thinking about you,' I said, a little sharply, I imagine.

'How goes it, Nicholas?' he drawled. 'Have you got through your fifty K yet?'

'Not yet. How goes it with you?'

'Oh, you know. It drags on. *Africa*, what can I tell you?'

'The office building.'

'What?'

'The lease on the building. Still problems?'

'Oh, definitely. The lease is a total bugger.'

'Randolph H. Randolph not helping to cut through all the red tape?'

'Who?'

'The lawyer. You had to bribe him. He took you to a bar.'

'Oh, *him*. No. He's actually out of the picture now. There's a new guy.'

'Really? Who's that then?'

'Oh, you know. Another lawyer. Another lawyer with his snout in the trough.'

'What's this one called?'

'Sorry?'

'What's his name?'

'His *name*?' There was a pause. 'Dunhill.'

'Dunhill.'

'Dunhill. Yeah. He's the bod. We're doing all our talking to Dunhill now. Anyhow, how are things in London? Everyone calm and poised? All ready for the off?'

I fell silent. I guess I couldn't do it any more.

'Nicholas. You've gone dead on me. Are you still there? Shit, I think the line's fucked.'

Eventually I said, 'You just read that off the side of a cigarette packet.'

'Sorry?'

'Dunhill. You got that name off a cigarette packet. There is no Dunhill, is there?'

'Not with you, Nicholas.'

'There's no Dunhill. No Africa. No *nothing*. Wanker searched your flat, Jay. He found the flight itinerary to Miami. The two tickets. For you and. You and . . .'

It seemed I couldn't complete the sentence.

'Fuck. This is a shocking line. Are you there, Nicholas?'

'*You fucking heard*,' I yelled at him. '*Don't fucking lie to me.*'

'Nope. It's no good. If you can still hear me, I'll try again later. What a bloody hopeless country, honestly.'

'Just tell me,' I persisted. 'Did you plan it like this from the start? Or did you just get greedy at the end?'

There was a pause. I heard him take a breath. I *knew* he'd heard my question. Heard everything. Then a sigh.

'Poor Nicholas,' he said, like he might have been talking to someone else. And then the line cut.

It was the last time I spoke to him.

4

'And Sandy calls us from Sheffield. What's on your mind, Sand?'

'I just want to say that I think you're a lot of smug southern tossers. Especially her, from that magazine. That were rubbish, what she said about turps and talcum powder getting piss stains off leather. I've tried it, and it don't work. And that astrologer is a plonker and all. I'm a Virgo, and I've had a crap week.'

'Is that it?'

'Yeah. It is actually.'

'Sandy from Sheffield. As ever, a joy to listen to her warm humour and sagacity. Back after this, my fellow tortilla chips.'

It was day eight. I felt curiously light-headed. Now that Wanker's deadline had expired, it felt as if the fear too had lifted, and there remained only a philosophical acceptance. I was indifferent to my fate, I fancied. Whatever Wanker planned to do to my body, it seemed Jay Bryant – and Caroline – had already done to my mind. In some way, perhaps, I longed for it. Maybe a few broken bones were what I deserved, I reasoned. Possibly, they might even yield that mysterious condition: closure. For the first time, I could see the truth in that quotation of John Osbourne's: 'Once I gave up all hope, I began to feel a lot better.' Certainly there seemed no difficulty in spouting the first thing that came into my head on the radio show.

The inmates in Clyde Folger's vivarium that afternoon were: a stain-removal expert from a women's magazine, an internet astrologer, a former Assistant Chief Constable of Devon and Cornwall who'd written a book about coming to terms with sleep apnoea, and a bloke who'd gone round the world photographing people's feet. And me.

A familiar grey cloud of cigar smoke hung over the studio.

'Something about swedes next,' said Clyde, waving a newspaper clipping under the Anglepoise.

'Stand by,' barked a voice from the control room. A station jingle played and the red light snapped back on.

'Yack FM for a Friday afternoon, your old mucker from way back, Clyde Folger, stirring the pot. Now hear this. Swede could prolong your life. That's swede the tuberous vegetable, not the sort with the blonde hair and the penchant for birch twigs. No, my friends, eat enough swede, and you could end up with a telegram from Brenda. So says new research. Panel . . . follow my lead, draw a bead on swede.'

The expert from the women's magazine said swede, along with most vegetable stains, could be removed with warm water and a damp cloth, although aubergine was trickier on account of oil absorption. Anything involving turmeric was a 'bitch on stilts'.

The astrologer claimed swede was particularly interesting because it started off pale yellow, but on cooking turned orange. 'And when you think about it, that's what happens to our own sun through the course of the day.'

The former Assistant Chief Constable of Devon and Cornwall cited swede as a healthy option within a balanced diet; obesity being the main cause of sleep apnoea.

And the man who travelled the world photographing people's feet said that in Sweden, swede was actually fed to cattle. He made the point that some Swedes had long, pale feet with extended spatulate toes.

'Was this research commissioned by the Swede Information

Council by any chance, Clyde?' I asked when it was time to chuck in my tuppence worth.

The great broadcaster peered at the cutting through his half moon specs as though it were a speck of dirt beneath a fingernail.

'Got it in one, monsieur,' he announced.

I did a little speech about tainted news. How the Council's job was to promote swede consumption. How they were probably involved in a nasty little shit-fight with the turnip people. How they wouldn't rush to spread the news if they found excessive swede-eating caused cancers in mice.

'Point taken, amigo.' Clyde allowed the press clipping to drift from his fingers and join the others on the carpet. He selected a fresh one. 'Okay, here's a big thought to take away into the weekend. Other universes could exist in parallel to our own,' he boomed. 'So says a top space boffin. Such parallel universes could exist alongside our universe, but wrapped up in six dimensions on a scale perhaps a billion billion times smaller than an atomic nucleus. Pick the bones out of that, Mr Pitt.'

'Time is nature's way of preventing everything happening at once,' I quipped. 'And God invented space so that not everything had to happen in Birmingham.'

'What about removing stains in a parallel universe?' Clyde enquired, with a bit of a gleam in his red-rimmed eyes. 'I bet there are some weird planets where you rub and you don't blot.'

The topic promoted a lively discussion. Walid phoned in from Lancaster to talk about something called the cosmological anthropic principle, which apparently was another way of saying that if there were many universes – some habitable, others not – we shouldn't be surprised to find ourselves in a habitable one. Colin from Newton-Le-Willows pointed out that TV signals from the 1950s had now travelled more than fifty light years out into space, so alien life-forms with the right equipment could actually be tuning into episodes of *I Love Lucy*. Munro from Kelvinside called to say he'd actually visited a nearby galaxy. The local residents resembled 'wee fried eggs. But not so greasy.'

After an hour, I felt the hand on my shoulder. I was replaced by a woman who'd written a book about the dating secrets of Young Conservatives.

As I walked through the Yack FM car park, I saw it. Parked a few spaces from my own vehicle. A dark blue Rover. Far enough away that I could pretend I had noticed neither the car nor the cadaverous figure who sat behind the wheel reading what looked awfully like the *Daily Mail*.

But now, here was the funny thing. All that stuff about closure; acceptance; indifference to my fate. The feeling that I might relish a fracture or two, the better to integrate the psychic and the somatic fallout from the trauma.

It was bollocks. All of it.

A vision of Wanker's face swam before me: his dark eyeballs gleaming as the blade of the cricket bat came to rest briefly behind his head. My injured rib howled its protest.

I did not walk gladly to my destiny.

My guts turned to custard — and I fled.

5

Clyde Folger was incredibly accommodating when I informed him of my predicament.

After a bit of a pantomime in the car park for Wanker's benefit – *oh shit, I've forgotten that important thing that I needed to remember* – I returned to the building, where I locked myself in a toilet stall for half an hour while I waited for the show to end. Thoughtfully, they piped the station's programming into the bathroom at Yack FM, so I could follow the sparkling twists and turns of the debate (French air traffic controllers' strike; head lice; genetically modified lager; jailing of minor TV personality for sexual indiscretions).

At 6 p.m., when the last of the rent-a-gobs had been turfed out at the end of *The Big Yack*, I put my head round the door of Clyde's studio, and found it unusually ablaze with light. And there he was, broom in hand, sweeping drifts of takeaway cartons, press releases and newspaper cuttings into a pile in the corner.

'Rule One: Always leave the studio as you'd wish to find it,' the great man boomed. 'Nobody knows what Rule Two is. Rule Three: Never eat anything sent in by a listener. Can't tell you the number of times that one's saved me a trip to the dispensary. What keeps you hanging around this shit-hole?'

It was the first time I'd ever seen him standing up. In a shameful yellow cardigan and baggy cords, he looked even more peculiar, the unnaturally large head tapering into sloping shoulders, shading – who could say at exactly what point? – into a trunk, ballooning catastrophically at the waistline, and finally bifurcating into a pair of stumpy little legs. The overall effect was that of a suburban troll. With a bit of a shock, I realised he was wearing carpet slippers.

Nonetheless, he inspired something within me that made me feel I could trust him. Perhaps it was pity. I told him there was someone outside who wished me ill. Specifically, I feared for the integrity of my bone structure. I made reference to a cricket bat. Could he perhaps smuggle me out a back way?

'Fanny-trouble, is it?' he asked, blinking above the half-moons.

'Sorry?'

He tapped the side of his nose. 'Old man todger been visiting certain moist, warm caves he shouldn't have been visiting.'

'Not that, actually.'

'Doesn't matter to me, old son. I was a horny little so-and-so at your age. I was up everything. I was up there faster than you can say knife. How fast can you say knife? Go on. How fast can you say it?'

Clyde stared at me, his fat little fingers linked across his belly-stroke-chest.

'Sorry. What, kni—'

'I was up there faster than that, feller. Meet me at the canteen door in five. I'll bring the wheels.'

It was a big guy's car. A BMW or some such, the driver's seat pushed right up to the steering wheel so he could reach the pedals. I crouched on the floor as Clyde piloted us through the Yack FM car park and out on to the North Circular.

'We're clear,' he said after a bit. 'No one's tailing us.'

'Thanks, Clyde,' I replied, surfacing. 'Sorry to get you mixed up in this ridiculous . . .'

'Not at all, old love. Actually, I haven't had so much fun since I was forced to flee the family nesting grounds, five minutes ahead of the bailiffs, back in Adelaide many moons ago. Of course we've all passed a lot of water since then.' After a pause he added, 'I don't suppose you can go home now. He'll be waiting for you, I guess.'

'I guess he will.'

'Stay with us tonight. There's stacks of room. I'm sure Carrie would like to meet you.'

I gazed upon my unlikely rescuer. The chubby little fingers resting on the wheel, a signet ring jammed on a pinkie; patchy fuzzy beard garlanding the lower part of his face like ivy round a ruin. His wonderfully deep, dark voice. I thought to myself: *He may look like a freak, and spout the most appalling drivel, but somehow I love this man.*

'It's too much trouble, Clyde. I'll find a hotel . . .'

'Bollocks, hotel. You're coming with me, old love.'

'All right. But let's stop on the way, and I'll buy some booze.'

'Consider it a done deal. Care for some classic rock?'

'Love some.'

Clyde poked a cassette down a hole, slipped into fifth, and we tooled off north to *Who's Next* by The Who, played at almost ear-splitting volume. The number called 'Won't Get Fooled Again' seemed particularly apposite that evening. I asked him to put it on again.

'You can't fucking beat it,' boomed Clyde during the tape hiss up to the opening chords. 'A Kraut car, the open road, and Pete Townshend on guitar. You were in nappies when this first came out. And the year, in case you were wondering . . . was 1971.'

The whole vehicle seemed to bounce on the tarmac as the track crashed in. A small smile played on Clyde's face. He was happy. It was a perfect DJ talk-up.

6

Clyde's place turned out to be a big old house in Bounds Green littered with books, magazines and a huge collection of vinyl records, 'from my days as a music jock in steam radio. Before it was all done by school-leavers and bloody computers.' There was a familiar background aroma of curry and cigars.

Equipped with brimming glasses of Teacher's, we settled into armchairs in his agreeably disordered sitting room and toasted one another's health. Clyde knocked his drink back in one, turned an interesting colour for a few seconds, and immediately refilled.

'Right, that's wet the pipework. Now let's get started.'

The second glass of Teacher's largely followed the format of the first. I began to get a sense of how the veteran broadcaster may have ended up in the shape he had. Beached on his recliner – his feet didn't reach the floor – Clyde resembled not so much a human as an obese hobbit.

'What did you think of the show today?' he asked.

'I though the Assistant Chief Constable was a bit of a waste of space. And that woman about the stains—'

'It's all *balls*, of course,' he boomed suddenly. 'Utter balls.'

I took a sip of Scotch. It was difficult to argue with that last remark.

'You know what the hardest part of my job is?'

I shook my head.

'Staying awake.'

I laughed.

'It's true, old love. Some afternoons, it's the most titanic struggle to keep from zizzing off. Here's mud in your gusset.'

'Cheers.'

'Marvellous drink, whisky. Can drink pints of it to no visible effect. You ready for another?'

'I'm fine, thanks.'

'The irony is that that bloody show is the only thing that keeps me ticking. And Carrie, of course.'

'That would be Mrs Folger . . . ?'

My host began to shake (amusement, I took it).

'No one's laboured under that title since The Beatles split up. Carrie's a special friend. Hang fire. If I'm not mistaken . . .'

There followed the sound of the front door opening.

'. . . this will be the little lady in person. Carrie, say hello to Nicholas Pitt. Gentleman, man about town and refugee from the war between the sexes.' He winked at me lewdly.

And in walked Carrie. Not, as I'd expected, a woman perhaps ten years younger than my host; homely and nurse-like. But a slender, dark-haired creature in her early twenties; hardly a galloping beauty, but in her odd, awkward way – her gaze didn't quite meet mine, she couldn't entirely decide which leg to stand on – undeniably attractive, and yes, even *sexy*, damn it.

'Pleased to meet you,' I offered. We shook hands (a wholly new custom to her, apparently) and Clyde boomed, 'Carrie's my good-luck charm, aren't you, honeybunny?' When her small, dark eyes fleetingly caught my own, they were filled, I noticed, with an unnameable thrill.

And I thought, *Jesus Christ. She can't actually be doing it with him, can she?*

Over dinner, I decided that quite possibly she could.

The three of us ate in the kitchen, at a long wooden table that Clyde cleared by sliding all the stuff on it down to one end.

'How's your cottage pie?' he enquired.

'Delightful,' I responded. 'Very reassuring.'

'Carrie makes a damn fine cottage pie. Her cottage pie craps over all other cottage pies. Quite literally.'

The recipient of these compliments smiled furtively and gazed at the short, fat broadcaster with something close to adoration on her face.

'Nicholas has been a naughty boy,' he said after a prolonged spell of shovelling of mashed potato and other ingredients.

Carrie giggled.

'What did he do?' she asked (like I wasn't there or something).

'He did a naughty thing with a lady that he shouldn't have, and now some man wants to bash him up.'

Carrie positively cackled with pleasure. She shivered at the naughtiness of it all.

I began to object, 'Actually, that's not entirely—'

'We're not here to moralise, old love. Mr Todger is the one-eyed gentleman who knows nothing of morals. Or trigonometry, come to that.'

'You've got it a little wrong, actually . . .' (I think he was a bit pissed now.)

'*Mr Todger . . .!*' he boomed theatrically, and then trailed off for dramatic effect. 'Mr Todger,' he resumed more quietly, 'is an impatient creature of the dark who has little regard for rules and proprieties. Top me up, would you, sweetheart.'

Carrie re-charged Clyde's schooner of Albanian cabernet sauvignon from the Sainsbury's wine box.

I felt bold enough to enquire, 'How did you two actually . . . meet one another?'

'Tell the man, honeybunny.'

'I came to interview him,' said Carrie in her small, strangled voice.

'For a docco called *Leg Ends of Radio*.'

'Legends,' she said, a bit embarrassed. 'It was part of my media studies degree.'

'All balls, of course. We were self-taught, in those days. People took baths then. Poor as they were.'

Carrie rolled her eyes and made a *tsk* noise.

'Shall I let you into a little secret?' said Clyde. 'How I never need to take a leak through six hours of live radio?'

Carrie tried to shush him, but he wouldn't be shushed.

'Would you like to know?'

'I had wondered,' I replied.

'Supreme urological control,' he boomed. 'Learnt it in the days of the three-minute pop single. You couldn't nip to the khazi and be back before the record ended. So you either pissed in a bottle or re-educated your urological muscles. "Bohemian Rhapsody" changed all that, of course. Five minutes forty-eight. Plenty of time. "Stairway to Heaven". Eight minutes and three seconds. You could take a dump in "Stairway to Heaven" if you knew what you were doing.' The great broadcaster shook his head. 'All the old skills have gone. I feel like a dinosaur, Nicholas. That's what she calls me, her pet dinosaur. Creature from a lost world.'

Carrie and I must have been staring at the dinosaur a little open-mouthed because suddenly he drained his glass.

'You two look like a pair of baby birds. Come on. Let's hunker down in the other room and have a drink.'

7

We lolled about for a bit, watching TV, flipping between the snooker and a new constructed reality programme where the members of two families were muddled about, so that Dad A lived with Mum B, and the siblings all ended up in the wrong bedrooms. The show was presided over by an annoying character in heavy orange make-up who seemed to have been on telly for ever.

'He's a great survivor,' growled Clyde from his lounger. 'You'd think he would have been put against a wall and shot years ago. What's his secret, Nicholas?'

'I read in a magazine that he shrinks the bags under his eyes with pile-reducing cream. That could be part of it.'

Carrie sniggered and wiggled about on the sofa and I felt another unforgivable surge of desire for the stringy, awkward creature.

'I've got an idea for a TV show,' said Clyde.

Oh shit, I thought. Hasn't everyone. 'Really?'

'It's a post-modern chat show with a twist. The telly-nabobs will hate it of course because it doesn't work without me, and I'm nobody's idea of a conventional telly star.'

Carrie started to object.

'But look at Homer Simpson,' he barked 'Look at Dr David bloody Starkey. Look at Sister Wendy. I'll run it by you some time, Nicholas.'

'I'd be very interested.' I replied. But my heart – and my estimation of my host – sank a little. Somehow I'd imagined Clyde would be above, or in view of his stature and his shape, perhaps *beyond* such vanities.

'I fancy a little grappa,' he announced. 'A small *digestif* to put the cap on the evening.'

He did in a third of a bottle. Along the way, there were further offerings from his personal philosophy: 'Never – but *never* – trust anyone in a bow-tie.' 'If you break wind in someone's bathroom, don't strike a match, set fire to a *newspaper*.' And my personal favourite, 'A man is never drunk if he can lie on the floor without holding on.'

On the way to bed, I was given the guided tour. Framed old records on the walls – 'Presented to WXZY's Clyde Folger in recognition of his role in making *Chirpy Chirpy Cheep Cheep* a success in Australia' – black-and-white publicity shots dating from when he was younger and thinner, more an actual human, less a forest feature.

I followed as he waddled through the upstairs part of the house, pointing to various doors. 'My room. Carrie's room. The bathroom.'

Carrie's room. So perhaps they didn't . . .

'Here's your bedroom. This room we don't talk about. And this here is the water closet. Love that one . . .' He savoured the words again, '*Water closet*. If there are no questions . . . I'll bid you goodnight.'

'Thanks, Clyde. You got me out of a jam tonight . . .'

'No probs, old love. You know what they say about jam, don't you?'

'What?'

He tottered off without telling.

I was trying to read for a bit – why is there *always* a Muriel Spark novel in people's spare bedrooms, do you suppose? – when it occurred to me to dial up my flat from my mobile.

There were three messages. Squeaky — a tastelessly chirpy tone about her — to say that a policeman had rung asking about my whereabouts (she'd said she didn't know, 'which was perfectly true as it happens'). She and Rollie would be out tonight, she reported. Rollie had tickets for Brian Wilson at the Royal Festival Hall, Rollie being something of a Beach Boys fan, apparently. Next, a Detective Inspector Somebody from the Fraud Squad at Scotland Yard. One of those growly old bastard voices, redolent of forty-a-day and a bottle of Scotch in the filing cabinet. Would I mind giving him a call in connection with a complaint regarding the alleged disappearance of a 'known associate' of mine and a sum of money believed to be in the region of one and a quarter million pounds. There were some questions he'd like to ask me. Next was Wanker, sounding slightly defeated, I was cheered to hear. 'It's Colin Wilkes, Nicholas,' he said. 'I'd appreciate a call when you have a moment.'

With the distinct feeling of the vultures falling into a holding pattern over my head, I deleted the messages and closed my eyes. Not for the first time in this narrative, I thought to myself, *what the fuck am I doing here?* Once upon a time, I had a girlfriend (fuck, nearly a *fiancée*). A newspaper column. Something close to what you'd call a career. And then, out of a sunny blue sky, Jay Bryant and Caroline Stamp walked back into my life. Now I was being sought on all fronts. Firstly for questioning by the police. And secondly for special torture by a boy I went to school with who was caught masturbating in a loo. In addition, I was sleeping under the roof of a bearded troll who referred to the male organ as 'Mr Todger'.

It didn't look good.

Even worse in some ways, the above-mentioned troll was the apparent love object of a gauche yet undeniably attractive member of the opposite species.

'People are weird,' Clyde had intoned shortly before calling it a night. Fixing me woozily from the cushions of his lounger, he grew suddenly serious, as a fresh riptide of grappa turned his thoughts towards the mystery of life.

'Never underestimate the weirdness of folk,' he said. 'However weird someone is, you'll always find someone a hundred per cent weirder. A thousand per cent.'

He was right. People *were* weird.

People were weird, and I had pissed on my chips. Who had said that to me recently? I wondered. I couldn't remember. But I recalled the image. The crisp golden-brown potatoes, hosed by the warm, acrid vinegar of wee-wee. It was the last picture in my head when I drifted off to sleep. But when I next woke, at 2 a.m. by the light from my Indiglo watch, there were . . . yes, there were; I could hear *noises*. The click of a door latch. Scrabbling, scuffling and whispering. And then, hideously, a slap. As in skin impacting against skin. A gasp. Followed by suppressed giggling.

What the fuck was I doing here? Listening to . . . to whatever unfolding horror it was that I was listening to.

There were further muffled sounds. At one point, a human (female) voice clearly employed the word 'kumquat'.

A few moments later, the other one (male) said, 'Beating about the bush?'

A long pause, and then the male again: 'Horsefly.'

'The British are coming.' (Her, excited.)

I could resist no longer. I crept into the darkened corridor as silently as I could. Heart thudding, I lowered an eye to the illuminated keyhole of the door next to mine.

Clyde and Carrie sat side by side in a large double bed, completing a crossword in a newspaper. The younger woman had her head against the older man's neck (or shoulder, or whatever you would properly call it).

'Sea cucumber,' she murmured. He inked in the letters.

They both appeared indecently content.

8

Around 4 a.m., I was woken by the unmistakable sound effects of vigorous sexual congress between consenting adults.

'Oh, crumbs,' he seemed to mutter at the moment of climax (it was hard to tell, even with one's ear pressed against the plasterboard).

'Honeybunny,' she moaned.

By eleven, when I next surfaced, all was silent. Downstairs, I found Carrie sipping tea at the kitchen table. She was in jeans and a T-shirt, flipping though a pile of daily papers. It was a Saturday morning in the suburbs. Oddly, my problems felt a long way off.

'Clyde's gone out,' she said, blushing. 'He says you're to help yourself to breakfast.'

'Thank you.'

'He's visiting a friend in hospital. He says I'm not to let you disappear.' If her face had turned any redder it would have vanished from the visible spectrum. Was it obvious that I'd heard . . . what I'd heard, last night? I wondered.

I fiddled about with the kettle and the toaster for a bit, shooting her a glance every so often. Pale arms emerged from the short sleeves of the T-shirt; there was an intriguing gap at the top of her jeans. Once, when I looked over, I caught her sneaking a peek at me. Her eyes darted back behind the *Mirror*, but it was too late; I clocked the puzzled look on her face. There really was something dreadfully . . . *awkward* about this girl. Something needy, and quite possibly unhealthy. It occurred to me that perhaps she thought it was normal to sleep with tree stumps.

I said, 'So you came to interview Clyde . . . and became friends like that.'

'I used to listen to his show.'

Of course. 'You were a fan.'

She sniggered. 'I used to write to him. One day he invited me to visit the studios. It all sprang from there really.'

You were a groupie.

'Was he what you were expecting?' *A little cruel, perhaps.* 'People are never like their voices, are they?'

She didn't answer. Stared at me for a bit, then said, 'Are you really in trouble because of a woman?'

'No. Not really.'

'I didn't think you could be.' Her hand flew to her mouth. 'Not that I mean . . . that it couldn't happen, or anything.'

'It's actually a bit more complicated than that.'

She was staring at me, her lips parted, small brown eyes glittering. So I found myself telling the story. The one that started with an old schoolfriend who I hadn't seen for years. Someone I'd always admired, perhaps even hero-worshipped a little. How he'd hatched an idea for us all to grow rich together. Her mouth went slack and her breath slowed as I explained how we'd flown to Majorca to meet the sad widower and his Levantine banker. How eventually we'd been given the money. How it even passed through my bank account before vanishing . . . along with my schoolfriend. And then, how things turned nasty. How the pornographer had tied me up, put my head down the toilet and attacked me with a cricket bat. How this same chap had been waiting outside the radio station for me last night. How the police would like to ask me some questions too.

I didn't bother telling her about Squeaky and the Goddess and all that side of things.

'It's a mess,' I admitted.

'It is, isn't it?' she agreed. 'What are you going to do?'

'I don't know.'

'Have you thought about suicide?'

I laughed. 'Actually, I haven't.'

'You should talk to Clyde. He's a genius.'

Carrie and I passed an uneasy morning, drinking tea and reading the papers. To make conversation, I found amusing little items to read out aloud: the pet duck who stepped on a shotgun trigger and killed its owner in Canada (she didn't think it was funny). The reclusive old lady who left ten million quid to the local cats' home in her will (she wouldn't get drawn in). The monkey in the language research laboratory in Tucson, Arizona, which had just completed its first novel.

'What's it called?' she asked.

'It doesn't say. *The Apes of Wrath*?' I suggested.

A slow smile spread itself across her face. 'It's a joke, right?' She giggled uncertainly, and again I had an appalling urge to ask her if she'd like to come upstairs and do the crossword with me.

Around lunchtime, Clyde returned.

'What me and Miss Phillips generally like to do at this stage on a Saturday is grab a bite and take in a movie. That suit, Nicholas?'

I found I couldn't raise a single objection. So it was that Clyde drove us off to a nearby shopping complex, where we consumed an indecent amount of barbecued chicken wings before hitting the multiscreen's confectionery concession. There, Clyde, apparently working to a pre-ordained plan, methodically filled a large popcorn container with a terrifying selection of jelly beans, allsorts, fruity chews, chocolate bonbons, toffees, sherbet flying saucers, peppermint humbugs, liquorice whorls, even some of those clingy rubbery things that looked like lizards; even some popcorn.

He parked himself between Carrie and me, and urged us to dig into the sweetie barrel.

'I love the movies,' he said, squeezing her leg, popping a sugared almond and sending me a wink.

We sucked, we crunched, we chewed our way through the new Woody Allen – plus whatever you call it when you have to prise a sticky mass off the back of your teeth with your tongue. When it finished, Clyde suggested we 'repo a bit sharpish' to Screen Eight, where the new Nicole Kidman vehicle was about to start.

'I love lovely Nicole,' he offered when we had settled into our new seats. 'I love her tiny little teeth. She craps over most other actresses.'

Carrie giggled. At Clyde's prompting, I reached for the last sweetie . . . except it turned out to be his thumb wrapped in silver paper, poking through a hole in the bottom of the container.

'The old ones are the old ones,' he gurgled as the certificate proclaimed that the following presentation had been checked and it was okay for us to watch it.

It felt rather like going to the cinema with daddy and a kid sister.

I felt oddly happy.

9

When we returned, Clyde declared that tonight he was going to do 'one of my famous barbecues'. Carrie clapped her hands in delight.

'It's a warm evening, we can sit on the deck, drink wine, and choke in animal fat fumes. How does that grab you, old love?'

I confirmed that I could not think of anything I'd rather do. Clyde revealed that a friend of his would be joining us – 'an old mucker from way back. You're sure to like him. He's a PLU.'

'PLU?'

'People Like Us.'

Clyde disappeared upstairs for a bit, Carrie following a few minutes later. I took the opportunity to call the flat. One message from a faintly hysterical-sounding Squeaky.

'Nicholas. The police were here this morning, asking questions about you. A large unpleasant one who said he was from Scotland Yard, and a smaller unpleasant one; but they could have been anyone really. Rollie had to ask them to produce their warrant cards. It was terribly embarrassing; they got it into their thick skulls that you were Rollie. Or rather that Rollie was you. They were actually quite off with him until he could prove who he was. It seems rather funny now, but it wasn't at the time. Rollie got very annoyed. Was calling you all sorts of names. Anyhow, I told them I didn't know where you were. Oops, got to go. Rollie's parked in a residents' bay and we're going to look at some curtains for his new flat. Bye, Nicholas. Look after yourself.'

Well that was it, wasn't it? Plainly Rollie had stayed the night after the Brian bloody Wilson concert. And now they were picking fucking curtains together. I helped myself to a grappa from Clyde's supply and dropped into an armchair to consider my position. Weighed up, and looked at from all angles and what-have-you, it seemed to boil down to the fact that I'd been deserted by everyone except the talking tree stump and his moronic para-mour. I swallowed another grappa and allowed a few minutes to pass until I found I didn't care quite so much.

After a while, the lovers returned. Clyde started fussing with charcoal and firelighters. Carrie – was it my imagination or was there a *mark* on her neck? – Carrie avoided my eye and chopped vegetables.

'Nicholas,' called the great man, 'if you could attend to the sounds and crack open some of the old vino collapso, it would be greatly appreciated.'

I fired up an Elvis CD, pulled the cork on a Libyan merlot, and dispensed brimming glassfuls to all the interested parties. Clyde clinked mine roughly, the dark red fluid spilling into the hairs on his wrist.

'Mud in your gusset, mate.'

'Mud,' I responded.

I took myself on a tour of the grounds. It was the completely bog-standard carpet of ill-kempt lawn, cat shit in the flowerbeds, a few sad rose bushes, plus a tree of some variety. In the tangle of undergrowth at the end, I noticed a few beer tins peppered with air-gun pellet holes. I turned and looked back on the scene of suburban domesticity. Through the kitchen window, a young woman could be viewed performing slicing actions. On the patio, a short fat man wearing an apron was consigning huge quanti-ties of chops, steaks, cutlets, chicken portions, sausages and who knew what else to the leaping flames of the barbecue.

I felt a sharp pang of longing. For the Happy Homestead, I guess.

'How do you like your meat?' asked Clyde when I wandered over to join him. 'I like it burnt to all fuckery on the outside, still twitching in the middle.'

'I'm more of a medium to well-done man myself,' I confided.

'Takes all sorts, and that's a fact, old love.'

Clyde's 'mucker from way back', when he turned up, was a reedy old boy with liver spots and sparse grey hair.

'Nicholas, this is Bob Holman. Bob and I were pups together in Canberra; that was when radio was radio. Bob was a leg end too, weren't you, Bob?'

Bob smiled sadly. Magnified brown eyes flickered behind huge lenses. 'Been out of the game a while now,' he said in a thin voice.

'Bob was king of the live ad. The jocks voiced the ads live in those days; Bob could do three hundred and eighty words a minute, each one clear as a bloody bell.'

'That's a lot, is it, three hundred and eighty words in a minute?' I enquired.

'Your average newsreader does a hundred and eighty,' said Clyde. 'Bob could give you two hundred extra words a minute. He was king of the live ads. What are you drinking, Bob?'

The king of the live ads fluttered his hand and requested 'Just a juice, thanks, Clyde.'

'Juice, bollocks. Give the man a proper drink.'

The sun went down. Bob, Carrie and I sat around the white plastic garden table as Clyde poked, raddled and banged his barbecue, producing dramatic showers of sparks and sudden alarming swags of smoke.

'I hope you're hungry, fellas,' he shouted, 'because we got a ton of tucker to get through here.'

Bob looked like he might have taken his last meal through a tube. With a bit of a shock, I realised he must be Clyde's age. Or more to the point, that Clyde must be his.

Our host set a platter of carbonised animal flesh before us.

'It's every man for himself round here, and that includes the women.'

Carrie had a surprisingly robust appetite, putting away several chops and sausages without much difficulty. The king of the live ads did what he could with a chicken leg, while the chef ploughed his way through a mound of dead beast portions, pausing only to apply more sauces and relishes and to re-fill the ever-emptying glass.

In the shadows beyond the patio lights, a cat stalked slowly across the grass. With surprising agility, Clyde hurled a chicken bone at it. 'Choke on that, you little fucker!' he boomed into the darkness.

10

'What now? Cheese? Chocs? More meat for anyone?'

The moon had risen. Several more empty bottles of Libyan merlot had made their way into the recycling box.

'If I eat any more meat, I may grow hoofs,' I tossed in weakly.

'Bob, show Nicholas your new toy. And top me up, would you, sweetheart.'

Bob's new toy was a state-of-the-art miniature video camera. Small and sexy, it was gun-metal grey, the size of a fag packet.

'Bought it in Honkers on the way over to see me brother,' he croaked. 'I've been using it to record him at the hozzie. Just lying there, talking and stuff. It's for the grand-kids really. He talked a lot about our childhood. Mum and Dad. Our sister. Lot of things *I'd* forgotten . . .'

Bob trailed off and blinked at the powerful little gadget resting in his trembling fingers.

'You got any brothers or sisters, Nicholas?' Clyde asked.

'Actually, no. No, I haven't.'

'Nor me. They broke the mould before they made me.'

Bob emitted a feeble chuckle (heard it before, I expect).

'Miss Phillips was telling me about this mucker of yours, Jay Somebody. Dropped you in the cack big-time.'

I laughed. 'You could say that, yeah.'

'Care to talk about it?'

'What's to talk about? Jay was an old pal of mine. To cut a

long story short, he seems to have disappeared with all the money.'

Clyde shook his head. 'There were a few of those back in Adelaide in the sixties. Remember, Bob? They found one of the guys out on Tonga. He'd bought himself a fucking harem.'

'Tropical fever did him in the end,' muttered Bob. 'Died happy, though, I expect.' Bob didn't sound like he meant it.

'Want to tell your uncle Clyde the whole tale, Nicholas? It's too early to break up the party, and it's all cack on the telly.'

Heavy sigh. 'I don't know . . .'

'Come on, mate. You know what they say. A friend in need is a pain in the arse.'

'Honestly, I wouldn't know where to start . . .'

'Cough it up, old chum. Start at the beginning. It's often easier that way.'

'The beginning. Is that the reunion? Or when Jay Bryant joined our class?'

'Your call, mate, I'm all ears. Not *only* ears, obviously. But you get my drift.'

For the second time in a day, I told the story. For some reason, on this occasion, I began it in our classroom on the first day of term.

'We have a new boy joining us this year, Jay Bryant,' said Mr Debenham. 'I hope you're all going to make him feel welcome . . .'

11

After I finished, there was a long silence. From somewhere nearby, an owl called (who would have thought there'd be owls in Bounds Green?). Clyde sighed a heavy sigh. Bob, who I could no longer see beyond the glare of the patio lights, may have fallen asleep, I figured. Carrie had taken herself off indoors some time ago.

'You trusted this guy, huh?'

'Completely.'

'You admired him. Put him on a pedestal.'

'I guess I did.'

'Maybe you even loved him a little bit . . .'

'Did I? Perhaps I did.'

'I sense a little love in there, Nicholas. Don't get me wrong . . .'

'No.'

'. . . I'm talking about the right sort of love. Nothing unsavoury.'

'No.'

'It can be natural for a man to feel love for another man. The love between a father and son. Between two brothers. Between a man and his dog, even. A male dog, we're talking here.'

'Yes.'

'Perhaps Jay Bryant was the bigger, older, handsome brother you never had.'

'Perhaps he was.'

'But he betrayed you.'

I had to clear my throat to reply. 'Seems like it.'

'Seems he intended to all along.'

'I don't know . . .'

'He used the bug-eyed woman to draw you in.'

'Caroline? I'm really not sure . . .'

'He used his cellmate, the viscount, to find the money man.'

'Hmm.'

'He used all of you.'

'You *could* construe the facts that way.'

'It was a scam, all the way down the line.'

'We were serious . . .'

'None of you knew anything about remote data processing.'

'We would have found out.'

'You said yourself the proposal document was – what was your phrase? – "bollocks and flim-flam". I quote.'

'One needed to sound confident. Upbeat . . .'

'It was a cute idea, one that would find backers. But there was never any intention of following it through.'

'Jay was very enthusiastic . . .'

'It was a lie, Nicholas.'

'Perhaps.'

'It was all a lie.'

I fell silent.

'What was in it for you?' he asked.

'For me? The money, I guess. A crack at some serious money.'

'How about spreading wealth from the first world to the third?'

'And that too, obviously.'

'The money went through your bank account.'

'It did.'

'Unfortunate.'

'Sorry?'

'It won't look good.'

'No?'

'I'm not a criminal lawyer, but I'd say the money trail puts your fingers firmly in the tucker bag. In my estimation, you're in it up to your eyebrows, mate.'

'Thank you.'

There was another long silence. In a quiet voice Clyde said, 'I think you know what you have to do, Nicholas.'

'W-what?'

'Use your imagination. Do you want another session with the wank-mag man and his cricket bat? Or would you rather tell PC Plod all about it in a nice warm police station over a cup of tea?'

'Shit, Clyde.'

'I don't think you got an alternative. Not one that I can see.'

Heavy sigh.

Softly he asked, 'Are you going to come quietly, old love?'

Heavier sigh. The heaviest yet. 'I guess so.'

A pause. Suddenly Clyde barked, 'Officer! Your cue.'

The sound of glass doors sliding open. I looked round to see a uniformed policewoman step on to the patio. Except it couldn't have been a policewoman. Surely no proper WPC would ever wear such a short skirt on duty (or high heels, now I came to notice them). Nor, I imagined, did the dress code of the Metropolitan force allow a female constable's tunic to flap about unbuttoned, revealing an expanse of underwired cleavage. She strode up to my chair, planting her legs apart in the manner of some floor-show artiste.

It was Carrie.

'Cuff him, baby,' said Clyde.

'Excuse me,' I stuttered. 'Sorry, *what's* going on?'

Before I knew what was happening, Carrie had attached my

wrists to the arms of the white plastic garden chair. The hand-cuffs, I noticed, were covered in pink fur.

'Are those from a sex shop?' I enquired.

'And that,' said Clyde, 'concludes this pilot episode of *Cough It Up To Clyde*, a new factual confessional format from Clyde Folger Entertainment. Till the next time, amigos, happy trails.'

There was a long – and on my part, stunned – pause.

'And . . . *cut*. Did you get all that, Bob?'

'Spinning back to take a look, Clyde.'

'Good man.'

'Er, Clyde?'

'Yes, Nicholas?'

'Sorry. *What* is this?'

'Showbiz, old love. There are no people like show people. And you know why? Because they smile, mate. Even when they're in a turkey.'

NINE

One year later

1

I came to realise that my entire life fell apart in sixty-six days. A shockingly brief time for the architecture of one's existence to disintegrate; the duration, perhaps, in that chilling phrase, of 'a short illness'. Yet when I checked the dates in my diary – from the reunion at the Carpenters Arms to the first interview at the police station – sixty-six days was what it boiled down to.

It struck me as grotesque. That one moment you could have a job, a career, a girlfriend; then an old schoolfriend turns up with a big grin on his face; and the next thing, you're staring at the yellowed fingers of a police detective as they drag a biro across the pages of your witness statement. Then the trial. Then what followed . . .

But actually Jay Bryant was right. Being in prison really wasn't so terrible. Rather like the long-put-off visit to the dentist, the anticipation was much worse than the reality.

Frabbage Hill wasn't even officially classified as a prison. It was a Mature Offenders' Centre, an experimental new category the Home Office had thought up for those who were no longer – or never – considered to be a danger to society. The regime was so light-touch it was almost laughable. The screws didn't wear uniforms, they were polite and helpful for the most part; our rooms (impossible to call them cells) were not locked, and one pretty much had the freedom of the place morning, noon and night. I've stayed in four-star hotels with a more repressive atmosphere.

Nor was the food as bad as one dreaded; the head chef used to work in a posh Paris restaurant, and prided himself on what he and his team could produce on a limited budget. Regrettably, alcohol wasn't as readily available as on the outside, though you could get hold of every kind of drug. I became quite partial to a variety of home-grown weed that was cultivated on an allotment in the village, and 'cured' in the prison laundry.

My room – my cell – my peter, in the argot – commanded a pleasant if unexceptional view over fields to the Norman church tower at Icke. I had books – the book club was reading *The Lord of the Rings* when I joined – I had access to TV, radio, the internet, daily newspapers and periodicals, plus a fascinating new social circle who I would never have come into contact with in my previous existence. There were four former Members of Parliament, a dozen businessmen – some quite prominent – a chap who used to run a privatised railway company, a disgraced TV performer, and scores of ordinary career cons who'd been making their way through the prison system, Frabbage Hill being the last stop before release.

In fact, after the initial shock, disbelief, and disappointment had worn off, I came to think that perhaps a spell in jail might do me good. The work was not onerous – I quickly found a job editing the prison newsletter – I was fitter than I had ever been, and I slept better too. In the fullness of time, even sexual frustration ceased to be a problem (I shall get to that).

The only cloud on the horizon was my impending jam roll (sorry, parole). The thought of freedom, of going back to the wreckage of my old life, filled me with faint dread.

Chad Butterick and I used to chat about the radical change in our circumstances over tea in the recreation hall after rehearsals. The 'once much-loved family entertainer' (as they put it in accounts of his trial) was producing, directing and starring in the Frabbage Hall Christmas panto, and I'd been helping him with a few of the gags. (He pleaded guilty to reduced charges in the end and copped a three.)

'This is *so* much nicer than doing telly,' he said, the famous cheeky-chappie visage lit by a bright smile.

'One meets a more interesting class of people.'

'Oh, infinitely. And there simply isn't the fear and loathing. You don't spend your entire day worrying that they're going to cancel your show, or replace you with Chris Tarrant. It's been a revelation. By the way, are you sure you don't want a part in this thing?'

'I'm happy to help with the script, Chad.'

'Because my Buttons is still a bit iffy. If his EDR gets brought forward, we could be in the clag.'

I was aware of Chad's concern regarding this performer's Earliest Date of Release.

'You don't miss telly a tiny bit?'

'The girls, of course. But I've got my magazines . . .'

'No. Stop. Too much information, Chad. Please don't tell me.'

2

Funnily enough, Chad Butterick's last TV appearance – after the revelations in the paper and before his arrest – was on *Cough It Up To Clyde*.

Twelve months after making the pilot episode in his back garden, Clyde Folger's confessional programme had become a modest ratings success for the television channel that commissioned a series. Within the prison system, however, the show was massive, large audiences forming in communal TV rooms for his weekly one-on-one confrontations with those he called 'the fallen', individuals, as he put it, 'who need to accept their guilt and move on'. Of course it was marvellous what they could do with lighting and camera angles and so forth. Clyde was only ever shown from the solar plexus up, and then half in darkness, rather like Marlon Brando in *Apocalypse Now*, his face looming out of the shadows, confronting his subjects with their innermost demons. Among the people he'd interviewed were a self-destructed footballer, an imploded tycoon, a former gangland villain (famously making Tony 'Blowlamp' Molloy weep like an infant when he recalled what he did to Sammy 'Sherbet' Lemons in an upstairs room at the Fiddler's Apprentice in 1969) and a disc jockey who fell from grace after his 'my cocaine hell' story in a Sunday newspaper was exposed as career-development bullshit (the guy put nothing stronger up his nose than a Vicks inhaler).

I liked to think I had played some small part in Clyde's revival. Indeed, when I first washed up at Frabbage Hill, he sent me a splendid hamper of cheeses and cooked meats from Fortnum and Mason. The note attached read: 'With fondest regards, some posh tucker courtesy of your old mucker from way back. Enjoy, old love.'

As well as finding favour in the criminal fraternity, I read in one of the media trade mags that *Cough It Up To Clyde* performed particularly well in the key 25–34 demographic and that 'Carrie with the Cuffs' who appeared at the 'acceptance of guilt' moment each week had become a gay icon. Apparently the only episode they had to scrap – because the guest failed to recognise he'd done anything wrong – was the one with Jeffrey Archer.

The 'taster' tape that Bob, the king of the live ads, shot in Clyde's back garden went down well enough with the TV channel, but was eventually ruled inadmissible by the judge at my trial, after a half-day of legal submissions. It was my counsel's one triumph.

My trial.

What can I say about my trial?

Somehow, during those four days in court, the question that troubled me most – more almost than whether or not I was going to be found guilty – was the one that Clyde had raised. Was it all a lie from the start? Did Jay know at the outset he was going to make off with the loot? I worried away at this problem endlessly, but essentially my view didn't change. I didn't really believe he *set out* to rip us off. I think most probably he was making it up, as he always did, as he went along. Of course in the continuing absence of the . . . I nearly typed, of the *boy* himself . . . we can never know for sure.

It did cross my mind that he could be dead. Murdered in an alley behind a dodgy club in Accra, his body never discovered. But then both the defence and the Crown agreed that there was no evidence that Jay had ever visited Ghana. And there was the enduring mystery of what had happened to the money, of which, once it was cleared out of that account in the Channel Islands, no trace was ever found.

My own feeling was that it would be out of character for Jay to be dead. I was reasonably certain it didn't figure in his plans. I was forced therefore to speculate about exactly when – and why – it occurred to him to cut loose with the spoils. And about the fifty thousand that remained in my bank account. Was it designed to forestall my suspicions? Or was it a token of his appreciation? Or of his guilt, perhaps?

And what about my own guilt? There was the question of technical guilt – guilt in the eyes of the law, that the jury would shortly come to a verdict upon – but also moral guilt. Here I felt on shakier ground. I felt like I had been caught up in what the French call a *coup de foudre* – a thunderbolt – the fuse lit when Jay Bryant came sauntering into the upstairs room at the Carpenters Arms, exploding a few days later when he brought Caroline round to dinner.

In my head, as I tried to pick it all apart, the commercial 'crimes' were intertwined with the Caroline 'crimes', if I may put it that way. It was true that in my enthusiasm to become an international business type I had closed my eyes to exaggerations in Wanker's brochure; had ignored false representations that were made about our skills and backgrounds. But equally crushingly, it seemed to me, I had allowed my interest in – okay, obsession with – Caroline to overpower my sense of self-preservation.

Clyde's words in his back garden in Bounds Green came back to me repeatedly.

'*He used the bug-eyed woman to draw you in.*'

Did he?

Another quote ran round my brain. What Caroline had said to me in the ruins of the old Arab fortress.

'*I always had a funny feeling about you.*'

Did she? Did she really?

Or was it a con? A con, if not from the get-go, then at least from some point in the proceedings.

She, of course, was mute on the subject.

It turned out that ten days after she'd flown to Miami in seat 2B, Caroline had returned to London. She'd then immediately left for Paris, where, according to her statement, she passed a month in a friend's apartment, 'mooching and scribbling'. Jay had asked her to go with him to the States, 'to help put another piece of the Ghana jigsaw in place. On the customer side,' he'd told her. Except that when they got there, all he seemed to want to do was smoke grass and go shark-fishing. 'Fishing bores me profoundly,' she told the police. 'Even from power boats.' Frustrated by his evasions and apparent lack of serious application – and the fishing thing – she flew to Europe to 'await developments'.

As there was no evidence that Caroline had received any payment from what was continuously (and to my mind annoyingly) described in court as 'the plot', and despite the 'embroidery' in her CV in the scheme's business plan ('Exhibit A' as it became known), the Crown Prosecution Service decided that a conviction against her was unlikely to be obtained.

Similarly, no case was brought against Wanker, his lawyers maintaining that far from being one of the perpetrators of the fraud, in fact he was a *victim* of the piece. For a time, it depressed me that Wanker had walked away with the best part of my fifty grand. My initial instinct was to incriminate the cadaverous pornographer with an account of the violent extortion he had carried out in his downstairs bathroom and later with his son's cricket bat. In the end, however, my solicitor felt that without witnesses, such evidence would only come across to the jury as 'thieves falling out amongst themselves' and advised against.

I mused ruefully that £46,000 was perhaps an appropriate sum in compensation for the years of abuse that – if I hadn't actually been responsible for – I had at least been party to.

Anyhow, it was clear that a view had been taken, in the circles that these views are taken in, that of the three of us – Caroline, Wanker and self – I was the one, in Clyde Folger's memorable metaphor, whose fingers were most deeply in the tucker bag.

When the trial began, neither legal team thought it would be fruitful to call the not-viscount as a witness, the potential alienation of the jurors being taken to be the critical factor. 'They'll think he's a posh prat,' said my solicitor. It was hard to dissent.

Similarly Wanker did not appear. I fancy the Crown may have had a hard time deciding whether he should be called as a prosecution witness – or thrown in chains and put in the dock alongside me.

So Caroline was the star. The court reporters enjoyed her long, deliberate silences with full side-orders of lip-sliding and eyeball action. In theory she was on the defence roster, there to lend strength to the notion that Jay Bryant was an essentially untrustworthy personage who could easily have hoodwinked his partners in commerce. Somehow, however, it didn't quite play out like that. When questioned, she professed a long-standing and fundamental indifference to his motives, born of once having had a relationship with – as the *Standard* put it – the 'shadowy and charismatic missing alleged fraudster at the centre of the case'.

'Would you say he let you down?' asked my genius of a defence counsel.

Caroline left a pause you could have driven a bus through. Two buses. Followed by a third, even (they do all arrive at once).

'Nothing's ever quite that simple, is it?' she replied.

And in cross-examination, when the Crown's brief asked her silkily, 'Miss Stamp, is it possible that you are still a little in love with Mr Bryant?' she allowed a full thirty-five seconds to pass (I timed it on my watch) before admitting, 'Mr Cudworth, the human heart has several chambers, and the valves between them are rarely a perfect seal.'

Even the judge wrote that one down.

3

One of my earliest visitors in prison was Deano. His eyes roamed about the visitors' room, taking in the tacked-up government posters, mostly on embarrassing public health themes.

'I hope you haven't come to gloat,' I said.

His expression seemed to contain affection and disappointment in roughly equal measure.

'I want you to know that you and Anita are still invited round for dinner. When you get out of here,' he added a little thoughtlessly.

'Thanks. Sorry. It was good of you to come. Actually, Deano. About Anita. That's all finished, actually.'

Deano pulled a face. 'We liked her. We thought you and she might have . . .' He trailed off.

'Yeah. It's true. We might have. I seemed to lack the necessary will, however.'

Deano shrugged. He looked down the long line of tables across which my fellow inmates were receiving their visitations from the outside world.

'Are they treating you okay here?' he asked. 'It's not exactly Alcatraz, is it?'

I was about to do the speech about what a jolly place Frabbage Hill was, full of marvellous characters and intriguing lunch choices. But instead I said to my old schoolfriend, 'It seems you were right. About Jay, I mean. About him being a bullshitter and everything.'

'You were incautious,' he replied.

'Being a scientist, you had a greater respect for facts, we decided.'

'So-called scientific facts are far more bendy than people would imagine.'

It didn't feel like the moment to open a discussion about epistemology and the nature of Truth.

'You wouldn't cheat on the cross-country runs,' I reminded him.

Deano crimped his mouth and gazed up at a skylight. A streak of bird shit dappled the frosted glass. 'I guess I just wanted to test my limits.'

I smiled at the scientist.

'I was an idiot, wasn't I?'

'Incautious, as I say . . .'

'I was a bloody fool, Deano.'

His eyebrows parked themselves at the setting marked YES YOU WERE ACTUALLY.

'He made a fool of me.' Heavy sigh. 'So did she.'

'The girl.' The way he said it made her sound like . . . like just some girl.

'And Wanker. Honestly, that fucking *wanker*, Wanker.'

Deano laughed. I hadn't felt able to tell anyone – beyond my legal adviser, and then only in the most general of terms – about the humiliation I had suffered at the hands of the former masturbator. Now, for some reason, I spilled the whole story. The German cistern, the cricket bat – my rib still twinged when I came to the bit about the cricket bat – the forty-six thousand quid through the letterbox, everything. Deano was suitably amazed.

'Jesus Christ,' he said.

'What do you think I should do? About the cash, I mean.'

Deano looked at me squarely. Weighing things up, deliberating, and all that other empirical scientific stuff. 'If you want my opinion, Nicholas,' he said finally, 'I should forget about it. I should make sure you never set eyes on . . . well, I guess we can't call him Wanker any more.'

'No. I expect you're right.' It was disappointing, but it felt like sage advice. 'How about cunt-face? We could call him that.'

Deano laughed. 'Wanker did suit him.'

'Deano. Listen. You're smart. What do you think? That evening at my flat, when Jay told us about the data processing thing for the first time. Do you think he knew *then* that it was all going to be a con? Or did it happen somewhere along the line; did it just suddenly occur to him to take the money and run? I suppose what I'm asking is, was he taking us – taking me – for a mug all along?'

Deano did that thing with his lips and the contours of his cheeks to denote thinking about it.

'Impossible to say, isn't it,' he pronounced eventually. 'But absence of evidence isn't evidence of absence, as we say in scientific circles.'

We sat in silence for a while.

'I should like to come over for dinner, actually. When I – when I get the chance.'

'We'd be pleased to have you.'

'Won't be with Squeaky. Anita, I mean.'

'Bring whoever you like. Come by yourself.'

'Be nice to meet Megan properly. And your kids.'

'They'll probably be in bed.'

'Of course.'

'Though our boy would be very excited to see you. He's obsessed with robbers and jails and policemen at the moment.'

'You could tell him I was a reformed master criminal.'

'He'd love that.'

'Now a useful member of society.'

'Perfect.'

'Battling wrongdoing wherever it shows its wicked face.'

'He's only six, but he's not a fool, Nicholas.'

For some reason, I suddenly felt a little emotional.

'It won't be for a while, of course,' I said.

'Of course.'

'He'll probably be into . . . *girls* or something by then.'

'I doubt it.'

'But I could come and see you all.'

'Definitely.'

A minute or two passed while I blew my nose and stared at the bird shit on the skylight and generally tried to avoid meeting my visitor's gaze on account of the tears that seemed to be rolling down my face.

'Colindale,' I said eventually.

'You remembered.'

'On the Northern Line.'

'Indeed.'

'That's nowhere near Mill Hill, is it?'

'Different branch.'

'Thank fuck for that.'

4

Perhaps the most annoying thing about the trial – more so than its conclusion and the sentence – was the way Squeaky stood by me throughout. Every morning, she'd be there in the public gallery, light glinting off her spectacles, making a big show of smiling and Being There For Me and generally enjoying the grim theatre of it all. I suppose I should have been grateful that I had at least one supporter in the wider world. Yet all I felt was embarrassed. As though she was my mother, who any minute might make me spit on a hankie and proceed to wipe the dirt off my face. I guess when you're feeling low and disgusted with yourself, you're going to take a dim view of anyone who's prepared to stick up for you.

It appeared that the growing *tendresse* with Rollie hadn't worked out in the end, despite everything they supposedly had in common. In particular, she discovered she didn't really like him 'in that way', which I took to be a reference to an ill-conceived attempt to poke his leathery old tongue down her throat.

On the day of the judge's summing-up, Squeaky wore her smartest business-lady suit and sat in the front row, twisting a hankie between her fingers. The beak – a truly ghastly old toad – told the jury he'd listened most carefully to the arguments of counsel (part of the job description, I should have thought). Of the witnesses, he'd been particularly struck by the testimony of

Miss Stamp, who'd given her evidence, he said, 'with great dignity, from a sticky place' – interesting choice of phrase, no? – 'pinioned between loyalty and fury towards an ex-lover'. However, 'regarding the defendant in this case', he glowered at me, 'I see no such moral torment. Only greed, opportunism and a flagrant disregard for the truth.'

He went on to remind everyone, in case they'd forgotten, of the four hundred and eighty-seven separate 'bald-faced lies, factual inaccuracies, misstatements, errors and wild guesses' that the Crown had identified in the proposal document that Jay and I had concocted. To employ Mr Cudworth's colourful phrase, 'This wasn't a business plan; nor does the expression "*flight* of fantasy" do it justice. This was nothing less than the full round-trip, with stopovers.' (Laughter.) The judge was also 'greatly persuaded' by the fact that all the money at issue passed through my bank account before it vanished, 'a version of events that no side in this case disputes'. When he got to the bit about how I'd gone on a 'reckless spending spree', commissioning expensive hand-made suits, giant TV sets and luxury furnishings, I noticed my barrister circling various items on a takeaway sandwich menu.

The jury took less than twenty minutes to deliver its verdict.

My brief, wiping a smear of mustard off his chops, argued that I'd been of previously blameless character, was not a danger to society, and a custodial sentence would be wholly inappropriate.

The judge took another view. 'Theft is a crime against the whole community,' he concluded, though he never showed his working-out in the margin.

5

Still, as I say, being in prison had much to recommend it. There were no heating bills, one didn't have to cook, and there were never any puzzling moments in the day where one couldn't decide what to do with oneself. To be honest, the most frustrating features of my confinement were the visits from the outside world. Indeed, if it wasn't for well-intentioned people turning up to remind me, it might have been possible to forget one was actually incarcerated.

Every fortnight, Squeaky set out on the long drive up, sometimes making a day of it with a side trip to a nearby National Trust property or garden centre. In the long, smoke-filled room where we received our guests, she got more than her fair share of attention from fellow inmates.

'That skinny bint your missus?' I was asked by a transferee from C-Cats (Category C institutions hold those, according to the useful Home Office guide to prison life, 'who cannot be trusted in open conditions but who would not have the ability or resources to make a determined escape attempt').

'Bit of a long story, actually,' I replied.

'I prefer more meat on 'em myself. Still, I wouldn't say no to a gobble if she were offering.'

Squeaky liked to bring me little gift packages. Nothing useful, of course, like drink, drugs or burn (local patois for tobacco). They usually contained soaps, bath gel, bars of posh chocolate, tins of preserved chestnuts, and once a muslin bag of pot-pourri ('to make your cell smell nice').

It was during one of these visits that she explained about Rollie going back to his wife.

'So you didn't . . . ?'

'No,' Squeaky replied quickly.

'And there isn't . . . ?'

'No, there isn't.' There was a long, telling pause. 'Well, actually . . . there is someone. A friend of a friend of Chloe's. He seems quite keen.'

'Good.'

I was surprised to discover that I was genuinely pleased for her. But Squeaky looked at me a little sourly.

'I don't know what I think of him yet,' she said.

'You mustn't keep coming to visit me, you know. It's miles . . .'

'I rather enjoy it, actually. It's nice to get out of town. There are some very sweet little villages round and about. And, you know,' she coloured slightly, 'it's nice to know that . . . that you're okay.'

'What are you worried about? That I'll be anally raped? This is the softest option in the entire penal system. If the regime here were any softer, they'd have to reclassify it as a health farm.'

Squeaky bristled slightly at the phrase (anally raped, not health farm).

'Do you ever hear from *her*?' she asked.

There was no doubt in my mind who she meant.

'I haven't seen her since her day in court,' I replied.

This was technically true. I hadn't seen her. But I did receive a postcard, several months after I began my sentence. It was from Belize; the photo showed a general view of Belize City.

'Dear Nicholas,' it read. 'Rain forest very beautiful, despite terrifying crabs that bite through Land Rover tyres. Been on jungle treks (saw tarantulas and wild boar), visited Mayan ruins, eaten strange food (roast iguana; quite plausible, actually). Scuba diving sublime. Swam with delightful shoal of little blue fish. They sucked our goggles. Thinking of you CX.'

I carried the card around on me for ages; I must have read it a hundred times. And then, remembering the trouble that Karen's postcard had brought me, I tore it into as many small pieces as I was able to.

Our goggles, it said.

They sucked *our* goggles.

In time, I came to accept that I would never fully solve the enigma of Jay and Caroline.

My best guess was this: they were two people – two lovers – who had made the painful discovery that they couldn't be together; but neither could they be apart for too long.

6

It was the *Frabbage Hill Leader* that now kept my literary pretensions under control. Frankly, it was a bit of a tired old rag before I was made editor; full of AA and NA meeting times and messages from the Governor, plus the odd poem from a reformed killer or repentant swindler. I quickly recruited a chief reporter; there was a chap at the book group called Lee, a bit of a rough diamond – he thought Frodo was 'a little toerag who needed a slap' – but he always seemed to know everything that was going on. I liked to think that with Lee's ear for news and my experience in the mid-market tabloid sector we turned the old *Leader* into required reading for inmate and screw alike.

One of my first innovations was to launch a lifestyle section called 'Bird' (rather nicely spare, don't you think?). We regularly reviewed prison meals – the chef welcomed it, he was an artist, after all – though the description of his *ragout d'agneau Angoulême* as 'brave, heroic even, but ultimately unconvincing' prompted a stinging Letter to the Editor in which he characterised our anonymous reviewer (a former art dealer who became . . . over-ambitious, shall we say) as a 'pompous, ignorant fool who I would cheerfully ban from my establishment, were it within my power'. Another popular feature was 'Peter of the Week'. Each issue we ran a picture spread of an inmate in his peter, a master shot together with smaller pictures detailing some of the *objects* and artworks he chose to surround himself with, plus details of where to get them and how much they cost.

The most popular feature in the *Leader* was compiled by Lee. 'Weather Notes' was a small box on an inside page purporting to contain the latest midday temperatures for various neighbourhoods and villages in the locality. The figures, however, bore no relation to actual Centigrades or Fahrenheits, nor indeed to the locations mentioned. As everyone knew, they referred instead to the market price of narcotics currently available within the prison system, Whixton standing for weed; Rothenworthy for resin; Eyn Bridge for ecstasy (you get the idea).

Lee was a more brilliant journalist than any I had ever met. On the Wednesday before press day, he took a couple of hours to stroll round the grounds, stopping to chat with his various mates, associates and contacts, and inevitably came back with enough material to fill the *Leader*'s news pages. He told me the stories; I translated them into journalese and banged them straight into the computer.

'Fuckin' doddle, this newspaper lark,' he remarked one morning as I was turning his account of Warden Hitchcock's secret battle with obsessive compulsive disorder into fifteen pars for the front-page splash.

'You have a gift for it,' I replied. 'Did you say he used to wash his hands until they *bled*? Is that possible?'

'That's what he said.'

'I guess if you really *scrubbed*.'

Lee put his feet up on the desk and lit another roll-up.

'The condition made his life a misery,' I continued, speaking as I typed, 'until he discovered an ancient Chinese herbal remedy.

'This week, the popular prison officer exclusively told . . . no, revealed, no . . . *confessed* to the *Frabbage Hill Leader* how "I wasted years of my life in meaningless repetitive behaviour."'

Lee blew a cloud of smoke over my keyboard. 'All you got to do is talk to people. Simple, innit?'

'Hardly anyone does, you know. Mostly, they make it all up.'

'You're having a laugh.'

'It's true, I promise you. What was that thing he said about his wife?'

'If it wasn't for his old lady, he'd have topped his-self long ago. Got quite teary about it, silly sod.'

'Known to all as "Hitch", the Frabbage Hill veteran wept . . . no, sobbed, as he told how "the love of a good woman" saved him from suicide . . .'

7

It came as a surprise to learn that there was an annual award for the best newspaper produced in one of Her Majesty's Prisons; and an even greater one when it was announced that we had won it. The Governor positively glowed at the news.

'This is recognition, Nicholas,' he told me over a cup of tea and a chocolate biscuit in his office. 'An affirmation of the sorts of things that I'm . . . that *we're* trying to do here.'

He glanced down at a file on his desk. 'I see you're already entitled to maximum privileges so there's nothing very much we can offer by way of a well done.'

Lee's words came into my head. 'See if you can talk the dozy cunt into giving us a piss-up.'

'Some sort of . . . public *ceremony* might go down well.'

The Governor eyed me with interest. 'Go on.'

'Well. Let's see. There could be speeches. Handshakes. The evening paper might send a photographer if it was a quiet news day. Weekends are best – papers are usually desperate for something to run on Mondays . . .'

So it was that on a bright Saturday afternoon in the autumn of the year, a marquee stood within the grounds of Frabbage Hill Mature Offenders' Centre. Under the canvas, selected inmates, specially invited guests and a small number of the general public mingled, made conversation and sipped from plastic beakers of warm wine. Members of the body that presented the award had travelled up from London for the occasion: the perspex obelisk that was in their annual gift stood on a side table for all to admire, its stylistic motif being a graphical intertwining of typewriter keys and cell bars. The Governor, who had taken the opportunity to invite various cronies from the liberal wing of the Prison Service, was especially gratified by the media presence the event had drawn. The evening paper's photographer had turned up as predicted; so too had a BBC regional radio chappie who was diligently roaming the tent in huge headphones in search of people to interview. I heard the Governor tell him, 'Naturally one is proud when one's whole approach to the penal process has been honoured in this way . . .'

A pile of the current issue of the *Frabbage Hill Leader* sat on a chair by the entrance flap. The masthead had been amended to include the banner: PRISON NEWSPAPER OF THE YEAR.

'Are you having a nice time?' I asked Squeaky. 'Who have you been talking to?'

'That beastly man with the narrow face just said the most appalling thing to me.'

'Lee? He's the chief reporter. What?'

Squeaky's fingers tightened on her plastic cup. 'He asked if I liked it . . . doggy-fashion.'

I couldn't help it. I sniggered.

'It's not funny, Nicholas.' But I could see she was trying not to smile.

'What did you tell him?'

'Oh, *please*.'

'How's Hugo?' I enquired after a bit.

'Fine. He should be here any minute.'

I was looking forward to meeting the new man in Squeaky's life.

'Rollie taking it well?'

'I think he might be having a mid-life crisis. He's been

turning up to work in those terrible trousers with pockets at the knees . . .'

'Combats.'

'And he's been pestering me to see him again.'

'I thought he'd gone back to Mrs Rollie.'

'I think he's obsessed.'

'Silly old fool. It's not as if you actually slept with him . . .'

There was a long pause. Squeaky suddenly became very interested in one of her fingernails.

'I thought you didn't. I thought you said—'

'I never said I didn't. I did. We did.'

'How many times?'

'Nicholas . . .'

'I'm curious.'

'Hardly at all. Not many times.'

'I thought you said you didn't like him *that way*. How many times is not many?'

Squeaky looked at me blankly. 'Eight, nine?'

'*Eight* or *nine*? Jesus, what would have happened if you'd actually *liked* the fat fucker?'

'It was all a stupid mistake. He isn't fat.'

'If I may ask . . . what took you so long to find out you didn't like him *that way*?'

'I don't see how it would help.'

'Indulge me. It's my special day.'

Squeaky dealt me what I'd call an ironic look. A new one in her repertoire.

'Are you making a speech?' she asked.

'Please. Was he pervy? Did he like you to dress up? Or talk dirty? What *was* it?'

There was a long pause. 'Actually,' she said, 'if you really want to know, he was uncomfortably large. There. Happy now?'

* * *

Uncomfortably large. The phrase rang through my head like a mantra. It became hard to concentrate on anything else.

'Bloody decent of you to come, Guy,' I told the not-viscount.

'Not at all. Prison only holds happy memories for me. Companionship, larks and so forth. This plonk is a bit rough, wouldn't you say?'

Oddly, it was something of a treat to see the bird-faced faux-aristocrat again. He was in posh country casual; tweedy jacket, lemon cords, and a pair of sublimely expensive-looking oxblood brogues.

'How's Teddy?' I asked.

'Happy as can be,' he replied with a twinkle. 'He's living in the oldest, dampest house in Machynlleth. He told me on the telephone the other day that it hadn't stopped raining for a fortnight. Could barely keep the joy out of his voice.'

'I feel ghastly about what happened to his money, Guy.'

'Oh I shouldn't, overly. He's been terribly sweet to me about it. There's plenty more, one gathers.'

'Jay rather took us for a ride, apparently.'

'Did he? I suppose he did,' reflected the not-v, wistfully.

'You haven't heard from him?'

'There was a postcard.'

'Belize?'

'That's the spot. Something about giant crabs.'

'He'll have moved on by now, won't he?'

'Yes, a restless spirit. But a fine fellow to share a cell with.'

'You're not incredibly pissed off at him?'

'Good Lord, no. Why? These things happen all the time, surely.'

'Do they?'

'Oh, I would have thought so.'

The tent was thronging nicely now. A tall, dark-haired woman with a striking face ducked as she came through the entrance flap. For some reason my stomach did a little swan-dive as she stood there for a moment, surveying the scene.

'Nicholas,' said Guy, 'I've brought you a little something. It's in my pocket.'

'Really?'

'We shall need to be discreet, surrounded by criminals as we are.'

When we had arranged ourselves suitably, the not-viscount palmed me a small paper packet and a rolled-up banknote.

'I'm most grateful.'

'Not at all. Congrats on the award and all that. I shall take a copy to Frabbage tomorrow. I'm driving over to visit the Abbey. According to Pevsner, the antependium is one of the finest in the county.'

Clyde Folger and Carrie were the undoubted celebrities of the occasion. The broadcaster and his muse were rapturously received on arrival, particularly by the MPs, who were clearly alive to the rehabilitative opportunities presented by an appearance on his TV show.

'We seem to have been travelling for days, old love. Jesus, the trains are shit in this country. Mud in your gusset.'

He crashed his plastic beaker against mine.

'I'm thrilled you could make it. Your show's a big hit here.'

'Hear that, honeybunny? My happiness is complete. What creature's piss am I drinking, by the way?'

I felt an unaccountable wave of warmth for the oddly proportioned confessor figure.

'Listen, amigo. Would you consider doing a slot on the old steam radio? We'll call it "Nick from the Nick".'

'Er. I'm not sure the rules actually allow that one, Clyde . . .'

'Just pulling your todger, old love. Did you know Miss Phillips is a gay icon?' The toadstool's paramour affected an awkward smile. 'It's a chains thing, apparently.'

The pair went off to shake hands and pose for photographs.

*   *   *

I marched up to the woman with the dark hair and the striking face.

'You look awfully familiar,' I told her. 'Are you Italian?'

For two reasons, this ranked as more or less the stupidest thing I have ever said: firstly, I didn't know any Italians. And secondly, even as the words tumbled from my lips, I realised who she was.

It was Karen.

The Girl With The Biggest Nose In The World.

Except that this nose – prominent, certainly; even large, you might say; adventurously so, some might claim – this nose seemed all of a piece with the face in which it sat.

'Oh my God.'

'Yes, Nicholas.'

'It's *you*.'

'Clever boy.'

'Jesus Christ. What are you doing here? I mean, it's wonderful to see you and everything, but. But. But.'

My brain swam. This was not the stalky, gawky giant-beak-on-legs of distant memory, but an altogether more glamorous creature; as I say, almost Italianate in looks. Powerful dark eyes shone either side of the – yes, there was no getting round it, it was a big nose all right; but one now in keeping with the rest of the topography. Her figure too had mellowed; where once there were bony extrusions, now curves held sway. And instead of the student rags she always wore – well, I'm not a fashion writer, but there seemed to be a sexy, stylish glamour about her current get-up; a whiff of posh perfume too, as opposed to chip fat and the lingering odour of Dreft. I realised with a mixture of regret and excitement that I very much wanted her.

'There was an advert for the award ceremony in the local paper,' she explained. 'I hope you don't mind me turning up like this. Actually, I'll go if you prefer. You seem a bit shocked.'

'No. Not at all. You look so . . . so *different*.'

'You've put on some weight yourself. Less hair than I remember . . .'

My fingers reflexively stroked the thinning thatch-work.

'I shouldn't worry about that,' she said, with a bit of a wicked expression. 'Apparently Jack Nicholson . . .'

'Yeah, yeah. Jack Nicholson. All the women he still gets at his age.'

'I read all about what happened,' she said.

'The court case.'

'I was rather thrilled to know someone who'd gone to prison. I've lost count of the number of people I told: *You know that bloke who stole all that stolen money? I went out with him at university*.'

'I made the most awful balls of things, Karen.'

'You did rather.'

'The phrase *five-star, twenty-four-carat cock-up* wouldn't be over-egging the pudding.'

'Your old schoolfriend really dropped you in it.'

'Big-time.'

'Probably not such a great idea to revisit one's . . . well, you're still young, so I can't say *youth*.'

'One's past.'

'There's usually a good reason why people lose touch.'

'People change, move on, sort of thing.'

'They grow up. Grow apart.'

'I'm glad we've met up again, though.'

'Oh?' Karen took the weight off her left leg, and splayed an ankle at a playful angle. As she raised a plastic beaker of warm chardonnay to her lips, I became aware of the delicate silver chain that lay across the blue veins in her wrist.

'What I mean is. If we hadn't. If I hadn't. Found that post-card, I mean. Attempted to revisit. Well . . .'

Wry amusement lay behind her striking dark eyes. 'Yes?'

'Well, we'd never have met like this, would we?'

'At your party. In prison.'

'No. I mean, yes.'

'Who's that oily-looking bloke with all the chins?'

'He used to be an MP.'

'I knew I'd seen him before. He was asking me about my work.'

'Ah.'

'Which is more than you seem to have done, by the way.'

'Sorry, Karen. What sort of work are you in?'

'If you really want to know, I'm Britain's – no, why be modest? – I'm Europe's leading authority on Britain's only fish-eating bat.'

There was a long pause during which she smiled at me pleasantly and I tried to think of something sensible to say.

'There's a research station at Whixton,' she added, when I still hadn't come up with anything after a bit.

No. Still nothing.

'We tag them. Follow their flight patterns. Feeding habits.'

Finally I managed, 'Where do they get the fish from, then?'

She looked at me like I was stupid or something. 'From rivers. Where fish are generally found.'

'There must be quite a lot to it,' I stuttered. 'Once you start delving.'

She gave me a bit of a look.

'So what else?' I enquired. 'What else about you, apart from the bats?'

She paused. There was something about the angle of her head – and by extension her nose – with respect to the vertical that suggested a playfulness. Maybe even a flirtatiousness. Her ankle, pivoting about on its heel, only underscored the idea.

'What would you like to know?' she asked.

I came right out with it. 'Are you married at all? Or . . . ?'

The beak tilted another two degrees off true. 'Or what?'

'Or . . . or seeing anyone special?'

I tried to keep it light, but I'm afraid my voice choked on the word *special*, and I was forced to clear my throat noisily.

'No. No to both, actually.'

'Excellent.'

'Sorry?'

'No. I don't mean it like that. What I mean is. I don't mean excellent that there isn't. What I. Oh fuck it, Karen. I *do* mean excellent.'

A small furrow appeared in the roof space above the beak.

'Actually, I was wondering whether you might be free for dinner some time.'

'Dinner,' she said. As though she was unfamiliar with the concept.

'Dinner. You know. In a restaurant.'

'Will you be alone, Nicholas, or shackled to a warder?'

'When I'm out of here. In five months' time. When my jam . . . when my parole comes through.'

'That's the most romantic offer I've had in weeks.' She didn't look like she meant it, to be honest.

'I know it's rather a long time away, but. But if you didn't have any other plans . . .'

'I'm afraid I haven't brought my diary with me for next year.'

'Golly. It will be, won't it? Next year. Fuck. What a thought.'

She smiled. 'Perhaps I'll leave you my phone number. If you still want to, when the time comes . . .'

'Oh, I definitely will. Want to.'

The pivoting ankle came to rest. But now the other one began to swivel on its heel. Her nose — her head, I mean — it too returned to the vertical, but no sooner had it arrived than it set off again, in the other direction this time. It stopped at about twenty degrees (if I'd had a protractor, I could have done the measurements).

She said, 'I'm not the same person you used to know, you know.'

'I know,' I replied, deliberately repeating the word *know*.

'I'm not such a—'

'Doormat.'

'I was going to say sponge, actually.'

'I've changed as well,' I added quickly. 'I'm not even the same person I was a year ago.'

'You don't seem all *that* different, to be honest.'

'It'll be like two new people. When we have dinner, we'll be two new people meeting for the first time.' I was quite excited about the idea.

'Meeting *again* for the first time.'

'A fresh start. A new beginning. A second chance to make a first impression.' An opportunity to rewrite the ending, was what I meant.

'You've lost none of your old . . . enthusiasm.' Bullshit, was what she meant.

I appealed to her. 'You won't go and do anything silly, like find a boyfriend, will you?'

She smiled. 'We shall just have to wait and see, won't we?'

Squeaky seemed unduly pleased by the arrival of a tall young man with enviably floppy hair. She rushed over to the entrance flap where he was standing about looking a little lost, and – yes, fuck, they did – they kissed.

'This is Hugo,' she trilled, after she'd hauled him over to say hello.

'Hugo Dittisham,' he said politely, offering a paw.

'And you would be the friend of the friend of that silly cow Chloe. Who is now shagging Squeaky, I presume.'

I didn't say it. But it was what I was thinking.

'Hugo's been visiting his mother at Eyn Bridge,' cheeped my ex.

'It's about half an hour away,' Hugo informed me. 'I thought I'd take Anita over to see the Abbey at Frabbage while we're up here.'

'I should. I hear it has one of the finest antependiums in the county,' I told him. 'Or do I mean antependia?'

Squeaky and Hugo looked at me pityingly.

'Sorry,' I said. 'It's this wine. And stress. I have to make a speech in a minute, and those always fill me with dread. It's good to meet you, Hugo. Anita mentioned that you'd be coming.'

I wanted to like the bloke. And to be frank, he did seem to be perfectly likeable; handsome – better looking than me, certainly – with an easy manner, and a pleasant, open face.

'Hugo had to make a speech for his company last week. Didn't you, Hugo?'

Hugo rolled his eyes, which made me warm to him somewhat. 'We do fund management. I had to speak to a seminar of pension managers. Gripping stuff, as you might imagine.'

Squeaky practically *glowed* with happiness. She radiated it. You could have read a magazine in the luminance that was coming off her. I knew now with absolute certainty that these two had had sex, and I was simultaneously pleased and depressed about it.

When Hugo went off to find refreshments, I told her, 'I like him.'

'I'm glad you approve,' she replied, still glowing (I think it was the phrase *we do fund management* that so thrilled her).

'No, I do. Really,' I insisted.

'He's terribly keen, actually.'

'And he's not . . . ?' Uncomfortably large. 'He's not . . . too dull? About pensions and that.'

'Not at all. Rather interesting, in fact.'

'Could he be . . . The One, perhaps?'

Squeaky shivered with pleasure at the thought.

'Early days, of course,' I added.

'Far too soon,' she replied. But from the look on her face, I could tell that the prospect did not dismay her.

'Can I be a bridesmaid?'

Squeaky peered at me rather earnestly. Then burst into a carillon of silvery pealing.

'You are such a silly sausage.'

'Listen. Seriously. There's something I want to say to you.' I took a deep breath. 'Maybe it's true that you and I weren't meant to be together. You know, *together*-together. Till death us do part, and all that. But I'd really like it if we could stay friends. Because plenty don't. And because we *did* have fun while it lasted. And because. And because. And because I don't think I could quite bear it if we never saw one another again. There. That's it.'

Squeaky looked a bit flushed by the end of my little speech.

'I agree, Nicholas,' she said quietly. 'Actually . . .' She sighed. 'Actually, I gave up on you rather a long time ago. It was meeting Hugo that made me realise how useless you were.'

A silvery peal followed. A little muted, maybe, but it was an SP nonetheless.

'Thank you,' I replied.

'He absolutely adores me. As a matter of fact, he's said he'd marry me tomorrow if I'd agree.'

I resisted the urge to yell: *well what the fuck are you waiting for?*

'And?'

'I'm considering it.'

'Too early to know.'

'Actually, I've known him for well over a year now.'

'Ah.'

'We met at one of Chloe's supper parties.'

'You did.' When she was still officially going out with me, was what she meant.

'We didn't do anything. Anyway, he was still with Thomasina. That's his ex.'

'I see.'

'Though we did have a bit of a snog in the garden.' Her hand flew to her mouth and she let slip a giggle. 'We both sort of knew then.'

'Knew.'

'He told me later that that was when he knew. And I already knew.'

'That you fancied him.'

'There was Thomasina, of course.'

'And Rollie, presumably.'

She fanned the air in front of her face with her fingers. 'I don't know why I'm telling you all this, Nicholas.'

'It's the spirit of redemption and release. They're big on that in prisons. Anything else you'd like to confess to while you're about it?'

As we stared at one another under the canvas roof of the marquee, I realised it was one of those moments. The tall blonde Englishwoman had moved out of my life. Our road had bifurcated. This was clearly a good thing if we weren't meant to be – and we weren't – yet at the same time, it was undeniably sad. It was an ending. A movie reel began to play in my head, highlights of the Squeaky and Nicholas story: on holiday in Greece, Squeaky rising from the blue Aegean. In Soho, the early days of our courtship, the two of us wandering the streets, holding hands. In the flat, Squeaky leaning against the kitchen top with a wineglass in her hand, laughing. At the cinema, her head on my shoulder. In bed, the climactic shudder.

I took a pace forward and hugged her.

'Oh Squeaky,' I murmured into her neck.

She hugged back. 'Oh Fishface,' she sighed.

We clung to one another for a few moments. When we broke apart, she began tugging at her jacket and smoothing her skirt and such-like activities.

'Squeaky, did you say?'

'My little joke.'

'Like a rusty gate.'

'Not at all. Anyhow . . . *Fishface*?'

She giggled. 'It's our nickname for you, Chloe and me.'

'Fishface.'

'There were others, but that one sort of stuck. You're not upset, are you?'

'No. Not at all.'

'It's quite affectionate really.'

'I see.'

'Better than Shitface.'

'Undoubtedly.'

'There was another—'

'Don't go on.'

'Nicholas, who is that very striking woman over there? You were talking to her earlier.'

'Her? Oh, that's, er, Karen. Funnily enough, I used to know her about a million years ago.'

'Really?'

Karen had been surrounded by a quartet of corrupt MPs. They were clearly showing off; the beak was bobbing up and down respectfully.

'You think she's striking, then?'

'A corker.'

'You don't think that nose is . . . a bit on the over-developed side?'

'Not at all. Is she Italian?'

The Governor made a reasonably lengthy address; the man from the BBC was obliged to change the batteries in his tape recorder, I noticed. The award, he concluded, was his pleasure to accept on behalf of the entire Frabbage Hill community, which it had been his honour and privilege to mould and then to serve. Brandishing the slab of perspex, he said, 'I just want to thank each and every one of you. Humbly, yet with enormous pride. This, in a sense, is yours too.'

When he called upon 'the editor to say a few words', I found a curious calm within myself. I realised I didn't give a shit about the shameless way the Governor had hijacked our award. During the polite pattering of applause, my eye flicked round the marquee, alighting everywhere on smiling dyads in positions of postural symmetry. Here were Squeaky and Hugo shoulder to shoulder, right elbows cupped in left hands, glasses of wine raised to chest height, their heads drooping together like sleepy children. Clyde Folger had thrown an arm round Carrie's waist and she had followed suit, though 'waist' in the case of the spherical broadcaster was an entirely historical concept. Even Karen and the not-viscount had managed a sort of nose congruence, their twin conks sailing proudly aloft.

'Life is strange,' I heard myself saying. 'And I've got this funny feeling that landing up at Frabbage Hill could turn out to be the best thing that's ever happened to me.' I took a deep breath. 'A friend of mine once said, if we want to discover new lands, we must first be prepared to lose sight of the shore . . .'

Epilogue

I waited until several days after the party before I called the number.

There was such a thing as unsupervised voluntary work, I explained. Inmates reaching the end of their sentence were encouraged to apply for it as a way of reacquainting themselves with the notion of gainful employment in society. Were there perhaps some light duties I could carry out at the research station? Sweeping up the bat droppings, or carting away the fish heads. Whatever it was, I was willing to help. There was a bit of an unpleasant pause – but she agreed to think about it.

'What's to think about?' I asked. 'You're in charge, aren't you?'

'I need to think about whether I want you in my life again.'

It turned out she was at least prepared to consider the idea.

Thus it was that three times a week, I took the bus from Frabbage Hill Mature Offenders' Centre to Whixton and the fish-eating bat research station. Today it amuses me to think of myself on that journey, my fellow passengers and I threading our way through those dismal placenames under the sort of lowering sky you get in this part of England. Icke, Rothenworthy, Eyn Bridge, Little Wantington (the third 't' on the road sign graffitoed to read as a 'k'), Parsloe, Grenolds Brook, Cottisbury, Morkton Parva, Fossy. Whoever had described this chain of comatose settlements on the old Roman road as 'pearls on a necklace' in the official county guidebook possessed an impressively black sense of humour.

My work at the research station was suitably menial: refilling the coffee machine and unjamming the photocopier were two of the more challenging tasks. The station itself — *station!* — was a low redbrick building that housed a number of earnest-looking young people who, I discovered, were the project's 'field researchers', individuals whose job it was to squat by the river-bank and jot down the names of any fish-eating bats who stopped by for a bite of supper. As the diners in question were exclusively nocturnal, I usually came across the researchers in the morning, rubbing their eyes and swapping details of the exciting night just passed ('Elizabeth Hurley took a small perch').

Karen, befitting her status, worked office hours. And once the young bat-spotters had gone off home to hang upside down from their bedroom ceilings, it was mainly just the two of us. She would spend the day analysing the overnight data, or tapping away at her latest fish-eating-bat-related treatise. I would try to find excuses to insinuate myself into her office and distract her.

'Karen?'

'Mmm.'

'Something's been bothering me.'

'Mmm.'

'You know these fish-eating bats of yours . . . ?'

Slowly, the beak would rise. Two powerful dark eyes would regard me humorously. 'Ye-es?'

'Why isn't there a bat-eating fish? You'd think nature would have come up with one by now.'

A pause. Then, 'Nicholas, would you be a sweetie and check the batteries in the tracking kits for tonight?'

Her nose fascinated me. I loved the way it poked through the two curtains of hair that fell across her face as she pecked at her PC keyboard. It was sexy; its stabbing protuberance a visual taunt, a reminder that I too wished to do some stabbing, some protruding of my own.

A climate of ironic flirtiness developed between us, a sort of delicately freighted backchat that I felt desperate to move beyond. Karen, however, seemed content to play it cool, joshing in an intelligent way, but nothing I could construe as a direct come-on. I, meanwhile, could never forget that I remained a guest of HM Prison Service. An overt approach was out of the question.

Weeks, then months passed in this fashion. And then one lunchtime it happened. Instead of the usual soup and sandwich run to The Village Baker at Rothenworthy — another of my un-supervised voluntary duties — Karen said, 'Come on. I've got a surprise for you.'

She drove us to her house; her cottage, I should say, about ten minutes away through deserted country roads. It was a cosy, flagstoned, low-beamed affair, filled with interesting *objets* and pictures.

Across an oak table in the kitchen, two places had been laid. A candle sat in a holder.

'Open some wine, would you,' she said, dragging a wooden spoon through a resistive medium in an iron pot on the stove. 'There's a white Rioja in the fridge.'

She'd made paella.

We clinked glasses, and when I looked into her face, I thought I saw something that hadn't been there in the morning. Or on any of the other days we'd spent together at the research station.

'I decided I couldn't really wait for you to invite me to dinner,' she said.

'Really?' I replied. I could barely get the word out.

'You've changed.'

'Have I?'

'You don't seem quite so full of crap.'

'I'm flattered.'

'I like you more this way. Even though you haven't compli-mented me on my cooking yet.'

'Haven't I? Sorry. It's lovely.'

'Lovely.'

'You know, nice to eat. Yummy. Did you know I was a food critic once?'

She laughed. 'Yummy?'

'Yes, yummy.'

'I haven't had this since I was in Spain.'

'I see.'

'Oh holiday.'

'Really.'

'On *that* holiday.'

'Ah.'

'When I sent the—'

'The postcard.'

'That one.'

'Ah.'

We ate on in silence for a few moments.

'So, er. When are you going to give me the guided tour, then?' I asked for some reason.

She set down her fork.

I followed her up the narrow wooden staircase. At the bedroom window, we paused to admire the view. Below us in the garden, standing in the long grass between a pair of twisty old apple trees, were two white beehives. Beige cattle loitered in the fields beyond. And beyond them, a long way away, was a low range of hills.

'On a clear day you can see the Abbey at Frabbage,' she said. 'There.' She pointed.

I followed the direction her arm was indicating. In the far distance, the pile sat on its mound like a broken tooth.

'I believe it has the finest antependium in the county,' I remarked.

We turned to look at one another. A loud and unmistakable message passed between us. It was headed 'Unfinished Business'.

'Antependium, bollocks,' she said.

'You're dead right there,' I replied.

I moved towards the beak, and the beak moved towards me. As we drew nearer, it altered its course, moving ten degrees off to the east. I trimmed my own angle of approach accordingly. The gap between us slowly closed, until the garden, the fields, the cattle, the hills, the Abbey, and finally everything else was blotted from view.

I am writing these words at a desk below the window I have just described. Downstairs, I can hear Karen tapping into her own laptop; a paper she's presenting at the forthcoming European Bat Symposium. The smell of tonight's paella drifts through the cottage. It's become 'our' dish, since I was granted my parole and came to stay; initially for a week or two, 'just while you get things settled', but for what has now turned out to be six months.

I still haven't decided what to do about getting a job, although Karen is putting no pressure on me. There seem to be three immediate options: Nigel, who edited the section that 'Aimless Days' appeared in, has been made features editor of another mid-market tabloid. He says he might take a column off me. 'City boy who chucks it all in to live in the sticks could be fun,' he said. 'Smartarse metropolitan type mixing it with the country bumpkins sort of thing.' He has asked me to 'play with the idea'. There's also a possibility of an opening at the local paper, *The Rothenworthy Recorder*, which, frankly, looks like it could do with a decent lifestyle section. And finally the farmer up the road who owns the beige cows says he can always 'do with some help around the place' – although to be honest, I don't know whether or not he's taking the piss.

This weekend, Squeaky and Hugo are coming up to visit. They seem terribly well suited, completely up a tree with each other, as the saying goes, and it can only be a matter of time before he gets down on one knee and makes the speech containing the M-word. Somehow, I think I should feel more churned up about it all than I actually do. What I feel mostly is numb. Still, I guess some relationships are like that. They end, the dust settles and you think: well, what was all *that* about?

Perhaps it's called growing up.

Karen has asked me to drive all the way over to Morkton Parva tomorrow. To the chemist's. To buy a testing kit. She says if I go to the Boots at Rothenworthy, by teatime half the village will be giving her the old raised eyebrows treatment: *Well? Are you?*

Our official position is that neither of us minds if we are. That is, both of us would be pleased if we were – and daunted, obviously – but not overly disappointed if we weren't.

Unofficially, I've been surprised to discover that secretly, I would be disappointed if we weren't. If she isn't.

I don't even care whose nose it gets.

In about half an hour, the beige cattle will start plodding back across the meadow to the farm gate. It's the point in the afternoon when the bees kick up a gear, laying on extra flights before deciding to call it a day.

Living with a zoologist, I've learned a lot about bees. How they've been around for 150 million years. How they need to visit two million flowers to make one pound of honey. How the worker bees communicate where the best flowers are by wiggle-dancing in front of the others when they return from a mission. A vertical, straight-up-and-down dance means: fly in the direction of the sun. An off-vertical dance indicates the number of degrees away from the sun. Distance is represented by the wiggling abdomen. The more furious the wiggle, the further they have to go.

There is something about that last detail I strongly relate to. *The more furious the wiggle, the further you have to go.*

For the time being, at least, I seem to have stopped wiggling.

Every time I look up from my keyboard, I see the bees arriving and departing on their fascinating flight paths. They do their work. I do mine. The days pass. Pollen accretes to the cells of their honeycomb, words to the hard disk of my laptop.

It feels curiously like happiness.

PAUL REIZIN

Dumping Hilary?

For Michael, hungover, the wrong side of thirty, working in the fickle world of TV, life is not what it should be. Even his relationship with cheerful, intelligent Hilary has reached the stage where he knows what she's going to say before she does. So, ever the man of action, he writes the list which will change his life:

Give up smoking
Dump Hilary
Get Yasmin (unobtainable Office Goddess)
Be nicer to parents
Think of really good – untraceable – revenge on Clive (girlfriend-pincher and career-wrecker)

When Michael manages to fix a trip to New York with Yasmin it all begins to look as if it might just work out. But Michael is about to discover that what you want and what you think you want are not necessarily the same thing.

'A well-observed insight into a man's brain' *New Woman*

'Very funny indeed' *Hello!*

'A great example of a hit-and-miss formula hitting the nail on the head . . . I giggled the whole way through' *Mirror*

'If you've ever wanted to know: a) What men are really thinking; b) How come there's so much crap on TV; c) Why you shouldn't have another Vodka Martini, read this hilarious novel!' Imogen Parker (author of *The Men in Her Life*)

0 7472 6670 0

review

You can buy any of these other **Review** titles from your bookshop or *direct from the publisher*.

FREE P&P AND UK DELIVERY
(Overseas and Ireland £3.50 per book)

Sitting Practice	Caroline Adderson	£6.99
Ghost Music	Candida Clark	£6.99
Intuition	Peter Jinks	£6.99
This is Not a Novel	Jennifer Johnston	£6.99
The Song of Names	Norman Lebrecht	£6.99
Nightdancing	Elizabeth Garner	£6.99
The Secret Life of Bees	Sue Monk Kidd	£6.99
My Lover's Lover	Maggie O'Farrell	£6.99
Blue Noon	Robert Ryan	£6.99
Revenge	Mary Stanley	£6.99
The Hound in the Left-Hand Corner	Giles Waterfield	£6.99
The Woman Who Painted Her Dreams	Isla Dewar	£6.99

TO ORDER SIMPLY CALL THIS NUMBER

01235 400 414

or visit our website: www.madaboutbooks.com

Prices and availability subject to change without notice.